QUINTESSENCE

QUINTESSENCE

David Walton

A TOM DOHERTY ASSOCIATES BOOK · NEW YORK

QUINTESSENCE

A Tor Book
Published by Tom Doherty Associates, LLC
175 Fifth Avenue
New York, NY 10010

Tor® is a registered trademark of Tom Doherty Associates, LLC.

ISBN 978-0-7653-3090-1

Printed in the United States of America

Acknowledgments

Writing is a solitary business. Novels are generally written by one person, spending many hours alone with his own imagination. It's a delight, therefore, when other people add their various insights and skills to bring a book to its final form.

Many thanks to my beta-readers, whose critiques were invaluable: Karen Walton, Mike Shultz, John Brown, Nancy Fulda, Chad and Jill Wilson, and David Cantine. Thanks as well to the many members of the Codex writers group for all their support and good advice, particularly Matt Rotundo, Christine Amsden, and Jessica Otis for her insights on sixteenth-century period details.

You probably picked the book off the shelf in the first place because of the beautiful cover art from Kekai Kotaki. And you would not be holding this book in your hand without the efforts of my stellar agent, Eleanor Wood, or without the faith and hard work of the editors at Tor: David Hartwell, Stacy Hague-Hill, and Marco Palmieri. Thanks to all of you.

B y the time Lord Chelsey's ship reached the mouth of the Thames, only thirteen men were still alive.

Chelsey stood at the bow of the *Western Star*, staring mutely at the familiar stretch of English coastline. The coal fire in North Foreland's octagonal lighthouse tower burned, just as it had when they'd left, guiding ships into the sheltered estuary. The silted islands were the same, with the same sailboats, dinghies, and barges wending through the maze of sandbanks, carrying trade goods between Essex and Kent. After seeing the great Western Ocean crashing headlong over the edge of the world, it seemed impossible that these familiar sights should remain. As if nothing had changed.

"Nearly home," said the first mate, the eighth young man to hold that post since leaving London three years before. He was seventeen years old.

Chelsey didn't answer. He didn't insult the boy by promising a joyous reunion with family and friends. They would see London again, but they wouldn't be permitted to step ashore. It was almost worse than failure, this tantalizing view of home, where life stumbled on in ignorance and peace.

But he hadn't failed. He had campaigned for years to convince King Henry there were treasures to be found at the Western Edge, and he had been right. The barrels and chests that crammed the ship's hold should be proof of that, at least. Treasures beyond even his imagining, not just gold and cinnamon and cloves, but precious materials never before seen, animals so strange they could hardly be described, and best of all, the miraculous water. Oh, yes, he had been right. At least he would be remembered for that.

Black-headed gulls screamed and dove around them. Through the morning mist, Chelsey spotted the seawalls of the Essex shoreline, only miles from Rochford, where he'd been raised.

He shifted painfully from one leg to the other. It wouldn't be long for him. He'd witnessed it enough by now to know. Once the elbows and knees stiffened, the wrists and fingers would lock soon after, followed by the jaw, making eating impossible. One by one, they had turned into statues. And the pain—the pain was beyond description.

They sailed on. Marshlands gave way to the endless hamlets and islands and tributaries of the twisting Thames, the river increasingly choked with traffic. At last they circled the Isle of Dogs and came into sight of London Bridge and the Tower of London, beyond which sprawled the greatest city in the world.

"Admiral?" It was the first mate. "You'd best come down, sir. It's a terrible thing."

Chelsey wondered what could possibly be described as terrible that hadn't already happened. He followed the mate down into the hold, gritting his teeth as he tried to bend joints that felt as if they might snap. Two other sailors were there already. They had pried open several of the chests and spilled their contents. Where there should have been fistfuls of gold and diamonds and fragrant sacks of spices, there were only rocks and sand.

His mind didn't want to believe it. It wasn't fair. He had traveled to the ends of the earth and found the fruit of the Garden of Paradise. God couldn't take it away from him, not now.

"Are all of them like this?"

"We don't know."

"Open them!"

They hurried to obey, and Chelsey joined in the effort. Wood splintered; bent nails screeched free. They found no treasure. Only sand and dirt, rocks and seawater. He ran his fingers through an open crate, furrowing the coarse sand inside. It was not possible. All this distance, and so many dead—it couldn't be for nothing.

"What happened to it?" he whispered.

No one answered.

He had failed after all. Soon he would die like all the others, and no one would remember his name.

He tried to kick the crate, but his leg cramped, turning the defiant gesture into something weak and pitiful. God would not allow him even that much. Lord Robert Chelsey, Admiral of the Western Seas, collapsed in agony on the stained wooden floor. He had lost everything. Worse, he would never know why.

Chapter One

THERE was something wrong with the body. There was no smell, for one thing. Stephen Parris had been around enough corpses to know the aroma well. Its limbs were stiff, its joints were locked, and the eyes were shrunken in their sockets—all evidence of death at least a day old—but the skin looked as fresh as if the man had died an hour ago, and the flesh was still firm. As if the body had refused to decay.

Parris felt a thrill in his gut. An anomaly in a corpse meant something new to learn. Perhaps a particular imbalance of the humors caused this effect, or a shock, or an unknown disease. Parris was physic to King Edward VI of England, master of all his profession had to teach, but for all his education and experience, the human body was still a mystery. His best attempts to heal still felt like trying to piece together a broken vase in the dark without knowing what it had looked like in the first place.

Most people in London, even his colleagues, would find the idea of cutting up a dead person shocking. He didn't care. The only way to find out how the body worked was to look inside.

"Where did you get him?" Parris asked the squat man who had dropped the body on his table like a sack of grain.

"Special, ain't he?" said the man, whose name was Felbrigg, revealing teeth with more decay than the corpse. "From the Mad Admiral's boat, that one is."

"You took this from the *Western Star*?" Parris was genuinely surprised and took a step back from the table.

"Now then, I never knew you for a superstitious man," Felbrigg said. "He's in good shape, just what you pay me for. Heavy as an ox, too."

The *Western Star* had returned to London three days before with only thirteen men still alive on a ship littered with corpses. Quite mad, Lord Chelsey seemed to think he had brought an immense treasure back from the fabled Island of Columbus, but the chests were filled with dirt and stones. He also claimed to have found a survivor from the *Santa Maria* on the island, still alive and young sixty years after his ship had plummeted over the edge of the world. But whatever they had found out there, it wasn't the Fountain of Youth. Less than a day after they had arrived in London, Chelsey and his twelve sailors were all dead.

"They haven't moved the bodies?"

Felbrigg laughed. "Nobody goes near it."

"They let it sit at anchor with corpses aboard? The harbor master can't be pleased. I'd think Chelsey's widow would have it scoured from top to bottom by now."

"Lady Chelsey don't own it no more. Title's passed to Christopher Sinclair," Felbrigg said.

"Sinclair? I don't know him."

"An alchemist. The very devil, so they say. I hear he swindled Lady Chelsey out of the price of the boat by telling her stories of demons living in the hold that would turn an African pale. And no mistake, he's a scary one. A scar straight down across his mouth, and eyes as orange as an India tiger."

"I know the type." Parris waved a hand. "Counterfeiters and frauds."

"Maybe so. But I wouldn't want to catch his eye."

Parris shook his head. "The only way those swindlers make gold from base metals is by mixing silver and copper together until they get the color and weight close enough to pass it off as currency. If he's a serious practitioner, why have I never heard of him?"

"He lived abroad for a time," Felbrigg said.

"I should say so. Probably left the last place with a sword at his back."

"Some say Abyssinia, some Cathay, some the Holy Land. For certain he has a Mussulman servant with a curved sword and eyes that never blink."

"If so much is true, I'm amazed you had the mettle to rob his boat."

Felbrigg looked wounded. "I'm no widow, to be cowed by superstitious prattle."

"Did anyone see you?"

"Not a soul, I swear it."

A sudden rustling from outside made them both jump. Silently, Felbrigg crept to the window and shifted the curtain.

"Just a bird."

"You're certain?"

"A bloody great crow, that's all."

Satisfied, Parris picked up his knife. Good as his intentions were, he had no desire to be discovered while cutting up a corpse. It was the worst sort of devilry, from most people's point of view. Witchcraft. Satan worship. A means to call up the spawn of hell to make young men infertile and murder babies in the womb. No, they wouldn't understand at all.

Felbrigg fished in his cloak and pulled out a chunk of bread and a flask, showing no inclination to leave. Parris didn't mind. He was already trusting Felbrigg with his life, and it was good to have the company. The rest of the house was empty. Joan and Catherine were at a ball in the country for the Earl of Leicester's birthday celebration, and would be gone all weekend, thank heaven.

He turned the knife over in his hand, lowered it to the corpse's throat, and cut a deep slash from neck to groin. The body looked so fresh that he almost expected blood to spurt, but nothing but a thin fluid welled up from the cut. He drove an iron bar into the gap, wrenched until he heard a snap, and pulled aside the cracked breastbone.

It was all wrong inside. A fine grit permeated the flesh, trapped in the lining of the organs. The heart and lungs and liver and stomach were all in their right places, but the texture felt dry and rough. What could have happened to this man?

Dozens of candles flickered in stands that Parris had drawn up all around the table, giving it the look of an altar with a ghoulish sacrifice. Outside the windows, all was dark. He began removing the organs one by one and setting them on the table, making notes of size and color and weight in his book. With so little decay, he could clearly see the difference between the veins and the arteries. He traced them with his fingers, from their origin in the heart and liver toward the extremities, where the blood was consumed by the rest of the body. He consulted ancient diagrams from Hippocrates and Galen to identify the smaller features.

There was a Belgian, Andreas Vesalius, who claimed that Galen was wrong, that the veins did not originate from the liver, but from the heart, just like the arteries. Saying Galen was wrong about anatomy was akin to saying the Pope was wrong about religion, but of course many people in England said that, too, these days. It was a new world. Parris lifted the lungs out of the way, and could see that Vesalius was right. Never before had he managed so clean and clear a view. He traced a major vein down toward the pelvis.

"Look at this," Parris said, mostly to himself, but Felbrigg got up to see, wiping his beard and scattering crumbs into the dead man's abdominal cavity. "The intestines are encrusted with white." Parris touched a loop with his finger, and then tasted it. "Salt."

"What was he doing, drinking seawater?" Felbrigg said.

"Only if he was a fool."

"A thirsty man will do foolish things sometimes."

Parris was thoughtful. "Maybe he did drink salt water. Maybe that's why the body is so preserved."

He lifted out the stomach, which was distended. The man had eaten a full meal before dying. Maybe what he ate would give a clue to his condition.

Parris slit the stomach and peeled it open, the grit that covered everything sticking to his hands. He stared at the contents, astonished.

"What is it?" Felbrigg asked.

In answer, Parris turned the stomach over, pouring a pile of pebbles and sand out onto the table.

Felbrigg laughed. "Maybe he thought he could turn stones into bread—and seawater into wine!" This put him into such convulsions of laughter that he choked and coughed for several minutes.

Parris ignored him. What had happened on that boat? This was not the body of a man who hadn't eaten for days; he was fit and well nourished. What had motivated him to eat rocks and drink seawater? Was it suicide? Or had they all gone mad?

The sound of carriage wheels and the trot of a horse on packed earth interrupted his thoughts. Parris saw the fear in Felbrigg's eyes and knew it was reflected in his own. The body could be hidden, perhaps, but the table was streaked with gore, and gobbets of gray tissue stained the sheet he had spread out on the floor. His clothes were sticky and his hands and knife fouled with dead flesh. King Edward had brought many religious reforms in his young reign, but he would not take Parris's side on this. It was criminal desecration, if not sorcery. Men had been burned for less.

Parris started blowing out candles, hoping at least to darken the room, but he was too late. There were footsteps on the front steps. The door swung open.

But it wasn't the sheriff, as he had feared. It was his wife.

Joan didn't scream at the sight. To his knowledge she had never screamed, nor fainted, nor cried, not for any reason. Her eyes swept the room, taking in the scene, the body, the knife in his hands. For a moment they stood frozen, staring at each other. Then her eyes blazed.

"Get out," she said, her voice brimming with fury. At first Felbrigg didn't move, not realizing she was talking to him. "Get out of my house!"

"If you can bring any more like this one, I'll pay you double," Parris whispered.

Felbrigg nodded. He hurried past Joan, bowing apologies, and ran down the steps.

"How is it you're traveling home at this hour?" said Parris. "Is the celebration over? Where's Catherine?"

Another figure appeared in the doorway behind Joan, but it wasn't his daughter. It was a man, dressed in a scarlet cloak hung rakishly off one shoulder, velvet hose, and a Spanish doublet with froths of lace erupting from the sleeves. Parris scowled. It was Francis Vaughan, a first cousin on his mother's side, and it was not a face he wanted to see. Vaughan's education had been funded by Parris's father, but he had long since abandoned any career, preferring the life of a professional courtier. He was a flatterer, a gossipmonger, living off the king's generosity and an occasional blackmail. His eyes swept the room, excitedly taking in the spectacle of the corpse and Parris still holding the knife.

"What are you doing here?" Parris said. The only time he ever saw his cousin was when Vaughan was short of cash and asking for another "loan," which he would never repay.

"Your wife and daughter needed to return home in a hurry," Vaughan said. "I was good enough to escort them." He rubbed his hands together. "Cousin? Are you in trouble?"

"Not if you leave now and keep your mouth shut."

"I'm not sure I can do that. Discovering the king's own physic involved in . . . well. It's big news. I think the king would want to know."

Parris knew what Vaughan was after, and he didn't want to haggle. He pulled a purse out of a drawer and tossed it to him. Vaughan caught it out of the air and peered inside. He grinned and disappeared back down the steps.

Joan glared at Parris, at the room, at the body. "Clean it up," she hissed. "And for love of your life and mine, don't miss anything." The stairs thundered with her retreat.

But Parris had no intention of stopping. Not now, not when he was learning so much. He could deal with Vaughan. He'd have to give him more money, but Vaughan came by every few weeks or so asking for money anyway. He wasn't ambitious enough to cause him real problems.

There were risks, yes. People were ever ready to attack and destroy what they didn't understand, and young King Edward, devout as he was, would conclude the worst if he found out. But how would that ever change if no one was willing to try? He had a responsibility. Few doctors were as experienced as he was, few as well read or well connected with colleagues on the Continent. He'd even communicated with a few Mussulman doctors from Istanbul and Africa who had an extraordinary understanding of the human body.

And that was the key—communication. Alchemists claimed to have vast knowledge, but it was hard to tell for sure, since they spent most of their time hiding what they knew or recording it in arcane ciphers. As a result, alchemical tomes were inscrutable puzzles that always hinted at knowledge without actually revealing it. Parris believed those with knowledge should publish it freely, so that others could make it grow.

But Joan didn't understand any of this. All she cared about his profession was that it brought the king's favor, particularly if it might lead to a good marriage for Catherine. And by "good," she meant someone rich, with lands and prospects and a title. Someone who could raise their family a little bit higher. She was constantly pestering him to ask the king or the Duke of Northumberland for help in this regard, which was ludicrous. He was the king's physic, the third son of a minor lord who had only inherited any land at all because his older two brothers had died. His contact with His Majesty was limited to poultices and bloodletting, not begging for the son of an earl for his only daughter.

He continued cutting and cataloging, amazed at how easily he could separate the organs and see their connections. Nearly finished, a thought occurred to him: What if, instead of being consumed by the flesh, the blood transported some essential mineral to it through the arteries, and then returned to the heart through the veins? Or instead of a mineral, perhaps it was heat the blood brought, since it began a hot red in the heart and returned to it blue as ice. He would write a letter to Vesalius.

When he was finished, he wrapped what was left of the body in a canvas bag and began to sew it shut. In the morning, his manservant would take it to a pauper's grave, where no one would ask any questions, and bury it. As he sewed, unwanted images flashed through his mind. A blood-soaked sheet. A young hand grasped tightly in his. A brow beaded with sweat. A dark mound of earth.

He must not think on it. Peter's death was not his fault. There was no way he could have known.

His conscience mocked him. He was physic to the King of England! A master of the healing arts! And yet he couldn't preserve the life of his own son, the one life more precious to him than any other?

No. He must not think on it.

Parris gritted his teeth and kept the bone needle moving up and down, up and down. Why had God given him this calling, and yet not given him enough knowledge to truly heal? There were answers to be found in the body; he knew there were, but they were too slow in coming. Too slow by far.

Chapter Two

CHRISTOPHER Sinclair needed money, and he needed it fast. Once Lady Chelsey discovered he couldn't really pay her what he'd promised, he would lose the *Western Star* and his chance along with it. He made a modest living thrilling the rich with exotic stories of foreign lands, and he could always sell off trinkets from his journeys if business was slow, but it wasn't nearly enough to buy a ship.

He stood motionless in the cabin that used to be Lord Chelsey's, listening to the brackish water of the Thames slapping softly against the ship. Outside, the night was black. The only illumination came from a brazier on the weathered table, over which a clear liquid slowly came to a boil. Sinclair's back and legs ached from standing, but he had long ago realized he could ignore any pain or discomfort that didn't suit his purposes.

He refused to consider the possibility of failure. All those years of wandering through Africa and Asia, all of the dead ends and wild-goose chases after clues buried in ancient texts: it all led him to this moment and the *Western Star*. She had traveled farther, explored more ocean, seen more wonders than any other ship in the world. Only the *Niña, Pinta,* and *Santa Maria* might have seen as much, but their mariners had never returned to tell the tale. If man could truly unlock the secrets of the universe, transform base metals to gold and conquer death, then the answers would be found in the places where this ship had been.

The liquid began to bubble violently. It was the "seawater" that had been discovered in barrels on the ship, though no one besides him had bothered to test the claim. It smelled and tasted of salt, true, but it wasn't like any seawater Sinclair had ever seen. For instance, it burned as well as any lamp oil when soaked into a wick. No salt water could do that.

Which made it a substance beyond his knowledge, and there was no substance from England to Cathay that was beyond the knowledge of Christopher Sinclair. This was something new.

It bubbled in a retort with a long spout that led to a coiled glass tube. After the liquid boiled into vapor, it would condense in the tube and then drip into a trough as a liquid again. Through this process, it would leave its impurities behind in the flask and reappear again purer than before.

Distillation was the heart of what he loved about alchemy: this slow, silent ritual, ripe with philosophical musings, in which a gross material vanished into its spiritual form and returned again, better than before. This was true religion. The subtle spirit liberated from gross matter. He could stand motionless for hours, performing occasional repetitive motions with his hands, alone with his thoughts.

But not tonight. He paced, unable to concentrate. The cost of this ship was more gold than he had ever owned in his life, never mind the thousands of crowns it would take to make her seaworthy again, hire a crew, and provision her for a journey of months. He would have to do something drastic. Something desperate.

Because he would sail on this ship no matter what it cost. No more searching vainly through ancient books. He'd wasted years of his life poring over the tomes of alchemical symbols and codes in which so much knowledge seemed to be buried, but his reading had just led to deeper and deeper mysteries. He refused to be consumed by them anymore. Obviously, none of their authors had discovered the secret of immortality. They were all dead.

Drops of liquid dribbled slowly along the coiled tube, stretched, and dropped into the trough. It was the oldest tool of the alchemist, this purifying of baser substances. Distill wine, and you produced alcohol, which could invigorate the human body and prevent meat from rotting. Distill vitriol, and you made it strong enough to dissolve just about anything. But what if you could purify the right essence, and keep purifying, and purifying, and purifying some more, until you found the very purest, most fundamental substance of the universe? Could not that substance be used to transmute any base substance to its purer form? Lead to gold? Death to life?

The substance had many names: the *aqua vitae*, the elixir of life, the philosopher's stone, the aether of the heavens, the fifth essence. Quintessence. Sinclair knew it must exist. He had spent his life trying to find it. Aristotle said it was found in the moon and the stars; the medieval alchemists said it came from distillations of the three elemental ingredients: salt, sulfur, and mercury.

Before Lord Chelsey and his sailors died, Sinclair had spoken with each of them. They were in obvious pain and fading quickly, but he didn't dismiss their words as raving, the way most people did. Sinclair had seen more of the world than most, and he had heard sailors' tales before. These men were telling the truth, or what they thought was the truth. And where better to find quintessence than at the horizon of the world, where the heavens curved down to meet the earth?

From somewhere on the ship a thud sounded, and then a louder clattering sound. It was still before dawn. There would be few people on the docks at this time, and certainly no one was expected aboard the *Western Star*.

Sinclair stepped quietly out of the captain's cabin, through the officers' cabins, and out onto the main deck. The sky was growing lighter, but the fog was thick. He stood in the shadow of the mast with his cloak drawn close about him, all but invisible in the gloom. He liked being unseen. He liked to watch people go about their business, unaware of his presence. It gave him power.

There it was—a dim shape heaving itself over the rail. The moon made his features plain: a sturdy laborer with a coarse face and thick beard, well muscled but not strong enough for a smith. An ironmonger, perhaps, or an armourer. Maybe just a brute who made a living staving in heads. Sinclair didn't know what he was doing here, but he could guess. Last night a corpse had disappeared from its place on the forecastle. A thief, then. Back to steal something from his ship again.

It was not technically Sinclair's ship yet, not by law, but it would be soon. He was the only one who saw its value, the only one not turned aside by foolish tales of haunting. Dead men there were in abundance, but no ghosts. Sinclair had never believed in ghosts.

The trespasser lit a tallow candle and sneaked toward the forecastle. Sinclair followed him, a soundless phantom.

His quarry reached the ladder. Sinclair, a step behind him, snatched the candle from his hand. The man spun, and Sinclair thrust both the candle and his dagger into the intruder's face, forcing him back against the wall and eliciting a shout of surprise and fear.

Sinclair was no fighter, and this man probably had twice his strength, so he spoke fast and in lordly tones, trying to maintain the advantages of surprise and fear.

"What's your name? Answer me!"

The man's eyes were wide, but he stammered, "Felbrigg."

"What is your business on my boat?"

"Your boat, my lord? I thought it belonged to——"

"Never mind what you thought. Account for your trespass."

"Just a little treasure hunting. A man's got to put bread in his poor children's hungry mouths."

"Is that why you took a body yesterday? To feed your children?"

Felbrigg gaped and stammered all the more. "I never——"

"Don't lie to me." Sinclair pressed the edge of his dagger against Felbrigg's lips. "This smells of devil worship. You brought it to a witch, no doubt. You seek a potion for love, or wealth, or to sire a son."

"Nothing like that! I swear it!"

"I promise you, the Lord Protector shall hear of this."

"No, my lord, I beg of you."

"You'll burn, I guarantee it. You and all your wicked cabal."

"It's for a man——a physic. He likes to . . . I don't know what he does with them. He pays me to get them. That's all I know."

"What's his name?"

"I don't know his name. He meets me in darkness; I give him the body, and he——"

Sinclair turned the point of the dagger and pressed it hard into Felbrigg's throat, drawing blood. "There are many corpses on this boat already. I don't suppose one more will cause much comment."

Felbrigg gasped and sputtered. "Parris. Parris, as God is my witness, but he's no devil worshipper. He's a physic. He cuts 'em open to see how they work."

Sinclair raised his eyebrows. "*Stephen* Parris?"

"That's him. Nice as you please. A real gentleman."

"Stephen Parris, who holds the king's life in his hands?"

"I told you, didn't I?" Felbrigg twisted his body, trying to work his neck away from the blade.

Sinclair thought fast. A rich man with something to hide could solve all his problems. Parris had more than enough money to refit the *Western Star* and supply it for a voyage.

He released Felbrigg. "It's Parris I want. I'll keep your name out of it. But if I find out he's been warned . . ."

"Yes, my lord. I understand." Felbrigg felt his neck and backed away.

Sinclair tossed a gold half sovereign to the deck, where Felbrigg picked it up. "I suggest you leave London."

"Right away, my lord. You won't see me again."

After Felbrigg had gone, Sinclair walked his ship again, making sure everything was as it should be. His past explorations had revealed several remarkable items, and he was afraid trespassers would find and steal them. Besides Felbrigg, he'd never seen anyone else on the ship, but he was constantly feeling like someone was standing right behind him. Many times he'd seen movement out of the corner of his eye, but when he turned, nothing was there. Perhaps it was simply the creepiness of being on board ship with sixty corpses.

He thought of Stephen Parris: intelligent, well educated, and apparently interested in discovering truth. Perhaps he would prove useful in ways other than his money. Sinclair had no qualms about manipulating someone for a necessary purpose. His aims were higher than the benefit of just one man. The cause was just, greater than any in history. Parris would thank him eventually. If he survived.

Sinclair chuckled at this small irony and blew out the candle, leaving the ship wrapped in gray fog. He returned to the captain's cabin, following the light from the brazier.

The distillation was complete. All of the liquid had boiled up into the tube, leaving a dull white sludge behind. Sinclair tipped the condensation trough, pouring the newly purified liquid into another flask. He turned it, letting the light of the fire refract through it. Curious.

He turned his back on the brazier, which was the only source of illumination save for a faint shimmer of moonlight in the fog outside. In the darkest corner of the cabin, he hunched his body over the flask and studied it in the blackness. The liquid glowed faintly, a clear white light that illuminated his hands and face. His heart beat faster. Several of Chelsey's men had said the very water on the island could heal injury and disease. Could it be that he had found it already? That Lord Chelsey had brought quintessence home with him on this very ship?

Tentatively at first, then with growing confidence, Sinclair lifted the flask to his lips and drank.

Chapter Three

PARRIS tiptoed downstairs, expecting his wife and daughter to be long asleep. It was almost dawn. Instead, he found Catherine sitting erect by the window in her dressing gown, every angle of her face and arms accentuating her delicate beauty. He hadn't seen much of her lately. When had she grown from a grubby, romping child into this fragile flower? He remembered her rolling on the floor in this very room, wrestling with a puppy.

He was tempted to walk right past, but he steeled himself to approach her. He couldn't go on forever not speaking to his daughter. His only child now, though the admission still made his throat feel tight. He reached her chair and stood behind it, looking with her out the window at the brightening sky.

"Good morning, Father."

"And to you, daughter. Why up so early?"

"Lady Hungate says a girl must always rise to greet the dawn. She says it is slothful to stay abed." Her tone was light, but Parris noticed the bitter edge.

"And what is Lady Hungate to you?"

"Oh, she's a great woman, as you well know. Her son is heir to a baronetcy. If I am to make a good match, I must behave as a lady, must I not?"

Parris walked around the chair to face her and saw that her eyes were red. "What happened? Why are you home so soon?"

"Mother was tired."

That was nonsense. Joan never tired of opportunities to pair Catherine up with promising young men. Parris felt the familiar panic rising in his stomach, as it had every time he'd tried to speak with Catherine in the last year.

"Did you enjoy the ball?" he tried.

She laughed in the false manner of society women, as if he'd just uttered a witticism. "Everyone enjoys a ball," she said. "How could I not enjoy it?"

There was something wrong. "What happened, Catherine?"

She looked at him frankly, and for a moment he thought she might confide in him. Then she looked away. "There was a splendid masque. Music and dancing. And that magician, Christopher Sinclair."

Sinclair again. "A magician?"

"Oh, yes. Haven't you heard of him? He's a dashing gentleman, and confounds us all with the most amazing tricks. Do you know he turned a walking stick into a snake and then back into a stick again, like Moses? I was so terrified!"

She didn't look at all terrified; she looked excited at the memory. She was such an innocent. Too naive to be thrown to the rapacious wolves that filled a royal court, greedy for power and wealth and all too willing to use a trusting young girl. The way Felbrigg had described him, Parris had imagined Sinclair as an ugly man, a dwarf perhaps, his face mutilated. It seemed he was just another fancy courtier, with a repertoire of flattery and legerdemain to amaze an impressionable young girl. Parris prayed God would keep his daughter out of the path of fortune hunters. He couldn't bear to see Catherine swept away by such a man.

He found he was clenching his fists so tightly he left fingernail marks in his skin. Not trusting himself to speak again, he left with a murmured good night. She was like that porcelain brought from Cathay along the Silk Road: rare and precious, but easily broken, and, once broken, irreplaceable. It made him angry to think of anyone hurting her, but that was fine. Anger was a safe emotion. Better anger than the grief he could sense like a deep well underneath, calling him to drown.

He retreated to his bedchamber, hoping for an hour of sleep before dawn, but Joan, too, was awake.

She sat rigid in a chair by their bed, knitting. The needles clashed in her lap like tiny swords, giving shape to a pair of hose that hung down below them.

"Haven't you slept?" Parris said.

No answer.

"I confirmed Vesalius," he told her, knowing she didn't care, but unable to help himself. "He corrected Galen, if you can believe it. A lot of people won't be happy about that."

"It's my happiness you ought to be concerned about." Her needles kept flashing.

Parris knew she was angry about the corpse. He gripped the back of his neck and massaged it. "How can I heal the body if I don't know how it works?" It was an old argument, raised more out of habit than any hope she would be moved by it.

"We agreed that you would stop bringing . . . the dead . . . into my house."

"*You* agreed."

"It won't bring him back, Stephen."

Parris retreated to the hearth. "I know that. Ten times over, I know it." He didn't want to have this conversation. He picked up the poker and gripped it in both hands as if he would bend it in half.

It always came back to Peter. Before his death, things had made sense. The future had been clear: Catherine would marry into a good family; Peter would inherit land and wealth and carry on the family name. Parris and Joan had been fond of each other, and their goals—Parris's to be London's preeminent physic and Joan's to establish their family in London society—had been well matched.

Then Peter died, and everything turned upside down. Joan, sensing her family's stability slipping away, had thrown herself into finding a match for Catherine, as if to pull them back on solid ground again. To Parris, it had the opposite effect: he no longer cared what people thought. His reputation as a physic was worthless if he couldn't truly heal. He retreated into his studies, pursuing more and more radical methods in his thirst for understanding.

Joan didn't understand this, but she didn't know the whole truth, either. It was too horrible to tell her—to tell anyone. Only Parris knew, and it ate away at his soul. He had killed his own son.

Day after day, while Peter grew sicker, Parris had given him capsules filled with elemental mercury. Mercury was widely used, a long-accepted treatment for a wide variety of diseases. The ancients had praised its medicinal powers. He had learned its uses at Cambridge. Every physic of his acquaintance had prescribed it at some point in their careers.

But the week after Peter's death, a letter had come from a physic in

Florence named Vecchio. Vecchio had performed experimental studies on the effects of mercury on healthy individuals. The results were sweating, racing heartbeat, muscular weakness, the skin peeling off in layers, the loss of hair, teeth, and nails. All of Peter's symptoms. It was a poison, and Parris had given it to his own son through sheer, unforgivable ignorance.

Joan still hadn't looked up from her knitting.

"What are you making?" he asked, to shift the conversation into safer territory.

"Hose for Catherine. What does it look like?"

Knitting was a strange new craft, but Joan had found someone to teach her how to do it. It allowed woolen hose to fit a woman's leg more neatly, and Joan was wild to have Catherine fitted out in the latest styles.

"No one will see them anyway, under her gown," he said.

She paused, dropping her hands in her lap. "What nonsense you talk. Her ankles will be visible."

"To whom will they be visible?"

"She's a young lady, Stephen. She needs to be out in society, finding a man to marry, raising a family."

He stared at the poker in his hands. No topic of conversation was simple anymore. "She's only sixteen."

"Old enough." The venom in Joan's voice made him look up.

"Why did you come home? What happened?" he said.

"She has a young man. At least, she fancies she does. The oldest son of Baron Hungate."

"And? You're always angling to find her a good match."

"Thomas Hungate is *too* good. And he's not courting her openly. I found them alone in the courtyard garden."

Parris felt a slow burn begin in his chest. "Doing what?"

"Nothing but sweet words, so far as I could see. But there's no chance he means to marry her. This is your fault. If you would take a hand in her future, she wouldn't be so vulnerable. She needs you."

"What she needs is to stay home."

"She's not a boy. She can't make her own way. She needs a man who will provide for her, and the older she gets, the harder that will be. You need to be involved in her life."

Joan continued to look at her clashing needles instead of at him, which somehow annoyed him even more than her chiding. He felt his voice getting louder. "I won't parade my little girl through a ballroom like a horse at auction."

"I'm not asking you to. Talk to your peers. Arrange a match with a good man, one who will take care of her."

"I will not. She's too young."

"She means nothing to you, then."

"She means everything to me."

"Only as a shadow of what you've lost."

Parris bit back a retort and swung the poker in a short arc through the air. For the last year, conversations with Joan had been a maze, every path leading to the same dead end. And perhaps there was some truth to it. Catherine was hurting, too, but his own pain had prevented him from getting too close to her. If she had been a boy, he could have included her in his work, taught her a physic's profession. But because she was a girl, the best thing he could do was keep her safe.

Even his work for the king was frustrating. The king—a boy only slightly older than Catherine—was dying, and there was nothing he could do about it. Edward could no longer disguise his bloody cough, and the disease had wasted deep grooves in his cheeks. Parris and his other physics bled him daily and gave him soothing draughts, but it made little difference. The consumption was eating him alive. It was only a matter of time.

Parris could diagnose ailments, provide relief from pain and discomfort, sometimes even slow the course of a disease, but cure it? Only rarely, and in such situations it was never clear if the cure was the result of anything he had done, or simply the favor of God. If he were a barber-surgeon, then at least he might cut out the offending part, but inflicting that kind of pain on another human being was more than he could stomach. Besides, surgeons killed their patients as often as they helped them, if not from the procedure itself, then from the fevers that inevitably followed.

And what about the soul? Did it really exist? Of course it must—the Bible was clear on that subject—but if so, where was it? Could it be measured and cut open? Was it located in the heart, or the liver, or the inscrutable gray matter of the brain? When the body died, how did the soul get out? Did it blow away like a gas, or glide through some other, unknown dimension?

He had tried to find out. When any of his patients died, he prepared experiments to detect their souls' passing. He weighed their bodies as precisely as possible before and after death. He filled the air with flour dust and watched for any unexpected movement of the air. He devised instruments to detect sudden changes of temperature. Nothing worked. And the fact that he couldn't measure the soul made it difficult for him to believe that it existed at all. To believe that the boy he had loved lived on.

In England, caught up as it was in the politics of religion, such questions were dangerous. Questions of doctrine were questions of state, and many a theologian had gone to the block for asking the wrong ones. More than once, his colleagues had cautioned him to choose a safer field of inquiry.

He realized Joan was looking at him. "The questions won't go away," he said.

She sighed. "There are questions that don't have answers."

"I won't accept that."

Finally, the needles stopped moving, and she set the hose aside. As she did so, a slim object slipped out from between the folds and clattered on the floor. She reached for it, but Parris was quicker, and swept it up before she could. It was a rosary.

"What is this?"

"You know what it is."

He thumbed the beads. "This is Mariolatry. Popish superstition."

She stood and faced him down. "That was my grandmother's, and her grandmother's before that. Our families have been praying to the Virgin for generations, and you think now just because some *king* decides—"

"It's not about the king, Joan. It's the Scriptures. They never speak of Mary as anything but a simple woman."

"You don't pray to Mary anymore?"

"Of course not."

She dropped her voice until he could scarcely hear her. "And our son? Do you pray for our son?"

Parris stood rooted in front of her, wanting to take her hands in his but knowing she would reject the gesture. "Peter is dead," he said, the words tearing a piece out of his heart even now. "If he's with the Lord, he doesn't need our prayers. If he isn't, there's nothing our prayers can do for him."

She cried out and slapped his face. He caught her wrists and held them. "Death is a great evil," he said. "Don't you see? We need to fight it. To hold it at bay, even conquer it, if we can. How can I fight it unless I study it?"

"I can't live in constant dread that my husband will be locked in the Tower." She pulled her hands away and crossed them over her chest.

"It's important work. It has to be done. And precious few have the knowledge or skill to do it."

"Is it more important than your wife? Or your daughter?"

Parris knew this was the point in the conversation when he was supposed to break. When he consoled her that she was more important than anything, when he made empty promises he had no intention of keeping. But this time he felt so very tired of the charade. "Yes," he said. "It is more important."

She drew in her breath, and he knew a line had been crossed in their marriage, maybe one he could never step back over.

Her eyes were cold. "Not in the house. If I find a body in my house again, I'll go to my sister's and never come back."

Parris wondered if she could actually do it. She loved London, loved the society, and finding a noble match for Catherine was her only goal in life. How could she do that from Derbyshire? Nevertheless, he bowed his acquiescence. He was exhausted, but the prospect of climbing into bed while she stared down at him with reproachful eyes and clacking needles was too unpleasant. When his manservant, Henshawe, tapped at the door, he was only too happy to leave the room.

"What is it?" Parris said, shutting the door behind him.

"A messenger, sir. He says he has a gift from his master, a man named Christopher Sinclair."

Chapter Four

THE messenger was the darkest African Parris had ever seen. It took Parris a few moments even to make out his outline in the dim dawn light. He wore dark livery broken only by a thin red cross on the chest. He was impressively muscled, and at his waist hung a curved sword.

"He wouldn't come in, sir," Henshawe said. "He insisted on waiting outside for you."

"You are the surgeon," the African said in a voice exotic with accent.

"I'm Stephen Parris. A physic, not a surgeon."

"At least during the day." His visitor laughed without showing his teeth, a disturbing rumble that didn't crack his stone face.

Parris didn't smile. What could this stranger know of what he did at night? The African held out a pale wooden box banded with iron.

"This is the gift from your master?"

The African shook his head. "It is not a gift, and he is not my master."

Parris looked at Henshawe and then back again. "I thought—"

"Never mind. Take good care of it."

Parris took the box. "What is it?"

"That is not part of the message." The African turned to go. "My 'master' will call on you later this morning."

"What does he want with me?" Parris called after him.

No response. The African mounted his horse and spurred it away. The clatter of hooves echoed down the road and then faded from hearing.

Parris stared at the wooden box, which was nicked and worn, the iron bands rusted in places and held by a simple swinging clasp. The wood itself was strange, so pale as to resemble ivory, but soft, a bit sticky, and aromatic. Parris opened it.

At once he clapped the lid back down, startled to find something alive inside. He brought the box into the house and opened it again more carefully, peering through the crack.

It was a beetle.

Its body was shaped in a smooth dome the size of a silver half crown, its wing covers hard and shiny black. Moving its legs with slow purpose, it tried ineffectually to scale the sides of the box. Tiny curlicues of pale green traced along its wing covers and head. The insect itself was intriguing, but not nearly as baffling as the question of what it was doing here. Why would Sinclair, a stranger, send him an insect in a box, regardless of how exotic?

The creature was still bravely scrabbling at the wall of its prison. There was an indistinct mark on its head, and Parris turned around to see it better in the sunlight now slanting through his window. As he turned, the beetle changed direction and began an assault on the opposite wall of the box, still leaving its head in shadow. Parris tried again, and again the beetle turned. No matter how he spun it about, the beetle changed direction so that it faced away from the sun.

Intriguing. Was it avoiding the light? He held a candle to the box instead, and the beetle did not change direction, allowing him to examine the marking on its head more clearly. It was the sun it didn't like, then. He blocked the sunlight with his body, putting the beetle into shadow, and turned the box around in his hands. Still, no matter how he oriented the box, the beetle faithfully crawled directly away from the window. Somehow it could sense the direction of the sun, even without seeing it.

Did it have to be the sun? Maybe the beetle always walked toward the west, regardless of the time of day. He wouldn't know for sure until evening, when the sun was on the opposite side of the sky.

His thoughts drifted back to Sinclair. As enjoyable as it was to apply logic to the mystery of the beetle's movements, that could hardly be the reason for the gift. Why had it been sent?

A servant brought a breakfast plate of bread, cheese, and thinly sliced meat, and Parris realized he hadn't eaten since the previous afternoon. He ate everything, and as an afterthought dropped a few crumbs of bread and cheese into the box for the beetle. He had no idea what it ate— green plants, probably—but perhaps the crumbs would keep it alive.

Before he could close the box, however, the beetle lifted its wing covers, extended its frail filament wings, and took buzzing flight. Parris held up the plate to stop it and corral it back toward the box, but the beetle flew straight through the plate and out the other side. It was impossible. He would have doubted his eyes before believing such a thing could happen, except that the beetle then flew straight through the wall as well, still aimed unfailingly west.

He ran to the wall and felt around the spot, telling himself it had simply landed and stopped buzzing, but knowing it wasn't true. He searched for cracks and crevices into which it might have crawled, but found none. On the other side of the wall was a storeroom, filled with jars of preserved food and household supplies, but there was no sign of the beetle there, either. It must have passed through the next wall and out of the house. The walls were made of stone, finely cut and mortared. It was solid rock, and the beetle had flown right through it.

⊰✦✦⊱

TWO hours later, Henshawe showed Christopher Sinclair into the parlor, and Parris had to revise his impressions again. Sinclair was not a polished courtier with powder and lace like Francis Vaughan. He had a vertical scar across his mouth and oddly colored eyes which, though not truly as orange as a tiger's as Felbrigg had claimed, shone with an animal energy. He wore a robe and turban like a Mussulman. Younger than Parris expected, he was probably in his thirties, though the turban hid the color of his hair. He was tall and strong and restless, with a face not handsome, but intriguing, full of expression, full of life.

"You send enigmatic messages," Parris said. "I received your gift, but I still don't know why you're here."

"A proposition," Sinclair said. His voice was deep and bold. "One you are uniquely suited to appreciate."

Henshawe took Sinclair's cloak, but Sinclair insisted on keeping his walking stick, a heavy staff of black wood, carved roughly and not very skillfully into the form of a snake.

They sat near the fire on oaken armchairs, a carved table between them on which the servants had provided a variety of cheeses and small Moroccan sweets. A triangle of morning light shone through the red damask curtains, making the room feel bright and cheerful.

"I want to interest you in an expedition," Sinclair said, "to Chelsey's island."

Parris barked a laugh. "Come, now," he said. "Voyages to the west have hardly been a sound financial investment."

"Bad luck," Sinclair said, shrugging. "There's plenty of gold and spice to be had at the edge of the world. But that's not, I think, where your interests lie."

His bright eyes danced, and Parris wondered how much he knew. It was from Sinclair's boat, after all, that Felbrigg had stolen the corpse.

"What do you mean?" he asked.

"Chelsey's island holds more wonders than you can dream of. Lead transmuted to gold, iron made as light as balsa wood, paper impenetrable, walls invisible. Sickness healed. Death defeated."

"How do you know all this? From Chelsey? The ravings of a madman?"

"Did you not open the box?"

"I did, but—"

Sinclair clapped his hands. "Give it to me."

Irked by this patronizing gesture, Parris took the pale box from his pocket and handed it over without a word. Sinclair opened it a crack and peered inside. The eyes that met Parris's over the lid were dark.

"Where is it?"

"It flew away." Parris dared not say it flew through a solid wall; he assumed Sinclair knew this and had sent it to him for that reason, but if not, he didn't want to look like an idiot. Besides, the more time passed, the more he'd been able to convince himself the whole thing was a trick of his mind. It had been dark, after all, and he'd been exhausted, his mind strained by worry.

Sinclair slammed the box on the table. "What were you playing at? Do you think I keep dozens of mystery beetles in my pockets?"

"How was I to know what was in there?"

"You could have taken better care."

Parris wasn't in the mood to be lectured about his care of a beetle. "I should have killed it."

Sinclair gave a slow laugh, made more sinister by the scar across his mouth. "You should have tried," he said. "Then you would know more than you do now."

"Master Sinclair!" a musical voice called from above. Behind them, an open stairway led to the second floor, and at the top stood Catherine, beaming. "I thought it was you," she said. She ran lightly down the stairs and swept into the room, her blond hair loose and falling about her face.

◄┼┼►

CATHERINE felt alive for the first time in months. Peter's death had loomed over everything for so long, she almost didn't remember what it was like to think and talk normally. It wasn't Thomas Hungate's sweet whisperings at the ball that made her feel that way, either, no matter what Mother might think. She had enjoyed the attention, but Thomas was ultimately as dreary as all the other young men at court, even if he was heir to a baronetcy.

No, what had woken her excitement was Christopher Sinclair. Master Sinclair's magic at the ball had made her forget, if only for an instant, the dread that had been with her so long, like a rock stuck halfway down her throat that couldn't be dislodged. He had made her feel again the enthusiasm for the future that had seemed so easy when her brother was alive and so impossible when he was gone. And now here he was, actually in their home, talking with Father in the parlor.

"Are you trying to convince Father to come on your expedition?" she asked him.

Sinclair smiled at her indulgently. "And will you not come, too, my dear?"

She laughed. "What would you have me do on a remote island?"

"I would have you inspire us with your beauty."

Catherine bowed her head, pretending modesty, but she was delighted at the praise, all the more so because it would irritate Father. He didn't approve of such banter, at least not where she was involved. She didn't care. Father rarely talked to her anymore except to forbid her to do things. He was fanatic about keeping her safe—whatever that meant. Probably because of Peter, though he never said so.

No one ever spoke of Peter. It was a forbidden subject, like Father's medical experiments, like Mother's secret Catholicism. He was in every argument, in every awkward silence, sitting at his empty place at the supper table, more obvious than when he'd been alive, yet never mentioned. Sometimes it made her want to scream.

It had been Peter who understood her love of forbidden topics, the worlds of politics and theology and science that were only allowed to men. He answered questions her tutors thought indecorous for a lady to ask, and taught her things she wasn't supposed to know. Master Sinclair, in subtle ways, reminded her of Peter—he didn't care much about propriety, either.

"If I came, would you teach me how to perform your miracles?" she said.

"You can perform one right now, if you like." Sinclair lifted his walking stick from the side of his chair and handed it to her. She gasped and took a step back. Father looked from one to the other of them suspiciously.

"Take it, *ma chérie*," Sinclair said.

"Will it . . . ?"

"It's perfectly safe."

She took the stick gingerly. It was solid wood, carved in simple lines. It didn't feel dangerous, but she had seen this trick before.

"Set it down," Sinclair said. "Don't throw it or drop it; just place it on the floor."

Catherine gently set it down. "Just what is happening here?" Father said, but as soon as she drew her hands away, he didn't need to ask. The stick, made of dead wood, transformed into a very real and living snake.

Even though she knew what was coming, Catherine gave a shriek and jumped back. She had touched the stick; there was no way it had been a snake held stiff by paralysis or in some kind of trance. It had been wood, not flesh. But now . . .

The black snake glided across the floor, its movement so smooth that it seemed to grow longer at the head and shorter at the tail. After a moment, Master Sinclair sprang across the room and snatched the snake, not by the tail as in the Moses story, but by the head. It hung limply from his hand, and Catherine couldn't see that anything had changed until he tapped it on the floor, and it was hard and unyielding again.

"How do you do it?" she said.

"Me?" Sinclair said. "You're the magician today. I had nothing to do with it."

"It's from the island," Father said. "Just like the beetle." He took the stick from Sinclair and turned it over in his hands. "Incredible. Is the snake alive in there, inside the wood?"

"I believe the snake *is* the wood. Where else would the wood come from?" Sinclair said.

"But wood is dead, and the snake is alive. That would mean it dies and comes back to life each time it changes."

"Unless its outer flesh hardens and then relaxes while it remains a snake inside," Sinclair said.

"But it's not even warm," Father said.

"Does it weigh the same before and after the change? Have you measured it?" Catherine asked.

Both men looked at her. Father seemed surprised to hear her speak, but Sinclair's eyes were merry. "As a snake, it weighs almost twice what it does as a stick."

"It isn't a trick, is it?" she said. "This snake turns into wood and back in the wild."

Sinclair swept her another bow. "Parris, your daughter is sharper than most men. You have it right: I'm a charlatan."

"So it's not a miracle at all. It's just what the snake does."

"Not at all," Father said.

"Exactly right," Sinclair said at the same time.

Father glared at him. "A miracle is something that violates the natural order of the world, as this creature clearly does."

"Not so. This snake is as natural as a fox or a hare. Just as a hare will prick its ears and bolt for a hole to escape danger, so this snake transforms into a harmless stick when it feels threatened."

"But it's not possible. Flesh doesn't change into wood."

"Clearly it *is* possible."

"Not according to the rules of nature."

"Maybe the rules of nature are different than you think."

Mother appeared in the doorway. "Catherine Parris, what do you think you're about?"

Catherine felt heat rush to her cheeks. Trust Mother to come in just as things were getting interesting.

"Your daughter is charming," Sinclair said. "She has been delighting us with her company."

"Thank you," Mother said, "but she's too old to be seen in polite society with her hair down. Catherine, go back upstairs and get Blanche to dress you in a proper gown and arrange your hood."

"I'm only talking," she said. "Master Sinclair doesn't mind."

"Just because he's too polite to point out your unseemly behavior doesn't mean you should persist in it." She pointed at the stairs.

Catherine didn't move. "Master Sinclair is taking an expedition to Lord Chelsey's island. He invited me to come along."

Mother's stern gaze snapped to Sinclair, though the polite smile never left her face. "Ah, the life of a woman in a colony," she said. "Living in a wooden shanty, working your hands to calluses, never enough to eat. Exotic, isn't it?"

"Lady Parris—" Sinclair said.

"I thank you not to fill my daughter's head with foolish fancies. Catherine, the men don't need you here, and certainly not dressed like that. Upstairs. At once."

Catherine trudged up the stairs, obedient. It was almost as if Mother purposely denied her any small pleasure that might distract her from her grief. Mother didn't want her to learn about medicine, or read about politics, or even see certain parts of London.

"What you want," Mother had told her once, "is to be a man. You want to be independent and educated, to fight battles and achieve great things. Every woman wants that at some point in her life. But it will only bring you grief. Men will not permit it. You can influence and seduce and manipulate a man, but you can't claim his place, or he'll destroy you. Put these things out of your mind."

But Catherine couldn't put them out of her mind. She wanted to make her own choices, follow her own inclinations, determine her own future. Father decided everything about her life, from the clothes she wore to the interests she was permitted to pursue. When she married, it would be the same, only her husband would be in command.

Not that she had any real prospects. The only young man of her acquaintance whose conversation had any real substance to it was Matthew Marcheford, the bishop's son, but he hardly counted. He was going to be a clergyman, like his father. She could never marry a clergyman.

She flushed, thinking of the things Thomas Hungate had said to her in the garden, before Mother had discovered them. He'd promised a cathedral wedding, a honeymoon in Venice, a house in the country. It wasn't like she believed him. The conversations at balls were all fluff and gossip, the dances monotonous, and the boys dull. But his sweet whispers had made her heart beat faster and her face grow hot. She couldn't imagine Matthew Marcheford ever saying things like *that*.

At the top of the stairs, she paused. Mother had already left the room, and the men weren't looking at her. Catherine sat, concealing herself behind the banister, and peeked down between the rails.

PARRIS was still trying to wrap his mind around the snake-turned-walking-stick when Sinclair pulled a box of pale wood out of his pocket. Parris recognized it as a twin of the one the African had delivered to him that morning. Sinclair opened it, and there was the beetle.

"You found it again," Parris said. "How could you possibly——"

"I didn't. This is another, and the only one I have left. Pray do not lose it again."

Sinclair crossed the room and set the box on its side on a heavy oak table. The beetle crawled out of the box and along the surface of the table. Sinclair placed a book on end in front of it. It crawled right through.

When Parris didn't react, Sinclair smiled. "Good," he said. "Now, how about this?"

He held a stack of books over the beetle and dropped them with a thump, raising a puff of dust. The beetle walked out unscathed, then walked through an inkwell without a pause. Next, Sinclair set a carafe of water in front of it. It walked through the glass, appeared in the water, swimming, and emerged through the opposite side. Parris stalked the beetle down the length of the table, watching it pass through everything in its way. At the far end, he laid his hand on the table so the beetle could clamber onto his palm, but instead it walked straight through. He didn't feel so much as a tickle.

"Why don't you show this to the king?" Parris said.

"You should know the answer to that."

Parris did know. King Edward wouldn't see the wonder in a mystery like this any more than he saw it in a dissected human body. "Black magic," he said.

"There's a fine line between wonder and witchcraft, but this is definitely over it." Sinclair scooped the beetle up in the box and snapped it shut.

"That box—the beetle can't escape through it?"

Sinclair kissed it. "Chelsey brought thirty different species of animals home with him: beasts like monkeys, beasts like birds, beasts like nothing any man has ever seen before. The snake and the beetle I have. All the rest are missing. Dead, perhaps, or transformed into sand with the rest. Not so much as a skeleton left to tell their tale."

Parris fell back into a chair, feeling dazed. He had no explanation for an insect that defied the substance of matter. An insect that defied death itself. An insect that, hard as it was to believe, implied that everything the Mad Admiral had claimed about this island might actually be true.

"A miracle," he said.

"No miracle. There are reasons for everything."

"Surely some things are decreed by God to be as they are."

"And what if they're not?" Sinclair's eyes were fever-bright. "What if everything in the universe is *not* guided by some unseen hand, but instead acts according to natural rules that never change?"

Parris was astonished. "You're a Copernican."

"Copernicus proved that the earth is flat, not round like the Greeks would have had us believe. He showed us the rules that govern the sun and the stars. He gave us their reasons."

"But he's been denounced. By Martin Luther *and* the Pope."

"If the world was created by a rational God, why should we be surprised to find it governed by rational rules? Copernicus wasn't content to know that the sun dissolved each night at the western edge of the earth and re-formed each morning in the east; he asked how it did so. And why."

"We already knew why. God re-creates it daily with his power."

"Yes, yes, but why? Why do fermented wine and soda ash bubble when mixed? Why are seashells found embedded in rocks in the high mountains of Tuscany? How does a blind seed buried in darkness know which way to grow to find the light?"

"The answers are the same. God directs them."

"Yet there are rules. This island of Chelsey's is no different. The man who understands its rules gains its power. For instance"—Sinclair rattled the box—"why doesn't my friend here crawl right out of his prison? Because the box is made of wood from the island. Wood from a tree the beetle lives in and from which it eats leaves."

"How could you know that? From Chelsey?"

"I know it eats leaves because that's what I've been feeding it. As for the rest: simple logic. A beetle can't take off from the ground; it must climb to a height in order to fly. If this beetle always passed through everything, it couldn't climb, and thus it couldn't get high enough to fly or find its food or hide from its predators."

"Predators? What could eat such a thing?"

Sinclair smiled. "A bird with tricks of its own."

"But it doesn't fall through my table," Parris objected. "My table wasn't made with wood from Chelsey's island."

"Now you're asking the right questions. Just what can and can't this creature pass through?"

Despite himself, Parris found himself growing excited. For the next half hour, they set the beetle to walk on every material they could find in the house: glass, cotton, paper, oak, yew, beech, tallow, straw, iron, brass, wax, porcelain, silk, earth. Parris wrote down their findings in the precise hand he used to record observations about the body when dissecting. By the end, they had discovered several things:

1. The beetle could walk through every material they tested except for wax and earth.

2. The table was not special. Once Parris scraped away the waxy resin that had been used to treat the tabletop, the beetle fell straight through it to be caught in the box he held underneath.

3. The pale wood of the beetle's box had not been treated, but the inside was covered with a natural waxy oil that imprisoned the beetle just as effectively.

4. The beetle could pass *into* the box, but not out of it—which didn't make any sense at all, but made an effective trap. Sinclair could slam the closed box down on top of the beetle, or slide the box along the table into it, forcing it to pass through into a prison from which it could not escape. Sinclair tried it several times, apparently pleased with the theatricality.

The fourth point was especially intriguing. How could the wax work to trap the beetle in one direction, but not in the other? Either it could pass through wax or it couldn't. The direction shouldn't matter. Was it possible the beetle had control over its ability? In which case . . . it wanted to be in the box? It was one possible theory, but not a very satisfying one. In any event, the waxy wood seemed a necessary part of the beetle's ability to survive.

"You must still admit the hand of God who created the tree to exude such an oil," Parris said.

Sinclair shrugged. "Just another mystery, to which we must pose questions. What does the tree gain from the oil? Perhaps protection from creatures that would eat its bark. Or perhaps the beetle itself provides some value to the tree."

Parris laughed. "Are you saying the tree *decided* to exude the oil to encourage the beetle to nest in its branches?"

"It's a mystery, as I said. And one we must travel there to solve."

⭤+⭤

CATHERINE shifted on the stairs, annoyed. Here she was, peeking through the banister like a child up past bedtime, while they were investigating one of the most remarkable animals ever seen. It was no use getting dressed and then trying to join them. It would take Blanche half an hour to arrange her gown and hair to Mother's satisfaction, and by that time the men's conversation would be over. Or if it wasn't, Mother would find some other reason to pull her away.

She itched to ask her own questions. Where did the beetle go, when it passed through a solid object? It implied there was some *other* place, some spirit world parallel to their own, into which it could momentarily pass. She wondered what would happen if two such beetles met on their way through a solid object. Would each beetle pass through the other? Or would they collide?

The light through the windows darkened, and wind whipped at the shutters. It would storm soon. A shadow behind Master Sinclair deepened, and she peered more closely at it. It had an odd shape, like a man crouched very still. It was too small to be a man, though, and it had what looked like huge claws extending from its hands. The light filtering through the red curtains gave the impression of red fur tipped with black. Catherine was not prone to fits of fancy or to imagining goblins in dark corners, but it looked real. Then its eyes flicked open, revealing large yellow irises around pupils of deep black, and she screamed.

As soon as she did so, the creature vanished. The men ran toward her, but Mother was quicker, bursting through the door and up the stairs with Henshawe right behind her. Catherine stood there like a fool, still pointing at the corner with a hand over her mouth.

Mother felt her cheeks and head. "She's flushed."

"What did you see?" Father said.

Catherine looked from one of her parents to the other. "Nothing. I'm sorry." She stumbled up the top steps and fled to her room.

⇥✦⇤

PARRIS stoked the sitting room fire, relishing the warmth and the sharp smell of burning wood. It gave him something to look at besides his wife, who was knitting again.

"Sinclair showed me something from Chelsey's island," he said. "A beetle that couldn't be trapped or killed. It flew straight through solid matter as sure as the Lady Mary is a Papist."

He waited, not looking at her. There was no sound but the crackle of the fire and the steady, soft click of her needles.

"This island," he said, trying again. "What if it holds the answers? The truth about the soul and life and death?"

"Folly," Joan said. "We have enough troubles here in London without seeking more at the edge of the world."

"Sinclair plans to form a colony. Chelsey left half his crew behind, so there should already be the rudiments of a settlement. He'll be taking families, men and women, as many as want to go."

"And you're saying what? That you want to go with him?"

"What if I do? He's looking for the same answers I am."

"Don't be a fool," Joan said. "He's just after your money."

Parris stole a glance at her. "We may not be able to stay in England anyway. The king won't live for long, and when he dies, Mary will take the throne. I'm not as important as a Cranmer or a Ridley, but my day will come. When it does, I'd better be out of the country."

"Rubbish. Who are you? You're a physic, not a bishop. You're not even a minister."

"But my name is on the Articles."

Her needles fell silent. "What?" she whispered.

"I was at the king's bedside when they were written. I signed my name to them as witness."

"The Forty-two Articles?"

"Yes."

"The refutation of Roman doctrine? *Cranmer's* Articles?"

"Yes, the very same! They were true. I believed them. I would sign them again."

Joan pursed her lips and shook her head. "So sign a recantation. Swallow your pride and return to the Church."

"I can't. I won't yield to Popery."

"You won't yield. Oh, yes, the *physic* will take a stand beside the archbishops and theologians. Please, Stephen. Greater men than you have bent in the wind."

Parris had known this wouldn't be easy. "We will have to flee London, one way or another."

"So this is your plan? You're serious? To drag your wife and daughter on this doomed expedition? The last people to go to this island *died*."

"We might die if we stay. We could return to our lands in Derbyshire and lie low, but it would be a risk."

"And what about Catherine?"

"She must come, too, of course."

"Don't be ridiculous."

"It'll be good for her. She'll see new things, experience more of life."

Joan counted on shaking fingers. "Disease? Malnutrition? Untamed jungle, dirt, and mosquitoes? Or the company of sailors and adventurers? Tell me, Stephen, which of these will be good for her?"

"There is more to life than comforts."

For a moment Parris thought she was actually going to cry. "This is no escape," she said. "To run to a place from which no one has returned alive. This is a death sentence of a different kind."

"It has its dangers," Parris said, "but it may also have its rewards."

"Well then, I shall look forward to seeing you on your return: mad as a March hare and dead within a fortnight."

"It won't be like that."

"Not for Catherine and me, it won't. We'll stay with my sister."

"Woman, you'll do as I say!" His voice broke at this, and he coughed to get it back under control. "If not for the king's illness, I would leave you and Catherine here. But you would be held hostage against my return. It wouldn't matter that you had nothing to do with the Articles."

She regarded him coldly. "As usual, men do as they will, and women must bear the consequences."

"Believe me, I would spare you this if I could."

She flashed him a hard, bitter smile. "You should have thought of that before now."

Henshawe knocked lightly and then pushed open the door. "Two gentlemen to see you, sir."

"Who is it?" Joan said.

"The master's cousin, Francis Vaughan, with a Spaniard."

Parris sighed. "Show them to the parlor," he said, but Henshawe didn't have a chance to obey. Vaughan strode into the room uninvited, his Spanish friend right behind him.

Chapter Five

CATHERINE felt like a fool. No one would have believed her if she'd told them what she'd seen. But there *had* been something in the corner. Only it wasn't there a moment later, leaving her to wonder if she'd imagined the whole thing. But if snakes could turn to wood and beetles could turn intangible, surely a creature with fur and claws might disappear.

She held herself erect while Blanche, her young maidservant, laced up her corset. Women's gowns were not as comfortable as girls', but now that she was sixteen, Mother insisted she wear them. The new gowns announced that she was a woman grown, old enough to marry. Old enough to attract looks from men of all ages.

Mother was constantly reminding her how important marriage was, how much could be gained with wealth and a title, how they had to make good use of Father's favor with the king before he did something foolish enough to lose it. But no one she met at Mother's balls was half as interesting as that little beetle she'd watched crawl over the parlor table.

She inhaled so Blanche could pull the laces as tight as possible. Blanche had been with her for over a year, and was now much better at her work. At the start, recently come from France, she'd known only a few words of English and hadn't been very skilled. Of course, Catherine spoke French, and she could tell that Blanche—though she tried to hide it—understood Latin. It was unusual for a servant girl. She suspected Blanche had a secret past, and amused herself by imagining what it might be. Blanche worked hard, though, both at her tasks and at her English. Catherine liked having a girl her own age around, so she never complained.

The gown came over her head, and Blanche arranged the French hood to frame her face. Catherine spun in front of a large mirror of polished tin, trying to catch a glimpse of what she must look like. The distorted reflection was hardly like the real thing, but it was enough. Father had scowled when Mother gave her this dress, warning that she was too young to be out in society. She thought Mother and Father should strike a deal: he would let her pick the dresses, and she would let him cut up dead bodies as much as he wanted.

Mother didn't think she knew about the dead bodies, but she did. Of course she knew. It was shocking, but that didn't bother her. The world was changing. Even religion was changing, with Englishmen boldly biting their thumbs at the power of Rome. Bishop Marcheford had called the Pope an antichrist from the pulpit on Sunday and denounced Papists as worse than pagans. In such a world, Father's secret experiments seemed thrilling, not frightening: a defiance of old institutions.

She might even have revered him, if he had spoken to her from time to time. As it was, he mostly irritated her, with his pompous speeches about how she wasn't ready to be out in society. How did he know what she was ready for? He barely knew her anymore.

Once, a few months earlier, she had told Matthew Marcheford that she hated her father. She had just been angry at some incident she couldn't even remember now, but Matthew had been appalled. He was a good friend, but she should have thought twice before making shocking confessions to the son of a bishop. He was going to be just like his father: educated, eloquent, brilliant . . . and so upright and honorable it made her sick.

Catherine dipped her fingers in a basin by the mirror and touched the cool water to her eyelids. When she opened them again, the red creature sat in the corner behind her writing desk. A scream leaped into her throat, but she fought it back down. She was not going to cause another commotion only to have it disappear again. The creature was about her size and had a startlingly human face. Its long, curved claws curved toward each other like a crab's pincers, and she could see now that it had many tails—at least six—that waved back and forth behind and above it. One of the tails, much thicker than the others, ended in a bony spine that looked needle-sharp.

Catherine whispered to Blanche as quietly as she could. "Look over there by the desk."

Blanche turned too quickly, and the creature sprang away and disappeared into the wall. Blanche narrowed her eyes. "I saw something." She approached the corner, which was now clearly empty, and waved her foot where the creature had been. "Was it a mouse?"

Catherine shook her head. At least Blanche had seen the movement—which meant Catherine wasn't crazy. "Come with me," she said.

Father's library was filled with books, scrolls, unbound sheafs of parchment, and boxes full of letters from all around the world. She trolled the shelves until she found what she was looking for: the thirty-seven volumes of Pliny the Elder's *Naturalis Historia,* the last work he completed before dying in the eruption of Vesuvius. She pulled out the eighth volume—*On Beastes*—and paged through it until she found what she was looking for.

She read the Latin out loud. "Likewise there is a beast which he calleth *Manticoras,* having three ranks of teeth, which when they meet together are one within another like the teeth of combs: with the face and ears of a man, with red eyes; of color sanguine, bodied like a lion, but having a tail armed with a sting like a scorpion: his voice resembleth the noise of a flute and trumpet sounded together: very swift he is"—she paused and looked up at Blanche as she finished the sentence—"and man's flesh of all others he most desireth."

Blanche's eyes were wide. "Is that what you saw?"

"It didn't have red eyes," Catherine said. "They were human eyes, like yours or mine. And I couldn't see its teeth."

"But . . . in the house? Was it real?"

Catherine pursed her lips. "I have to tell Father."

They raced together into the sitting room. Catherine burst through without knocking, clutching the book, and then stopped dead at the sight of both her parents talking with Cousin Vaughan and a stranger with a massive head of black curls and dead eyes. Blanche, coming through the door right behind her, gasped and clapped a hand over her mouth.

Catherine had once thought Vaughan handsome, with his lavish red Spanish cloak and lacy cuffs and that elegant little pointed beard. But the looks he'd given her over the past year made her uncomfortable. A few months back, he had cornered her in an alcove and told her she was growing more beautiful every day. He might have done more, but the sound of a door closing had spooked him, and he'd run off.

The stranger wore an acre of black cloth more like a priest's cassock than a gentleman's cloak. He had a large jaw and deep-set eyes that scanned the room relentlessly. Blanche shrank back until she was half hidden behind Catherine.

Vaughan swept an ostrich-feather hat from his head and gave her a deep bow. "Miss Catherine." He turned back to Father and indicated the stranger. "This is Diego de Tavera, an aide and friend to the Spanish ambassador."

Father nodded his head somewhat curtly, and Catherine dropped a curtsy.

"I have private business with you, cousin," Vaughan said.

"I have nothing more to give you," Father said.

Vaughan's smile was not friendly. "I'm not after money."

They held each other's gaze until Father said, "Very well." He walked out of the room with Vaughan following, leaving Catherine, Blanche, and Mother alone with the Spaniard.

They all stared at each other, no one moving. Catherine hadn't been pleased to see Cousin Vaughan, but this stranger with the dead eyes frightened her even more.

◆┼◆┼◆

PARRIS slammed the parlor door and glared at Vaughan. "What do you want?"

"How is the king?" Vaughan asked.

"He's well."

"Really?"

"The picture of health."

"You see, I am just returned from Framlingham."

Parris froze. "To see the Princess Mary," he said. It wasn't a question.

"Her Grace must know." Vaughan's voice was barely audible, a breath in his ear. "She must be prepared."

So Vaughan wasn't looking for money, after all. This subject was far more dangerous, and it was not a conversation Parris wanted to be anywhere near. "No one can say when the king will die, least of all me," Parris said. "Pray God he lives to seventy and sires many sons for England." He moved to leave the room, but Vaughan caught his arm.

"Come, now, cousin. Everyone knows the king doesn't have long to live. What I want to know is, who will the king will name as his successor?"

"*You* want to know? Or your Spanish friend does?"

"Tavera is Mary's confidant. Once she takes the throne, Catholic Spain will be our strongest ally."

"Then why ask me?"

Vaughan released his arm and began to pace. "There are rumors. The Duke of Northumberland may pressure King Edward into disinheriting Mary and naming a Protestant heir instead."

"Nonsense," Parris said.

"All too probable. Northumberland will not relinquish power easily. Her Grace will be in danger. She must know what he plans."

Parris did know what Northumberland planned, but he wasn't about to tell Vaughan. The nobles of the land were arming against the day of the king's death. Mary had the best claim to the throne, but the country was divided, some longing for the return of the old faith, some wanting to avoid it at all costs. Parris himself wanted a Protestant monarch to continue Edward's reforms, but he didn't want to be part of the fight.

"You're in his rooms all the time; you hear what he and the duke talk about in their secret conferences." Vaughan sidled up to him and hissed in his ear again. "Or must I tell the king about your guest last night?"

Vaughan wore the self-satisfied smile he used when he knew he had someone's complete attention. He was no fool, despite his foppish appearance; the man spoke Latin, Greek, and French, and had a keen mind for politics. But Parris knew what Vaughan did not: that the king might not even survive long enough to be told. He was at his palace in Greenwich now, seeing almost no one, and waiting for the end.

"This is treason," Parris said. "Please leave."

Vaughan laughed. "It'll be the talk of the court. Stephen Parris, the king's physic, a demon worshipper. Mutilating the dead to cast the king's horoscope. You'll be lucky to last the night."

"No matter. I'm the king's man."

"I don't think the king will see it that way."

Parris held the door open. "You're finished here."

"No second chances."

Parris made no reply. Vaughan tipped his ostrich-feather hat and sauntered out.

◆◆◆

CATHERINE wanted to leave, but she was afraid to turn her back on Tavera. His gaze seemed to bore through her whenever he looked her way. He spoke mostly with Mother, but his eyes moved constantly. Blanche continued to cower behind Catherine's back.

"I have only been in the country for a few months," Tavera said, his

Spanish accent pronounced. "I tried to pay my respects at the palace, but I was not allowed an audience."

"Few are, these days," Mother said. "The king has not been well."

Tavera's pale eyes betrayed no emotion. "In what particulars? Has your husband told you anything?"

"Only that we should pray for the king's health."

"Are you sure? Perhaps he let slip when he thinks the king will die?"

"Stephen would never say such a thing."

"Of course not. Excuse me, I forget my manners." Tavera's eyes traveled the room. "But you would tell us, would you not?" His voice was like gravel.

"Sir?"

"Your cousin has told me of your loyalty to the True Faith. You would tell us if you knew anything of the king." His eyes flicked to the wall, to the door, back to her. "In these dark times, those of us who are still friends of the Princess Mary must remain faithful."

Mother regarded him steadily. "And how might the friends of the princess be rewarded?"

A smile crept across Tavera's face, but it didn't make him look any more cheerful. "She is ever ready to reward those who love her. Any stains on your family name would be . . . forgotten . . . if your service is valuable to Her Grace."

"And if my husband . . . ?"

"The princess understands what it is to be a woman," Tavera said. "She spent much of her life submitting to the whims of an evil father. Act soon, and she will be your ally."

Mother swept her fingers at Catherine as if brushing her out the door. "Master Tavera and I must talk alone."

Catherine stared at her. "But——"

"Now, Catherine."

Catherine curtsied and made to leave, but before she could, Cousin Vaughan returned, with Father just behind him. "My lady," Vaughan said, "we must take our leave."

"So soon?" Mother said. Vaughan kissed her hand, and the two men left.

Father's face was like thunder. He and Mother glared at each other for several moments until Father's mouth twisted and he chuckled.

"I don't see what's funny," Mother said.

Father shook his head. "That fool is climbing into deep waters."

Catherine remembered the creature and the book in her hand. "Father?"

Mother pressed her fingers to her temples. "Leave us, Catherine. Say no more of this."

✦✦✦

CATHERINE retreated to her room, Blanche right behind her. As soon as the door was shut, Catherine cornered her.

"You knew him, didn't you?"

Blanche's dark hair had pulled loose from under her cap, and her eyes were wide and frightened. "Who?" she whispered, almost too low for Catherine to hear.

"That huge Spaniard. Who is he?"

Blanche's lip trembled. "You heard his name."

Catherine studied her. "You're from Spain, aren't you? Not from France."

Blanche's eyes darted fearfully. She put a knuckle to her mouth and bit on it.

"I know you're a Jew," Catherine said gently. "I've seen your prayers on Saturdays. And the foods you avoid."

Blanche covered her face in her hands and began to cry. Catherine touched her shoulder. "I won't tell. It's our secret, honest."

"I did live in France. For three years, in Calais. With my father."

"And before that?"

"I was born in Valladolid, Castile."

"What's your real name?"

"Blanca."

Catherine smiled. "Of course." She guided Blanche—Blanca—to the bed and helped her sit down.

Blanca wiped away tears. When she could speak again, she told her story in a shaky voice.

"Diego de Tavera came to our town three years ago. He brought many priests and soldiers with him and announced what he called a 'Term of Grace.' We were *conversos*, outwardly Christian, but everyone knew it was a sham. We had ten days to burn our Talmud and convert to Christianity, or Tavera said he would burn my father to death and then torture my mother and sisters and me until we recanted.

"My father brought me with him to court in Toledo to petition the emperor to stop Tavera. While we were gone, there was a procession in the streets to honor the Virgin Mary. My youngest sister emptied a basin of dirty water out the window without looking, and it splashed on a statue of the Virgin.

"A mob stormed our home and set it on fire. They grabbed my mother and sisters when they ran out and dragged them to Tavera. By the time my Father and I returned home with the emperor's letter, it was too late. Tavera had burned them all at the stake."

Blanca was crying again. "Juana, my youngest sister, was only seven years old. We left Spain that night and fled to France."

Catherine clasped Blanca's hand. "What happened to Tavera?"

"Nothing. He went on to do the same thing at the next town."

"You started over? Learned a new language?"

"I already knew French. It was the language of the court, even in Spain. My father taught me when I was small."

"Where is your father now?"

"Our neighbors in Calais started to get suspicious. We claimed to be Christians, but they knew. We boarded a ship for London to start over again, but my father died on the voyage."

Catherine had never known any of this. She had imagined a romantic past for Blanca—a French princess on the run, perhaps, waiting for her true love to pass her a message that it was safe to return. This was different. This was real. Blanca couldn't have been more than thirteen years old when her mother and sisters had been killed, and only sixteen when she lost her father. Catherine blushed to think of this daughter of a rich and important Spanish family waiting on her hand and foot.

A servant brought a platter into the room: sliced bread and meats, lentils, a cake of raisins, cheese, and wine. Blanca arranged the meal on a small sitting table.

"What was your home like?" Catherine asked.

Blanca busied herself serving, until Catherine wondered if she'd heard the question.

"Happy," she said finally. "We had everything we wished for: meat on the table, pretty things to wear, sweets on feast days. Though we had to pretend to be Christians, and follow our own customs as best as we could in secret.

"My father was an important man of business. I didn't understand what he did, but it was something to do with foreign trade. Many people owed him money. They treated him with respect, though most people knew we were Jews." Blanca laid a cloth in Catherine's lap. "I didn't realize until that day how much they hated us."

The meal served, Blanca left for the kitchen, where she would eat her own lunch with the other servants.

Catherine thought of Blanca's memories and wondered about Father. She was aware enough of political realities to know Father could be executed if his human dissections were found out. At the least, he would lose his place at court. Would they have to leave the country and wander from place to place like Blanca, pretending to be someone else, fearing for their lives?

She didn't know what to think of Father's crime. Perhaps it truly was evil of him to rob those men of a proper Christian burial—most people would think so. When she thought of it, though, she was more curious than appalled. What did the body look like inside? How did it work? Were the arms and legs controlled by strings from some central location, like a marionette?

When she finished her meal, there was plenty left over, and she thought again of the manticore, if that's what it was. As far as she knew, it was still in the house. It had turned invisible, or something very like it. Was it a ghost, then? Or a demon?

If Father didn't have time to solve this mystery, maybe she could. The first thing to figure out was whether it was a spirit or real flesh and blood. That was easy. If it was flesh and blood, then it would need to eat.

She placed the platter of leftover food on the floor. Then she left her sitting area and retreated to the far side of the room, where she settled on her bed to wait.

The afternoon light dimmed, and wind rattled the windowpane. Rain began to spatter the sill and soon became a hypnotizing downpour. She was sleepy, and keeping a sharp watch on the food became difficult. Just as her eyelids began to close, the cake of raisins jerked and disappeared.

Her breathing quickened, but she forced herself to remain still. The storm muted the day's light, but not so much that she couldn't see her room clearly. There was nothing there. Yet the meat began to twitch, and a corner tore away and vanished. In a few minutes the meat was almost gone, and Catherine still couldn't see even a hint of the thing eating it.

She waited. Slowly, like the first stars appearing in the night sky, the barest sense of the manticore appeared. The outline sharpened, and the colors became distinct, but she could still see the wall through its body. She would have sworn it was a ghost, had a piece of her sliced meat not been hanging from its mouth.

It chewed and swallowed, now as solid as she was. Despite its shockingly human face, it wore no clothes, and its body was covered with brilliant orange-red hair, as bright as any tropical bird. Instead of hands, each arm ended in sharp pincers, and each of its back legs ended in a pair of curved hooks that seemed ill-suited for walking. Its multiple tails waved and intertwined around a thicker, spiked one. Despite all of these oddities, its most striking feature was its yellow eyes—not the color of corn or wheat, but brilliant, like sunshine. They were blazing straight at her.

It snapped up the last of the meat with its pincer-hands, never taking its gaze away from her. Catherine began to wonder if it could distinguish between the meat on the platter and the meat on her bones. She had heard of the cannibals of the Indies, wild men who ate their own children. Maybe this hadn't been such a good idea. She took a small pillow from her bed and threw it, hoping to startle the manticore away, but to her amazement, the pillow flew right through its body.

The manticore didn't move. How could it pick up and eat solid food, and yet not be touched by a pillow? It didn't even seem to have noticed.

Hooves clattered against the courtyard outside, and the manticore tensed, poised for flight. Catherine rushed to the window. It was Father, riding out to attend on the king, his cloak streaming with rain.

Only then did she realize she had turned her back on the manticore. She whirled, but it wasn't by the meat platter anymore. Where had it gone? She felt motion behind her, and turned again to see the manticore's spiked tail swinging toward her, aimed at her back. She screamed and dodged away just in time.

She ran for the door, made it through, and careened down the stairs, not daring to look behind her. On the last step, she tripped and fell onto the stone landing, scraping her elbow, but she barely felt it. She jumped to her feet again and kept running. Mother appeared and called after her, but Catherine had only one thought: she had to reach Father. Mother wouldn't understand, wouldn't believe her. She raced to the stables and climbed onto her horse, not bothering with a saddle, and galloped out into the rain.

Mother and Henshawe ran out behind her, shouting, but she ignored them. The pelting water was cold and streamed into her eyes. Halfway across the courtyard, a shadow flew toward her, only visible because of the disturbance it made in the water. The horse reared. Its back was wet, and she reached for its mane, but clutched only empty air. She fell hard to the paving stones and rolled away from the thrashing hooves. Her right leg twisted beneath her, on fire with pain. She tried to stand and found her leg wouldn't support her weight.

Henshawe eased a halter over the frightened horse's neck and led it back toward the stable. Mother helped Catherine walk, her reprimands lost in the noise of the rain. Father rode out of sight, unaware of what had happened. Leaving Catherine to face the manticore alone.

⧾⧾⧾

INSIDE, Blanca helped Catherine out of her wet clothes, and Mother wrapped her in a thick blanket. She pressed a steaming cup of chocolate into Catherine's hands, a bitter drink recently imported from Spain and gaining popularity at court. Mother dismissed Blanca and pulled up a chair to sit across from Catherine.

"You love your father, don't you?"

Catherine nodded, wary of the direction this conversation might take.

"I love him, too," her mother continued. "No, don't give me that look. I love him more than you know." She wrapped her thin fingers around her own cup of chocolate and breathed in the vapors. "Did I ever tell you he was there when you were born? He was actually present, at the birth. The midwives were horrified. They ranted and screeched at him, but he wouldn't budge. Ever the physic, he had to see for himself how the body worked.

"Of course, the midwives told everyone, and it was a great scandal, but I loved him for it. He was there, you see. He wasn't off riding or shooting or making a business deal. He was right in the thick of it, next to me, looking at everything, asking questions, cheering me on. When they finally lifted you out, bloody and squalling, the tears were running down his cheeks."

Catherine took a sip from the bitter chocolate, scalding her lips, and wondered why her mother was telling her this. If she loved Father so much, why did she scold him all the time? Why did they barely touch anymore? Saying what she thought around her mother could lead to a long lecture, but Catherine took the risk. "He's the same man now," she said. "Still searching for the truth."

Mother shook her head. "It was an admirable trait before. Now it's an obsession. He'll keep throwing himself against that stone wall until he destroys himself, and us with him."

"Is that why you always fight?"

"Someday you'll understand. You'll have your own children, and they'll mean more to you than the world. A wife has to defend her children, even against her own husband." She put a hand on Catherine's knee with a wry smile. "Not that I expect you to be easily cowed. But sometimes, despite all you say and do, your husband won't be dissuaded from folly. When that happens, as a mother you have to close ranks. Your first responsibility is to your children. To salvage what you can." She wasn't even looking at Catherine anymore. "Even if they hate you for it."

Catherine laughed and clasped her mother's hand. "I don't hate you."

"Just remember that, whatever I do, it's out of love for you. I know you don't want me to find you a husband. I know what you want: to run your own life, to discuss politics and money and be the equal of a man. You don't see what I see. You haven't lived long enough. Romantic stories end badly, more often than not."

Catherine relaxed. So that was what this was all about. "Don't worry. I know better than to fall for Thomas Hungate."

Her mother's eyes drifted past Catherine again, as if seeing something in the far distance. "I know you do," she said.

Chapter Six

PARRIS took a wherry to Greenwich. He preferred the water route, especially on a day like this, when the storm left the roads awash in mud. The boat's canopy kept the rain off, and the Thames was only marginally slower than the traffic-clogged Dover Road.

The boat maneuvered between the massive starlings of London Bridge, under the shadow of its shops and houses, and continued on toward the wharfs, where oceangoing vessels too tall to pass under the bridge stopped to unload their cargo. A forest of masts crowded the riverbanks as the ships jostled for room, the queues backing up past Wapping and Rotherhithe and clear around the Isle of Dogs.

He found himself reading the names of the ships: the *Katryn Belle,* the *Plenty,* the *Sancta Clara,* the *Black George.* Then he saw it: the *Western Star,* tied up at anchor and rocking gently against the pier. Parris knew little of ships, but he could tell this was a carrack, the workhorse of trade with distant lands like Africa, the Indies, and Cathay. He noticed how warped its planking was, how the ends of boards stuck out from the line of the hull, though he didn't know if such damage was superficial or serious. Its sails were weathered and gray, its decks deserted.

It was still full of preserved corpses, too, unless something had changed. Which was odd in more than one way. Under normal circumstances, a crew would sew their dead into sacks of sailcloth and tip them into the sea, not transport them home. They must have died so quickly and in such numbers that the others had not the strength or the stomach to dispose of them properly. Fear of ghosts or no, he was surprised that the harbormaster hadn't ordered the ship cleaned by now, or even burned. Perhaps he had, and Sinclair had somehow prevented it.

At Greenwich, they tied up at the king's pier. Servants held the palace doors open wide, and Parris navigated through sumptuous rooms to the private chambers where the boy king was spending his final days. He met another of the king's physicians, George Owen, just leaving the room.

"How is he?" Parris asked.

"A bit stronger today. He's hearing a suit and arguing about it with the duke."

"Whose suit?"

"Some fool who wants funding to repeat the Mad Admiral's expedition."

Parris gaped. "Christopher Sinclair?"

"That's the name."

"He's in there right now?"

Owen nodded. "I'd slip in quietly."

Parris thanked him, opened the door, and tred softly past the posted guards. The cavernous bedroom was decorated in the Italian Renaissance style, not yet touched by Tudor renovations. Tall gilded mirrors faced ancient portraits over acres of red carpet, and on the ceiling Endymion reclined in the arms of Morpheus, the god of sleep.

Edward was sitting propped up in bed, his frail form lost under layers of rich cloaks. The bed was draped in damask and cloth-of-gold, and cherubs cavorted with peacocks on its high wooden panels. A servant hovered nearby with a cool cloth for the king's head and another to wipe his face when he coughed. On Edward's right was the Duke of Northumberland, an imposing gray-haired man with a reputation for political ruthlessness, who ruled as Edward's regent until he came of age. To his left was Sinclair, still wearing his robe and turban, orange eyes alight with passion.

"I'd sooner have this man drawn and quartered than furnished with further coin," Northumberland said.

Sinclair chuckled as if this were a jest. "My lord, I seek only to enrich the crown."

"With dirt and salt water, sir? Where is the profit from the crown's first investment?" Northumberland said.

"The profit is only delayed."

Parris padded quietly to the side of the bed, avoiding eye contact. Edward shifted aside the fur cloaks and unlaced his doublet to reveal his sunken chest. Parris made a neat incision, just above the lungs that caused the king such distress. With tongs, he lifted a leech from a leather pouch and placed its greedy mouth over the wound. Physics were divided over the use of leeches, but Parris found that no other method so cleanly and swiftly drew out the blood.

The king coughed hard several times, then spoke in a weak voice. "Master Sinclair."

"Your Majesty?"

"Lord Chelsey's voyage took three years. We wish to know how you propose to return in one."

"Your Majesty, Chelsey was charting unknown seas, conquering a wild climate, and hewing a settlement out of the wilderness. At the very edge of the world, he found an island which he named Horizon. He left half his men there in a thriving colony, stockpiling gold and spices. A ship need only load the cargo and return home."

"Forgive my ignorance," drawled Northumberland, "but Chelsey's cargo was a ship full of dirt. You *claim* he left a colony. But like any street charlatan with a foolproof method to make gold from goose feathers, you ask us to pay handsomely now for a wonder yet to come. How can we be sure these riches will not simply transform to dirt again? If they ever existed at all."

"Because not everything transformed," Sinclair said. At this, he produced from his pocket a golden fruit the size and shape of a fig, round at the bottom but rising into a thinner stemmed neck. It was exquisitely made, with a minutely carved gold stem and subtle vertical striping.

"Are you asking us to believe that this grew from a tree?" Northumberland said.

Sinclair held it as delicately as a blossom. He proffered it to the king. "Touch it, Your Majesty."

The king took it and gasped in surprise. Parris tried to keep his eyes on his work, but he couldn't help watching. The fruit was airy and fragile, like a thing made of eggshells instead of gold.

"How did such a thing come into your keeping? And why was it not produced before now to support Lord Chelsey's lunatic claims?" Northumberland said.

"Chelsey gave it to me before he died. He lived only hours and was in great pain and confusion."

"It is marvelous," the king said, still turning the fruit in his hands.

"Peel it, Your Majesty."

King Edward pressed his thumbs into the fruit and pulled the edges apart. The thin gold tore, revealing another layer. The king took an eating knife and neatly cut the fruit in half, revealing a shining latticework of golden seeds and rind. His face showed his amazement. "We have never seen such a thing before."

He passed the wonder up to Northumberland, who took it between two fingers as if it might soil his hands. "How many of these do you have?"

"Only the one," Sinclair said.

Northumberland crushed the fruit in one meaty fist. He opened his hand to reveal a tiny crumpled golden ball, hardly bigger than a grape. "This wouldn't pay for my supper," he said. He threw it on the floor at Sinclair's feet.

Parris doused the leech with vinegar to make it loose its hold, then pressed a cloth to the wound. Edward coughed shallowly, unable to clear the fluids that were drowning him.

"The king is tired," Northumberland said, but Edward held up his hand.

"How many of these trees are on the island?" the king asked.

"I don't know," Sinclair said. "Perhaps hundreds."

"And there are spice trees as well, you say?"

"Cloves, cinnamon, pepper, sandalwood. We have only to send ships to gather them in."

"Then we see no reason why you should not do so."

"Majesty," Northumberland said, "the expense of such a venture . . . we do not have the coin."

"Then take the coin from somewhere else. We believe in Master Sinclair."

Northumberland's voice was smooth. "It is not possible. There is important business of state and law to which our coin is committed: think of the reforms, Your Grace."

Parris saw the boy king's face slump, and knew that as always, Northumberland's word would stand. Parris was surprised Edward had crossed Northumberland as much as he had. If Sinclair really wanted this venture to succeed, he should have directed his energy into convincing the duke, not the king.

"I would not dream of asking the realm to bear the burden for this venture," Sinclair said. "That is why I requested that Stephen Parris be present."

Parris jumped. His shifts attending the king were determined by the palace chamberlain and not, as far as he knew, at the whims of eccentric explorers.

Edward seemed to see Parris for the first time. "My physic?"

"Yes, my lord. It has come to my knowledge that Master Parris has corpses brought in secret to his home, where he desecrates them and performs unnatural rituals."

Parris couldn't move. He stared in shock at Sinclair, who met his gaze calmly. Why would Sinclair betray him? It didn't make any sense. Parris fell to his knees in front of the king and tried to speak, but no words came out. Edward might be under Northumberland's thumb, but he was still a Tudor, and his rage was a fearful thing. He was not much older than Catherine, but if he chose to order Parris's execution, no one would stop him.

Edward's face flushed and his hand flew to the incision on his chest. He started coughing into a cloth and couldn't stop; by the time he caught his breath again the cloth was bright red. The servant took the bloody cloth and gave him a goblet of wine.

Rage shook Edward's boyish voice. "Is this true?"

Parris thought furiously. If he lied, he'd be in much worse trouble when he was found out. Better to stick to the truth. "I perform studies of natural philosophy. It is for the education of the mind only."

"What other reason could there be than to consult demons about the hour of your majesty's death?" Sinclair said.

"No, Your Grace! I am your faithful servant."

"I can produce witnesses," Sinclair said. "Ask him where the bodies are now that were delivered to his home."

Parris said nothing. He could hardly tell the king they were cut into pieces and buried in an unmarked grave.

"I trusted you with my life," the king said. "And you repay me with treachery?"

"Perhaps it is fortuitous," Sinclair said.

Edward regarded him incredulously. "Fortuitous?"

"We were speaking, after all, of my expedition."

"What possible value does a treasonous physic have to your proposed voyage?"

"If he has committed treason," Sinclair said, "then all of his possessions are forfeit to the throne."

The king smiled slowly. "They are indeed."

"A considerable estate in Derbyshire, so I'm told, and lands with forests and two coal mines besides."

Now Parris understood. This morning he'd thought Sinclair a friend who valued his input. Now it was clear the man only wanted to rob him. He threw himself at the king's feet. "Your Majesty, I beg to speak."

"What's more," Sinclair said, "I have need of a man like Master Parris on my voyage."

The king frowned. "There are many physics in England."

"It is not for his knowledge of physic that I need him. It would seem he is also knowledgeable in the dark arts."

Edward's frown deepened. "That does not commend him for any righteous task."

"But Your Grace, I am told there are native peoples on this island. I wish to evangelize them and bring them to the knowledge of the true Protestant faith of the Church of England."

"A worthy mission," the king said with passion.

"But the devil is strong in such faraway places. He will fight our progress with invisible spirits and all his wiles. If I take a man such as this along—in chains, of course, as my prisoner—he may see the work of the devil for what it is, and so give me warning. Besides"—Sinclair's scarred mouth twisted into a frightening smile—"such exile is a worthy punishment for one who has betrayed you so wickedly."

"I like this plan," the king said. "It is just and fair, and it will aid in furthering the gospel to the ends of the earth. Go, with my blessing."

"Your Grace!" Parris said. "Have mercy, I beg you. It's true that corpses were brought to my home, but not for devil worship!"

Northumberland laughed. "He condemns himself with his own mouth. Take him away."

Soldiers grabbed his shoulders, but Parris shook them off. "No! Your Grace!"

The hilt of a sword slammed against his head, dazing him. He felt himself hauled to his feet by strong hands under his arms. Sinclair spoke in a whisper: "Well done, but don't overdo it. Come out quietly."

Parris lashed out with his fists and struck Sinclair in the head once, twice. Sinclair staggered. His turban slipped off his head and onto the rug.

Parris tried to hit him again, but the soldiers wrenched his arms behind his back and held a bayonet in his face. Sinclair scooped up the turban and put it back, but not before Parris saw what it was meant to hide. Sinclair's bald head was traced with a glowing filigree of light that shone through his skin in organic loops and whorls like a thousand fingerprints intertwined.

The king and the duke had not seen; their view was blocked by the soldiers. What could it mean? Parris had never seen anything like it.

"I will take Master Parris into my own custody," Sinclair announced. He bowed. "I thank Your Majesty for your most gracious support."

Parris stumbled through the palace, dragged along by the soldiers. Sinclair's African servant awaited them.

"Leave him with me," Sinclair told the soldiers. "Maasha Kaatra will make certain he doesn't escape."

Parris took one look at the African's cold dark eyes and had no doubt it was true.

Chapter Seven

PARRIS couldn't believe it. Sinclair had betrayed him completely, and now he was laughing as if he would never stop. The African, too, was grinning broadly. Sinclair clapped him on the back. "I could have cut glass on your glare," he said. "You had half the court terrified. And you!" He gestured at Parris. "You looked about to tear my throat out, and that punch! Very convincing, though a bit painful." He rubbed at his head where Parris had struck him.

They rode back toward the city through the ankle-deep mud of Dover Road. The ancient track was part of what had once been a Roman road connecting London to Canterbury. The mud was so thick the horses' hooves made sucking noises as they stepped their way through.

"You find it funny to ruin a man's life?" Parris said.

"You're serious? Come, man, it's what you want. You were planning to come along anyway."

"That doesn't mean you had to force me."

"Your secret's getting out. That cousin of yours has been dropping hints around the court; it was only a matter of time. If anyone else had told the king, you would have woken up in the Tower, and that wouldn't have helped either of us."

"And my fortune? My lands?"

Sinclair shrugged. "You would have invested anyway."

"Not *all* of it."

"So we'll leave you an estate. Relax. This was the way it had to happen."

Parris was still angry, but he felt some of the panic bleeding away. Sinclair was right; in fact, he had already planned to liquidate some of his holdings to finance the expedition. But he didn't like to be manipulated.

"I forget myself," Sinclair said. "Stephen Parris, this is my friend and fellow conspirator, Maasha Kaatra."

Parris eyed the African warily. "Why do you call him that?" he asked Sinclair. "It's an unusual choice." Most slaves were given proper English names like James or William.

"That's his name," Sinclair said. "And he's no slave. He was a prince in Nubia, before his brother sold him and his family to the Portuguese."

"Why does he wear livery, then?"

"It is sometimes convenient to appear to be what others expect," Maasha Kaatra said.

"You should have warned me," Parris said. "Why didn't you show me that golden fruit before, when you were at my house?"

Now it was Maasha Kaatra's turn to laugh. "That fruit never came from a golden tree. It was crafted in Sumatra. Stolen from a pagan temple by the same Portuguese raiders who took me from my home."

Parris blinked rapidly and coughed. "You swindled the King of England?"

"For a good cause." Sinclair said. "Horizon holds more wonders than those provincials at court could ever dream of. My message was in essence true."

"And now what? Am I to be confined on the ship?"

"What nonsense you speak. Go home to your family. Tomorrow, we begin. There is much to do before we can sail."

As they neared the city, Parris could see the lights of Whitehall Palace and Westminster behind it. To his right, two cows wallowed, escaped from nearby fields. He imagined Joan waiting at the door for him, anxious for his safety, but she wasn't that kind of woman. He found her in a rocking chair by the kitchen fire, almost a mirror to how he had left her: still knitting, the chair groaning a slow rhythm while the flames crackled. She didn't even look at him.

Parris eased himself into a chair and pulled off his muddy shoes. He set them by the fireplace to dry. "Where's Catherine?"

"Up in bed. She's hurt." The words were delivered like daggers. "She fell off a horse, trying to follow you."

"Is she all right now?"

"Better. The physic gave her a draught."

"What physic was here?"

"Dr. Weeks."

"Weeks? He's a barber-surgeon, and the worst of the lot. You let *Weeks* put his hands on my daughter?"

"I thought she might have broken her ankle, but it was just a sprain. You weren't here."

"He's a charlatan. He wouldn't know a hangnail from a kidney stone. What kind of a draught did he give her?"

"Stephen, you weren't here!"

Her voice rang in the sudden silence. The firelight cast half of her face in flickering red, the other half in shadow. Her chair and hands were still.

"The king knows," Parris said. "Sinclair told him everything."

She shook her head. "You fool."

"I don't know how he found out. Vaughan must have talked."

"Of course he did. It was inevitable. That's how you always are, Stephen. I warn you, and you don't listen. You follow your obsessions like a horse with a feed bag, oblivious to everyone around you."

"The world doesn't understand my work. Someday it will."

"Your important work, yes, I know. More important than your wife and daughter. You told me."

Parris bit back his reply. He wanted to explain that it was Joan and Catherine whom his work was meant to protect, but explanations wouldn't make any difference now. He stared into the fire.

"You haven't heard my sentence."

That got her attention. "Sentence? The king pardoned you . . . or you wouldn't be here. Do you mean a fine?"

"I am to finance Sinclair's expedition."

She coughed. "At what cost? Are we to sell everything we own and pay as much as this Sinclair wants to take?"

"Worse. The king has already taken all our lands and given them to Sinclair."

For once, Joan was speechless. Her lips worked, but no sound came out. Finally, she whispered, "Everything?"

"Everything."

"What will we do?"

"We'll join the expedition, as we planned. This changes nothing."

Joan dropped her knitting on the floor and stood. "Are you mad? It changes everything. He robbed you. It was suicide to begin with, but now . . ."

"It doesn't matter. We must go." Parris crossed his arms in front of his chest. "It's the other half of my sentence. I am commanded to go along."

He thought she might fly into a rage, but instead she gave him the disgusted look she usually reserved for incompetent servants. "So you've ruined everything."

"If I could leave you and Catherine behind, I would. But it is not safe for you here without me, and it's impossible for me to stay."

She gave him a frank look. "Not if the king dies."

Parris glanced quickly around their empty room. "Hush!"

"Don't hush me. The king will die before Sinclair leaves, won't he? Once he dies, you're free."

"If Mary takes the throne, my life is forfeit anyway. If Northumberland stays in power, the king's decision remains in effect."

"Northumberland can't stay in power."

"That remains to be seen." He lowered his voice. "The king wants the Lady Jane Grey to succeed him. He's signed it into law."

"He can't do that. Mary is next, and Elizabeth after her. He can't just change the bloodline."

"He'll rule both of his sisters to be illegitimate children—he can't really do one without the other—removing them from consideration. Jane is the granddaughter of Henry VIII's sister. She's the next closest."

Joan gasped. "Jane's wedding last month. To Northumberland's son."

"Part of the plan."

"A sweet-faced teenager with royal blood, loyally Protestant, more interested in books than in politics. Northumberland will string her as a puppet. And he'll lock the unsuspecting princesses in the Tower before the king's body is cold."

Parris nodded. "Either way, my sentence holds."

Joan walked away from him and faced the window. "It's not right. Mary should be queen."

—+++—

CATHERINE dreamed of manticores. Thick trees in a dim forest, and manticores invisible, but all around her.

When she woke, it took her several moments to recognize her own bedroom. Weak sunlight filtered through the window above her head, casting vague shadows. Then, in a rush, she remembered turning her back on the manticore, seeing its horrible spiked tail swinging toward her spine . . .

She sat up and pressed her back against the wall, scanning the room frantically. What if it was still here? Looking around her perfectly normal room, it seemed absurd that there could be an invisible creature lurking there, but how could she tell? The platter of food was still on the floor where she'd left it, along with some scattered crumbs.

The door opened, and Catherine yelped, but it was only Blanca, carrying a basin of warm water and a cloth. She sidestepped the platter with a puzzled look and set the basin on the dresser.

"Are you all right, my lady?"

"I . . . I'm fine. You gave me a start, is all."

She considered telling Blanca about the manticore attack, but couldn't quite bring herself to do it. It would just worry her, and to no purpose. It was Father she needed to tell. He should be home now, back from attending the king.

She hobbled down the stairs, favoring her injured ankle. It was stiff, but it wasn't broken, and it would heal soon. The barber-surgeon had at first refused to touch her on the grounds that it was indecent for a man to put his hands on a woman's leg, but Mother had bullied him into it, saying she was only sixteen years old and a child. That was amusing, since Mother had spent the last year telling all and sundry she was sixteen years old and a woman grown. Ripe for the picking, as Matthew Marcheford had waggishly put it. Catherine doubted his father, the bishop, would have approved.

Father was in the library. He sat at his writing desk, quill in hand, scratching at a parchment, and he didn't see her come in. She hesitated. Would he take her seriously? She wanted him to think of her as intelligent and sensible, someone he could share his work with, like he had with Peter. If she ran to him with wild tales of invisible monsters in her room, he might dismiss her as a flighty girl jumping at shadows. She had to speak to him in the language he understood.

She carried the volume of *Naturalis Historia* to his desk and set it next to him, propped open to the passage about the manticore. He set his quill down and looked at her, one eyebrow cocked.

"Have you ever seen a creature like this?" she asked. "Or did Master Sinclair speak of one?"

He peered at the text, reading quickly, then regarded her again, worry clearly etched in his face. "No," he said. "What's this about, Catherine?"

Feeling jumpy, she sat on a nearby chair. "May I have a parchment and quill, please?"

He paused a second, and she thought he might press her, but he handed them over. He lifted the inkwell out of the desk and set it on a tea table next to her. On the top half of the parchment, she sketched the manticore's face. She added unkempt hair, a hunched body, hooked feet, pincer hands, and a multitude of tails, until she had drawn him completely. Not bad, she thought. She was no Hans Holbein, but it was unquestionably the manticore.

He watched her while she sketched. When she was done, she turned it around to face him. "I saw this creature in the parlor," she said. "That's why I screamed when Master Sinclair first came. I saw it again yesterday in my room."

He tensed. "In your room?"

"Yes. It can turn invisible." She swallowed, knowing how unbelievable that sounded, but hoping that the beetle and the snake had provided enough precedent. "And it can pass through solid objects—but it's real. It can pick up solid objects, too." She explained about the experiment she had performed with the platter of food. She kept her voice calm and tried to sound rational.

"So it could pass through things when it was invisible?" he said.

"No. Here, look."

On the bottom half of the parchment, she drew a square and divided it into four quadrants. In the top left, she wrote the word *visible*; in the top right, *invisible*. She struggled for the right word for a moment, and then in the bottom quadrants wrote *substantial* and *insubstantial*.

"Those are the four states I've seen the manticore take. Invisible most of the time, but occasionally visible. Insubstantial when the pillow I threw passed through him, but substantial when he picked up the meat."

Dipping her quill again, she drew a line connecting the word *invisible* to the word *substantial*. He had taken a piece of meat while invisible, so she knew he could be both at once. This was where things got hard to understand. The invisible things in her experience—beams of light, smells, water vapor, wind—were also insubstantial. It was hard to think of them as separate concepts. She supposed a strong enough wind could be substantial enough to knock things down, but that wasn't the same as picking up a piece of meat.

She drew another line connecting *visible* to *substantial* and *visible* to *insubstantial*. It stood to reason that the remaining connection, *invisible* to *insubstantial*, was also true, but there was no way to be sure.

She was still scared, but it was easier to bear when she could think through the problem clearly. The exercise helped relax her mind, but she still hadn't told her father everything.

"Yesterday . . . it tried to stab me"—she pointed at the spiked tail in her sketch—"with that. I only just got away." Though she didn't understand why. If it had wanted to kill her, it could have done it easily while she was sleeping. "I tried to ride after you, to tell you, but the horse spooked—I think it might have seen the manticore—and threw me off."

Father stared at the parchment silently for a long time. He tapped where she had written *insubstantial*. "You saw Sinclair's beetle?"

"I saw it. This manticore is just as real."

He seemed to come to a decision and stood abruptly. "We'll search the house. Wherever you go, I want Henshawe with you, or one of the other servants. Someone is to sleep with you at all times. If you see it again, or even think you do, scream for help."

"How will you search the house for something invisible?"

"Maybe Sinclair will know." He pointed a finger at Catherine. "But no more experiments. I don't want you luring this thing anywhere near you."

"If I set out more meat, it might come again. You could see it yourself, and we could try to catch it."

"No. That's an order, Catherine. I'll talk to Sinclair, but in the meantime, I want you safe."

⊰✦⊱

SINCLAIR was in his study when Bishop Marcheford, of all people, paid him a visit.

He kept Marcheford waiting for ten minutes, just on principle, and when he finally entered the drawing room, he found the bishop standing at the fireplace mantel, running a finger along the bright feathers of a headdress from Nubia.

"Be careful. That belonged to a witch doctor," Sinclair said.

Marcheford was a slim man, but with a craggy appearance, his face deeply lined and his hands spidery and gaunt. "A child of God has nothing to fear from demons," he said. "Much less from a tool used in ignorant worship of them."

"You're not afraid of the devil, then?"

" 'The Lord is the strength of my life,' " Marcheford quoted. " 'Of whom shall I be afraid?' "

"Of plague," Sinclair said. "Of famine. Of civil war."

"All possibilities. But all under the rule of God."

Sinclair opened his mouth to respond, then stopped. He wanted to say that this made God our enemy, and it was high time man took the business of life and death into his own hands. But there was no point in saying this to Marcheford. Especially not if Sinclair wanted the king's continued support.

"What can I do for the Church?" he said instead.

Marcheford's sharp gaze seemed to penetrate his forehead and see into his mind. Sinclair was not usually unsettled, but this man's grave demeanor unnerved him.

"I want to know if you will grant safe passage to men of my choosing when the time is right," Marcheford said.

"Safe? You do know we are bound for Chelsey's island."

"That will do as well as any other place. God is there as much as in England, but I daresay there are no Papists."

"Are Papists really so bad? They may disagree with your theology, but they're not as likely to starve or drown you as an ocean voyage."

"Have you been to Spain?" Marcheford said. "I was there for a year as an ambassador for the king. I saw the Inquisition there firsthand." His voice dropped to an urgent whisper. "Men rounded up in the middle of the night with sacks over their heads, burned with irons or broken with hammers until they would admit to anything. Women and children, too, hung by their arms for days, or drowned nearly to death again and again. The lucky ones were merely burned at the stake." Marcheford's eyes burned into Sinclair's. "If Mary becomes queen, the same persecutions will come here."

"She's a woman," Sinclair said. "She won't have the stomach for such ruthlessness."

"Spain is already looking to pull her strings. There is a man, Diego de Tavera, here in the guise of an ambassador's aide. He is one of their chief inquisitors, and a bloody and brutal man. Diplomacy is not his forte. The moment Mary takes the throne, she will be under pressure to crush the Protestant Church."

"And what business is that of mine?"

He'd been hoping to prod Marcheford into anger, but the bishop fixed him with his eyes. "Are you not a Protestant, sir?"

"I owe no vow to the devil in Rome, if that's what you mean." Though neither did he love the Cromwells and Cranmers of the world. What good had it done to steal lands and goods away from the monasteries and give them to the high lords, to drape their tables with altar cloths and decorate their walls with the portraits of saints? Now that the monks had been turned out into the streets, where were the safe houses for travelers to rest and receive a meal and a bed? Where were the hospitals and apothecaries? The Reformers might teach the doctrine of charity, but the poor were hardly the better off for it.

"Then surely you would save any you could," Marcheford said.

Sinclair shrugged. "I have passenger berths still unclaimed, meant for colonists who wish to stay with us. Anyone with strong arms and a willing spirit is welcome."

"It's decided, then," Marcheford said. "I'll give you a list of passengers. But you must be ready to sail."

"How much time do I have?" It was a treasonous question, but this whole conversation was probably treason.

"Less than you think." Marcheford's face was grim. "The king died an hour ago."

Chapter Eight

PARRIS didn't need to go looking for Sinclair. Before he could finish instructing the servants on the need to keep Catherine under close watch, Sinclair appeared at his doorstep, pounding on the door like he would break it down. Parris opened it to find him spattered with mud and breathing hard.

It was well after sunrise, but the fog obscured the morning light. Parris opened the door to let Sinclair in, but before he could speak, Parris thrust Catherine's sketch of the manticore in his face. "Have you ever seen this before?"

"What is it?"

"Another of your mystery creatures, it would seem. It walks through walls, just like the beetle."

Sinclair studied the sketch. "Where did you see it?"

"Catherine saw it. Right here in my house." Parris put steel in his voice. "In her bedchamber."

Sinclair scratched his chin. "I may have seen it."

"Let me guess. On Chelsey's ship?"

"It was just a flash. A shadow, two or three times. But now that I see this picture . . ."

"It must have followed you here."

Sinclair walked past Parris into the room and waved a dismissive hand. "It doesn't matter now."

Parris caught his arm. "What do you mean, it doesn't matter? That thing attacked my daughter!"

"I came here to tell you to pack your bags."

"What are you talking about?"

"We need to leave. We have only days before our ship must depart."

"Is that possible? Is the ship even ready?"

"No. There are many repairs needed, and many supplies to be gathered. Nevertheless, we must leave. I would set sail tonight if I could."

Parris pointed at a chair. "Sit down and start making sense. What's happened?"

Sinclair sat and clasped twitching fingers. "The king is dead."

"What? Was it announced? When?"

"No announcement. Nor will there be."

"I don't understand."

"You know of the king's design for the succession? How he names the Lady Jane as the next queen?"

Parris fell into a chair across from him. "I do. How is it that *you* know?"

"I had it from Bishop Marcheford. Northumberland plans to suppress the king's death as long as possible. In the meantime, he'll bully the peers and bishops in London to sign their support of the device, and arrest the Princess Mary before she knows her brother is dead."

The door creaked, and both men jumped to their feet. Parris realized they'd been whispering, their heads together like a pair of conspirators. They turned to see Catherine peeking into the room.

"I thought it was you," she said. She limped into the room, favoring her bandaged ankle.

Sinclair swept her a bow. "Always a delight, mademoiselle."

"Won't you stay and break your fast with us?" she said.

"I couldn't impose on your mother."

"It was Mother's idea. She said I should ask you."

Parris raised his eyebrows at this. Joan, asking Sinclair to stay?

"I'm sorry, I must take my leave," Sinclair said. "Our ship departs, and there is much to do."

"Departs?" Catherine said. "When?"

"As soon as possible."

Parris heard the sound of galloping in the courtyard. He looked out the window and saw Henshawe riding away hard. What errand was he off on with such haste?

"Catherine?" Parris approached her, suspicious. "Did your mother send you in here to talk with us?"

"She said I should make Master Sinclair feel welcome until she was ready to—"

"Joan!" Parris charged through the door and nearly ran into Joan in the hallway.

She curtsied. "My lord."

"Where is Henshawe going?"

"I sent him on an errand." Her voice was calm, matter-of-fact.

"To whom?"

"Your cousin, Francis Vaughan."

"With what message?"

She smiled sweetly. "That the king is dead."

Parris stared at her, feeling like he'd just found a snake in his bed. "What have you done?"

"Probably saved the princess's life. Don't tell me they're not sending someone to kill her."

"Kill her? No. Capture her, yes. But they wouldn't kill a royal princess."

Joan raised an eyebrow. "You're a bigger fool than I thought."

"I'm your husband. Fool or not, you're to obey me."

She curtsied again. "Forgive me, lord. I didn't realize you'd forbidden me to speak to your own cousin."

"Do you even understand what you've done? With Mary captured, the Protestant monarchy would have continued in peace. With her free, it will be civil war. She'll run to Suffolk, raise an army. We'll be back to our grandfathers' time, family against family, north against south. Thousands will die."

"I doubt it. Mary is the rightful queen. The country will support her."

"You've ruined us. Haven't I told you what Mary will do to us if she takes the throne? Now we'll have to sail before we're ready."

"You will."

"What do you mean?"

"Maybe you still have to go on this lunatic voyage. But Catherine and I don't."

"Of course you do. You'll be just as . . ." He trailed off, comprehension dawning. "You bought your safety."

"Thanks to my warning, Mary will escape and rally the people behind her. When she takes her rightful place as queen, it will be in part because of me."

Parris's fists clenched, and he towered over her. "But it may be at the cost of my life! Did you consider that?"

"Not if you sail soon."

"You betrayed me."

She shrugged. "This was more important. You should know all about that, seeing how important your work is."

"I can't believe you did this."

"You started it, Stephen. I'm just trying to protect Catherine. That's all I care about."

—◄┼┼►—

THERE wasn't enough time. Parris's lands were quickly sold at bargain prices, his family houses and possessions scattered to strangers. But there was too much work to be done to mourn the loss. The *Western Star* was already in dry dock at the Deptford shipyards with a crew hired to refit her, but she was badly damaged from her journey. Besides the repairs, supplies needed to be purchased, and a crew of eighty men had to be hired to sail her—a difficult task, giving the looming possibility of war and the ship's reputation.

Princess Mary escaped capture and fled to Suffolk, where thousands flocked to her banner. Queen Jane's authority was sanctioned by the privy councillors, the lord mayor, the judges, and the nobility in London, but no one knew how long it would last. The city prepared for war.

Sinclair worked on the ship with the crew, overseeing the work with seemingly limitless energy, ducking under ropes and around bales of sailcloth, checking lists, and employing terms like "mizzenmast" and "lateen rigging," the meaning of which Parris had only the vaguest idea. Some of the refitting instructions were eccentric enough to cause rumor. The ship was to have not one, but two cookhouses on its main deck, the second designed as an alchemical distillery. It was also to have an expanded brig, with multiple metal-caged cells of varying sizes that could only be intended for captured animals. This last caused some wag to christen it Christopher's Ark, and the name could be heard about London society gatherings.

The sheer scale of the enterprise was breathtaking. Men dangled like spiders over the sides of the ship, swinging from ropes as they pounded planking onto the hull. Shirtless and barefoot, they swarmed the rigging, raising lines, fastening, hammering, some so high it made Parris dizzy to look at them.

As the workmen were leaving for the night, Sinclair appeared behind Parris and said, "I'm curious."

"About what?"

"When you opened up the corpse, what did you find?"

Parris hesitated, fearing a trap. "What are you talking about?"

"Your black sorcery—what else?" Sinclair grinned like a predator. "Come, you know by now I'm not squeamish. The men on this ship died for a reason. I want to know what you found."

"His stomach was full of stones. His intestines were laden with salt. As if he'd been so starved he'd resorted to eating rocks and drinking seawater—though his flesh showed no sign of malnutrition."

Sinclair nodded, unsurprised. "Less than most sailors after a long voyage, in fact."

It was true. Parris hadn't thought about it, but most sailors returning home from long sea voyages were sickly, diseased, half starved. The man he'd dissected, besides being dead, looked like a man who'd been enjoying rich fare in the comfort of his home.

"It's not the only place we found rocks when we expected something else," Sinclair said.

"You mean the treasure? You think these men ate food that transformed into rocks?"

Sinclair nodded. "And fresh water that turned to salt water. They stocked their storehouses with food and water from Horizon, but when they sailed too far, it transformed, just like the gold and diamonds."

Parris grew still, thinking of the grit that had permeated everything in the man's body. He had presumably eaten Horizon food not just on the journey, but the entire time that he was on the island. It had passed into his blood, insinuated into his very flesh.

So this was a one-way journey after all. If what Sinclair had said was true, there was no coming back alive.

◄+++►

NINE days after Edward's death, Queen Jane's monarchy collapsed. When Princess Mary arrived at the city gates accompanied by an army of peasants thousands strong, the councillors opened the gates to her and tore up the oaths they'd signed to Jane. Northumberland was thrown in the Tower, and Mary I took the throne, loved by the people, proud, regal, and every inch a queen. In a day, the Roman Church was restored and Protestantism declared a dangerous heresy, worthy of imprisonment or death.

Parris's last meal with his family was rushed and tense. The dry dock had been dug out, floating the ship again with water from the Thames. They would sail in the morning—ready or not—and finish provisioning in the Azores.

"She imprisoned Bishop Ridley," Parris said when he arrived, slamming the door behind him.

Joan took his cloak. "Sit and eat your supper."

"He went to ask Mary's pardon. Can you believe it? Ridley, who vowed never to recant. And *Cranmer* signed a letter acknowledging the Pope as God's representative on earth."

"As I wish you would do," Joan said. "A piece of paper is a worthy trade for a man's life. Now sit."

"Much good it did them. Mary won't accept their confessions. They're both in the Tower, awaiting her pleasure."

Joan steered him into his chair and ladled beef broth into his trencher. Parris sat reluctantly, still seething.

Catherine arrived at the table and sat in her place, pretty in a blue gown, with little froths of lace around her neatly folded hands. "Who is in the Tower, Father?"

"Practically everyone. Cranmer, Ridley, Latimer, Bradford, Coverdale—who *isn't* in the Tower?"

"You are not," Joan said, "and if you leave tomorrow as you plan, you'll keep it that way. Now give the blessing while the food is hot."

Parris prayed, begging for succor for those unjustly imprisoned and for the overthrow of the Papist Queen, ". . . to the sovereign God be all glory forever, Amen and Amen." He wondered what the morning would bring, now that Marcheford was trying to turn the expedition into a Protestant lifeboat.

Catherine took a bite from a broth-soaked chunk of bread, elegantly dabbed her napkin on her beautiful lips, and cleared her throat. "Father?"

"Yes, child."

"I want to go to Horizon with you."

"No," Joan said. "I secured your safety. You are not going to that place."

"I have no prospects here," Catherine said. "Without our fortune, no one will want to marry me."

"You think there will be prospects on a desert island?"

"It's not a desert. There are towering trees and birds and pools and the biggest flowers you've ever seen . . ."

"We don't know that," Parris said.

"I've seen it in my dreams."

Parris grew concerned. "Have the servants been watching you, as I asked? Staying up with you at night?"

"Yes. None of us have seen the manticore again."

Joan looked from one to the other of them. "Whatever are you talking about?"

Catherine's expression was unreadable. "I've been having strange dreams."

"What kind of dreams?"

"Of a faraway country. A green place overlooking the ocean from a beautiful forest."

"You're dreaming of Derbyshire," Joan said, raising an eyebrow at Parris as if daring him to disagree. "Memories from your childhood."

Catherine shook her head. "It's not Derbyshire. The forest is tall and strange and *old,* and there are creatures that definitely don't live in England. I think it's . . ." She looked at Joan's hard eyes, then turned to Parris instead, who tried to smile encouragingly. "I think it's Horizon."

Joan glared at Parris, and he wondered if she was holding him responsible for his daughter's dreams. Joan took one of Catherine's hands and spoke gently. "Perhaps you're not well."

"There are beautiful cliffs with waves throwing spray into the air, and stars like fireballs at night, so big you can see like it's day, and the manticores—"

"Enough," Joan said. "Don't let your imagination run wild, girl. Wake up. What could you do in a colony? Chop wood? Build houses? Hunt?"

"I could study the animals. I could learn how they live. I could find the secrets of things, like Father does."

Parris was touched by her loyalty, but he had to put a stop to this. She was only setting herself up for disappointment. "It won't work, Catherine. It takes a lot of education to understand things like—"

Catherine stood suddenly, the scrape of her chair against the stone floor cutting him off. Her eyes were wet.

"Never mind," she said.

"Catherine—"

"I'll be in my room." She stormed up the stairs.

"See what you've done," Joan said.

◆+◆+◆

CATHERINE stood at the window, looking out toward the west. She would not be left behind, even if Father didn't want her. Master Sinclair had invited her on the expedition, and she was going to go.

She remembered the feeling of setting down his walking stick and seeing it slide into life under her hand. Simultaneous attraction and repugnance, exhilaration and terror, but what secrets such a creature must hold! It meant anything was possible. If a living snake could change its very nature and cheat death, surely a young woman could escape the trap of her life and make herself into something new.

Mother would do anything to prevent her from going, but she couldn't stop her, could she? Catherine was, after all, sixteen. A woman grown.

Chapter Nine

EARLY the next morning, Henshawe carried Parris's cases down to a growing mound in the front parlor. Parris had already given the servants notice that he wouldn't be able to employ them any longer. Once Parris was on the boat, Henshawe would return to Derbyshire and seek work from the new owners of Parris's lands.

"Stephen!" Joan's panicked voice called his name from another room. He rushed to find her, alerted by her tone of voice that there was some emergency. He found her in Catherine's room.

"Where is she?" Joan asked.

"I don't know. Did you check downstairs?"

"Use your eyes!"

He looked around and saw what Joan had seen. The drawers were open and had been picked through in a hurry. Clothes were missing. The top of the dressing table had been cleared.

Henshawe appeared breathless in the doorway. "My lady, her horse is gone."

"It's all those ideas you've been putting in her head," Joan said.

Parris raised his hands in protest. "I told her no."

"Your friend Sinclair, then, with his impossible stories and magic tricks. You heard her at supper last night, going on about wild creatures and green forests. I swear, Stephen, if you've—"

"Stop," Parris said. "Stop blaming me, and let's find her."

◄+++►

CATHERINE rode toward Deptford, reasoning that Master Sinclair would be at the dockyards making final preparations. She had tried to sneak out unseen, but Blanca had spotted her. Instead of telling her parents, Blanca insisted on coming along. Catherine explained that she wasn't planning to come back, but Blanca said that didn't matter. The family no longer had the funds to employ her, and she had no family and nowhere else to go. If Catherine was going to join this expedition, well then, Blanca would, too.

Blanca rode next to her on a nag assigned to the servants for errands, but she rode with more grace and style than Catherine did on her young mare. Spain was known for its horses, and Catherine wondered what breeds Blanca had ridden as a child. She imagined her galloping through the Spanish hills with her sisters in the innocent days before the Inquisition, laughing as they glimpsed the distant ocean and smelled salt on the breeze.

Catherine had never visited the dockyards before. The commotion thrilled her: men with odd clothes and strange appearances, crates and boxes and barrels with mysterious contents being hauled to and fro. She saw Mussulmen with bright cloths wrapped about their heads and even two Cathayans with their black hair in long, braided queues.

A hundred ships sailed up the Thames each day, carrying cloves from the Moluccas; camphor and tortoiseshells from Borneo; ivory and dark-skinned slaves from Africa; porcelain from Cathay; damask from Persia. The ships' masts bristled over the tops of the buildings. Catherine had never been far from home, not even as far as Wales. She wondered when she would return again, or if she ever would.

She turned a corner, and there it was: the *Western Star,* its marvelous lines drifting with the current and her masts scraping the sky. The ship was so *enormous,* its stacked sails as big as houses, that she could hardly look at it in its entirety, but flitted her gaze from gleaming hull to the triple crow's nests barely visible in the sun's glare. At the very pinnacle, sailors in loose calf-length trousers and knit caps climbed the riggings, tying off sails with elbows hooked around the ropes, heedless of the drop. The air was crisp. Gulls screamed and dove.

She felt exhilarated. Her parents would be after her; she knew that. They would guess exactly where she'd gone. She had to persuade Master Sinclair to let her stay. If he agreed, then surely she could convince Father as well. She didn't want to marry a poor farmer from Derbyshire and spend her life churning butter and hanging laundry out to dry. She wanted to discover the world. Mother didn't need to understand, as long as she didn't stop her.

A flash of red hair flew under her horse, distracting her. She looked around to see what it was, and felt something heavy land on the horse behind her. She tried to turn, but this time, on the horse, she couldn't move quickly enough. She screamed as she felt something pierce her back, but at the contact, something *clicked* in her mind, like a carriage and harness coupling together. There was no pain, only a muddled sense of unreality, as if she were falling asleep.

Her perspective shifted. . . .

She could see her own body, lying on the ground, apparently fallen from the horse. Blanca leaned over it, calling her name. She stood back from the scene, frightened, ready to bolt at any sudden move. She felt another mind, confused and terrified, intersecting her own.

+++

IT was all wrong. The girl-child had given him food, thus making him an offer of kinship. It was vulgar without the dance or the sun or the quicksilver rite, but he was so desperate to understand this strange world that he had accepted her offer anyway. She had pulled away at first, as was common with the young on the first attempt. When she came to the boat, he tried again, thinking she would lead him home. Instead, she acted confused and afraid, even though she had made the first offer.

He had thought she might help him, but now she lay on the ground like a fallen leaf and didn't move. She wasn't dead——he could sense her mind flitting through his own——but with no picture sayings, only words in a strange tongue. She didn't speak to him, almost as if she didn't realize they were kin at all.

This was not how it was meant to be. He was supposed to bond with the leaders of the hairless tribe, not a frightened girl. He was here to forge an alliance between their people, to gain their support against his tribe's enemies and to lay a foundation for a profitable trade relationship. But the men he had come with on the ship were all dead.

Everything was so foreign and strange here. The sun was so distant he could barely feel its power. Staying invisible exhausted him, but he dared not reveal his presence before he had a better sense of the goals and desires of the hairless ones around him.

He needed to connect, to communicate, but now he was linked to this girl-child, with no way to break the bond.

What if she didn't get up? What if she died?

+++

PARRIS and Joan found Catherine lying in the dirt surrounded by sailors and stevedores. Parris scattered them with a shout and knelt beside her.

She was still breathing. Some fool had thrown seawater on her to rouse her, soaking the front of her dress. Her head bled from a gash, but it didn't look serious. What worried him was that she wasn't conscious.

He scanned the wharf. "There—that inn. We need to get her inside."

Lifting her carefully, he carried her across the street into a run-down stone tavern striped with mud from ancient floods. He stumbled up the stairs, Joan on his heels. Once Catherine was stretched out on a bed, he examined her again. The wound on her head didn't seem bad enough to have knocked her out, but he knew there could be unseen damage.

"Go get a cloth and fresh water."

Joan glared, but obeyed. Catherine was chilled from the water and the wind, and her hands were like ice. He needed to get her out of this wet dress and under some blankets to keep her warm. He felt her forehead. No fever, thank goodness. He rolled her onto her stomach so he could unlace her dress.

Once the laces were loose enough, he pulled the two sides of cloth aside. In the center of her back was a large, circular welt, surrounded by a ring that looked like the marks leeches made on patients when he bled them. The welt glowed faintly, a clean color like sunlight, fresh as the dawn peeping through a closed curtain. He couldn't think what weapon or object might have made such a mark. But he recognized the glow.

Joan opened the door and came in with a basin and cloth. "What is that?"

"Help me." Together they pulled her dress off and wrapped her in the bed's wool blanket, rough but warm. Parris took the cloth from the basin, squeezed it out, and rubbed it gently across her face, washing away the dirt and salt.

"Stephen, what happened to her back?"

"I don't know."

A knock at the door startled them. Joan opened it to reveal Sinclair, with Catherine's maidservant, Blanche, by his side. Joan objected at first to allowing Sinclair to see Catherine's naked back, but Parris insisted, arguing that her life could depend on it.

Parris studied his face for any sign of recognition. "What does it remind you of?"

"You're referring to this." Sinclair unwrapped his turban.

Joan gasped. The glow had grown stronger since the last time Parris had seen it, or perhaps it was just the poor light in the room. Parris walked around him, studying the pattern and considering the differences between it and what he saw on Catherine's back. The glow was the same, but Catherine's marking was more like a puncture wound combined with a suction mark, whereas Sinclair's markings looked like they had grown out of his skin. He remembered Catherine's drawing of the manticore. Had it attacked her again, more successfully this time? Did this wound come from the spine on its tail?

"Tell us what you know, both of you," Parris said.

Blanche told how Catherine had screamed and fallen from her horse, but she had seen nothing to explain it. She said she knew about the manticore, but hadn't seen it herself.

Sinclair described how he had distilled the water found on the *Western Star* into an elixir, and how at first, when he drank it, it had seemed to do nothing. Every night he had distilled it still further, trying to produce its purest form, and drank it to no obvious effect. Until the skin of his head had begun to glow.

"You drank it with no idea what it would do to you? What if it had been poison?"

Sinclair shrugged. "Chelsey said that on Horizon it healed all injuries and diseases."

"This isn't Horizon."

"Would you prefer I had found a gullible child to test it on first?"

Catherine whimpered and turned over in the bed, but didn't wake up or respond to Joan's soft entreaties.

The old panic fluttered in Parris's chest like a caged bird fighting to break free. It had been the same with Peter. He didn't know what was wrong with her, so he didn't know how to help her. What if he tried the wrong thing? What if he gave her something that killed her? One thing was sure: this was no ordinary illness. It had something to do with Horizon.

Blanche brought Catherine's bags, and Parris rummaged through them, looking for the parchment drawing she had shown him before. He found it, smoothed it out, and showed it to Sinclair. "I think this is what happened to her. She was attacked by this creature."

Joan looked over his shoulder at the sketch and her eyes grew wide. "This *thing* is real?"

"It's one of the menagerie that Lord Chelsey captured and brought back to London. It must have followed Sinclair to our house."

"What are you going to do?" Joan asked. "How will you wake her up?"

"I don't know."

Sinclair consulted a pocket watch. "The ship must sail soon, before the crowds attract too much attention. We've escaped the queen's notice so far, but . . ."

"We'll have to take her along," Parris said.

Joan leaped to her feet. "What?"

"I must go on the ship. Whatever is wrong with Catherine, it's connected to Horizon. Perhaps a venom from this manticore creature, perhaps something even more peculiar. But no doctor in England will know what to do. We have to understand what's happened to her by understanding Horizon. She must come on the ship."

"No! No, you will not take her away from me. She'll wake up again in time."

"You don't know that."

"Please, Stephen. I bargained for her safety. She's all I care about. Don't do this to me."

Parris turned to Blanche. "You planned to board with Catherine, didn't you? Will you come and help me look after her?"

Blanche curtsied. "My lord, I would like nothing better."

"She is not going!" Joan said.

Parris shook her head. "There's no other choice. I'll bring her back to you, I promise."

"You are such a fool, Stephen Parris." She stood and backed toward the door. "You won't win this time. I won't let you."

"What are you going to do?"

She reached the door. "The same as you do. What I must." They heard her footsteps running down the stairs.

"Joan!" Parris looked at Sinclair. "She'll tell the queen."

Sinclair indicated Catherine's prone form. "Then bring your daughter, and let's go. There's no time to waste."

Chapter Ten

THE wharf thronged with people, pushing and shouting and trampling the boards. At the gangplank of the *Western Star*, private soldiers hired by Sinclair held them back with matchlocks and drawn swords while the ship's provost examined papers and checked passengers' names off his list.

Parris carried Catherine in his arms, followed by Blanche and three stevedores hauling their baggage. Sinclair led the way ahead of them, forging a path.

"Why are all these people here?" Parris shouted.

"They want to board the ship," Sinclair shouted back.

"But who are they?"

He shrugged. "Protestants."

At the gangplank, they found Bishop Marcheford arguing with Maasha Kaatra. "Will you please tell your servant to give me the passenger manifest?" Marcheford said. "I have last minute changes to make, important men in danger for their lives. We can not leave them behind."

"Maasha Kaatra is in charge of boarding," Sinclair said. "No one gets on or off this ship without his permission. If you want to stay on the list yourself, I suggest you treat him more civilly."

Marcheford gaped. His son, Matthew, who had been standing behind him, noticed Catherine's limp form in Parris's arms.

He rushed forward, a worried look on his face. "What's wrong with her? Is she sick?"

Parris had no time to explain, but he let Matthew help him carry her up the shifting gangplank onto the deck. He was surprised at how much the ship swayed, even anchored here in the river. Probably nothing compared to ocean swells, but it was disconcerting to walk on such an unsteady platform.

When they reached the cabin, both Matthew and Blanche left, Matthew to rejoin his father, and Blanche to find a place for herself in the hold, where most of the passengers and future colonists would sleep. Parris's cabin was barely large enough to fit his luggage, but it was the quarters for a commissioned officer, and thus one of the best accommodations on the ship. It was meant for one man, with room for a small bunk and his sea chest, and perhaps a small writing desk. Parris lay Catherine on the bunk. He would hang a hammock for himself. The room was small, but it was private, and that was more than most could expect.

By the time his things were arranged, Blanche had returned. He left Catherine with her and returned to the main deck. The crowd on the wharf had grown, which made him nervous. For one thing, a mob would attract attention, and attention from the crown was the last thing they wanted. For another, there were far more people here than could possibly have passes to board, though many of them doubtless had strong reasons to leave England. They would have to be turned away.

Sinclair had hired an army officer named Oswyn Tate to be military adviser and commander to the expedition. A dozen men under Tate's command, wearing metal breastplates and helmets, guarded the gangplank. Tate himself stood at the fore, his oxlike build and bristling red beard lending added intimidation. So far, this measure had been sufficient to hold back the crowd, but Parris worried that twelve men wouldn't be enough if things turned ugly. Desperate people did desperate things.

He found Sinclair at the rail. On his left stood William Dryden, an imposing, muscular man who was the newly hired captain of the *Western Star*. Dryden had been a lucky find: a ten-year Royal Navy veteran with experience as the captain on two ships of war. He wore an embroidered royal blue coat with epaulets on the sleeves over white breeches and stockings and black shoes, along with a blue captain's hat. He peered down at Sinclair's dusty turban as if it offended him.

"Here they come," Sinclair said.

Parris followed his gaze and saw three of the queen's soldiers, clad in mail from neck to toe, pushing their way through the crowd. Sinclair strode down the gangplank and met them at the bottom. One of the soldiers handed papers to Sinclair, who gestured at the ship and seemed angry. They argued for several minutes, but their words were lost in the noise.

One of the soldiers took Sinclair by the arm. Sinclair punched him in the neck, knocking him into the others, and ran back up the gangplank, throwing the papers into the water. The soldiers tried to follow, but Tate's men blocked their way.

Captain Dryden met Sinclair at the top and grabbed his arm. "What are you doing? I'll not be a party to treason."

"I'm paying you to take us to Horizon," Sinclair said.

"What did those papers say?"

"It doesn't matter. We have a royal sanction for this voyage."

"The devil take you, liar. Those were the queen's soldiers you just assaulted. I'm throwing you off my ship."

"Come, now, Captain. You're a Protestant, in a ship full of wanted Protestant men trying to leave England. Do you really want to explain that to the queen? Your days will be as numbered as the rest."

The captain's face reddened and his grip tightened.

"On the other hand, if you sail with us as you agreed, you will return home the richest man in Christendom and a national hero."

"So you say. Maybe I won't return at all."

"We've been through this, Captain. And there's no time."

There were screams from the crowd and the clatter of hooves on stones. Two dozen more of the queen's soldiers trotted onto the wharf on horseback, forcing men and women to jump clear or be trampled.

"Cast off!" bellowed Dryden. "Raise the anchor!"

The bosun stalked aft, echoing Dryden's order. Four apprentice seamen labored at the capstan to hoist the anchor off the bottom, and sailors cut the lines that held the ship to the shore. Men ran to and fro in frenzied activity, hauling on ropes and shouting to each other. The sails fluttered and filled with air.

On the wharf, the cavalry drew up into formation and raised matchlocks to their shoulders. Before Parris could think, the air around him whistled, and he heard the roar of the report and saw smoke explode from the guns. He was so shocked they had actually *fired* on the ship that he just stood there until someone grabbed his arm and dragged him down to the deck.

A groan from behind caught his attention. Captain Dryden lay on the deck clutching his chest, his fingers wet with blood. Parris crawled over. The wound looked bad, and blood bubbled from Dryden's mouth.

Parris tore off his own cloak and stuffed a folded portion of it into the wound, pressing it down as tightly as he could.

An explosion rocked the ship, sending a fountain of water into the air just in front of them. The wharf was farther away now, the gap between them widening, but the queen's soldiers now commanded one of the defensive cannons along the water. With them stood a gaudily dressed man with an ostrich-feather hat and a dark giant with coils of black hair, both of them pointing at the ship and shouting. Francis Vaughan and the Spaniard, Diego de Tavera.

Slowly, the ship pulled farther away down the river. Too slowly. The gunners poured powder and rammed the next ball deep inside. The cannon swiveled and erupted in smoke and fire. This time the ball struck just short of the mizzenmast, smashing the rail and blowing a hole in the quarterdeck. A sailor screamed as he plummeted from the rigging into the water. Ropes swung loose, and a crossbeam tore away, toppling through yards of canvas to crash onto the deck in a shower of splintering wood.

The ship was in uproar, but the sails were full of air, and the ship picked up speed, finally leaving the wharf and the soldiers and the terrible cannon behind.

"Take him to the infirmary!" Parris shouted to two sailors who were trying to lift Dryden. He wasn't sure where the infirmary was, but that was where he would find the things he needed to treat wounds. As far as he knew, he was the only physic on board. The injured would be his responsibility.

Parris ran across the deck to the nearest propped trapdoor and climbed down a ladder into the hold. It was dark, smelled of salt and urine, and was unbearably hot. The cramped area was strung with hammocks, sometimes two or three on top of each other, and Parris realized this was the deck where most of the sailors slept. In fact, some were just climbing bleary-eyed out of their bunks, probably those on the night shift, woken by the noise and chaos. The oak planking creaked and sweated moisture. He could hear skitterings and gnawings from what could only be rats.

He found another ladder and descended it, then yet another. The ship was a maze of decks and ladders and cabins—the warrant officers' quarters, the officers' mess, the galley. Four decks down, Parris stopped. Here a single room stretched the whole length of the ship. It was packed with rolls of spare sails and rigging, casks of water and beer, tools and supplies they would need once they arrived, guns and gunpowder, and who knew what else. The sheer size of the ship was astonishing—there were more floors and rooms than in a king's palace.

Realizing he must have missed the infirmary, he climbed back up again, and finally found it tucked behind the officers' mess, crowded with groaning, bloody men. It was stocked with supplies, and Parris set to work cutting and bandaging. One man's arm, riddled with bullet fragments, needed to be amputated at the elbow. Three of his fellows held him down while he screamed through a cloth rag. Parris hated barber-surgeon work, but he was the only one available who could do it. The procedure was bloody, but quick and clean. He swabbed the wound with hot water and bound it as tightly as he could.

Only one person died. Captain Dryden had been hit in the lung, and had breathed his last before Parris had even found the infirmary. When Parris broke the news, Sinclair grunted and mumbled something about the quirks of fate. The next time Parris saw him, he was wearing Dryden's hat.

❖❖❖

THE ship left the Thames estuary and sailed into the more turbulent waters of the North Sea. For some reason, Parris had thought of it as a small body of water, tranquil compared to the wild ocean. Instead, the waves were like mountains, high enough to block view of the land. The ship scaled the side of each wave so steeply, he could fall over backward if he wasn't careful. They topped each crest with creaking sails and pitched downward into the next trough.

The cannon shot had left a mess on the quarterdeck. The masts were not seriously harmed, and when they stopped at the Azores to reprovision, they could have the damage repaired with minimal delay to their journey, but the queen had made her point clear. They were renegades now, traitors to the crown. There was no going back. Parris wondered if he would ever see Joan again.

Once the injured had been cared for, he returned to his cabin, where he was surprised to see Matthew Marcheford with Blanche, sitting over Catherine's motionless form. Parris sat with them, exhausted, and truthfully answered Matthew's questions as best he could, telling him about Catherine's sightings of the manticore and fall from her horse, with Blanche adding details as necessary.

Then he asked Matthew to leave so he could examine Catherine more closely. He pushed aside her dress and scrutinized her skin, looking for any unusual marks beyond the puncture wound in her back, but finding none. He touched her head, her hands, her feet, and thought her temperature seemed high. She had always been sanguine as a child, which had made her joyful and kind, but the excess of blood also made her prone to fever. He made a quick incision in her arm, not knowing what better to do, and attached a leech from his bag. It pulsed as it fed.

Parris stroked her damp hair. "Be still. I'm here now. Be still."

What else was there? Fever or not, the real problem had to do with an invisible creature that—presumably—was now hiding somewhere on the ship. Somehow it had reached inside her and pulled out some essential part of her consciousness. Her soul? Was that possible? He couldn't just wait until they arrived at the island. He had to study her, understand what had happened, and figure out how to free her. The trouble was, he had no idea how to start.

⊸+┼+⊷

CATHERINE couldn't wake up. She roamed the ship, but she had no control over her movements, and even her thoughts were barely her own. She clutched the high point of one of the masts, looking down over the ship from a dizzying height as the sun sank into the Western Ocean.

The girl-child could not separate her thoughts from his. Perhaps she was too young. She was physically larger than he was, so he had assumed she was old enough to handle a mind connection, but she flailed like a child, not holding a clear sense of her own mind as separate from his. He began to fear that she had not been a willing participant, that her offer of food had not been an offer of kinship, as he had thought. In fact, he was starting to suspect that the hairless ones had no mind communication at all. How they could be intelligent creatures without the ability to bond was hard to imagine. How would they pass learning from generation to generation? Such a race would necessarily be very primitive, and yet, the hairless ones seemed to have a complex civilization.

Perhaps, if he could get the girl-child to understand, she would still be able to help him. He needed to speak to her without the boundaries of language, to pull from her mind an understanding of the hairless ones and what they intended. Were they indeed returning to his home? What did they plan to do when they got there? Would they be friends to his people, or were they a threat?

Without her help, he couldn't even break the bond. Perhaps he should try again with another, someone older, someone who could learn the picture communication and tell him the things he needed to know. It was vulgar to consider forcing a bond on another unwilling person, but he didn't know what else to do.

For the moment, though, he had a more pressing concern. He was hungry.

Thoughts flew through Catherine's head that she didn't understand, but one thing emerged clearly: she was hungry.

She scrambled through the rigging, as natural as breathing, letting go of each rope entirely before grabbing the next. She jumped and slipped through decks and walls as if they were fog. She could smell food behind a storeroom door. A heavy bolt was drawn across it and locked, but she slipped through it as easily as through the others.

The first thing she saw was a piece of fish. She snatched it and tore a piece off with her teeth. She hated herself for stealing it, but where else was she to find food? When she had finished it—even crunching its bones—she found some raisins, wonderfully sweet after the fish, which had been so salty it had burned her tongue. A block of cheese went down after the raisins. Her hunger satisfied, she retreated above deck, where at least she could see the sky and the distant stars.

She wondered if she would live long enough to return home, to come once again within reach of the stars that breathed life into every creature and leaf and rock. She missed communing with her memory family, missed the land that was familiar to her, where things made sense. Ever since she had boarded the hairless ones' ship, everything had gone wrong.

The way had been long, and food, scarce. The men caged him and prodded him. A woman had been there, among the men, who spoke kindly to him and wept for her own troubles. He had thought she might help him, and so he had tried to bond with her, but she was weak from sickness, and she had died. When that happened, the men had shouted at him and had given him no more food.

He crossed the main deck and passed through another wall, this time into the small room where the girl-child's body lay with her sleeping father. At least this one had not died, not yet. Her mind was like a butterfly in a net, fluttering in panic, beautiful and fragile.

Catherine struggled to regain her own thoughts. She was in her own cabin, looking at her own sleeping form. She tried to turn her head, to walk away, anything to get free, but she had no control. She couldn't even move her eyes. On the bunk, she saw her body twist from side to side. She stopped trying to move, and her body on the bed stopped moving, too. This was no dream. She was trapped in the manticore's mind.

Chapter Eleven

As the ship's physic, Parris was one of the six top-ranking officers on board. Sinclair summoned them into his stateroom: Collard, the first mate; Tilghman, the sailing master; Battersby, the boatswain; and Thorpe, the purser. All four had donned clean uniforms and stood at formal attention. Parris, wearing stained traveling clothes, joined the line uncomfortably. He didn't want to be here. He wanted to be finding a way to wake Catherine.

The stateroom had been Dryden's, but Sinclair had moved in. Instead of steering charts and compasses, the decor was exotic: a tiger-skin rug in the doorway, tall pitchers in strange, asymmetric shapes, a pair of curved, jeweled swords mounted above an enormous chest of black wood, and everywhere the trophies of alien animals: horns, tusks, teeth, claws, and skins. Candles illuminated this butchered menagerie, casting ghastly shadows. Maasha Kaatra lurked in the background, looking like one of the shadows himself.

Sinclair remained seated. "I do not believe in frivolity or excessive intimacy in the running of a ship," he said. "I expect to be addressed as 'captain' or 'my lord' at all times, whether or not in the company of the petty officers and seamen. A casual attitude on the part of the officers leads to indolence on the part of the crew. Is that much clear?"

The officers nodded assent.

Collard cleared his throat. "My lord, will you be performing all the duties that Captain Dryden would have performed had he lived?"

"Yes, Master Collard. I thought that was evident. I understand that, as the first mate, you had reason to expect the position might have passed to you, but given the nature of our mission and my unique knowledge of our destination . . ."

Collard bowed. "I mean no disrespect, Captain. But Master Tilghman has been given no charts from which to navigate the vessel, nor any sailing plan to plot the course to our destination."

"We sail west, gentleman," Sinclair said.

The officers traded glances. Tilghman gave an embarrassed laugh. "My lord, it's not that simple. The prevailing winds, the currents, the depth of the water; all of these things must be——"

"Don't patronize me," Sinclair said. "I've spent most of my life at sea, and I'm well aware of the nuances of sailing a vessel of this size. What I mean to say is, there are no charts. You will have to rely on me for your sailing plan. I will direct the arrangement of the sails and our navigational calculations. I will provide Master Tilghman the headings from day to day, without explanation, and you will simply have to trust me."

The cabin was silent. Parris studied their faces, wondering how they would take it. It was hard enough that Sinclair, a civilian with no experience commanding a boat, had assumed the captaincy. Now he wanted them to follow his orders blindly?

Battersby, an ungainly man with a conspicuous adam's apple, swallowed. "Sir——"

"My lord," Sinclair corrected.

"My lord." He dipped his head. "How will you know how to find this island? Even with charts, ships have been known to miss their mark by hundreds of miles when crossing open sea out of sight of land. Without a chart . . ."

Sinclair stood. "Gentlemen, I will reveal my method on one condition. That knowledge of it does not leave this room. Can I rely on you?"

"Of course, my lord," Collard said. Parris furrowed his eyebrows, suspicious, but he nodded with the others. He had no one to tell.

"I received a vision," Sinclair said. "An angel appeared. He told me to bring his people to the ends of the earth, to the land he would show me. Then he placed his hands on my head, and immediately I knew the course we should take. Each night the angel returns, lays his hands on me, and gives me the knowledge I need for the next day."

It was the boldest lie Parris had ever heard, even worse than telling the king that Sumatran gold had come from Horizon. He doubted these veteran sailors would be taken in. Battersby crossed himself and kissed a crucifix he fished out from under his shirt, but the others looked skeptical.

"My lord," Collard said, "you ask us to trust our lives to this incredible tale. Do you have any proof?"

"I do," Sinclair said. He lifted the captain's hat from his head. Underneath, his bare head glowed with swirling lines of light. In the dimness of the cabin, it was truly impressive. Parris could almost believe Sinclair had been touched by an angel.

The officers gaped. Battersby clutched his crucifix with a trembling hand and murmured under his breath. Thorpe and Tilghman took several steps back, and Collard, though he held his ground, had no doubt left on his astonished face. Sinclair replaced his hat, and the light vanished.

Collard bowed low. "My lord. Forgive me. I had no idea. . . ."

"I understand the position this puts you in," Sinclair said, magnanimous now that he had their support. "Believe me, I do. But it is essential that I keep this a secret. I rely on your discipline to keep the men in hand."

The officers bowed again and started to go, but Sinclair held up a hand. "One more thing," he said. "Maasha Kaatra holds no official rank on this ship, but he speaks with my voice." As he spoke, Maasha Kaatra stepped forward. Parris jumped; he had forgotten that the African was in the room. "If he gives you a command, you are to obey it immediately and completely, as if I had given it, with no questions asked," Sinclair said. "Is that clear?"

The officers' faces were incredulous, but they nodded their assent.

"Thank you," Sinclair said. "You may go."

The men filed out, all except Parris, who could hardly keep his voice under control. "What do you think you're doing? You, touched by an angel? I've never heard such sacrilege in my life."

"I need them to trust me."

"And you do that by lying to them?"

Sinclair sat down again, unmoved, and began paging through a navigational log. "I can't tell them the truth. But there's no reason the story won't last. Can anyone prove that I haven't seen an angel?"

"I know you haven't. So tell me. The truth this time."

"You haven't figured that out yet?" Sinclair shook his head. "You disappoint me, Doctor."

"You're bluffing. I don't believe it. You really don't know where you're going, do you?"

With the air of a man sorely tried, Sinclair reached into a pocket and pulled out a familiar pale wooden box banded with iron. Carefully, he cracked it and showed Parris the contents. It was the beetle, still scrabbling against the wall of its prison. Sinclair slowly rotated the box, and the beetle changed direction to match. It always maneuvered to face directly toward the bow of the ship. The direction they were sailing.

It took Parris a moment to realize what Sinclair was showing him. "This is it. Your secret. The beetle is the compass—it always points west."

"Better. It always points toward Horizon. It's trying to get home."

Incredible. Parris watched it marching incessantly toward its goal. Such a small, unimpressive-looking animal, yet it could fly through walls and somehow, across hundreds of miles of ocean, know which way to go. "But this is wonderful! Why keep it a secret? Let the men know."

"How long do you think it would last, if I did? All it would take is one disgruntled person who wants to go back to England. The beetle would be dead, and we would be lost."

"It's not so easy to kill."

"But it's very easy to throw over the side."

Sinclair snapped the box closed and returned it to his pocket. Parris's gaze drifted to the balcony and the miles of water behind them. He thought of the miles ahead of them, seemingly without end, and he had to admit that Sinclair was right. The beetle was too precious and too fragile to risk its loss.

"There's no chance the officers will keep your glowing skin a secret," Parris said. "The whole ship will know by tomorrow morning."

"I'm counting on it."

"And Bishop Marcheford might have something to say about an angel visitation."

Sinclair sighed. "Marcheford is a problem," he said. "He needs to remember that he's not a bishop anymore. He has no authority aboard this boat."

"Unlike your African friend."

"Yes. That bothers you?"

"Do you really expect your officers to take orders from him?"

"Why shouldn't they?" Sinclair said.

"Well . . . because he's . . ."

"Black? Heathen? Barbarian?" Sinclair shook his head. "You've got to get your head out of your provincial little island. When I told you Maasha Kaatra was a prince, I don't mean he was some local chieftain's son. His father ruled a nation hundreds of years old. He grew up in a palace, speaks eight languages, was educated in Persia—where, by the way, they've been doing experimental science for centuries."

Parris wanted to object, but he knew it was true. Some of the best translations of Greek scientific texts came out of Persia, sometimes with remarkable improvements. "I don't care if he's the emperor of the world; they don't know him."

"They don't know me, either. I still require their loyalty."

"How about mine?"

Sinclair looked up from his papers, his brow wrinkled. "I need yours, too, of course."

The wrinkles cleared. Sinclair shut the logbook and stood. "Come with me."

Parris followed him down several ladders into the storage compartments in the hold. Sinclair lifted a lantern from a hook, and they climbed down still farther into the darkness of the bilge. It was damp and hot and smelled of feces, probably from the rats. Barrels of nonperishable provisions leaned against the curved walls.

Sinclair wended his way toward the bow, where he threw aside a canvas cover, revealing three long wooden boxes. Coffins.

Parris took a step back. "You're not serious."

With an iron bar he found on the floor, Sinclair began prying up one of the tops. "From the original voyage."

"They've been dead for weeks," Parris said. "They can't still be . . ."

The top screeched free of its nails and clattered to the side. The box contained what Parris expected: a dead body. Despite the passage of time, however, it was as well preserved as the one Parris had dissected before. There was no smell.

"I thought you had them buried."

"I saved a few for you."

Parris felt a flicker of hope. If these bodies were as perfect inside as the other had been, he might be able to learn a lot about Horizon and its workings. It might not tell him how to wake Catherine, but it was something, a start. He couldn't just sit around bleeding her. The more knowledge he could gain, the better chance he had.

Satisfied, Parris looked around. "I'll need more light."

⊹⊹⊹

AS night fell, Sinclair walked the decks, checking the sails, watching the dark water slip by. He kept to the shadows. He liked to watch the sailors about their business, unaware of his presence. He passed near a gang of sailors dicing and passing around a bottle of spirits, and he stopped, listening to their conversation.

". . . not what I signed up for," said an apprentice seaman, no more than eighteen years old. "I'm no Protestant, but if I go home, the queen'll lock me up all the same."

A gray-bearded sailor with a missing ear gave a sour laugh. "That's if we make it home."

"Home or not, I won't never see my Lizzie again," said the apprentice.

"Ah, I've seen your Lizzie. She's no great loss," Graybeard said.

The apprentice leaped to his feet, fists raised. "She's my betrothed. I won't hear talk like that." He kicked Graybeard, who rose smoothly to his feet, still laughing, and dodged a wild punch. The others hooted and shouted their approval or jumped up to join in the fray. The apprentice snatched up the bottle of spirits and swung it toward his opponent's head, but Sinclair stepped out of the shadows and snatched it out of his hand.

Seeing the captain, the sailors fell back and touched their foreheads, chorusing, "Pardon, my lord."

Sinclair sat in the circle and took a long swig from the bottle. "Join me, friends."

The sailors traded nervous glances, but he beckoned to them, and they cautiously sat. He couldn't leave them brooding. That sort of attitude would only feed on itself as the voyage progressed. He had to focus their attention on what lay ahead.

"Son, you'll see your girl again," Sinclair said. "You'll drape her neck with diamonds and her fingers with golden rings." He passed the bottle to the young apprentice, who took it uncertainly. "Of course, you'll have to survive the Cynocephali first."

"What's that, then?" the apprentice said.

"The worst sort of devils. Wild men of the islands. They have no heads, but one eye in each of their shoulders, and a mouth like a bloody gash in the middle of their breasts. They fall on their victims in packs and eat them alive."

The silence lasted for a moment before the sailors erupted into guffaws and clapped the apprentice on the back. He'd turned as pale as sailcloth.

"Gave him a fright, you did."

"I think he's going to be sick."

Sinclair pointed at each of them in turn. "Laugh if you will. But I've seen worse in my day. The mermaids, now, there's a creature I wouldn't see again." The sailors leaned forward, expectant. "Aye," Sinclair said, and let his eyes grow distant. "We were becalmed near Madeira. Trapped there for three days without a breath of wind to stir the sails. They came from the south, five of them, each more beautiful than her sisters, and the way they swam! Turning and twisting and leaping out of the waves, the water sluicing over their perfect bodies. We hadn't seen a woman in months. It was enough to drive a man mad."

The young apprentice's eyes were huge. "What did you do?"

"I? I gripped the rail and shut my eyes tight."

"Whatever for?"

" 'Cause them that didn't couldn't hold back. They threw themselves in the water and swam toward those vixens without thought for life or limb."

"And? What happened?"

"Why, they died, son. The mermaids wrapped them in their warm embrace and dragged them down into the deep to feast on their flesh."

The lad recoiled, coughing and covering his mouth with his hands while the other sailors laughed.

"And what manner of creatures will we find in the west?" Graybeard said. "Satyrs?"

"Gorgons!" said another.

"My brother saw an incubus once."

"Put aside this nonsense!" a new voice said. Bishop Marcheford clambered down the ladder from the forecastle, one rung at a time like a green recruit. Sinclair gave a deep sigh. Whatever Marcheford planned to say, it wasn't going to help.

"All this superstition and spreading of tales just causes unnecessary fear," Marcheford said, yanking his doublet straight again. "If we're going to survive this voyage, we have to keep our trust in God, who created and commands all things."

Sinclair rolled his eyes. Marcheford wasn't going to endear himself to professional seamen by giving them advice on how to make it through a long journey. He wondered if bringing him had been a mistake. As a high-ranking clergyman, Marcheford represented a rival source of authority, and one in direct opposition to Sinclair's goals. Sinclair didn't want his men contemplating eternity; he wanted them greedy for earthly gold. Success on this journey would come from those driven to line their pockets and sample the exotic delights of faraway lands, not from those trusting in a benign Creator for safety. He needed them voracious, willing to stop at nothing. Superstition fed that drive, as long as it was directed properly. Religion would ruin it.

"I hope in future——" Marcheford began to say, but Sinclair couldn't stand to hear more.

"Forgive the good preacher," he said. "He knows nothing of the far lands." He was gratified to see the yellow teeth of the sailors appearing again in smiles. Marcheford's mouth was amusingly agape.

"Terror awaits us, make no mistake," Sinclair said. "The dreadful and the horrible are our fate. But there's more. Have you not heard of the Sylphids? Sprites of the forest islands that never die? They love gold and jewels and collect them for centuries. You have only to follow one to its nest to find riches beyond your dreams."

The smiles were broader now, and the bottle began to be passed around again. Marcheford was forgotten.

"Or what of the Amazons? In that land, they have no men, for the women conceive by sipping water. They are as tall and beautiful as Aphrodite, and since they have no channel for their insatiable lusts, they yearn for nothing night and day but to lie with men."

Laughter and catcalls erupted around the circle, the sailors leering and elbowing one another. Sinclair ruffled the apprentice seaman's hair. "A young buck like you might find himself with two or three at once."

The lad blushed. Marcheford looked disgusted and opened his mouth to say more, but Sinclair rose, took his elbow, and steered him away.

"What are you doing?" Marcheford said. "You're filling those men's heads with lies."

"Useful lies," Sinclair said. "Which makes them a good deal better than your kind."

"The Scriptures, you mean?"

"I mean the tales of life after death that you fill men's heads with. Gates made of giant pearls, streets lined with gold, that sort of thing.

What good does it do them? I'll give them treasures here and now, in the real world."

Marcheford wagged his chin. "This world is but a shadow," he said. "The true reality comes after."

Sinclair thought of the men he'd seen die: from drowning, scurvy, consumption, by hanging, or by the sword. They were all gone. Ever since he was a child and watched his father waste away on his sickbed, watched the moment when all the intelligence and affection disappeared from his face, Sinclair had known the truth. There was nothing after death. Death was the absence of being. He had spent his life searching for a solution to that problem, but he didn't believe it was to be found in a mystical heaven that no one on earth had ever seen. No, he wanted a solution he could touch and taste and experiment with, one grounded in the reality of the only world he knew. And he would find it, even if God himself stood in his way.

He released Marcheford's arm. "Just stay away from my men," he said.

≺+╋+≻

TWO of the three corpses were the same as before: dry and gritty, but well preserved. Parris lost himself in the work, filling five books with notes and diagrams. Both corpses gave tremendous insight into the workings of the human body, but little more into Horizon. They were the same as any other corpse, only thoroughly salted.

He worried that he was wasting time, that none of this would help Catherine, but at least he was *doing* something. He pressed on, trusting that the more he knew about Chelsey's journey, the better chance he had of helping her.

The third body was different. For one thing, it was a woman.

"I can't cut her," he told Sinclair.

"Why not?"

"She's a woman. I can't . . . well . . ." He felt his face growing hot.

"She's dead. She won't be offended."

"Why was there a woman on the ship anyway?" He thought about it, then reached the obvious conclusion. He wondered from what port of call Chelsey had sweet-talked her aboard, and whether he'd told her where they were headed. "Did Lady Chelsey know?"

Sinclair shrugged. "I didn't bring it up."

"I don't want to touch her."

"I won't tell your wife."

"It's not that. It's just not . . ." *Decent,* he thought. *Appropriate. Honorable.* But he recognized the fallacy. To truly understand the body, he had to understand both sexes. He had watched Joan giving birth to Catherine, hadn't he? This wasn't all that different. Besides, for all he knew, a woman's organs were organized according to a different system altogether. Certainly there had to be room for a child; that implied a different mechanism, or at least a different structure. For some reason, though, this was one radical conclusion that didn't sit well with him. He might be able to desecrate a man's body, but to touch a woman in the same way made him feel sick.

He almost convinced himself that he couldn't learn any more from the third corpse than he had from the first two, but his worry for Catherine drove him to it. If there was any chance, he had to try.

As it turned out, it wasn't only the gender of the corpse that was different. Her body had the same rocky grit, the same effusion of salt, but she was somewhat decomposed, implying that she had died earlier than the others, and for a different reason. Only after the food and water in her system had transformed did the salt prevent further decay.

When he turned her over, he saw the welt. His heart thudded in his chest. It was the same as the one on Catherine's back, a puncture wound surrounded by a ring, only this one didn't glow. And another thing: her spine looked odd, like something had wrapped around it. He dug carefully with his knife, peeling back the skin. A thin cord spiraled around her vertebrae, beginning at the welt and stretching up to her neck. He'd never seen such a thing in any body before.

Leaving his knife, he raced up the ladders to his cabin, where Catherine still lay, pale and unmoving. Blanche stepped aside as he turned her over and opened her dress. There was the welt, as before. He ran his fingers up and down her spine, and yes—her flesh wasn't wasted like the corpse, so it wasn't as noticeable, but he could feel the cord twisting around her spine.

He sat back on his heels, panting from his run. What did it mean? Chelsey's mistress, if that was who she was, had clearly been attacked in the same way by the same creature. It was another piece of knowledge, but it didn't help. It wasn't knowledge he could use. By all appearances, Chelsey's mistress had never woken from her connection with the manticore. In fact, it had probably killed her. Maybe that cord was something planted by the manticore when it stabbed her, something that grew until it penetrated the victim's brain.

He forced himself to be calm. That didn't make any sense, at least none that he could think of. What possible advantage could it give a manticore to kill a victim over the course of days? Catherine had seen it eating meat, but no hunting animal would take so long to kill its prey. Nor would it help as protection against enemies. There must be another practical reason.

If only he could figure out what it was.

⧋⧋⧋

THE manticore was trying to speak to her. It took an effort for Catherine even to think of them as two different people: herself and the manticore, the manticore and herself. It wanted to know what was happening, where the ship was going, and what they would do when they got there. The questions weren't in any kind of language Catherine could understand, but the impressions were there, in pictures and memories.

I want to be free, she tried to think. *Let me go.*

What followed was a rush of anger and frustration and a river of consciousness that pulled her under.

It was his first mind ceremony. His pincers were filed sharp and wrapped with wreaths of white flowers. Both his blood family and his mind family were gathered. On the rain-drenched cliff edge, his blood father danced a salutation to the setting sun.

From this vantage point, standing right on the edge of the world, the sun seemed to fill the sky. The rain clouds overhead boiled in its heat, and billows of fog swept up from the void below. His blood father danced until the sun sank into the steam and finally disappeared.

He knew what was expected of him. His mind father approached and stood facing the void. In the dark, he clambered onto his back and for the first time drove his tail into his mind father's spine. Memories of generations past began to pour through the connection. He dreamed of births and deaths, wars and alliances, volcanic eruptions and landslides. The languages of faraway tribes flowed into understanding. The memory family he was joining was a rich and important one, unbroken for millennia.

His blood family lifted him into a woven sling threaded with fragrant flowers and traveled through the forest all night, carrying him. He saw a shining cascade bubbling up from among the rocks and running down into a smooth silver pool.

His mind father brought him a ladle filled with the thick silver liquid. Because of the bond between them, he had the disorienting sensation of seeing the scene from both his mind father's perspective and his own: one lifting the ladle; one leaning forward to drink. He opened his mouth, allowing the thick, heavy liquid to roll down his throat.

Intense pain shot through him. His vision disappeared in bright light. It felt as though a piece of his mind were being boiled away. He could feel the connection to his mind father being severed, and knew this was an essential part of the ritual, a way to keep the memories of generations without the dangers of maintaining a permanent bond.

Catherine surfaced from the memory like coming up for air, grasping at the threads of her own identity. She understood what the manticore was telling her. Striking her with his tail had been no attack. He had meant her no harm. Instead, it was his people's way of sharing thoughts and passing memories to family members. She understood, too, that the bond could be broken, but only with the silver liquid she had seen in the memory. With the human part of her mind, she recognized the liquid as something she had seen her father prepare in capsule form for Peter when he lay dying. Mercury.

Chapter Twelve

SINCLAIR could hear the shouting right through the floor of his cabin. It was dawn, earlier than he had planned to rise, but too late to bother going back to sleep.

He donned Dryden's hat, covering his glowing scalp, and went out onto the balcony, enjoying the spray of salt water. Below him, the rudder churned through the ocean swells. Above him stretched the taffrail, its aft lantern swinging. He breathed in the cool air.

The shouting continued. He sighed, threw on a cloak, and climbed down to see what the trouble was.

In the officers' mess he found Osywn Tate, the man he'd hired to command the expedition's soldiers, arguing with the first cook. Tate's muscled bulk seemed even larger in the cramped quarters belowdecks, and he towered over the cook, a stout, pugnacious man who had been blinded in an old knife fight and made no effort to patch or disguise his disfigured eye sockets. Both men were red in the face and stopped their shouting abruptly when Sinclair entered the room.

Tate bowed. "Beg pardon, my lord."

"What's the trouble?"

"He"—Tate pointed at the cook—"is accusing my men of theft."

"They're always taking more than their ration," the blind cook said. "Drawing extra beer like they're God's own angels. They think I can't tell, but I can."

Tate made an indignant noise. "Salute when you speak to the captain, and call him 'my lord.'"

The cook grudgingly touched his cap and said, "M'lord."

"What's your name?" Sinclair said.

"Piggott, sir. And any that calls me Piggy'll be scraping off the hogging, if you catch my meaning."

Sinclair turned to Tate. "The next time a man takes a ration of beer which is not his own, that man will feel the lash." Tate opened his mouth, but Sinclair put up a hand to stop his objection. "I don't care who it is. That kind of theft endangers us all."

"That's not all that's missing, lord," Piggott said. "There's a block of cheese gone, half a salted fish, and nine cakes of raisins."

Sinclair raised an eyebrow. "Nine?"

"I know my stock. Don't matter that I'm blind. Nothing goes missing in this galley without I know about it."

"Did you ask the purser?"

"Aye, and he says naught was done with it."

"Perhaps rats got in."

"Rats don't carry off a fish. And they leave scat."

"I told you, it was the ghost," Tate said.

Sinclair rounded on him. "What are you talking about?"

"Ask him. The door was locked. I'll bet my sword it was the ghost that took those things."

For a moment, Sinclair didn't answer. He knew now what must have taken the food, and it was no ghost. Trying to conscript sailors who weren't superstitious was like trying to hire a blacksmith without calluses. If the manticore stayed loose, it would cause fear and tension, and that he couldn't afford. "Ghosts don't eat raisins," he said.

"This one does," Tate said. "My men have seen it on watch. I saw it myself from the masthead, too—like a sailor high in the rigging, as insubstantial as mist, the stars shining right through him."

"Bosun's mate says his rum has gone missing, too," Piggott said. "You're telling me a ghost wants rum to drink?"

"I'm telling you what I saw," Tate said, his red beard sticking out from his chin. "Chelsey's whole crew died aboard this ship. Of course it's haunted."

"And I'm telling you, keep your men away from my stores."

"I don't take my orders from you."

"You do if you don't want to die of starvation halfway from here to Horizon," Piggott said. His ability to fix either of them with his mangled eyes as if he could see them perfectly well was unnerving.

Tate leaned toward him, his face growing red, and opened his mouth to speak, but Sinclair rapped on the table. "Mr. Tate, that's enough. I think you'll find that extra rations of beer and stolen rum are the reason for these ghost sightings. You are charged with keeping peace and order, not filling men's heads with a lot of superstitious nonsense." Of course, Sinclair had been filling men's heads with superstitious nonsense just the night before, but this was different. He didn't want the men afraid to do their work.

Tate was suddenly peaceable. "Yes, my lord."

"Mr. Piggott, back to your duties, and no more about this, if you please."

"Aye, sir," said Piggott. Feeling his way forward with a stout pole he used as a cane, he managed to bump heavily into Tate, and Sinclair felt sure that he'd done it on purpose. Tate growled, but didn't retaliate.

"Good day, men."

Sinclair ducked out of the mess, shaking his head. Despite his instructions to Tate and Piggott, everyone on board would hear the stories. The missing stores, however, had given him an idea. He found Parris in his cabin, caring for his still-unconscious daughter.

"I know how to help her," Sinclair said. "We need to catch the manticore."

Parris shrugged. "Yes, but how?"

"By making sure it can get into one of the storerooms but not out again."

"You think it's like the beetle. That it passes through some things and not others."

"Maybe even the same things."

Parris grinned and clapped him on the shoulder. "We'll need candles."

◄┼╂┼►

THE *Western Star* was built to carry enough stores to provision seventy crewmen and ninety passengers for a voyage of four months. Half of the honeycomb of compartments that made up the seven decks of the ship were dedicated to storing food and drink. Most of that space, however, was empty, since there hadn't been time to purchase enough fresh provisions before their hasty departure. Only two large storerooms contained the food for the first leg of their journey, and it was here that Parris and Sinclair set their trap.

They set out slats of wood on the floor edge to edge, careful to leave no space between them. With a bucket, they scooped wax from a bubbling pot of melted candles and drizzled it over the wood until it was completely covered. When the wax cooled, they separated the slats and meticulously scraped off any drops that had seeped through and hardened on the wrong side. Maasha Kaatra helped, working silently alongside them.

The African made Parris nervous. Partly it was his size and evident strength, and the curved sword he always wore at his belt, though Parris had rarely seen him draw it. In London, it was rare to see a black man armed with a weapon. Partly it was the deep blackness of his skin, as different from Parris's indoor pallor as it was possible to be. Most of all, though, was the simple fact that he had Sinclair's ear, and he had his trust. There was a history between the two of them that Parris didn't know, a friendship born of past adventures, which made it that much harder for Parris to predict or control what Sinclair might do.

When they ran out of candles and Sinclair went to search out some more, Parris took the opportunity to speak. "Why do you follow him?" he said.

Maasha Kaatra didn't need to ask what he meant. "When I was a boy, I read a book called *Theory of the Balance Of Nature* by Jabir ibn Hayyan."

"Geber the alchemist," Parris said.

"As he is known in the West. He sought a recipe for the creation of life. He even claimed to have created a snake from elemental substances."

Parris snorted.

"I know," Maasha Kaatra said. "It doesn't matter. He planted questions in my mind about life and death, questions that have never left me."

"And you think Sinclair will lead you to answers?"

Maasha Kaatra pulled his sword from his scabbard so suddenly that it was out before Parris noticed the motion. He met Parris's eyes. "Sinclair let me kill the men who bought me as a slave and killed my daughters. I put this sword through their bodies and watched them die. When I was finished, I turned the sword on myself, but Sinclair convinced me to live. We seek the same magic, he and I. To turn death into life." He slid the sword smoothly back into its scabbard. "Besides, my brother betrayed me to become ruler in my place, only to be overrun by the Blue Sultanate. I have no home to return to."

Parris swallowed, still watching the sword. He didn't know what to say, but Maasha Kaatra didn't seem to require a response. He picked up a slat and resumed scraping the wax.

When they completed the work, the ship's carpenters nailed the wooden slats in a crosshatch pattern on the inside walls, ceiling, floor, and across the opening of both storerooms, with the waxed side placed inward, toward the middle of the room. The hope was that the manticore would be able to pass through the scraped side of the wood into the room, but once there, would not be able to bypass the waxed wood to get out. Of course, they would have to tear down the slats before anyone could get any food from the storerooms again, but for the time being, it would do.

⊰+✦+⊱

CATHERINE was hungry. She was always hungry, and the food in this place never seemed to satisfy. She followed the smell and passed easily into the room as she did the others, though the opening had been blocked with bars of wood. She ate greedily. Sated for the moment—though it wouldn't last—she turned to leave and found her way blocked.

Trapped! He threw his body against the wood again and again, ignoring the pain, trying to break out. He screeched and climbed the walls, smashing shelves, looking for a gap. Nothing. But the wood slats across the opening weren't strong. He could break through them. He crashed into the bars again, and heard one snap.

⊰+✦+⊱

A MIDSHIPMAN pounded on the door to Parris's cabin to tell him he was wanted below. Parris raced down to the storerooms to find Sinclair there before him. One of the two rooms was wrecked. Shelves littered the floor in splintered pieces, mixed with the torn remains of food. The wooden slats on the walls and even the ceiling were gouged and split. The idea had worked, at least—the slats had apparently made its escape more difficult—but there was nothing inside.

The slats rattled. Parris jumped back with a shout.

Sinclair laughed. "Yes. It's still in there."

Parris peered through the gaps, angling his body to get a view, but he could see nothing. Not a shimmer, not even a shadow. The wood crashed with an unseen blow, startling him again. One of the boards split and hung loose. The wax might prevent it from passing through, but it wouldn't stop the creature from breaking out. Which meant the manticore, though unseen, was truly part of the material world. How could it be *both* tangible matter and invisible spirit? Substances could change from one form to another, as when water transformed into its spiritual form when heated, but nothing could be *both* physical and spiritual at the same time, could it? Yet this creature was. It was beginning to look to Parris like the whole world was as much of a mystery as the human body. By the time they reached Horizon, they might find that nothing they thought they knew was really true.

"We'll need to reinforce these slats," Sinclair said. "This won't hold it for long." He clambered up the ladder, shouting. In moments, one of the carpenters arrived with wood and nails. He crossed himself and murmured prayers under his breath, but he did the work.

Sinclair reappeared, carrying a bellows from the cookhouse and a sack of flour. Behind him, another sailor labored with a bucket of water. "Now let's see what our friend looks like," Sinclair said.

He lifted the bucket and hurled the water through the slats. Much of it landed on the floor, but a screech from inside told them some of it had hit its mark. Sinclair scooped a handful of flour from the sack and funneled it into the mouth of the bellows. He inserted the bellows between the slats and worked the handles up and down. Clouds of flour dust billowed into the storeroom.

White eddies spiraled in the air in the wake of the invisible thing inside. Parris's pulse quickened. As the white powder clung to it more and more, the manticore became increasingly agitated, twirling and shrieking and throwing itself against the walls. Soon they could tell it was about the size of a small man, though a dozen limbs flew in every direction, and it climbed up and down the walls with disconcerting speed.

It paused its mad charge in the middle of the storeroom, and they could see its chest heaving with exertion. Suddenly, beneath the clinging flour, the creature itself turned completely visible.

Parris stared at the brilliant red fur, the pincered front limbs and the hooked ones in back, the many entwining tails, and the all-too-human face. It was just like Catherine had drawn it, though now in living color. Its thicker tail, the one with the sharp tip, was ringed with a stiff flap of moist flesh like a cuff. If that tail was used to pierce flesh, the flap might provide the same suction as a leech's mouth, anchoring it to the wound. That would explain the shape of the mark on Catherine's back.

It was repulsive. Parris could hardly stand to look at it, knowing that those horrible limbs had wrapped themselves around his daughter's body and thrust themselves into her flesh.

"Kill it," Parris said. "Kill it now, before it figures out how to escape."

"We won't learn much if we kill it," Sinclair said.

Parris tried to keep the desperation out of his voice. "I don't care about that. That thing has Catherine in some kind of trance. If it escapes, we might never be able to catch it again. We can't see it; we can't touch it. It could murder everyone on this boat, and we couldn't do anything about it."

"What if we kill it and Catherine still doesn't wake up?" Sinclair said.

Parris had no answer to that.

"Wait. Be patient. We have to study it and learn."

—‡+‡‡—

SINCLAIR'S studies only frustrated Parris more. Sinclair seemed willing to take his time, instructing men to haul materials and devices from his alchemical distillery on the main deck, and then tinkering with them interminably. Once he began, his experiments were so tame that Parris despaired of finding any helpful results from them before it was too late for Catherine. When Sinclair began viewing the manticore through glasses of varying colors and thicknesses and recording the results, Parris couldn't stand any more.

"My daughter is dying," he said. "We have to *do* something!"

Sinclair peered at him through a sliver of red-tinted glass. "I am doing something. What else do you suggest?"

Parris threw up his hands and stormed back to his cabin, where Blanche was trying to spoon a thin broth into Catherine's mouth. Occasionally she would swallow small amounts of it, but it wasn't enough. She needed to eat. She was growing paler, and her hands felt thin and weak. Parris stroked Catherine's hair and talked to her, trying to reason things out. Trying to think what he could possibly do to the manticore to break the bond between them.

Chapter Thirteen

T HE *Western Star* reached the Azores. Parris refused to go ashore with the rest of the passengers and crew, unwilling to leave Catherine. Sinclair drove the loaders hard, anxious to continue the voyage, and in only three days they left the islands behind. The empty storerooms were now filled with hundreds of barrels of hardtack, haunches of salt pork and beef stacked to the deckhead, casks of salted fish, cheese, rice, nuts, raisins, dried peas, prunes, oatmeal, and butter—this mostly for the officers' table—and a small pen of live pigs and chickens to be kept on the forecastle. There were barrels of fresh water, as well as thousands of liters of beer, which would keep fresh on a long journey better than the water.

Sinclair invited a select few to his cabin to celebrate. They were passengers, mostly, intellectuals from various fields. A roasted pig lay across the center of the table, an apple in its mouth, circled by platters piled with fresh food. Parris sat by himself, eating his meal but not tasting it.

Sinclair rapped on the table with a knife. "Delicious as this food is, it's not why I invited you here. We need your help. As some of you may be aware, Stephen Parris's daughter is dying."

The cabin fell silent. Parris looked around, startled.

"What none of you are aware of is that his daughter's consciousness is trapped by a Horizon creature on board this ship. An invisible creature that can walk through walls."

"Superstition," said a portly gentleman in a vicar's black clothing. "That's not possible." His name was Andrew Kecilpenny, and he sat next to a gaunt man with a jovial smile named Gibbs. During the first half of the meal, Kecilpenny and Gibbs had argued constantly, apparently out of long habit.

"Of course it's possible," Gibbs said.

Kecilpenny opened his mouth to reply, but Sinclair raised a hand. "I assure you, it's not only possible, it's true. Parris and I have captured this creature and seen its qualities for ourselves. What we need are ideas." He briefly explained what they knew about the manticore and the need to release Catherine from its bond.

Parris gave Sinclair a grateful smile. There were ten men in the room. Surely, with all these minds working on the problem, they could come up with a solution.

"It must be a spirit," Kecilpenny said. "Physical creatures can't walk through matter. It's a known fact."

"You just mean Aristotle believed it to be a fact," Gibbs said. "That doesn't make it true."

"How can you disagree with Aristotle? Every philosopher for two thousand years has built on him. Demetrius. Galen. Thomas Aquinas. Even heathen Mussulmen like Avicenna. Everything we know about physics, anatomy, government, rhetoric, biology, all the physical sciences, came from Aristotle."

"Actually," Parris said, "I made a study of blood veins recently, and found that they originate from the heart, not from the liver. Galen was wrong about that. Aristotle, too."

"Aha!" Gibbs wagged a finger at his friend. "I told you. Aristotle was wrong."

"In that particular, anyway," Parris said.

"In every particular."

"It doesn't matter," Parris said. "The manticore is a physical creature. It eats meat, breaks wood, leaves footprints in flour."

"That doesn't mean it couldn't pass through matter," Gibbs said. "Like all physical things, it's made up of particles swimming in a void. With the right inducement, those particles could pass right by each other and out the other side."

Kecilpenny rolled his eyes. "Gibbs is an atomist. Never mind that Aristotle buried that philosophy two millennia ago."

Gibbs reached across the table and pulled the apple out of the pig's mouth. "Think about it. Let's say I cut this apple in half." He did so, slicing it neatly through the core. "Then I take one of the halves and cut that in half. I keep on cutting with a very sharp knife until I get down to the smallest possible piece that can't be divided. That's what Democritus called an atom—the uncuttable, most basic piece of matter."

Another man chimed in. "But why can't you divide it? Aristotle said matter was continuous. You can keep cutting infinitely."

"Infinitely?" Gibbs said. "If you cut something *infinitely*, you end up with *nothing*. Matter can't be composed of nothing."

Parris felt his spirits rising. He liked these two, and it helped him to hear others attacking the problem, even in these abstract terms. He had read Galen's commentary in which he had ridiculed atomism, but that didn't mean it couldn't be true—Parris had already shown that Galen could be wrong. It was hard to see how atomism could explain the bond with Catherine, but if it shed light on any of the manticore's mysterious abilities, that would be a start.

"If there are atoms," Parris said, "there must be something *between* the atoms."

"That's right," Gibbs said. "A void. Between the atoms, there's an empty void that the atoms pass through."

Was that how the manticore and the beetle did it? Did they somehow spread their constituent atoms apart so they could pass each other through the intervening void? "What do atoms look like?" Parris said.

"Too small to see, of course," Gibbs said. "But solids and liquids must look different. Democritus suggested that the atoms of solids have little hooks and eyes, or something like antlers, to entangle them and hold them together, but the atoms of liquids are slippery and run over each other, like when you pour a glass full of poppy seeds."

"Fanciful nonsense," Kecilpenny said. "As well say the atoms are tiny rabbits that jump around and bounce into each other."

"But solids can change into liquids," Parris said. "Perhaps it's simply the arrangement of the atoms that makes the difference between a solid and a liquid." As he said it, he thought of Sinclair's snake, and a chill went down his spine. "Or between flesh and wood," he added. "Or lead and gold."

"Everything that we experience," Gibbs said. "The texture of wool or glass, water, oil, smoke, vapor, the fact that every drop of vinegar behaves like every other drop of vinegar—can be explained by atoms moving through the void, bouncing off one another and sticking together and interacting."

"What about the mind?" Parris said, thinking of Catherine. "What about the soul?"

Kecilpenny clapped his hands. "Therein lies the problem. It's a godless philosophy. It eliminates the spiritual."

"I don't know about that," Parris said. "Even if atoms exist, they must still have been created by God."

"But if you explain everything by mechanism, nothing is left to God's intervention. You relegate God to the role of spectator, watching his machine tick along. But why do you feel the need to invent the machine? God has the power to run it all himself."

As the conversation stretched on, Parris's excitement ebbed. It was all talk, no action, and these philosophical arguments had been running for centuries. They weren't going to conclude in time to save Catherine.

He slipped out, leaving them to their talk, and returned to his cabin. Catherine was so thin he could see the outline of the bones in her face and neck. He could hear her breath only faintly. He held her hand and spoke softly to her, not knowing if she could hear him or not.

Hours later, as the sky outside grew dark, Sinclair knocked on the cabin door. "You left too soon. We figured it out."

"You're serious?"

"I should have thought of it earlier," Sinclair said. "Come with me."

Hardly daring to hope, Parris followed him out to the main deck and into the alchemical distillery. The walls and floor were brick, and the room resembled a kitchen more than anything else. Most of the space was filled with a brick furnace with tiered openings of various sizes. A wooden workbench was strewn with books and charts, glass retorts, alembics, cucurbits, jars with variously colored powders and liquids, and a large brazier. The other walls contained shelves with more jars, most of them unlabeled. Several books were scattered about with titles like *Concerning the Making of Things by Fire* or *On the Hindering of the Accident of Old Age*. One massive volume on the table nearest Parris, its binding grimed in soot and spotted with stains, was labeled *The Secret of Secrets*.

"It's obvious, once you think of it," Sinclair said, rummaging in a drawer of the workbench. "It's one of the fundamental elements, and it's a metal—an element of earth—whereas quintessence is its antithesis, an element of the heavens. It stands to reason they should repel each other."

He came up holding something which he offered to Parris with an open palm.

"Have her take this," Sinclair said. "If you can get her to swallow it, I think there's a good chance she'll recover."

Parris's heart leaped. Sinclair had found the answer. Against all odds, he'd discovered a cure. Then he looked into Sinclair's hand and saw a shiny, metallic capsule that he recognized immediately. A mercury pill.

It was too much. All Parris's stress and fear came rushing out at once. "That's poison, you fool." He slapped the pill away and rushed back out into the night.

He didn't go back to his cabin. Instead, he scrambled down the ladders to the storeroom where the manticore was trapped. He was tired of waiting. He couldn't trust Catherine's life to a room full of intellectuals. He had to do something himself, and—crazy as it was—this was the only thing he could think of to do. If Catherine died, he didn't want to be alive to see it anyway.

He peered inside and saw the manticore, fully visible now, though it seemed to be asleep. He picked up the hammer the carpenter had left behind and began prying out nails. When he had cleared enough of the slats away, he squeezed between them and climbed inside.

The manticore's yellow eyes opened. Without any warning, it sprang, one instant reclining on the floor, the next instant on top of him. It was what Parris had intended to happen, but even so, the swiftness and violence of it overwhelmed him. He shrieked and clawed at it, but it was too fast and strong.

It wrapped its tails around his body, pinioning his arms. The tips of the tails actually seemed to slip through his skin without resistance or pain, but once inside his flesh, they regained the usual nature of matter, so that they worked like barbs. He couldn't pull away. When Parris was so thoroughly bound he couldn't move at all, the manticore's thicker tail, held coiled over its back, straightened and plunged downward into his spine.

For a brief moment, it occurred to Parris that this had been a very bad idea. Then he was pulled into a different place and time and lost track of who he was.

＋＋＋＋

LEAVING *the hairless one behind on the floor, he leaped through the hole in his cage and was free. He climbed to the highest part of the ship, as far away as possible from the cage in its belly. The hairless ones had tricked him. Instead of using food as an invitation to kinship, as was proper, they had used it as a trap. But this one had come inside as if he intended kinship after all. The young one was learning to talk, though if she remained bonded much longer, she would die. Perhaps this one could learn to talk, too.*

Parris's mind whirled as they climbed higher and higher in the rigging, the deck dwindling to a tiny, pitching platform far below. He had understood that Catherine's consciousness was somehow trapped by the manticore's, but he hadn't imagined anything like this. He had no control over its movements. He could hardly even keep track of his own thoughts.

Father?

The voice appeared in his mind without sound, but he recognized it anyway. Catherine? And yet, who was Catherine? Something important, very important. He couldn't think. Why didn't he have any hands?

Father, it's me, Catherine.

He had flashes of vision: the ship from high above; a fountain of pure, elemental mercury; Catherine lying prone on her bed; himself lying on the floor of the storeroom.

You can talk to me with your thoughts. Just think about what you want to say.

He wanted to answer, but he couldn't think of who she was, or who he was, or how he got there. He had been captured, that was right, tricked by Chelsey's sailors. But no, that was someone else.

A fountain of mercury . . . the memory of his first memory ceremony blew through his mind like a breath of wind. Mercury. That was what he needed. Sinclair had been right.

He laughed, a long and bitter laugh, though he couldn't tell what body was doing the laughing. He was trapped now, just like Catherine. He should have let Sinclair give her the pill. He knew the truth now, but he couldn't do anything about it. He would watch Catherine starve to death, and then he'd starve to death himself.

The pain caught him by surprise. It was agony, and he screamed. What were the hairless ones doing to him now? They were trying to pull him out of his body, trying to steal his soul.

"Wake up!"

Parris's perspective lurched sickeningly. Someone was slapping him. Dizzy, he opened his eyes to see Sinclair leaning over him, his hand raised. Another blow landed, snapping his head to one side.

"I'm awake!" he said before Sinclair could slap him again.

Sinclair hauled him to his feet. He was inside the storeroom. He was Stephen Parris, not a manticore, and he was alive. He tasted something sharp and metallic.

He swayed, but Sinclair grabbed his arm.

"What were you thinking?" Sinclair said. "You let the manticore go free!"

"You gave me mercury," Parris said, dazed.

"Yes," Sinclair said. "Brought you out of it, though, didn't it?"

Parris snapped to full awareness. "You have more, don't you?" He dragged Sinclair toward the ladder. "Come on!"

⊹⊹⊹

HE knew it would be bad, but he hadn't expected this. Catherine arched and writhed and thrashed about, her body stiff, her face contorted in expressions of pain. It had seemed so quick while he was in the manticore's mind. But he'd only been connected for such a short time; maybe it took longer in proportion to the duration of the bond. He held her as well as he could, but her body shook more powerfully than he could control.

What if it was too late? What if her mind was so thoroughly fused with the manticore's that breaking her away would kill her? She arched so violently he thought her head would touch her feet, and screamed until her lungs were empty. Then, finally, her taut body relaxed and she collapsed against the bed.

She opened her eyes and looked around, blinking slowly. "Father?"

He lifted her and squeezed her tightly. "It's all right," he said, as much to himself as to her. His eyes were wet. "It's all right now. You're free."

⊹⊹⊹

THEY were two weeks sailing west of the Azores before they realized the problem. Sinclair was in his cabin, preparing for bed, when a sharp knock interrupted him. Sighing, he donned his captain's hat, threw on a cloak, and opened the door to find the blind cook, Piggott. "A word, Captain?"

Sinclair stepped aside to let him in. "What is it?"

"The food from the Azores."

"What's wrong with it? Is it going bad?"

"Nay, it's fresh enough. Only it's not all there. They promised twenty barrels of salted fish; they only gave us ten. Some of the crates are only half full. The Madeira wine is missing altogether."

Sinclair slammed his fist against the wall. "Where's Thorpe? Why were the stores not checked?"

"They *were* checked, my lord. We counted every barrel and opened every crate. Everything was accounted for."

"Then how—"

"It was Chandler, my lord, the purser's mate. He directed the loading and storing. We think he was paid off to remove or swap the stores after they were loaded."

"Well, where's Chandler, then? Get him in here! I'll have him whipped until his skin hangs in ribbons."

"I'd have stripped his hide for you, my lord, if I could. He's gone."

"Gone?"

"Ain't no one seen him since we left. He stayed behind, in the Azores. Of course, he would have to stay, wouldn't he? Not much good getting all that money if he just came along with us."

Piggott left him a complete accounting of what stores were actually aboard, and Sinclair worked the numbers at his writing desk, seething. He would not turn around. They were too far along, and the season was late already. To return was to risk sickness, strain on the ship, and the loss of crew. By his reckoning, they would still have enough food to reach Horizon, with disciplined rationing. They would just have to make it last.

✦✦✦

CATHERINE felt wonderful. Her memories of the beginning of the voyage were scrambled and confused. Now, however, she was just where she wanted to be: away from home and sailing to the edge of the world. She was growing stronger every day. Captain Sinclair had invited her to eat at his table with Father, so the better food could revive her more quickly.

She ate a cracker topped with quince jam. "How did you know to use mercury?" she asked.

Sinclair chewed thoughtfully and swallowed before replying. "There are three fundamental elements in alchemy: salt, sulfur, and mercury. Many alchemists have thought a combination of these three would ultimately yield quintessence, though all attempts have failed. I thought that instead of being an ingredient of quintessence, perhaps mercury would neutralize it." He shrugged. "It seemed worth a try."

Catherine wiped her mouth with her napkin. "Are you saying the manticore put quintessence *inside* me? Is that what made the wounds glow?"

"I think that's how it disappears and walks through walls—its flesh is full of quintessence. The beetle, too, and the snake—maybe any creature from Horizon. It's even in their water. I tried to distill it, and I think I partially succeeded, but it doesn't work on me. It obviously entered my flesh when I drank it, but it gave me no special powers."

"So, then . . . quintessence also allows two minds to form a bond," Catherine said. "To share memories and experiences."

"I don't think we've found the limit to what quintessence makes possible," Sinclair said. "It's the *prima materia*. The original material from which God made the world. As far as we know, it could do anything."

"Which is only any good if you know how to use it," Father said.

"Of course." Sinclair pushed the plates aside and brushed away the crumbs. In the open space, he laid out a parchment. With a wink at Catherine, he said, "Take a look at this."

It was a variation of the box with four quadrants that Catherine had drawn at home. He had combined her quadrants into two, labeled *Visibility* and *Substance*, and had added two of his own: *Transmutation* and *Psyche*. These were the four categories—that they knew of so far—that animals from Horizon could alter. In the first box, he had written *manticore*; in the second, *manticore and beetle*; in the third, *snake and mantis*; and in the fourth, *manticore*.

Catherine clapped her hands. But . . .

"What mantis are you talking about?" Father asked.

Sinclair's eyes twinkled. "One of the passengers—a six-year-old boy—found it in a crack in the hold. I don't know how he spotted it, but he did."

He produced a small box and lifted the lid. Catherine eagerly peered inside, but saw nothing. The box was empty.

"Is it invisible?" she asked.

Sinclair shook his head. He reached in with an open palm, as if to let something crawl onto his hand. She saw a flash of movement, but when she blinked, it was gone. He lifted his hand.

"Do you see it?"

They both looked carefully, until Father made a noise of astonishment. "You have six fingers," he said.

Catherine counted—it was true. Now that Father had pointed it out, she could tell which one didn't belong. A second pinkie finger protruded next to the real one. As she looked closely, she could make out tiny legs and wings held close to a long body, and a flat head in the place of the fingernail. Its coloring and texture were identical to Sinclair's other fingers. "Is that . . . ?"

Sinclair grasped the extra finger and pulled it away from his hand. As he did so, it changed color to a brilliant green and brown and spread its wings for flight. She could see why he'd called it a mantis—it had long, jointed limbs and a triangular head. Sinclair kept it trapped in his cupped hand.

"It's extraordinary," Father said, peering close.

"It's just like the snake," Sinclair said. "It doesn't just *look* like other substances. It transforms into them."

He dropped the mantis onto his porcelain dinner plate. Instantly it all but disappeared, flattening itself along the rim and taking on the same off-white color. They could still see it—it made a bulge that clearly didn't belong—but it appeared to be a defect in the plate rather than an insect lying on top of it. Sinclair bent his middle finger back with his thumb and flicked the mantis, hard. The plate rang with the impact. Catherine reached out a tentative finger and touched, then flicked it herself. It was made of porcelain.

Sinclair took a gold crown and slid the insect onto it, where it took on the exact appearance and texture of the gold. "If it looks like gold and feels like gold and acts like gold . . . it must be gold," he said, smiling.

"But it's not," Catherine said. "Some part of it remembers that it's really a mantis. Even when it's gold, it's not the same as the coin, because it can change back again."

Father was nodding. "Implying that it has a component besides its physical body," he said. He looked at Catherine and then at Sinclair. "This insect has a soul."

Sinclair dropped the mantis back in the box. "Don't jump ahead of yourself, Doctor." He shut the lid with a snap.

But Father couldn't be discouraged. "Until now, we've been chasing shadows. Mere traces of the power behind the universe." He gazed at the box with wonder in his eyes. "This tiny creature knows more of the world than the wisest of men."

"There must be more," Catherine said. "If these are just the animals that ended up on the boat, Horizon must be teeming with them."

The idea was thrilling, but something else pleased her even more. Her father was talking to her, listening to her, and smiling at her in a way she hadn't seen him do since Peter had died. With pride.

He kept looking at her, as if to satisfy himself that she was still there. She caught his eye and grinned at him, and he winked. She was happier than she had been in a long time, but she couldn't help thinking of Mother, left behind with no son, no daughter, no husband. What would she do? Her whole life had been wrapped up in Catherine and her future.

One other thing bothered her. Although she hadn't seen it, the manticore was still loose on the ship. She'd had no more dreams, nor had Father, but she'd been in the manticore's mind too long to forget it was out there. Lonely and confused, far from anything it knew, it feared being captured again, but it was also determined to understand the humans. It would try again.

⊰╋╋⊱

IT visited her that night.

When Catherine woke, disturbed by a movement, she found it there, perched silently on the foot of her bunk. She gave a little shriek, and Father startled awake, looking around with bleary eyes, until he saw the manticore and froze.

Catherine understood that its attack had not been meant to harm. It had seen her as a potential friend, an ally who might help it. Even so, she dared not let it touch her again. Good intentions or not, it had nearly killed her.

In its mind, she had seen pictures of its life, both past and present: glimpses of Horizon, glimpses of London from its point of view. She wondered if the process worked both ways. Had it seen memories of her youth in Derbyshire, of London balls and parties, of Thomas Hungate's flirtations? If so, it had probably found her mind just as incomprehensible.

Slowly, Father eased himself out of his hammock. "What do you want?" he asked the manticore.

The manticore cocked its head, and Catherine's heart thudded violently. "I don't think it understands English," she said. The manticore opened its lips and mirrored her expression. Was it imitating her? Slowly, she raised a hand and spread five fingers wide. It raised its own forelimb in response and reached forward. Its pincered hands opened, and something dropped onto the bed. She picked it up. It was a cluster of raisins.

"Thank you," she said, and bowed her head in a gesture she hoped it would interpret as thanks.

The manticore bobbed its head several times in response, then performed a complex series of movements with two of its tails and vanished. Catherine held her breath. After a few moments, she reached out under the blanket with a tentative foot, but she felt nothing. It was gone.

Catherine remembered the sensation of leaping from branch to branch through tall forests, looking through gaps in the foliage at the gigantic sun, or gazing down from a dizzying height over the very edge of the world, an endless cliff that descended into darkness and void. Then also, quite suddenly, she remembered a name. *Chichirico.* The sound included a harsher teeth-snapping noise than she could reproduce, but she said it aloud anyway. "His name is *Chichirico.*"

Father reached out, plucked a raisin from the cluster, and ate it. "Tastes fine," he said. "It seems Chichirico brought you a gift."

"Why?" Catherine said.

Father considered. Catherine knew he was remembering his time in the manticore's mind. She understood that Chichirico's original mission had been a diplomatic one.

"I think he's trying to make friends," Father said. "I should probably tell Sinclair, but I don't think I'm going to just yet. He's not really the diplomatic type, and I don't want Chichirico experimented on anymore. When we get to this island, we may very well need his help. So"—he met Catherine's eyes—"our secret for now?"

"Our secret," Catherine said.

Chapter Fourteen

CATHERINE hadn't expected to find Matthew Marcheford on board, and she wasn't sure she was glad to see him. She'd run away from her former life to re-create herself as someone new, and she didn't need someone who already had fixed notions of what she was like. Matthew knew her too well. Their mothers had been friends for years, and Catherine and Matthew had played together as children, back when they were young enough to run and toss hoops and throw balls, before she was too old for outside games and Mother confined her to dresses and needlepoint.

She liked Matthew, but she always suspected he liked her a bit more. He was too polite to say anything, too old-fashioned to take any step without the formal interaction of fathers on both sides, but she could tell. Despite that, he'd been a safe friend, because she knew he wasn't rich enough for Mother to approve him as a potential match. Now things were different.

There was no avoiding him, though. Besides Blanca, he was the only other passenger on board her age. Some of the younger sailors were in the same range, but they worked and socialized in different spheres. She was stuck with him, and would be for a long time.

She leaned back against the rail at the stern of the ship, enjoying the play of the salty breeze through her hair and watching the helmsman pull on the wheel. Matthew leaned beside her in the unadorned black jerkin and hose of a good Protestant, with unruly sand-colored hair, an abundance of freckles, and hands and feet rather too large for the rest of him. On her other side, Blanca stood upright with her hands folded in front of her, quiet but with a smile on her face.

Catherine had told no one about the visits from Chichirico. He'd continued to come to her cabin at night, usually with some small gift of food he'd stolen from the stores. They traded signs and words in a poor attempt to communicate. He never stayed long before some sound or movement spooked him and he vanished. She longed to tell someone, but she wasn't sure what reaction she'd get. Blanca would just be scared, and Matthew would probably tell his father.

Catherine turned around and leaned over the back rail—the *stern* rail, she corrected herself—looking down on the white water churning up from the rudder. The ship's wash trailed out behind them. The ocean behind them was empty. They weren't heading for the Continent, or even around it to Africa or the Indies, like any other ships would. They were striking out across a desert of water, with no guarantee they would ever find land at all.

"Did you sail on a ship like this when you came from Spain?" she asked Blanca.

"No," Blanca said. "I came over land to France. When I sailed to England, it was just across the channel, and the boat was much smaller."

Catherine laughed. "I've never been on a ship before."

"Never?"

"Well . . . just the wherries up and down the river. Never on a sailing ship like this."

"I sailed to France with my father when I was young," Matthew said. "I hardly remember it, though." He chuckled. "The only thing I remember is vomiting in his lap."

"You didn't." The image of the dignified Bishop Marcheford mopping up such a mess made her smile.

"I think that's why he didn't take me on any more voyages."

It was a chance comment, lightly delivered, but it made Catherine wonder how well Matthew got along with his father. He was like Bishop Marcheford in many ways, but that didn't mean they were close.

"What do you think will happen to us?" Blanca asked.

Matthew, as usual, took the question at face value. "We'll join the Horizon colony," he said. "It will be hard work, but with God's grace, we'll survive. Eventually Queen Mary will be overthrown, the Princess Elizabeth will bring the true faith back to England, and it will be safe to return."

"You've got it all planned," Catherine said.

"What if we can't return?" Blanca said. "They say you can live forever on Horizon, but once there, you can never leave."

Matthew shook his head. "Just stories. I daresay we will find Horizon is a place in God's world, just like any other. A place where we will be free for a time to practice our faith and still be Englishmen, but nothing more."

"But Matthew," Catherine said, "I *saw* Master Sinclair turn a rod into a snake and back again."

"And I saw a street magician who could turn your silver shilling into an iron penny—though I noticed he never changed it back again."

"It's not a trick. If you saw it, you wouldn't think so."

"Then there's some explanation. It doesn't mean we'll find the Fountain of Youth."

"And I was bonded to the manticore. I shared its mind. You can't tell me that's normal."

"But is it magic? Does it mean all the stories of turning lead to gold and living forever are true?"

Catherine stamped her foot. "You don't know everything, Matthew Marcheford."

"I never said I did!"

"Go back to your Greek and Latin."

Catherine crossed her arms and looked out across the ship. As she did, she noticed a portly man in vicar's clothes standing farther down the rail, tinkering with a strange contraption. Several leather bands encircled his head, supporting a wooden rod that stuck straight out from one of his eyes. A vertical crosspiece was attached halfway along the contraption, and at the very end, beyond his reach, hung a tiny circle of colored glass.

"What's he doing?" Catherine asked.

Matthew shrugged. "No idea."

Catherine started walking toward the man, ignoring Matthew's suggestions that maybe they should leave him alone.

"What is that?" she asked when she reached him.

The man lifted a black patch that had covered one of his eyes and peered at her. He had a fleshy face with a hint of jowls. "Oh, good morning, Miss Parris. I don't believe we've met. I'm Andrew Kecilpenny." He gave her a short bow, which she returned in a curtsy. "This is a cross staff."

"It doesn't look like any cross staff I've ever seen," Matthew said, following behind with Blanca.

"That's because the only ones you've seen were for measuring the distance between the horizon and the North Star," Kecilpenny said.

"That's right. To calculate latitude."

Matthew was showing off again. Catherine was tempted to hit him. "What's yours for?" she asked Kecilpenny.

"To measure the size of the sun."

Catherine saw the surprise on Matthew's face, and knew it must be reflected in her own. The sun was, well, it was just the sun, wasn't it? It was the source of light and heat. It didn't have a *size*. Did it?

"How can you measure its size when you don't know how far away it is?" Matthew said.

"You caught me," Kecilpenny said. "I can't. But I can tell if it *changes* size."

He showed them how he could peer down the rod and slide the vertical crosspiece along it lengthwise until its height matched the height of the sun above the horizon. Then, using another rod, he tapped the tiny circle of glass, pushing it farther out until it exactly covered the sun, from his point of view. He then pulled the contraption off his head and marked the position of both crosspiece and glass.

"I don't understand," Blanca said. "The sun doesn't change size."

Matthew was quicker. "It will, though. The closer we get to the western edge of the world, the closer we'll be to where the sun sets, so it will seem bigger in the evening, and smaller in the morning."

Kecilpenny nodded. "The sky is a dome. As we move toward the edge of the dome, we'll be closer to the things on it—the sun and stars—when they pass through the west. So if I measure the relative position of these pieces at about the same time every day . . ."

"You'll know how close we're getting to the end of the world," said Catherine. She remembered her dreams of Horizon and how impossibly huge the sun and stars had looked in them. She had a feeling that by the time they arrived at the island, Master Kecilpenny wouldn't need a strange contraption to see that the sun was getting larger.

"What does it matter?" she said. "You don't know how big it gets. So you can't tell how close we are. Can you?"

A throaty laugh made them turn around. Behind them was a small, gaunt-looking man who nevertheless had such a jovial smile that

Catherine liked him on the spot. "No purpose in it at all, really," the man said, winking at Catherine. "Kecilpenny just likes to measure things."

The new man introduced himself as Gibbs and made several jokes at Kecilpenny's expense, making them all laugh, even Kecilpenny. Catherine took a deep breath of salty air and leaned back against the rail, reveling in the height of the mast above her and the might of the canvas sails, bloated with wind. Men moved in the rigging, keeping watch or repairing lines, looking tiny next to the massive scale of their vessel.

Above the men, she spotted something even higher and tinier that was not a man at all. A feeling of vertigo took her breath away.

"Look! There it is!" Blanca called, seeing it, too. She pointed.

Matthew tried to follow her gaze. "What?"

"The manticore. Can you see it?"

They all looked, and they all saw Chichirico, hanging from the tip of the highest topgallant.

"I wonder what it's been doing all this time," Matthew said.

◄╋╋►

SINCLAIR heard grumbling wherever he walked. He'd been forced to reduce rations to bare subsistence levels, only one meal a day, and no one was pleased. His officers grumbled more than any of them, since he'd insisted they should have the same portions as everyone else. A mistake, perhaps. Their discontent was spilling down to the working sailors, and his tales of immeasurable riches just over the next wave were starting to lose their effect.

He was no tyrant. He would rather motivate through charisma and manipulation than through brute force, but enthusiasm was fading. More and more people—sailors and passengers alike—talked about going back home, to Holland, perhaps, if not to England. To maintain discipline, he'd resorted to posting Tate and his soldiers to guard the storerooms and oversee the distribution of food.

He climbed up to the forecastle, skirting the empty meat pen, the cookhouse, and his alchemical distillery. Near the bowsprit, he gazed out over the western horizon with the wind in his hair, leaning against a cluster of large barrels stored between the ship's two bronze cannons. The barrels were from the original journey of the *Western Star*. Although they contained nothing but pebbles and fine sand, he had insisted on bringing them along, despite arguments by some that using the space for fresh water or food was more sensible. He liked to sit here and touch them to gain strength.

There was an alchemical reaction brewing on the ship, like two incompatible elements forced into the same retort. The officers resented his authority, and would resent Tate and his soldiers if they had to enforce it. The passengers, on the other hand, mostly educated men with no experience of life at sea, blamed the officers for the inevitable hardships of the voyage. Put both in the crucible of months on the open sea, and an explosion seemed inevitable.

Tonight, however, was cool and clear. Beyond the stacks of billowing canvas, he could see a thousand stars like glowing motes of dust, frozen in a windblown instant of time. The ropes creaked as the boat rose and fell. He listened to the sounds for several minutes before he realized he wasn't alone.

John Marcheford stood not far away, looking out over the black water, hands clasped behind his back. Most passengers spent at least some of their time on deck, standing at the rail, contemplating the rolling sea. Sinclair took note of where each one stood and which direction he looked, whether west, toward their destination, or east, toward home. He would have guessed John Marcheford for an east-looker, given the life of privilege and respect he had left behind in London, but the former bishop consistently stood at the very prow, shielding his eyes against the sun and peering toward the horizon.

As they stood in silence, each with his own thoughts, Sinclair could hear two sailors on watch in the rigging.

"I tell you the winds are all wrong," said one.

"Wrong? They're the devil's own," said the other, his voice deeper and gruffer than the first. "One moment from the east, the next from the south, then back around from the north. I never trimmed sails so often in my life."

"Captain says it's on account of the stars. He says we're getting closer."

"And how would he know? He ain't been there, neither. Far as I can see, this damnable ocean goes on forever."

Marcheford spoke softly, apparently to himself. " 'As far as the east is from the west, so far hath he removed our transgressions from us.' "

Sinclair recognized it as a biblical quote, though he couldn't have said what book or chapter. "That's not as far as it used to be," he said.

Marcheford seemed to see Sinclair for the first time. "What?"

"The east from the west. It used to mean an infinite span, a distance only God could reach." He gestured toward the horizon. "Now man has the same power."

He expected Marcheford to be shocked, but he only said mildly, "That remains to be seen, I suppose."

His calm annoyed Sinclair. "Trust me, Bishop, we'll get there. There's no limit to what we can conquer. The ocean. The air. Death itself."

"Death is already conquered," Marcheford said.

"I'm not using a spiritual metaphor. I mean death, real physical death, defeated. No more fathers wasting away to nothing while their sons keep helpless vigil. No more young kings cut down before they come of age. Somewhere at the heart of the universe is the secret to eternal life, and sooner or later, with or without God's help, I will find it."

"So that's what you're after. The philosopher's stone."

Sinclair turned away, unable to bear his life's ambition spoken of in such dismissive terms. Marcheford was a churchman, which, as far as Sinclair was concerned, made him an enemy of knowledge and progress. He'd pitched his tent on the side of revealed truth.

It didn't matter. He didn't need Marcheford's approval. He strained his eyes toward the horizon, wishing for land, though he knew it was far too soon. When they arrived, then everyone would know he'd been right. He just had to get them there alive.

+ + +

THE remaining fresh foods were quickly exhausted. The dry biscuits were so hard they had to be soaked in beer or water to make them edible. Weevils laid their eggs in the biscuits and the rats couldn't be kept out. Everyone was hungry, which meant everyone was bad-tempered and quick to fight.

Parris spent most of his time in the infirmary, caring for the sick. The passengers were especially susceptible. They were unaccustomed to the cramped and idle life aboard ship, each night a test of endurance in the hot lower decks with the rats and the stench.

Catherine, Blanca, and Matthew helped him bathe faces in cool water, distribute medicines, and apply compresses. The most common complaints were tooth pain, skin spots, and nosebleeds, which were early signs of scurvy. No one knew why travelers on long voyages were prone to the disease, and no one knew how to cure it. Bowel disorder and stomach cramps were frequent, too, some to the point of physical weakness.

John Gibbs succumbed more quickly than most, and Parris suspected intestinal worms. He treated him with an infusion of cloves, and then attached a leech to his arm. The leeches, at any rate, weren't starving. Andrew Kecilpenny hovered near his friend, thinking up new topics of conversation for them to argue about.

Gibbs seemed eager to respond, but his breath was labored, and his face looked pale. Parris used vinegar to detach the leech and shooed Kecilpenny out of the room. Throughout the conversation, Kecilpenny had seemed almost merry, enjoying the debate, but at the door he turned a pained face to Parris.

"He looks bad. Will he make it?"

Parris lowered his voice. "He's weak, but he's a big man, and he can still argue with you. He'll recover."

"He needs more food. Ever since the captain reduced rations again, there just hasn't been enough. Maybe if I gave him my portion . . . ?"

"No. Eat your own food. You have a wife and daughter, don't you?"

Kecilpenny smiled. "Mary. And Elizabeth is six. They're well, though. Hungry, but still healthy."

"Gibbs will pull through." Parris hoped it was true. Sinclair had reduced all their rations to a half share of hard biscuit and a quarter of a fish a day—provided enough fish were caught to go around. It wasn't enough. What little cheese, rice, and oatmeal remained were reserved for children and the sick. Not even Sinclair was eating better.

"Do you think we'll make it?" Kecilpenny said.

"What do you mean?"

"We can't just keep sailing west forever. If we don't find Horizon soon, we'll have to turn back, or we won't have enough to get home on."

"We're getting close," Parris said. "You've seen the sun." Kecilpenny's measurements had shown for weeks that the sun was changing size, but they could all see it now. When it rose behind them, it was tiny, its feeble light hardly penetrating the mists, and the mornings were dreary and chill. By each evening, however, it tripled in size, a fearsome inferno that painted the western sky in fiery hues. To avoid the heat, the passengers gathered above decks for fresh air, and the sailors, stripped down to their loincloths, sweated freely as they clambered through the rigging.

A knock on the door made them both jump. He opened the door and was surprised to see Collard, the first mate.

"Come back later, when he's awake again," Parris said to Kecilpenny. "Your visits help."

Collard shut the door the moment Kecilpenny left. "You have to talk to him. He has to see reason."

"Who?"

"Sinclair! We're lost, and he won't admit it."

"What do you mean, 'lost'?"

"I mean we don't know where we are. We're off course and sailing blind. The farther west we go, the more bizarre the sea becomes. Unexpected winds, unpredictable currents."

"But we're still headed west."

"Yes, but at what latitude? What longitude? Where is this island he promised us? The North Star has all but disappeared. It's been fading for weeks, and drifting east. Without the stars, there's no way to know where we are."

Parris knew he was right. The Great Bear wasn't even recognizable anymore. Tilghman prowled the deck every night with his astrolabe and star chart, but how could he calculate the ship's position from an unrecognizable sky? To most of the passengers, stars were little more than decorations in the night sky, but to sailors, they told the way home.

For men who had spent their lives harnessing the air and the sea, these changes were like the betrayal of a lover, disturbing to their very sense of self. Parris had overheard one sailor, suffering in the heat of the gigantic evening sun, grumble to a companion they were sailing straight for the fires of hell.

"An angel—" Parris began, but Collard cut him off.

"Don't feed me that nonsense. You have to talk to him. Or else something will have to be done."

"Such as what? Are you talking mutiny?"

"Not yet. But if you can't get through to him—"

"Why me?"

"Don't play the fool. He listens to you. He's leading this ship to disaster, and everyone knows it."

"You're the ranking officer. I suggest you raise your concerns with Captain Sinclair yourself."

"Spare me. He's no captain."

"Whatever you call it, he's the one with the right to give orders."

Collard spat. "I mean he didn't *earn* it. He's never commanded men at sea, never faced down an enemy's cannon without flinching. He doesn't know what a command *means*. And he doesn't know how to navigate on the open seas."

"Does it occur to you that perhaps *Captain* Sinclair has access to information that none of you knows about?"

The look on Collard's face made it clear he didn't find that likely.

"What experience do you have with magic islands?" Parris said. "Or with navigating at the edge of the world?"

"Nobody does. Everyone who's tried it is dead."

"Did you think it would be safe? A pleasant outing with sunshine and good fishing? Of *course* it's dangerous. Of *course* standard navigation won't get you there. If it were easy, it would have been done before."

"Enough." Collard opened the door again. "I can see you're Sinclair's man."

"No," Parris said. "No, I'm not. But he's gotten us this far, and I'm inclined to trust him for the rest."

Collard strode away, leaving Parris with his own uneasy thoughts. Was the beetle really leading them in the right direction? It suddenly seemed ludicrous that they were all trusting their lives to an insect. Maybe it wasn't really pointing toward Horizon. Or maybe it had died, and Sinclair was too stubborn to admit he didn't know where he was going.

Morale was important. It made sense to conceal the existence of the beetle, but only to a point. The officers needed some assurance that Sinclair knew what he was doing.

Unless he didn't know what he was doing. Unless he really was sailing blind.

Chapter Fifteen

CATHERINE hated to be trapped belowdecks. Some passengers rarely left the stuffy hold, uncomfortable around sailors and apprehensive of the heaving seas, but Catherine couldn't stand the suffocating heat and the stench. She needed to be out under the sky.

"Come on," she begged Matthew.

"It's raining," he said.

"Not that much. And it's fresh."

They sat among the rolls of sails in the hold, sheltering from the wet. The other passengers crowded the narrow space, talking together in their own corners or trying to steal some sleep. There was little distraction here from the subject that dominated everyone's thoughts: food.

Catherine's stomach hurt, and her joints ached. She felt tired all the time, and it became increasingly difficult to think about anything but their next meal. The key was to find useful things to do—there was always sailcloth to be mended, and the youngest sailors were glad to trade stories of life at sea in exchange for help with swabbing or sweeping—but it was hard to work up the energy to volunteer.

The least they could do was to go up on deck instead of lying around feeling sorry for themselves. She knew Blanca would come along, if she could convince Matthew. She persisted, talking about the benefits of fresh air until finally he hauled himself to his feet.

"If I must," he said.

The three of them clambered up through the maze of decks and ladders until they could see the sky, which was a surly, overcast gray. The rain had stopped for the moment, but it had left the deck beaded with droplets of water. They trudged forward to the bow and looked down on the choppy sea, leaning against the barrels of sand and pebbles that Captain Sinclair had brought along from Chelsey's original expedition. Blanca produced a brush and started to run it through Catherine's golden hair.

"You're not my servant anymore. You don't have to do that," Catherine said.

"I know. I like to. It's so beautiful when it's neat."

"Let her. It's been looking like a haystack, most days," Matthew said.

Catherine put her hands on her hips and narrowed her eyes at him.

"Do you think we'll actually make it?" Blanca said. "The ocean goes on and on forever, and we just get farther and farther away from home."

"We have to trust Captain Sinclair," Catherine said. It felt like a constant refrain. It was always the other two who voiced doubts and fears, leaving her to lift their spirits.

"Captain Sinclair is obsessed with this journey," Matthew said. "He'll never turn around, even if everyone else starves to death. Somebody should stand up to him. Collard. Or your father, maybe."

"Don't drag my father into it."

"He's the only one Captain Sinclair listens to even a little bit. He might be the only one who has a chance."

Catherine felt her cheeks going red. "But my father doesn't need to convince him. He trusts him. As we all should."

"Based on what?" Matthew slapped the barrels in front of them. "Based on rocks and sand? He's just stubbornly following his life's passion to the grave, and he doesn't care who he drags down with him."

"No one forced you to come."

"Well, actually, my father *did* force me, but . . ."

"Don't argue," Blanca said. "It only makes things worse."

"I mean, where's the proof? My father says he won't even tell the officers how he chooses his headings. The only evidence we have that this island even *exists* is a snake that does clever parlor tricks."

"Don't forget the manticore."

"Which no one ever sees. What help does the manticore give us to actually get there? It's not like it shows up and talks to people and tells them the way to its island."

Catherine turned away and stilled her face. She tried to relax into the soothing motion of Blanca's brush in her hair.

"Catherine?" Matthew said, his voice suspicious.

"What?"

"What aren't you telling us?"

"What do you mean?"

"You look like you're hiding something."

"I'm just tired of arguing about it, that's all."

Matthew walked around her and met her gaze. "Have you seen the manticore again lately? I mean, up close?"

Catherine sighed. She didn't want to tell him; it would only mean trouble. He would tell his father, who would interfere. But she didn't want to lie to him, either. "I talk to him almost every day," she said.

The shocked looks on their faces made her grin. "Catherine, that thing *attacked* you," Matthew said. "You were unconscious for days. You almost died!"

"My father talks to him, too. Besides, that was two months ago, and he was just trying to connect. He didn't know it would hurt me."

"He?"

"Yes; his name is Chichirico. He visits me at night, after most people are asleep. He never stays long—only a few minutes—and he never touches me."

"You should tell Sinclair. It's not safe."

"And what right do you have to dictate my safety, Matthew Marcheford? Nobody knows him as well as I do. I've been in his *mind*."

"What does he say to you?" Blanca asked.

Catherine winced as the brush hit a snag, but Blanca worked it out gently. "Not very much. I don't understand his language at all, and besides, it seems to be mixed up with motions. He's always moving his tails in complex ways when he makes sounds, as if it's part of how he communicates."

Matthew furrowed his brows, apparently wrestling with his thoughts. "You mean this creature has a language. It's not just an animal."

"Of course," Catherine said. "He's a person, no matter what he looks like. There are thousands of them on Horizon. Dozens of different tribes, spread all over the island. Their culture is complex and thousands of years old."

"And when we get there . . ."

"We'll have to be able to communicate with them."

He was quiet for a time, thinking. "I'm afraid for you," he said finally. "I don't want you to be hurt—"

"That's not your job."

"I know." He held up a hand. "I'm trying to say I think you're doing the right thing. We won't do well on the island if we can't communicate with the natives. They already know how to live there, and we don't. If we arrive, and this Chi . . ."

"Chichirico," Catherine said.

"If he tells them he's been mistreated, we could be in trouble. But if he's your friend . . ."

"Yes. That's what I think, too." She felt a rush of gratefulness to Matthew for understanding; she hadn't expected it. "But I can't tell Sinclair."

"No. I see that now. He'd just try to do experiments on him and scare him away."

"So you won't tell anyone?"

Matthew shook his head. "But be *careful*."

❖❖❖

IF anyone else but Parris had stormed into his cabin without knocking, Sinclair would have thrown him into the stocks. He growled, "Shut the door," and went back to the log where he was recording the day's progress.

"You can't keep going on like this," Parris said.

Sinclair was in a bad mood. It wasn't his fault that half their stores had been stolen. The rations were for everyone's good, to keep them alive, and yet they treated him like a villain. He didn't offer Parris a seat. "Going on like what?"

"Like an alchemist. Hiding your methods. Keeping secrets. Most of the passengers are inclined to trust you, but the sailors know things aren't right. They don't recognize the stars. They can't tell where they're going, and they think you can't, either."

Sinclair nodded agreement, hoping Parris would just go away.

"We've seen no signs of land," Parris said.

"There's still time."

"You're a fool. You don't have time. You should hear the conversations around the deck—most people are talking about turning around. Collard and Tilghman are openly predicting you'll lead us all to our deaths. If you don't give them some indication that you know what you're doing, they're going to kill you and take us home."

Sinclair slammed the quill into the inkwell. "And you? Is that what you think, too?"

"I've always believed you," Parris said. "It's the officers and crew you have to worry about."

"They need to obey, not understand," Sinclair said. "Now, if you'll excuse me, I have a ship to run."

He threw the door open and strode out of his cabin, only to trip over a pail that had been left in front of his door. It was one of those used by common sailors, who took turns preparing their meal rations with three or four others. The pail smelled bad and was half full of greasy liquid. In the center of the liquid floated a chunk of pork fat.

"What is the meaning of this?" he said.

Three midshipmen, standing nearby at attention, sprang to his side. "It's a cooking pail, Captain."

"I can see what it is. I want to know how it got here."

The man scraped his bare foot against the deck. "It's a . . . a protest, my lord."

"A protest?"

"This was the supper provided to the men after their work last night. I don't know who left it here, but perhaps they thought if you saw what they were given to eat . . ."

"It's outrageous." In fact, it was disgusting, and it turned Sinclair's stomach just to look at it. His command that the sailors be given the same portions as the officers obviously hadn't extended to the quality of the cut of meat. That wasn't good—it meant the officers were following the letter of the law while violating the spirit—but it wasn't as dangerous as the insubordination that this pail implied.

Parris appeared at the door, his face creased in worry. "Throw a feast," he said. "Invent a holiday and celebrate it with a big meal. Lift their spirits."

Sinclair gritted his teeth. He was surrounded by idiots. "We can't have a big meal. We don't have enough food. That's why we have rations in the first place."

"We'd lose a day's worth of food, maybe two. But you'll lose more than that if you don't have the sailors' loyalty."

"This isn't a matter of loyalty. It's a matter of obedience."

He couldn't afford to show sympathy anymore. The time to sit and pass the bottle with the sailors was gone. There wasn't enough to eat, and smiles and promises weren't working anymore. Parris was right. He couldn't keep going on like this. The sailors had to fear him more than they feared hunger. More than they feared death.

"Spread the word," Sinclair said to the midshipman. "If the man who left this pail by my door does not give himself up by sundown, I will flog every fourth man until he is apprehended."

The midshipman paled. "Yes, my lord."

"No!" Parris said. "They'll hate you for it."

"They hate me already. This will give them good reason for it."

—◆┼◆┼◆—

SINCLAIR stood sourly on the main deck as the men gathered in rows. The only sounds were the shuffling of bare feet and the creak of the boards. The gigantic sun encompassed most of the western sky, but when it slipped from sight, it left nothing behind but the endless desert of blue-black ocean. There was no moon, and the only light came from scattered lanterns swinging on decks around them. To Sinclair, it gave the impression the ship was just a fragile bubble of light floating in an empty universe.

Beside him, the red-bearded Oswyn Tate stood in a wide stance and fingered a cowhide whip trailing nine knotted lines.

"Some of you think yourself ill-treated," Sinclair said. "You think you aren't getting what you deserve. Well, it's going to get worse. If you toe the line, do your work, and accept your fair share, you'll come home richer than you ever dreamed. If you cross me, you'll wish you'd drowned the day you were born. One of you"—he looked from man to man—"isn't satisfied. He doesn't care how much the rest of you suffer, so long as he gets more. Master Collard, every fourth man, if you please."

"It was me!" A boy, no more than eighteen years old, scrambled forward out of line and cowered at Sinclair's feet, and Sinclair recognized the apprentice seaman who had been so frightened by stories of wild men and mermaids. He doubted the boy's fellows would have turned him in— they would have taken their chances at the lash rather than turn rat— but they would have known who the culprit was, and that he had kept silent. That pressure had been enough to force the boy to confess.

"It was my pail, my lord. I thought . . . I hoped . . . Forgive me. I'm so hungry, my lord."

"What's your name?"

"Merton."

"Merton, then. Twenty-five lashes."

The boy's eyes grew wide with terror. "Twenty-five . . . !"

Two of Tate's men grabbed the boy's arms in sudden violence and tied him over a raised hatch cover before he could resist. He was already shirtless, his back red and filthy like most of the men's, and he cried and pleaded as they made the knots tight. Tate stretched the whip's cords in his hands and loosened his arms. His face was grave.

Tate lifted his arm and let the whip fly. It struck with a wet snap and the boy screamed.

"Captain!" Bishop Marcheford scrambled down from the quarterdeck, then ran up to Sinclair, breathless. "You must stop this at once."

Sinclair glowered at him. "This is not your affair."

"He's just a hungry boy. He works his hands raw for you every day with nothing to eat but rancid fat, and this is how you treat him?"

"Close your mouth, or I'll put you under the lash."

"He deserves your praise, not—"

"Enough!" Sinclair rounded on him. Marcheford backed away, and Sinclair drove him farther with his arm, pinioning him against the rail. "You don't understand what you're talking about," he said, his voice intense yet too low to be heard by the crew. "This is the open sea. A hundred people boxed up in a wooden prison that feels smaller every day, and yes, food is scarce and tempers are frayed and many fear we're headed to our doom. But the only way—the *only* way—to get this ship safely to Horizon is for my authority to be absolutely unquestioned."

Marcheford stared at him, mouth open. Sinclair gave him another shove and turned back to the flogging. As the blows landed, the gathered sailors began to murmur, a sound that grew to an angry buzz.

"Collard," Sinclair said. "Silence this noise."

Collard didn't move.

"Master Collard, I gave you an order. Silence your men."

"Apologies, Captain," Collard said. "I don't hear anything."

"Pass along my order," Sinclair said. "The men are to make no noise."

Collard held his gaze for a beat, but he turned and called the command to the bosun, who shouted it down the ranks. The noise stopped.

When the flogging was over and his bonds untied, Merton collapsed to the deck. Sinclair ordered him carried to the infirmary. "Dismiss the men," Sinclair said to Collard. "Any sailor not on duty is to be in his bunk."

The men obeyed, but their faces were hard and their looks cold as they filed past him. They thought him a tyrant, but they didn't understand it had to be done, for the good of everyone.

Except, perhaps, for Merton. The boy moaned piteously as they maneuvered his torn body through the hatchway. Sinclair turned his back. It had been necessary. It was the only way.

–+ + +–

IN the dim lamplight of the infirmary, Parris soaked a rag in vinegar and salt water and bathed the flogged boy's wounds. His skin hung in ribbons, and blood still oozed darkly from dozens of ragged cuts. The vinegar and salt only inflicted more pain on the boy, but they were necessary for him to heal cleanly. The boy whimpered, his throat already scraped hoarse from screaming.

The infirmary was crowded with the undernourished, many of them too weak to talk. Gibbs was one of the few who had recovered and grown strong again. He and Kecilpenny still visited often to argue natural philosophy with Parris, a welcome distraction from the dying. Scurvy was now so advanced with some that their teeth fell out of soft, bleeding gums. Fifteen men and one woman had already succumbed to the disease and been buried at sea, sewn into canvas bags.

It was hard to keep faith. Sinclair's authority seemed to slip more every day, and with it everyone's confidence that he could actually bring them to Horizon alive. Parris dreaded the nights, when the pains in his stomach and joints kept him awake, but he hated even more waking to mornings without enough to eat or drink and nothing but endless water as far as the eye could see.

After bandaging the boy's wounds as best as he could, Parris left him in the infirmary to sleep and climbed the ladders to the main deck. He was exhausted, but unwilling to face his bunk just yet. At least on deck a cool wind blew and he could think in peace for a while.

A group of sailors stood fishing from the quarterdeck, murmuring softly together as they leaned on their lines. Shifts of men fished all hours of the day and night to supplement their meager stores, though they seemed to catch fewer and fewer the farther west they sailed.

A shout from one of the men drew his attention. The men exclaimed and pointed over the starboard rail. One of the sailors had a striped fish, no bigger than his foot, dancing on the end of his line. Despite its tiny size, he strained to lift it as if it took all his strength, the line as taut as if there were a whale on the other end.

The fish dangled, thrashing, just above the waves, but the sailor couldn't raise it. His fellows laughed and urged him on. Finally, by bracing the rod against the deck, he began to inch it higher, but before it was halfway up, the rod snapped, and fish, line, and broken rod disappeared into the waves.

The sailors burst into fresh laughter, but the fisherman was grave. "The devil's in these waters," he said.

Parris frowned, the omen disturbing him. He didn't believe in portents and signs, as a matter of course, but something odd had just happened. The little striped fish had pulled on the line as if it were made of cast iron, and Parris doubted it was incompetence on the part of the fisherman.

He retreated to the forecastle and gazed into the west, thinking about the fish. He supposed if Horizon had beetles and manticores with special properties, it might be surrounded by unusual sea creatures, too. If they were starting to see them, it meant they were close.

He squinted into the distance, willing a shoreline to appear. The dark horizon shimmered, an effect often mistaken by green conscripts as the evidence of distant land, but there was nothing there. There was never anything there.

Yet it was the only thing that could save them. No matter how many fish they caught, no matter how severe Sinclair's punishments became, the only way they could survive was if this endless ocean finally gave way to the one word that echoed in everyone's minds and hovered on the tips of their parched tongues.

Land. Land. Land.

Chapter Sixteen

I T wasn't land.

It appeared almost directly to port, a hazy green spot in the far distance. The lookout atop the mainmast saw it first, and his excited cries were echoed through the crisp morning air. Parris felt the swell of anticipation as those on deck pointed and shouted and hugged each other. Kecilpenny's wife, Mary, had tears on her cheeks as she held little Elizabeth high and showed her where to look.

The rigging sprang to life as sailors rushed to obey the bosun's shouted commands, adjusting the angles of stays and sails to point the ship in the right direction. Soon even Elizabeth could see the green smudge—too small to be Horizon, but any island with food and fresh water would be welcome.

The passengers crowded the forecastle, straining to see the spot grow more distinct. For once, the wind and currents cooperated, drawing them quickly the way they wanted to go. Cheers and applause broke out spontaneously and bottles of spirits were passed around.

The closer they sailed, however, the more concerned Parris became. Something bothered him about the shape, something that didn't look natural. For another thing, despite their speed, it didn't seem to be getting closer very fast. By the time they caught up to it, everyone could see the truth.

It was an animal so large it defied belief. A shapeless mountain of flesh scored with deep wrinkles, it floated not in the water, but above it, through the air. It had no legs, no ears, no tail, and no wings—nothing that explained how such a massive creature could stay aloft. A giant snout stuck out from one end, pitted with cavernous nostrils and topped with eyes the size of wagon wheels. The creature was a rich variegated green, as if covered with algae, and from one side its only limb lifted toward the sky like the stump of an arm, stretching an acre of loose skin it seemed to use as a sail. Or perhaps, Parris thought, as a sun shade during the searing brightness at the end of each day.

Sinclair named it the behemoth. Though it showed no interest in the ship whatsoever, the response among the sailors and passengers was universally hostile. They shouted at it and cursed it, and there was even talk of trying to kill it. At first Parris thought it was a reaction to the bitter disappointment that they had not reached land after all. After a time, though, he realized that it was the very *wrongness* of the thing that prompted such rancor. It floated impossibly through the sky, apparently free from the laws of nature that kept them bound to the water. They didn't understand it, and so they hated it.

Despite its great size, the behemoth moved slowly and seemed docile, occasionally drifting down to the surface of the water to scoop vast quantities of seaweed into its maw. For the next day and night it followed the ship, driven by the same winds, and caused no problems beyond the occasional sleep-destroying thunder of its grunting call.

Parris decided another meeting was needed. He invited Sinclair, of course, as well as Gibbs, Kecilpenny, and half a dozen others who seemed most interested in discussing and understanding the Horizon mysteries. Catherine insisted on coming along. It seemed odd to Parris to include a girl in an intellectual gathering of men, but he had to admit she had more experience with the mysteries of Horizon than most of them.

He produced the chart and added the behemoth to the *Transmutation* section, reasoning that it must change the flesh of its body into a material lighter than air.

"That's a big assumption," Gibbs said. "We don't know how it flies. I think we should make a new category."

Kecilpenny naturally disagreed, and a long argument ensued that came to no conclusion. Parris eventually interrupted and told them all about the striped fish he had seen that broke the sailor's fishing rod. Whether it should be categorized as *Transmutation* or not, he suggested it was similar to the behemoth's ability to fly. The behemoth altered itself to be lighter than seemed possible, while the fish—which he dubbed an ironfish—altered itself to be heavier than seemed possible when it was pulled out of the water.

"A fish like that would give a seabird a hard time," Catherine said.

"It certainly would," Sinclair said. "No doubt it was to foil predatory birds that it developed the ability in the first place."

This prompted a new round of debate as to whether animal abilities were learned, like a horse was trained to pull a cart, or endowed by a benevolent Creator who knew what the animal needed. Predatory instincts were, Kecilpenny said, the result of the Fall and the intrusion of sin into the world, so perhaps God had, in his mercy, given some prey animals the means to resist. The explanation didn't entirely sit well with Parris, who didn't understand how an animal like a tiger, every inch of it designed to hunt and kill, could have been originally created by God for any other purpose.

Parris took to watching the behemoth from on deck whenever he wasn't needed in the infirmary. It didn't do very much—it seemed to spend most of its day gliding down to the water's surface to feed—but it was so large and unusual that it drew his eye. Which was probably why he was the first to see a small striped fish leap out of the water and bite the underside of the behemoth, holding on with its teeth.

Parris laughed out loud to see it—the tiny ironfish had certainly set its sights high if it thought it could eat such a meal. But the fish was followed by another, and another, until a dozen fish hung by their teeth from the behemoth's flesh. It hadn't occurred to anyone on the ship that an ironfish might use its ability, not to avoid predators, but to catch its own prey.

Another dozen ironfish attached themselves, and the behemoth began to list. When its bulk touched the water, a frenzy of fish splashed at the surface, and the water turned red. The behemoth bellowed and rolled its eyes, but it had no defense. Over the course of the next hour, the school of ironfish, hundreds strong, dragged it under the waves, devouring it as it sank.

Scavengers arrived, other kinds of fish in countless colors and variety, to share in the bounty. The press of fish attracted larger predators that surged and cut through the masses, gorging themselves. From nowhere flocks of seabirds appeared, diving into the water to snap up pieces of meat. On deck, sailors and passengers alike dropped fishing lines, pulling up fresh fish almost as soon as their hooks touched the water. By evening the deck was strewn with meat, and while it was trimmed and salted, two sailors played merry jigs on pipe and fiddle while passengers danced. Both groups feted and cheered Sinclair, their miseries temporarily forgotten.

Parris sat quietly while the others made merry. He was annoyed by the fickleness of the sailors, who only remembered their loyalties when their bellies were full. The passengers and crew had all been disturbed by the behemoth, but the ironfish bothered Parris more than the behemoth ever had. The behemoth had never done anything but eat and grunt, but the school of ironfish had worked together to destroy something much bigger and stronger than themselves. He was glad for the much-needed food, but he wasn't sure it was time to celebrate.

◄┼ ┼►

THE next morning, Piggott knocked on Parris's door and presented him with a dead ironfish. The cook had been cutting open an ordinary fish to prepare a meal, and had found one of the small striped fish swallowed whole inside the larger fish's stomach. Piggott said none of the men would eat it—they called it a demon fish—and he would have thrown it overboard except that he knew Parris liked to cut things up.

Parris thanked him sincerely. As soon as Piggott left, he found a lonely corner and set the fish on a pile of folded sailcloth to work. It felt soft to the touch, like scales and meat, not iron, and it was as light as any other fish. He sliced it open from mouth to tail.

He peeled back the skin, expecting to see a skeleton made of iron, or at least the familiar quintessence glow. Instead, it just looked like a fish—meat, bones, and entrails, the same as any other.

He cut further, exposing the skull and jawbone. The teeth were layered like a shark's and razor-sharp, but it was the rest of the skull that drew his attention. From the jaw to the spine, the bone thinned, forked, forked again, then twisted and curled around itself in intricate whorls that made his eyes swim. Somewhere in the center of the pattern a light glowed, like a twinkling star peeping through a hole in the clouds.

"Quintessence," he whispered.

The jaw was hanging open, and Parris closed it with a snap. The hidden light blazed, and the fish's bones transformed to a hard gray metal. He tried to pick it up, but it was as heavy as a stone. He pulled the jaw open, the light faded, and the fish returned to a normal weight.

Astonishing. There was a muscle connecting the jawbone to the intricate skull, which implied that the fish could choose to close its mouth without transmuting, which it would have to do to chew its food without sinking to the bottom. The jaw mechanism allowed it to transmute the instant it grabbed hold of something in the air.

Parris peered past the curls of bone to the glowing pearl in the center, surrounded by tiny tendrils. It was lodged in the fish's brain, which was curious if its purpose was only to transmute. But quintessence could also form a mind connection between creatures, as with manticores. What if these fish shared a similar connection, so that when one of the group found prey, the others would come to help bring it down?

He spent hours studying it. Finally, to prove that it really was the pearl that gave it the power to change, he snapped the thin bone and removed the pearl. He exercised the jawbone, but nothing happened. He put it back in its spot, but it was too late—without the pearl attached, it no longer worked as before. At least he knew more than he had when he'd started. He threw the remains of the carcass overboard and went to look for Sinclair.

Parris found him on the forecastle, leaning as usual against his barrels of pebbles and sand.

"We're very, very close," Sinclair said. "No more than a few days distant."

"How can you know that?"

"All these wonders don't convince you?"

"If you know something, you should share it. People are afraid."

"Who's afraid?"

"Don't think that celebration last night solved all your problems. The men are yours again for now, but when the food runs short again, or something else threatens us, it'll be mutiny. You got lucky, but the general feeling around the ship is still in favor of going home. If you don't do something . . ."

"We're close," Sinclair repeated. "Have you seen how the water glows?"

Parris had. It was faint, like the glimmer of the moon on the water, only there was no moon. The light came from the water itself. "It's not enough," he said.

⇥✦⇤

PARRIS was the first to find an ironfish attached to the hull. It hung just out of reach, its jaws buried in the wood. He called for Tate, who fired a matchlock into it, blasting it to shreds. They found two more on the starboard side. Before these could be cut down, however, another three leaped from the water and fastened their teeth into the planking.

In minutes there were too many to count. The near ones they hacked off with knives; those farther down they shot, but they weren't fast enough. The sailors were terrified of the demon fish, but Sinclair bullied them into rappelling over the side with ropes around their waists. They slashed the fish down quickly, but each time a dead one fell into the water, two more leaped from the waves to replace it.

Soon the ship was wallowing, its forward motion all but stopped, the sails pulling so hard in the wind that the masts bent visibly forward. Sinclair ordered them furled, and sailors rushed to obey. Tate roared up and down the deck, handing out weapons. At his direction, two passengers wrestled a stockpot full of boiling brine to the deck and used their ration cups to pour it down on the ironfish.

It wasn't enough. Soon the ship's lumbering bulk barely cleared the swells. Shark fins cut through the waves, and seabirds wheeled overhead, expecting another feast.

Parris crowded the rail with the others, firing over the side. One of the ironfish missed its aim, leaped clear out onto the deck, and smashed down like a cannonball. Two sailors hauled it up between them, straining as if they carried a boulder instead of a fish.

"Wait!" Parris said. He ran over before they could tip it into the sea. "Leave that with me."

"They're weighing us down, my lord. Got to go over the side."

"This one won't make a difference. We need to figure out how to beat them before they pull us under."

The sailors traded a look, shrugged, and dropped the fish. It thunked onto the deck like an anchor.

Ignoring the furor around him, Parris knelt. Despite its impossible weight, the fish twitched like any other fish. Its mighty jaws, bunched with muscle, were still clenched tight. Parris slit its throat.

The twitching stilled; the jaws fell slack. Parris felt the difference immediately and lifted the fish with one hand.

A shadow fell over him. Sinclair, looming.

"What are you waiting for?" Sinclair said. "Open it up!"

Parris sliced open its belly and peeled back the skin up to its head. The panic around him was distracting. Men raced to and fro while water swept over the deck. Parris saw an ironfish leap from the sea and fasten itself on a sailor's arm. The sudden weight pulled him overboard before he could even scream.

Working faster, Parris exposed the skull and jawbone. As before, the curling patterns of bone hid a glowing pearl at their center. He snatched up a tool from the deck like a thin pair of pliers used to bend fishhooks. Inserting it between the curls of bone, he gripped the pearly bead and tore it free.

"What if all the ironfish in the school are linked, like the manticore?" he shouted over the din.

"They could attack efficiently as a group," Sinclair said. "But what good does that do us?" Then his eyes widened as he understood. "It's our only chance. Come on!"

They raced together toward the forecastle. Water flooded the main deck, washing around their ankles. Parris clambered up one-handed, still clutching the pliers and the glowing pearl. They burst into the alchemical distillery. From a crate, Sinclair pulled a stoppered vial containing a shiny silver globule. It was elemental mercury—a hundred times the amount used in a mercury pill.

He unstoppered the vial. Parris held the glowing pearl over its mouth and dropped it inside.

The instant the pearl touched the mercury, black foam erupted, a violent effervescence that shot out of the vial and splattered on Sinclair's face and hands. The vial shattered. Before either of them could react, the deck heaved, throwing them both into the air. Retorts smashed around them, raining them with broken glass. The ship leaped back above the waves like a cork from underwater, throwing men and ropes and barrels into the air.

Parris and Sinclair crawled out of the distillery. The ship was afloat again. Disappointed birds wheeled and shrieked above them. Picking himself up, Parris stumbled to the rail and looked into the water. Hundreds of dead ironfish floated on their sides, their jaws hanging open.

The forecastle was strewn with fish guts, oily black residue, and shards of glass, all of it soaked in seawater. Picking his way through the clutter, Parris spotted a flash of light and leaned in for a closer look. It was the quintessence pearl from the ironfish's head. Not only was it still glowing, but it was brighter than before, shining with a pure white light that was hard to look at directly. Parris fished it out of the water and held it up, shielding his eyes. He dropped it into a pouch he wore at his belt to study later. Men staggered about or lay on the deck, groaning. They would need his attention.

He called for those who could be moved to be brought belowdecks while he circulated, bandaging those with more serious injuries and pronouncing a few dead. After these were addressed, he descended to the increasingly crowded infirmary. The bandages originally stocked on the ship were gone, so he was forced to cut strips from the injured men's clothing to bind their wounds.

As he worked, he thought about what had happened. The quintessence pearl in the ironfish's skull gave the ironfish its ability to transmute—he knew that, because when he removed it, the change no longer worked. But the pearl retained its connection to the pearls in all the other fish. Just like the mercury had severed Catherine from her bond with the manticore, it had severed the ironfish's bonds with each other. He had hoped that breaking their connection might confuse them, or might at least slow their attack. He hadn't expected it to kill them all. And yet, the mercury hadn't destroyed the quintessence pearl. In fact, when he'd picked it up out of the wash on the deck, it was shining even brighter than before.

Several hours later, finally finished with the injured, he went to look for Sinclair. As he climbed above decks, however, he felt heat against his thigh. He reached down and found that his pouch was warm. He fished out the pearl, which was now blazing bright enough to blind and was hot to the touch. He dropped it back into the pouch and wondered what on earth was happening. The thing kept growing in energy. Had the mercury caused this? It didn't make any sense—Sinclair had described mercury as the antithesis of quintessence. It was supposed to have a neutralizing effect.

He climbed up onto the quarterdeck, where, at Sinclair's direction, sailors had piled dead ironfish in a growing heap around the mizzenmast. He bent down to examine one. Perhaps later that evening, when he wasn't so tired, he would dissect one again and see what else he could find.

A splintering noise erupted from behind him, and he was thrown to the deck. Shouts of warning came too late as another crash impacted the starboard beam. At first Parris thought maybe they had run aground on a hidden reef, but when he peered over the rail, he could see it was no reef. It was a fish.

A gleaming back a thousand times larger than any ironfish cut through the water, as large as the ship's hull turned upside down. The enormous fish twisted and then charged, ramming a head like the turret of a castle into their vulnerable starboard beam. Its head breached the water, revealing a long snout filled with rows of man-sized teeth.

"Leviathan," Parris whispered.

The men were weary, their will to resist spent. "It's the devil himself, come for us," said one.

"It's God's punishment," said another.

But Oswyn Tate marched from bow to stern, his red beard soaked with salt water, shouting commands. "If this be the devil, then we'll fight him. To arms!"

Whipped on by Tate, sailors grabbed matchlocks and harpoons and loaded the two bronze cannons with shot. They soon discovered that matchlocks did nothing: the bullets had no apparent effect on the beast. Cannons were hard to aim at such an angle, having been designed to loft across the water toward an enemy vessel. The first two shots fell wide, but then, as the leviathan circled back for another charge, a cannonball struck the water directly against its fearsome head. The monster bellowed, a deafening sound both deep and shrill at once that seemed to break open the air. It charged again. The boat tipped precipitously toward it and then rocked with the impact, sending men sliding along the suddenly steep deck. One of the precious cannons slid into the rail, smashed through it, and fell into the black sea, dragging a screaming gunner with it, one leg caught in its trestle.

Sinclair appeared and ran to Parris. "What does it want?" he shouted.

"A bellyful of meat. What else?"

Sinclair shook his head and pointed. Several men had fallen overboard and were treading water. The leviathan was ignoring them.

Parris raised his arms to signal his exasperation. "Maybe it eats wood," he said. "Or sailcloth, for that matter."

Harpoons flew at the monster, some lodging in its flesh, but doing little damage. It would do no good simply to anchor the beast; it was big enough to dive and drag the whole ship down by the ropes.

Parris saw Catherine near the bow, watching the action with her mouth open, her dress soaked and torn. "Get below!" he shouted. She didn't hear him, so he ran toward her, waving his arms. "Get to safety!"

The leviathan followed him. Inexplicably, it abandoned the spot it had been attacking, where the planks were weakened and splintering, to smash its body into a new section of the ship, directly under Parris. The impact tossed both him and Catherine to the deck. She rolled, screaming, and he rolled after her, both of them sliding into the rail.

He grabbed her face. "You shouldn't be here. Please, get below."

Another impact sent them reeling. Once again, the leviathan had adjusted its line of attack directly toward Parris. For an instant, he remembered the book of Jonah and wondered if this fish had been sent specifically for him. He dismissed the thought, but he still didn't understand what had just happened. Why would the leviathan swerve to target *him*?

Catherine scrambled away toward the hatch. He turned back to the fish, praying she would obey him and get out of harm's way. As he did so, he noticed again the heat at his side. He reached into his pouch and drew back his hand in shock and sudden pain. When he realized what it was, he laughed out loud. He took out the pearl, now so hot he could barely touch it. It shone like a miniature sun and seared his fingers, but he held on. He drew back his arm, and with all his strength, he hurled the pearl into the sea.

The leviathan erupted out of the water, long jaws snapping, enormous tail thrashing for height. It engulfed the tiny pearl in its mouth, and for a moment the entire fish shone as if from the inside, its bones shadows on its skin. It crashed back into the water. The ship tipped precariously on the resulting wave, but when it righted itself, the seas were calm. The crew gathered to stare over the starboard side, but they saw nothing. The leviathan was gone.

━◆◆◆━

BY the time those thrown overboard had been rescued and the wreck of lines and sails had been put to rights, the giant sun had disappeared in the west. The ship was safe again, but the revelry of the night before was gone. Despite getting no sleep during the day, those sailors assigned to night shift were forced to come on duty, and those coming off duty retired to their hammocks belowdecks. Catherine, not wanting to be alone, made her way down to the orlop deck to find Matthew or Blanca. The mood there was dark. Passengers curled up to sleep or sat in small groups, muttering over their beer.

"Did you see it?" she asked.

Both Matthew and Blanca shook their heads, eyes wide.

"Did you?" Matthew said. "Were you on deck?"

Catherine nodded. "It was nearly as big as the ship. A monster."

"We could only hear it," Blanca said. She pointed to the curved hull where it bowed unnaturally inward, some of the boards splintered or sprung loose. A steady stream of water trickled from the damaged area. The leak wasn't dangerous—there were a dozen such seepages around the ship already—but it would make the passengers' sleeping area even more damp and unpleasant. And it was testament to how close they had come to disaster.

"I'm afraid," Blanca said.

"I don't think it'll be back," Catherine said. She explained about the pearl that her father had thrown into the sea. "It wanted something, and once it had it, it left us alone."

"I don't mean that," Blanca said, lowering her voice to a barely audible whisper. "I'm afraid of the sailors."

Catherine frowned, remembering Maasha Kaatra's warning. "Why? Has one of them been bothering you?"

"Didn't you see on your way down? They're not going to sleep."

Catherine remembered. The sailors slept in stacked hammocks on the level just under the main deck, but they hadn't been sleeping. They'd been milling around, whispering and talking. That wasn't good.

She glanced at the end of the long compartment, where one of Tate's soldiers stood watch over the storerooms where ammunition and weapons were kept. He was still there, armed with pistol and sword, but Blanca's comment made her uneasy. Something was wrong.

⟝✦✦✦⟞

PARRIS noticed Collard and Tilghman slipping down a hatchway, which was odd. Neither had the night shift, so they should be heading to their bunks. The officers' cabins were on main deck level, under the raised quarterdeck. Why were they going below?

Suspicious, Parris followed, choosing a different ladder and making his way toward the infirmary. He saw groups of sailors whispering intently instead of retiring to their bunks. They fell silent and drifted apart when they saw Parris coming. Spooked, Parris ducked into the infirmary and shut the door behind him.

Trouble coming. He cracked the door and peered out. Far too much activity for sailors at the end of the day. He saw a gun being passed around, and then another.

He closed the door again. What to do? Should he find Tate? But Tate's cabin was forward, on the other side of the sailors' sleeping compartments. Sinclair was closer, still up on deck. He had to be warned.

But perhaps that wasn't wise. If he warned Sinclair, and mutiny broke out, he would be taken down with him, perhaps even killed. On the other hand, he was a known friend of Sinclair, and he'd defended him to Collard. He was likely to end up on the wrong side of the mutiny anyway, locked in the brig until they returned home. And with food in increasingly short supply, would they waste any on the prisoner? Better to do what he could while there was still time.

He put his hand on the door, then another idea stopped him. He could join the mutiny. If he did it now, he would be on their side when it mattered, and perhaps they would spare him. After all, what could Sinclair do to stop it, even if he were warned? There was nowhere to hide. Maasha Kaatra would stand with him, but what good would that do? And yet, Sinclair had performed miracles before.

It didn't matter. Parris knew what was right. Sinclair, for better or worse, was his friend. He believed in him. Despite his flaws, he believed Sinclair would succeed in leading them to the island.

Parris swung open the door. Feigning nonchalance, he strode out of the infirmary, down the passageway away from the growing knot of sailors, and up the ladder. His neck prickled. Someone called his name, but he just kept climbing.

⊰+⊹+⊱

CATHERINE didn't even hear them coming. Three sailors appeared around the corner, their bare feet making no noise on the wooden floor. They silently surrounded the soldier guarding the storeroom. Not recognizing the trouble until it was too late, the soldier drew his sword, but before it could clear its scabbard, the sailors fell on him, driving their knives into his body.

Catherine screamed. Passengers jumped to their feet and scrambled away, but Matthew, like a reckless fool, shouted and ran toward them. With no weapon at all, he tackled the nearest attacker around the waist and pulled him away. They tumbled to the floor together.

"No!" Catherine ran after him, frantic. "Matthew, don't!"

The sailor was wiry and strong. He twisted easily in Matthew's grasp and thrust with his knife, stabbing Matthew in the thigh. Matthew cried out and released his hold. The sailor jumped to his feet and joined his comrades, who were pulling guns out of the storeroom. "Let's go!"

They ran back the way they'd come, carrying the weapons. The soldier who had been left on guard lay in a pool of blood, his eyes staring sightlessly. Matthew was pale. A red patch soaked rapidly through his hose and flowed onto the floor. Catherine called for help and pressed her hands above the wound, trying to stop the flow. A passenger gave her a strip of cloth, which she tied as tightly as she could around Matthew's leg, as she'd seen her father do.

Matthew lifted his head, trying weakly to get up. "I'm good," he said. "I'll be fine."

"You're not fine, you idiot," Catherine said. "What did you think you were going to do?" She worried about what was happening upstairs. The sailors hadn't stolen those guns for target practice. Had they taken over the ship? Was Father safe?

The pool of blood under Matthew grew rapidly. He kept trying to talk, but he seemed confused, and his words were gibberish. Catherine started to cry, and pressed on his wound as hard as she could.

"Get my father," she said. "Please, someone! Get my father!"

Matthew's eyes lost focus, and his head hit the floor.

⊷+ +⊶

PARRIS scrambled out onto the main deck and slammed the hatchway cover down, afraid that sailors might be right behind him. It wasn't hard to find Sinclair. He was on the forecastle, right where he always was at night, gazing out to the west and leaning against his barrels. Parris could see him perfectly, since the seawater around them now glowed so brightly it illuminated the deck with a soft light.

"They're coming," Parris said, breathless.

Sinclair grinned. "Who? The mutineers?"

Parris stared. This wasn't a joke. If Sinclair already knew, then why wasn't he below, trying to put a stop to it? If he could arrest the leaders before they were organized, he might prevail, though the chance seemed small. Had he given up, just like that? "They're coming right *now*," Parris said. "They mean to kill you."

"I'm glad you're here," Sinclair said in a conversational tone. "I wanted to ask you: do you think a quintessence pearl is more like a container or a window? I can't figure it. Does it store its quintessence inside itself, or does the quintessence pass through it from some other place?"

Parris threw up his hands. "Do you even hear what I'm saying?"

That grin again. "I'm thinking more like a window. Otherwise, how could it increase as you described? In which case, perhaps the reaction with the mercury enlarged the opening, or somehow made it more potent."

Parris tried to get his breathing under control. "They have guns. Any moment, they're going to push up through that hatch, and it will be the end. It won't matter what quintessence is like, because we'll never get to see it."

"If the mercury did enlarge the opening," Sinclair said, "we could reproduce the effect. We might even learn to tap that energy for our own purposes."

A hatch on the main deck opened with a creak and a bang, followed by fast footfalls. Parris ran back to the rail to see a dozen sailors climbing both ladders onto the forecastle, each with a matchlock, and behind them, Collard.

Parris looked for a way out, but found none. He'd risked his life to warn Sinclair, but Sinclair had ignored him. He should have stayed in the infirmary.

The sailors formed a semicircle around them and aimed their weapons. Collard took his place at one end, nearest Sinclair, and leveled a pistol.

The sailors' faces were set. Collard's was twisted with unconcealed contempt. Parris raised his hands, shaking slightly, but Sinclair didn't move.

"You are relieved of command," Collard said.

Sinclair actually laughed. To Parris's amazement, he seemed totally at ease and genuinely amused. He made a show of counting the sailors arrayed around him. "Come, now," he said. "Did you really need to bring twelve armed men to subdue me? You must be more afraid of me than I thought."

"This voyage is over," Collard said. "We will turn around and sail for the Netherlands. If you don't resist, you will be imprisoned in the brig until we hold a sea trial to determine the extent of your guilt."

"And if I do resist?"

"We will execute you now."

Sinclair shook his head, a teacher disappointed in a misbehaving pupil. "Look around you," he said. "Look at the water, the sky, the creatures we've seen. We're close. You've come far and sacrificed much. Will you go back home with nothing?"

Collard's lip curled. His pistol trembled, and Parris feared he would shoot Sinclair right there. "No more discussion. There is nothing to the west but our certain deaths."

Sinclair's eyes swept the sailors, ignoring Collard. His voice was stern and confident. "Any one of you who lays down his weapon now will be spared the lash."

"Silence," Collard said, his voice rising in pitch. "Step forward and raise your hands in the air, or you will be shot."

Sinclair shut his mouth, but the corners curved in a wicked smile. He stepped forward. Very slowly, he spread his arms wide in a gesture of surrender. As he did so, he opened his hands, and a stream of glittering particles tumbled to the deck.

The sailors gasped. They rushed forward, a few of them abandoning their matchlocks, and scooped up what Sinclair had dropped. Diamonds.

"Leave them!" Collard said, but no one paid any attention.

"Check the barrels," Sinclair said.

The sailors raced to the barrels and wrenched the top off the first. With cheers, they pushed it over, pouring thousands of diamonds onto the deck in a coruscating flood. Another barrel came crashing down, and gold nuggets littered the boards. Men from below, hearing the cheers, poured onto the deck like rats, and the sailors in the rigging scrambled down.

Sinclair laughed loud and hard, watching the men scuffle over the treasure. Collard's face was mottled with fury. Parris saw the look in his eye and shouted a warning, but it was too late. Collard pressed the firing mechanism on his pistol, and it erupted in a cloud of gunpowder smoke and noise. In a frozen second, Parris saw Sinclair, mouth open and eyes wide, as his stomach erupted in red. He collapsed, clutching the wound, his clothing already soaked with blood. His captain's hat fell to the boards.

"I relieve you of command!" Collard shrieked. He threw the spent pistol away and pulled a second one from his belt, aiming again at Sinclair, but before he could fire, Maasha Kaatra appeared. His curved sword swung in a graceful arc that buried itself deep between Collard's neck and shoulder.

Parris rushed to Sinclair's side. Blood was everywhere. Parris had seen many wounds in his life, and he knew instantly that this one was fatal. Sinclair's hands twitched feebly at his sides. His eyes rolled up and glazed over.

The fool. Sinclair could have told the sailors about the diamonds as soon as he knew; he could have stopped Collard before he spoke a word. Instead, he had played with them, manipulating as he always did, creating volatile situations to turn them to his advantage. No one else Parris had ever known could lie and swindle as much as Sinclair and come out of every situation on top. He was lucky, more than anything, but this time his luck had run out.

Parris stripped off his doublet and jammed it into the wound, trying to stop the flow of blood, but he knew it was futile. This was the end, despite the diamonds. No one else could lead them to the island. Parris knew the secret of the beetle, but he could never command the vessel. No one would follow him. The remaining officers would take command and turn the ship for home.

The sailors' celebration had stopped cold. Men with handfuls of diamonds watched in shock as Sinclair's lifeblood poured out onto the deck. Maasha Kaatra dropped his sword and knelt at Sinclair's side. Wind ripped through the sails, Sinclair's hat skidding away. His bare head still glowed.

In fact, his blood glowed, too. Not as brightly, but it gleamed with a clear light which grew brighter as they watched. Soon it was obvious to everyone, dazzling, shimmering around the edges of the wound. It grew in strength, until the men had to shield their eyes. A bright flash, and then the light began to fade again. When they lowered their hands, they saw Sinclair climbing to his feet.

He stood before them, a triumphant smile on his face. His uncovered head blazed. The bullet wound in his stomach was completely gone.

No one moved or spoke. Sinclair laughed, his voice echoing eerily in the shocked silence. He raised his hands and spun before them, showing his perfectly whole body. He bent and scooped up handfuls of gold and diamonds from the deck and threw them high into the air. "Wonders beyond your imagination!" he shouted.

The shout broke them out of their trance. Men erupted into cheers and danced and hugged and poured diamonds over each other's heads. Sinclair stood over them all like a god, a halo shining from his head, the picture of supernatural strength. No one would dare cross him now.

A few good-natured fights broke out, and one man lost a tooth, but the scraps weren't serious. They all knew it was true now. Miracles could happen. There was an island, and all the treasures Sinclair had promised them would soon be theirs. The fact that they had no idea how to get them back to England seemed a minor point with diamonds shining in their fists.

◄╋╋►

CATHERINE searched Matthew's face for some sign of life. There was so much blood. What was happening above? Blanca had run up to find Father, but neither had returned. Had there been more murders? She bent and laid her head against Matthew's chest. She could hear him breathing, but faintly. Where was Father?

Finally, he came, leaning over Matthew, lifting his head and cradling it in his arms. He produced a vial of glowing liquid. "Here," he said. "Drink this."

Chapter Seventeen

PARRIS'S skills as a physic were no longer needed. He spent the day distributing glowing vials of Horizon seawater, drawn right from the ocean. It now tasted fresh and delicious instead of salty, and men hauled up bucketsful and filled empty beer barrels. They cut themselves with their knives, marveling as each wound glowed and knit together again, not even leaving a scar. Those in the infirmary for malnutrition were suddenly strong and energetic. Most ecstatic of all was the blind cook, Piggott, who responded to his drink by leaping madly across the deck, shouting profanities and smacking things with his cane. When they finally calmed him down enough to get some sense out of him, the reason for his mad dance became obvious. His mutilated eyes were round and clear and alive in their sockets. He could see again.

But all was not right. Relatively few sailors had actually participated in the mutiny, but the cultural rift between them and the passengers spread into a wide gulf of mistrust. Two of Tate's soldiers had been killed. The others had been attacked and injured, but the injuries had been quickly repaired by the miraculous water.

Those five sailors who had participated in murder were executed. There were plenty of witnesses, so there was no question of their guilt. Instead of hanging them, or even dragging them through the water behind the boat, as was common on sailing ships as a lesson to others, Sinclair had them shot by firing squad at the stern rail, their bodies falling backward over the rail and into the sea.

It was a good choice, Parris thought. It allowed the men whose colleagues had been killed to carry out the punishment, but it was over quickly and privately, leaving no evidence behind to increase the tension between passengers and crew. Though it did occur to Parris to wonder if the soldiers would aim for the heart. After all, a shot in the stomach or shoulder would pitch the killer into the sea just as effectively, but there the miraculous water would heal the wound, leaving him stranded in the ocean, hundreds of miles from land, with plenty to drink but nothing to eat. A death that an angry soldier might think more appropriate. He didn't ask, however, and the soldiers never mentioned it.

There was a sense on board now that Horizon was close. Passengers and sailors alike strained their eyes for sight of land, but now it was with eager expectation instead of despair. When the sailors addressed Sinclair, their salutes were lively and their voices awed. Far from hurting Sinclair's godlike reputation, his revelation of how he had been miraculously healed had raised him even higher in the reverent affection of the passengers and crew. They were invincible now. He'd made them all gods.

"I thought it might work that way," Sinclair said. He paced the quarterdeck, bouncing on the balls of his feet, unable to stand still. "Chelsey told me the water had healing properties."

"Healing *properties*?" Parris said. "It made a bullet wound evaporate!"

"I thought that since the rocks had turned back to diamonds, the water's properties might return as well."

"Just in time, too."

Parris worried about the water, though. Chelsey and his crew had drunk that water, and it had turned back to salt in their bodies on the voyage home. They were now committed to Horizon. The only way they could go home again was by solving the mystery of its transformation.

Sinclair rolled his sleeves into precise folds. "Are you ready to begin?"

The mountain of dead ironfish heaped against the mizzenmast had already begun to decay in the heat, and the stench was overpowering. No one was willing to cook and eat the meat, for fear it would turn to iron again in their stomachs, but Sinclair had forbidden anyone to throw the corpses overboard, in order to preserve them for study.

"As I'll ever be," Parris said. He spread out a length of sailcloth, selected one of the fish, and sat down. Sinclair sat opposite and took another. With boning knives borrowed from the fishing tackle, they set to work dissecting.

Parris took careful notes, setting each organ aside in orderly fashion and drawing it in his notebook before continuing. Sinclair hacked into each with abandon, tearing away bones and muscle. He had dismembered three of them before Parris was halfway through his first.

"Slow down," Parris said. "You'll never discover anything that way."

"I don't care about fish anatomy. I only care about this." Sinclair held up three faintly glowing pearls. So that was what he was doing. He wasn't trying to understand the fish at all; just *shelling* them to get the quintessence pearls.

"Don't you want to understand how the bones and muscles interact?"

Sinclair shrugged. "I'll leave that to your expertise. I want to study the quintessence itself."

"You knew we would find quintessence. Even before we left England. How did you know what it was? How did you even know it existed?"

Sinclair tore apart another skull with a splintering of bone. "It's been known for centuries. Aristotle identified the four elementary essences, Water, Earth, Fire, and Air, and theorized the existence of Quintessence, the fifth essence, as the aether in which the sun, moon, and stars moved. The medieval alchemists went on to describe what they thought were the three essential ingredients of quintessence—salt, sulfur, and mercury. But I don't think quintessence has any ingredients. I don't think it can be made. It's the *prima materia,* the original clay of Creation, as old as God himself."

"But what *is* it? Is it material? Spiritual?"

"That may not be a meaningful distinction."

Parris thought about the debates with Gibbs and Kecilpenny over atomism. "What if everything quintessence can do could be explained as a rearrangement of the smallest, most basic pieces of matter?"

Sinclair raised an eyebrow. "Been listening to John Gibbs lately?"

"I'm theorizing," Parris said. "Consider how the beetle and the manticores pass through walls. If atoms could be made to move around each other through the void"—he passed the fingers of one hand between the fingers of the other, demonstrating—"then two objects could pass through each other unharmed."

"Why don't the objects fall apart into little pieces, then?"

Parris shrugged. "We don't know what holds them together in the first place. Perhaps instead of being physically connected, they're simply attracted to each other, like a lodestone to iron. Once they pass through, they snap back into place.

"Transmutation can be explained with atoms, too. If the nature of a material is determined by the arrangement of its atoms, like Democritus said, then by rearranging them, you could transmute one material into another."

"It's a theory," Sinclair said. "Untested, but interesting. What about invisibility?"

Parris shrugged. "I don't see how moving atoms around could explain that."

"And what about sharing thoughts between two creatures? Light and thought aren't made of matter, and yet quintessence affects them. But we'll keep your theory in mind."

Sinclair scooped up the pile of pearls he had collected and stood up. "I'll be in the distillery," he said, and strode away, leaving Parris to continue his more careful dissections alone.

Parris had to admit he wasn't learning a whole lot. The ironfish were, for the most part, just fish, with gills, heart, liver, kidney, and intestines just where he would expect to find them. The skull was the only unique part, particularly the thin, forking spiral of bone that held the pearl.

For comparison, he cut up a salted fish head from the galley. The main difference, besides the spiral skull, was the location and manner in which the muscles connected it to the hinge of the jaw. Parris moved the jaw up and down, marveling at how the skeleton transmuted to gray metal and back again. Obviously the fish didn't need to be alive, or even recently dead, for the quintessence to work its magic.

He was getting used to thinking like Sinclair did—always looking for a reason to explain what happened in the world instead of calling it a miracle. Kecilpenny seemed to think that such reasoning left God out of the world, and indeed, Sinclair seemed to have little regard for God. He saw God, if anything, as a rival from whom power had to be wrested. But Parris didn't agree. Perhaps God *had* made the world as an intricate machine, but that didn't mean he wasn't involved in it. Parris believed that by trying to solve the riddle of sickness and death, he was doing God's work. Had not Christ risen from the dead? Then surely, by trying to preserve life, he was helping to fight that same battle.

A shadow across the sailcloth made him realize he had a visitor. Catherine stood watching him. "May I help?" she said.

Parris held out his notebook. "Definitely. If you make the drawings, you could save me a lot of time."

"No, I mean I want to cut."

He hesitated. Something in him recoiled at the thought of his daughter elbow-deep in fish remains, like when Sinclair had asked him to cut open Chelsey's mistress. She was a woman. It wasn't decent. But he recognized that the feeling had no place out here, thousands of miles from London society.

"Good," he said. "I'll show you how."

⪪+++⪫

SINCLAIR put the tiniest bead of mercury he could extract onto a circle of glass and used tongs to drop a quintessence pearl into it. As before, the mercury erupted in black foam. Unlike before, the pearl didn't glow any brighter. In fact, its light faded to a dull white. Perhaps it had to be removed from the mercury before it would work.

He pulled it out and watched it, giving it time to react, but it lay on the brick furnace, cold and inert. He tried another bead of mercury, but this time only a small amount of foam bubbled up from the contact. A third bead had no effect at all.

What was wrong? The first pearl had blazed like the evening sun and burned Parris's hand. But had it been that bright at first, or not until later? He tried to recall, but the moment was lost in the panic of the heaving ship and shattering glassware. The pearl had been thrown to the deck like everything else, where Parris had spotted its glow and plucked it out of the wash of broken glass and fish guts.

Salt. Of course. They had not yet reached the fresh water then, and the seawater on the deck was salty. The pearl had been lying in the salt water, and the pouch Parris had put it in had been soaked in brine along with everything else. It was the salt that had caused the change.

Sinclair filled a small vial with water, poured in some salt, and stirred. He dropped the pearl inside. Its glow returned and steadily grew brighter, and the vial felt warm. After a count of fifty, he could barely look at it anymore. After a count of one hundred, the water began to boil.

Sinclair plucked out the pearl and doused it with mercury, which again reduced its glow. He let the water cool, sniffed it, and then took a tentative drink. Fresh, or nearly so. The reaction that caused the pearl to glow had used up the salt.

Sinclair dumped it out and rinsed the vial. He had to be careful—he had no desire to attract another leviathan—but he repeated the experiment, just to make sure he could. Salt increased the glow, while mercury shut it off. Which made sense, considering how mercury had severed the connection between Catherine and the manticore, while the glowing salt water healed wounds. Salt and mercury. The one increased the effect of quintessence and the other reduced it.

It also explained how the seawater around them now was so fresh and full of quintessence. Somewhere deep in the water there must be a tremendous source of quintessence, or thousands of sources, enough to use all the salt in this part of the ocean. It had apparently reached some sort of equilibrium. New salt water would flow into the area from the east, and fresh water must flow out of the system somewhere to their west—presumably over the edge of the world. The new salt would fuel whatever quintessential reactions were going on deep underwater.

Salt and mercury. That left only one of the three essential alchemical ingredients not yet understood: sulfur. Sinclair spooned a few grains of sublimated sulfur into a vial. The yellow powder dissolved in neither water nor alcohol, so he stirred it into some terebinth, a strong-smelling resin. When he dropped a new pearl into the resulting liquid, there was no obvious change. Perhaps the sulfuric content wasn't strong enough. He sorted through his containers and found some oil of vitriol, a powerful dissolving agent made from sulfur and saltpeter. He'd lost most of his supply in the destruction when the ironfish died, and it would be a laborious process to make more, but this experiment was worth it. Careful not to spill, he measured a tiny amount into a dish and dropped in one of the pearls.

The light vanished. It didn't just fade, like with the mercury. Where the pearl had been before was just . . . a void. A tiny sphere of black nothingness, as if the pearl had been cut out of the world. So the void Gibbs always talked about existed after all. As Sinclair watched, transfixed, the void began to grow.

It grew to the size of his eye, then his fist. He was fascinated at first, and prodded it with a glass mixing rod. The end of the rod went into the void easily, but it didn't appear again on the other side, just as if he were pushing the rod into a hole. But a hole in what? The universe? He held the rod above the void and dropped it. It fell inside and never returned.

The void grew larger still, until it was the size of his head. He had to sweep things off the worktable to prevent them being swallowed up. He could sense a tremendous depth to it, like looking up at the night sky: an abyss of infinite, empty space. He felt dizzy, as if he might fall into it and keep falling and falling forever. And still it kept growing.

He couldn't stop it. He poured mercury on it, then salt, with no effect. He couldn't push it, move it, cover it, or contain it. Frantic, he started attacking it with whatever he could find: lead, copper, lime, alcohol, quartz, phosphorus, gold. It swallowed all of them without a trace. It grew larger, forcing him back. In moments, he would have to abandon the distillery. And then what? Would it swallow the whole ship? The world?

In a desperate last effort, he grabbed a horn of gunpowder and ran a short fuse. It was enough powder to demolish the distillery. The void was the size of the ship's wheel now, a perfect empty sphere, and the blackness seemed to call to him. He'd spent his whole life running from this. Nonexistence. The end of thought and reason that crouched waiting at the end of every man's life. It was the opposite of quintessence. This was the stuff of death.

Terror gripped him, and he struck at his flint again and again, unable to make a spark. The edges of the void stretched toward him. He pressed himself flat against the brick wall, unable to light the fuse, unable to flee. Frantically feeling around for something else to throw at it, Sinclair found the pale wooden box in his pocket, the beetle's home. It was precious, irreplaceable, but he threw it at the void anyway, desperate to survive.

The box flew into the center of the void, pulling the material world with it like a splash of spilled paint. The void stretched and deformed, rippling like the surface of a pond. It gave a final, violent swell and collapsed with a deafening pop that must been heard all over the ship. The beetle box, unharmed and still closed, landed on the deck.

It was gone. The flint tumbled from Sinclair's hand. He fell to the boards, his heart hammering, the vision of that bottomless void still fixed in his mind. In alchemical philosophy, the three substances symbolized aspects of the nature of man. Salt corresponded to the physical body, mercury to the spirit or will, and sulfur to the soul. Ever since, as a child, he'd watched his father die, he'd understood that his soul—that spark of being and personality that was uniquely Christopher Sinclair— was destined, at his death, for the void. Now he had actually seen it— nonexistence made visible—and it rattled him.

When Parris burst in, Sinclair was still huddled on the floor, shaking. The gunpowder horn, fuse, and flint lay where he'd dropped them. His worktable was split in two pieces, with instruments scattered everywhere. The brick furnace that dominated the room, however, was the most striking casualty. A large piece of it was carved away in a semispherical curve, the brick sheared off as smoothly as polished wood, with no sign of the missing portion. It was simply gone.

Seeing the expression of astonishment on Parris's face, Sinclair started to laugh, and once he started, it was hard to stop.

–◄+◄+►–

PARRIS found Gibbs and Kecilpenny in a corner of the orlop deck, soaking hardtack in their beer and then knocking it against the sides of their cups to dislodge the inevitable weevil larvae. Kecilpenny's wife Mary sat nearby with their six-year-old daughter Elizabeth, combing the tangles out of her hair. The little girl was thin and pale. As usual, Gibbs and Kecilpenny were locked in heated debate. Parris traded a glance with Mary, who rolled her eyes.

This time the debate was over whether God had first provided salvation for everyone and then chosen who would believe, or if he had first chosen who would believe and then provided salvation only for those few. Parris waited for them to finish and acknowledge him, but after listening to several volleys, he concluded that they might never finish.

"You were right," he said to Gibbs. As he suspected, this halted the conversation. Gibbs said, "Of course," just as Kecilpenny said, "Not likely."

"About what?" Gibbs said.

"About the atoms and the void. Well, at least about the void." Parris explained what had happened in the distillery, as thoroughly as a shaken Sinclair had been able to recount it to him. "So salt magnifies quintessence, mercury diminishes it, and sulfur seems to, I don't know, reverse it. Turn it inside out. The point is, it's possible for matter to be pushed out of the way and leave a void behind. It confirms Democritus."

"Hardly a rigorous experiment," Kecilpenny said. "Sinclair mixes some liquids and produces a black cloud, which expands and damages his equipment. A slim basis on which to rest a model of the universe, don't you think?"

"There's a solution for that," Gibbs said. "We have more ironfish and we have vitriol. We could reproduce it."

Parris remembered the neatly sculpted brick, the terror in Sinclair's eyes, and the tremor in his voice as he recalled the expanding void. Had the wood of the beetle's box stopped the void's growth? Could they be sure it would do so again?

"Maybe that's not such a good idea," Parris said.

⊰✦⊱

CATHERINE was still dissecting ironfish on the quarterdeck when Matthew found her. His knife wound had completely healed, thanks to the miraculous water. She had to admit it was brave of him to leap to the soldier's defense like he had, but it was also monumentally stupid. If not for the water, Matthew would be dead. It wasn't an instinct she would have expected of Matthew, though. He wasn't a fighter; he was a soft-spoken intellectual. Yet, faced with murder, he had jumped toward danger without a thought. All she had done was scream.

She made another cut in her latest attempt at ironfish dissection. She wasn't very good at it. The fish lay in front of her in a mess of slime and scales, and she couldn't tell one part from the next. She pushed the mess aside and reached for another fish.

"What are you doing?" Matthew said.

"Learning," she said. "Want to help?"

He sat down several paces away, wrinkling his nose. "They smell awful."

"That's why I need to do it now. They won't last much longer."

She cut open the belly, sawing to get through the tough bits. Father's cuts were always straight and precise, but hers were ragged. At least she hadn't sliced through any organs this time.

She pulled the skin back and fixed the corners to the planking with pins. She lifted out one piece at a time, trying to note the shape of each and how it connected to the larger systems.

"How's Chichirico?" Matthew asked. He always wanted to know about her meetings with the manticore.

"Frustrating," she said. "I can say dozens of his words now, and I can even wave my hands a little to approximate some of the motions that go with them. And he can speak a little English, too—actually better than I can manage his language. But we can't *say* anything. We can just point to things and name them. Half of the words I know are for kinds of food."

"It's a start."

"It's maddening, because both of us know there's a better way. I know so much about him and his life and his home from when——"

"You're not thinking of trying to bond with him again, are you?"

"Of course not. Though it wouldn't be so bad. We know how to break the bond now."

"We know how to break it once. There's no guarantee it would work again, and if it didn't, you'd be trapped. You'd die."

He was preaching at her. "I know what would happen, Matthew."

"All right. I just worry about you, alone with that thing."

"Well, don't."

Catherine removed most of the organs intact this time, leaving only the skeleton and the head. She cut through the face, exposing the intricate skull, and showed Matthew where the spark of quintessence was.

"It still works," she said. "Watch."

She closed the jawbone, and the skeleton transformed. The sudden increase in weight yanked it out of her hand and dropped it to the boards with a clunk. She lifted it with difficulty and pried open the jaw, making it light again. Matthew leaned closer to look, his curiosity overcoming his reticence.

"It's this muscle right here that controls it," she said. With her knife, she peeled the muscle away from where it attached to the skull, but the knife slipped, and she snapped off a piece of bone.

She grunted in disgust. "I always make a mistake. I should have cut when it was closed, like this." She slapped the jaw shut, and the skull transformed into metal again.

Matthew's mouth dropped open. "I don't believe it."

"Don't believe what? I just showed you a moment ago."

"No. Look." He reached past her and picked up the shard of bone she'd accidentally broken off. It was gray metal, just like the rest. "Open the jaw again," he said.

She did. Not only did the whole skeleton change back to bone, the detached fragment did as well, even though it wasn't touching the rest of the fish. She closed the jaw, and again the fragment changed.

"Keep doing that," Matthew said. "Open and close it every count of five."

"What are you doing?"

"I want to see how far away it still works." She snapped the jaw shut, counted to five, then opened it again. Matthew clambered down to the main deck and backed away from her across the bulk of the ship, holding the fragment. She assumed it was still changing, because he kept moving toward the bow. He climbed up to the forecastle and didn't stop until he was leaning against the bowsprit. To complete the experiment, she picked up the fish and made her way aft to the taffrail, as far away from him as she could possibly be on the ship. When she saw Matthew running toward her, she turned back and met him at the mizzenmast.

"It worked every time, no matter how far away." His face was flushed, and she grinned to see him so engaged.

"It's amazing," she admitted.

"How much farther might it go? For miles? What if it could reach all the way to England?"

"To England? I don't think so."

"Why not? We don't know how it works, so we don't know its limits. Just think what that would mean. . . ."

She shrugged. "It would mean quintessence can connect things that aren't physically connected. But we already know that."

"I'm not talking about what we *know*. I'm talking about what we can *do*." His eyes shone. "Can I have it?"

"What, the fish?"

"And the fragment."

She handed it over. "There's plenty to go around. What are you going to do?"

"I'll show you when it's done."

She watched him go, thinking how unlike his father he was at that moment. He was vulnerable in his excitement, with a carefree disregard for dignity that was very different from the preachy propriety he sometimes wore. She liked this Matthew a lot better.

❖❖❖

SINCLAIR stood at the forward rail, watching the water. The seas had grown high, and the boat pitched up and down as it crested each wave and dove into each trough. In the darkness, it was easy to see the water's luminescence, which made each rolling movement more unsettling. Most of the passengers were curled in the hold, sick or trying not to be. John Marcheford, however, stood clutching the bowsprit, gazing west as usual.

The weather wasn't really dangerous, at least not yet, but Sinclair had ordered the mainsails reefed and the sea anchor thrown out to reduce the chance of broaching. He trusted the helmsman to keep the boat faced into the waves, so for the moment there was nothing for him to do. He joined Marcheford at the bowsprit.

The man was an enigma. Stuffy, dignified, and unromantic—the last man in the world for a wilderness outpost—yet he awaited the ship's arrival with apparent eagerness.

"What do you expect to find on Horizon?" Sinclair asked.

"A sanctuary. A haven for the religiously oppressed." It was a quick answer and sounded rehearsed.

Sinclair crossed his arms and leaned back and forth against the motion of the ship. The rolling seas didn't bother him; he'd seen far worse. "That's what it is for your people. What is it for you?"

Marcheford regarded him, apparently deciding whether or not to speak. "The apostle Paul said his ambition was to preach the gospel where Christ had never been named." His expression grew wistful. "I've preached to believers all my adult life. But that's what I want: to preach to those who have never heard."

It took Sinclair a moment to figure out what Marcheford was talking about. When he did understand, he exploded into laughter. "You want to *evangelize* the *manticores?*"

Marcheford turned back to the waves. "Catherine Parris tells my son there are thousands of them. Dozens of tribes, isolated from the rest of the world. That means generations living and dying without a single messenger to share the gospel."

"Bishop, they're animals."

"You're not all that different from an ape yourself, taken from a physical point of view."

Sinclair grinned. "But I have a human mind and soul. These manticores will probably cut your throat just to watch the blood flow."

"Thanks to your healing water, it won't do them much good."

Sinclair was surprised Marcheford had even drunk the water—he'd expected the bishop to object on some kind of religious grounds. "Don't fool yourself. It won't bring you back from the dead. If Collard had shot me through the heart instead of the stomach, I wouldn't have gotten up again."

"And where would your human mind and soul be then?"

It was a loaded question, and Sinclair brushed it aside. "We're on different sides in that fight."

"I don't think so. We both want this colony to succeed."

"You want to bring more creatures under God's power. I want to steal God's power for myself. I want to bring the dead back to life."

"You're serious. Isn't that just a little bit arrogant?"

Sinclair laughed. "I've already turned a rod into a snake, healed the sick, cast a devil out of a young girl, and made a blind man see. You don't think I can learn to raise the dead?"

"I'll settle with you getting us safely to the island," Marcheford said.

"That you can count on."

Chapter Eighteen

THIS time, it was the real thing. Land. Sinclair could hardly keep his eyes from the vast green expanse that dominated the western horizon, though it was still many miles distant. This was it. Horizon Island. They sailed close enough to see fifty-foot cliffs surrounded by jagged rocks. Then the fog rolled in.

Thick and impenetrable, it seemed to rise from the sea like an enchantment. They could see neither ocean nor sky. Worse, the fog caught the reflection of the water's glow, so that shimmering lines danced eerily through the air, giving the impression that the ship was moving every way but forward. All sense of direction vanished. The currents pulled against the ship unpredictably, and the sailors took frequent soundings, anxious to avoid running aground on unseen reefs or shallows.

The mood on the ship turned dark again, as lookouts strained to see what lay ahead of them. Barrel staves tossed into the water drifted away in different directions, and the wind seemed to blow on them from all points at once.

The sky darkened and lightning flashed. A new, eerie wind blew in, filling their sails but not shifting the fog. The waves grew higher.

Tilghman jogged up to Sinclair and threw a quick salute. After Collard's death, Sinclair had reluctantly promoted the sailing master to first mate, despite suspecting that he'd been complicit in the mutiny. To be sure there was no trouble, Sinclair had taken to keeping Maasha Kaatra with him on deck, his curved sword never far from reach.

Tilghman shot Maasha Kaatra a nervous glance. "With your leave, Captain, we should reef the sails and lie ahull to wait out the storm."

"Not this storm. This storm never calms."

"All storms calm eventually," Tilghman said, not quite masking the scorn in his voice.

"Not one caused by the ocean's water pitching over the edge of the world. Unless you want to go over the edge, keep our sails spread and run this ship with the wind."

"But we're blind. If the coast is to our leeward, we'll be pounded into driftwood on the rocks."

"Chelsey made his colony on the shores of a quiet bay on the southern end of the island. There's a narrow entranceway between the cliffs. That's where we're heading."

Tilghman looked desperate. "Captain, it's suicide. Even on a familiar coast, with no fog, I wouldn't risk a leeward landing with winds of this strength."

"We have little choice. Trust me. I'll guide us straight into the bay."

"We'll run aground, my lord. Magic water is one thing, but this is the sea. Step down and let us do the sailing, sir."

Sinclair didn't have much height over the first mate, but he used what he had to loom over him. "Are you going to obey your orders or not?"

Tilghman didn't even flinch. "No, sir. Not to our deaths, sir."

"Then you're relieved. Bosun!" The fog was so thick that it was hard to see more than a few paces away across the deck. The bosun materialized out of the mist in response to Sinclair's shout. Tilghman flushed and looked as if he might still try to object, but Maasha Kaatra stepped between him and Sinclair, and Tilghman shut his mouth. Sinclair repeated his instructions, which the bosun bellowed out to the helmsman, and soon the ship was running from the wind with all her sails unfurled.

Several times, Sinclair thought he saw huge shapes cresting near the ship, but he couldn't be sure. A cold, driving rain drenched them, but still the fog didn't clear. Despite their speed, waves began breaking over the stern, and the helmsman fought with the wheel. Controlling their forward motion was crucial, allowing the waves to hit them at enough of an angle to reduce the impact, but not so much of an angle as to fling them sideways and capsize them.

Sinclair gave up on keeping the beetle box a secret. He no longer had the luxury of checking it in his cabin and then relaying changes of heading to the crew. He stood behind the helmsman, cracking the lid of the beetle box just enough to peer inside without drowning it. If he was seen, so be it—this was the moment of truth. He shouted slight adjustments to their heading, which the helmsman did his best to obey.

A shout from the bosun made Sinclair spin around. A gigantic wave yawned over them, far larger than the ship. Before he could grab hold of anything, it crashed down over them, knocking him to the deck. The ship tipped terrifyingly to port. It righted itself, but was now broadside to the waves. Then, just as it seemed they would capsize, the fog disappeared.

It didn't dissipate, or blow clear, or admit a ray of sun through a hole in the clouds. As if they'd crossed an invisible line, they left the fog behind and sailed into the blinding light of the gigantic evening sun. The sun filled the sky in front of them, so bright that for a moment Sinclair didn't see how near the horizon they had come.

The ocean current became a torrent, pulling them forward, toward the impossible point at which the water just stopped. Beyond it, there was nothing: no land, no water, just the dome of the sky. As they grew closer, they could hear the sound, like an enormous waterfall. It was the edge of the world, and the ship was spinning helplessly toward it like a cork caught in the rapids.

On the way, Kecilpenny had pointed out that if water flowed off the edge of the world, the oceans would soon drain dry. He suggested the world must be more like a bowl, with a rim that kept the water in.

Kecilpenny was wrong. Water was definitely flowing over the edge, and fast. Sinclair thought the bowl idea was probably right, only this was an overflowing bowl, implying that somewhere in the world, new water came into the system, either up out of springs or down from the sky as rain. Excess water flowed out over the rim.

But none of that would matter if they all died. They needed to find the entrance to Chelsey's bay, if it even existed. It was possible the settlement had been a delirious invention on the part of a dying man, but they had to try. Then he spotted it: a slim, dark opening in the cliff face coming up on their port side.

"Hard to port!" Sinclair screamed. "Now, now, now!"

The helmsman froze, staring at Sinclair with wild fear in his eyes. "You mean starboard."

"Port! Before we die!"

"That's straight into the cliffs!"

With a growl, Sinclair pushed him aside and grabbed the wheel. This was the only chance they had. If they couldn't regain control of the boat within the next several moments, they would be lost. He strained at the wheel, and both Maasha Kaatra and the helmsman joined him, combining their strength to fight against the current.

Slowly, the rudder cut the water, and the ship turned, but they flew even faster toward the edge. Men shouted in terror. The ship, broadside to the current, began to list alarmingly as it turned, the sails dipping perilously close to the water.

The gap in the cliff face grew larger. For a terrifying moment he thought they would miss it entirely, but then they sailed straight through, into a short waterway with towering cliffs on either side. The ocean still raged behind them, but ahead the turquoise water shone flat and calm. A warm breeze ruffled their hair and brought with it exotic scents of unfamiliar fruits. Birds soared and dove.

The ship emerged into a deep bay lined with sandy beaches under a clear sky.

❖❖❖

SINCLAIR was the first to see the dock. They sailed around the circumference of the bay, examining the shore with spyglasses in hopes of seeing evidence of the settlement Chelsey had left behind. A forest surrounded the bay, but the trees were unlike any he had seen anywhere else in the world. Some were topped with thick layers of moss, others with long green streamers that flapped in the wind. A few sent up enormous hovering leaves like kites, tethered by long stems that collected the sunlight and left their neighbors in shadow.

A wooden pier extended into the bay from a stretch of sandy beach near the mouth of a river. After food and shelter, a dock would be the first priority of a new settlement, because it would allow ships to be loaded with the trade goods that were the whole reason for the settlement to exist.

The dock was large enough and the water deep enough to accommodate a ship the size of the *Western Star,* but Sinclair chose to send the longboat instead. They didn't know what surprises might await them, and it was better not to find out when the ship was tied up at anchor.

He didn't trust anyone else to lead the landing party. For one thing, he came with papers that named him as the colony's governor, and he'd rather the settlers hear it from him than from anyone else. For another, no one else had his experience, his eye for detail, or his understanding of the possibilities of quintessence.

Unfortunately, he didn't really trust anyone else to stay and command the ship, either. The sailors had treated him with superstitious awe ever since his wound had so dramatically healed, but that kind of popularity could shift again as quickly as the wind. He didn't think Tilghman would sail off and strand him at this point, but just in case, he asked Maasha Kaatra to stay behind and shadow Tilghman.

They lowered the longboat from its berth into the water. Sinclair would go ashore with a team of Tate's soldiers to greet the settlers, then, if all was well, return to the ship. He was just about to climb down into the boat when a cry from a lookout brought him back on deck. "Ahoy! Boats in the water!"

It was true. Three small boats came toward them with five or six occupants each. Chelsey had left no more than thirty men behind, so this was at least half of them. Why send such a large delegation? Or were these the only survivors? Perhaps they were just excited to see fellow countrymen and couldn't hold back.

Sinclair examined the boats in his spyglass, then drew back in alarm. The boats were . . . He looked again. They weren't boats at all, but creatures with concave backs, each with a tall dorsal fin rising from the middle with a membrane stretched over a bony frame, catching the wind like a sail. Eyes and snouts protruded from the front, with long flat fins on each side. What the creatures looked like under the water, or how much of their bulk swam underneath, he couldn't tell, but on each of their backs sat five men.

No, not men. Manticores. Manticores wearing English clothes.

Chapter Nineteen

CATHERINE watched with apprehension as the manticores approached. She wasn't ready. Her conversations with Chichirico, if you could call them that, were still awkward and slow. She didn't know enough to act as a translator, much less as a diplomat. She'd be lucky to understand them at all.

Besides, the manticores were gray, not red like Chichirico. They were larger, and their faces were rounder, with heavier jaws. Chichirico had told her a little about the different tribes on the island. He said the grays were an enemy of his people who valued treachery and war and liked to gain riches through conquest. That could be just his own prejudice, of course, but it didn't seem good that these were the first manticores they were encountering.

The gray manticores sat motionless, apparently as unimpressed by their living boat as she would have been riding on a horse. Captain Sinclair raised his hand in what Catherine hoped would be interpreted as a friendly gesture and directed the men to throw rope ladders over the side.

The manticores ignored the ladders. Catherine couldn't tell if they didn't understand what they were for, or if they just chose to do things their own way, but they leaped right through the hull of the *Western Star* and emerged on deck behind most of the onlookers.

There were screams and panic and weapons raised. For most of the sailors and passengers, this was their first real look at these manticores.

"Hold your fire!" Sinclair called. "Stand aside."

The manticores made their way closer, swinging on the ship's low-hanging ropes and spars rather than walking. Each of them wore a single article of clothing: breeches, jerkin, doublet, or hose.

"We don't know what they want," Sinclair said. "Remain calm. Assume they mean us no harm."

He spoke peacefully enough, but Catherine saw Tate and his men checking their weapons. Now was the time.

Where was Chichirico? Was he just going to leave this to her and Father?

One of the grays, wearing not only breeches but a sailor's cap on his head, began to speak loudly, moving his tail in complicated ways. It was too fast to understand. Catherine could only pick up "hairless ones," their term for humans. As he spoke, the other manticores began fanning out, surrounding the gathered sailors and passengers, who shouted or backed away. Tate and his men advanced, their matchlocks ready.

"Wait!" Catherine pushed through the crowd. Father tried to stop her, but she twisted out of his grasp. She planted herself in front of the nearest manticore and used both her voice and her hands to say, "Safety, friend," the greeting Chichirico had taught her.

Her heart was pounding out of her chest, but she had to stifle a laugh at the dumbstruck look on Sinclair's face. *There,* she thought. *I can do things you never expected.* Everyone stared at her, frozen, waiting to see how the manticore would respond. It spoke and waved its tail again, but she couldn't tell if it was answering her with pleasantries or threats.

Father stepped forward. "Speak slowly," he said, a phrase common from their conversations with Chichirico.

Instead of answering, the one with the sailor's cap presented Sinclair with a bundle of cloth. He accepted it gravely and beckoned to four men, who hefted two chests forward and opened them. Inside were glass beads, small mirrors of burnished metal, and cheap jewelry. To the humans, they were not terribly valuable, but in this land they must be rare and unusual, like carvings and cloth from the Indies or Cathay were in Europe. The manticores ran their pincered hands through the items, speaking animatedly.

It was a cordial exchange of gifts, which seemed a good sign for future dealings. Catherine began to think her language skills wouldn't be necessary. Until Sinclair unwrapped the cloth.

It was an English cloak, the wool dyed a light green, and it was stained with blood.

⧓

SINCLAIR stared down at the cloak, the dried blood unmistakable. There were other explanations than murder. Perhaps the cloak's owner had killed an animal, soiling the cloak, and then decided to be rid of it. Or maybe he had died in an accident, and the manticores had simply found the cloak. But it didn't look good.

Sinclair had traveled to many places and had been on board when captains encountered new peoples for the first time. The trick was to impress the natives with the invincible, magical power of the English ship and its people. If they started to believe the English were weak, that all the rare treasures aboard were available for the taking, then the English would be in grave danger. Intimidation was the key.

He lifted both hands, palms out toward them, and said, "We come in friendship," in a loud and, he hoped, impressive voice. They ignored him. Catherine attempted more speech, but they ignored her, too.

He took a matchlock and powder horn out of the hands of one of his soldiers and showed it to the manticore with the sailor's cap, who seemed to be the leader among them, though it was hard to tell. The gun was already loaded and primed, so he blew on the match, dashed some powder on the pan, and raised the weapon.

"Wait!" Catherine said. She pointed. The red manticore, the one from their ship, had appeared from nowhere and was talking to the grays. Sinclair didn't know if that was good or bad. What would it tell them? That the humans had lured it with food and imprisoned it? If the manticores attacked, he didn't know if Tate and his soldiers could fire without hitting their own people.

He couldn't risk it. A demonstration of their weaponry was the best way to guarantee good behavior. A bird wheeled overhead. Sinclair aimed the matchlock quickly and fired. The weapon roared. The bird flew off unharmed, but the manticores reacted violently. They leaped high, clambered up into the rigging, and then, hanging upside down by their hooked feet, they let go, dropping straight through the deck just as if they were dropping into a hole.

A moment later, they reappeared, emerging through the gunports in the hull. Each carried an assortment of items: a doublet, a broach, an empty bottle, a length of rope, a knife. They leaped onto their living boat-creatures, which immediately began swimming back toward shore. He could see powerful tails churning under the waterline.

The passengers on deck shouted after the thieves. Tate lifted his weapon. "Should I fire on them, my lord?"

"No. Hold your fire. We don't want to start a war."

Thieving wasn't unusual among island natives, either, though most didn't have the advantage of being able to walk through walls. Finely woven cloth would be a rare treasure to them, as would steel and strong rope. What worried Sinclair was not what they had taken, but what they had left behind. He fingered the bloodstained woolen cloak, wondering about its owner, who was probably dead. The manticores might just have found his body, but it seemed more likely they had killed him.

He decided to delay the landing party until the next day. The group would have to be well chosen and well armed.

He pointed at Parris and Catherine. "You two. In my cabin."

They followed him. Parris beckoned to Matthew Marcheford, who came along, too, carrying what looked like two wooden boxes.

Once they were inside, Sinclair shut the door and faced them. "How did you do it?"

"We've been speaking to the manticore much of the voyage. Learning his language, trying to understand him," Parris said.

"How much can you communicate?" Sinclair said.

"It's slow going. We're getting better, but you saw what happened. Catherine tried to greet them, and they ignored her. I don't know if they understood what she said, but I certainly didn't understand what they said."

"Can you teach others what you know?"

Parris shrugged.

"We can try," Catherine said. "It's nothing, though, compared to what we could learn by bonding again."

"No." Both Parris and Matthew said it together. "It's too much of a risk," Parris said. Sinclair eyed Catherine, considering. Was she volunteering? Did she *want* to try to bond again? After all, they would need to communicate if they wanted to survive here.

"What did our manticore and the gray ones say to each other?" Sinclair said.

"Our manticore's name is Chichirico," she said. "The grays are from a different tribe. They weren't happy to see him. I know the word they use for humans—it means hairless—and they combined it with the word for 'like,' as in, 'I like raisins.' I think they were accusing him of being a human-lover."

They all considered this for a moment. "How sure are you?" Sinclair said.

She shrugged. "Not very. I mostly picked up the tone."

"Keep trying. We need to understand what's going on."

"There's one more thing," Parris said. "We wanted to show you these." He said it calmly, but his eyes were dancing—he was excited about something. He motioned Matthew forward, who produced the two wooden boxes, each with a handle and a bell attached.

"What are they?" Sinclair said.

"Devices for communication. Matthew made them."

Sinclair took a closer look. The boxes seemed identical. They were freshly and somewhat inexpertly constructed; the sides weren't entirely flush, and some of the nails were bent. On top of each was mounted a small bell. A string passed from the top of each bell through a hole in the top of each box. On the side of each box was a wooden lever.

"What do they do?" he asked.

"Pull one of the levers," Parris said.

Sinclair did so, expecting that perhaps the lever would pull the string and cause the bell to ring. And in fact, a bell did ring, so that at first he didn't realize what was happening. He pressed it a second time, and only then it struck him. The bell on the *other* box had rung.

He looked up in shock. Parris laughed. Matthew and Catherine failed to suppress smiles.

Sinclair reached over and pressed the lever on the second box, causing the bell on the first box to ring. He lifted one of them, examining it on every side. There was no connection whatsoever between the boxes. He walked onto his balcony with it and pressed the lever again, and again the other box rang.

He came back inside, aware that his mouth was hanging open. "This is incredible," he said.

Parris pushed Matthew forward. "Tell him."

Matthew explained what he and Catherine had discovered with the broken fragment of ironfish skull. "I attached a piece of jawbone from different ironfish to each lever. The rest of the skull from each fish is in the opposite box. So when I pull this lever"—he pulled the one on the table, causing the box in Sinclair's hands to ring—"it closes the jaw hinge here, causing the skull in that box to grow heavy enough to pull down on the string and ring the bell. When I release the lever, the bones turn light again, and the bell rights itself, lifting the skull back to the top of the box."

Sinclair thought of all the street magicians who claimed to be able to talk to people across England through their minds, or witch doctors whose supposed powers included the awareness of events happening far away. He held the real thing in his hands, and his mind flew to all the uses such a device could have. Advance warning of an approaching army. Calls for rescue from ships in trouble. Centuries of men had longed for such a power, and this boy had created it with wood, string, nails, and a few bits of dead fish.

"We could assign messages to certain numbers of rings. One ring for 'arrived safely,' two for 'in danger, need help'—like that," said Matthew, and a whole collection of new uses exploded into Sinclair's mind. Why stop at predetermined messages? Why not create a whole alphabet of rings and communicate anything at all?

"How far apart do they work?"

"We don't know," Parris said. "It works across the length of the ship, but we haven't been able to test it any farther."

Sinclair clapped Matthew on the shoulder. "I'll take one of these to shore tomorrow. You keep the other one here. We'll test it and see how far it can go."

Matthew nodded. They filed out, leaving the boxes behind. When they were gone, Sinclair placed one box at one end of his table and the other box at the other end. For a long time, while the sky outside grew dark, Sinclair sat in his chair, pulling the lever nearest him to hear the bell on the other side of the table ring.

hinge here, causing the skull in that box to grow heavy enough to pull
down on the string and ring the bell. When I release the lever, the bones
turn light again, and the... counterweight pulls the skull back to the top
of the box.

Sinclair thought of all those magicians who claimed to be able
to talk to people across England, or to read minds, or watch distros
whose supposed powers enabled them to see events happening far
away. He had the real thing in front of him, and his mind flew to all the uses
such a device could have. A fortress ring of an approaching army.
Calls for rescue from ships in trouble. Centuries of men had longed for
such a power, and this boy had created it with sound, string, nails, and a
few jars of dead fish.

Chapter Twenty

PARRIS clambered nervously into the longboat. It tipped perilously,
almost throwing him into the water, but a soldier grabbed his arm
and steadied him. Five of Tate's men were already aboard along with Sinclair. Their destination was the wooden dock Sinclair had spotted the
day before, and from there, the human settlement, if one existed.

They had seen no sign of humans. No one had spotted their ship in
the harbor and come waving a flag. They'd seen no smoke to indicate a
settlement was nearby. The most likely explanation was that the humans
were all dead.

The currents in the bay were sluggish and mild, and they reached the
dock easily. Built for large carracks like the *Western Star,* the dock was too
high off the water to be useful for their small boat, so they splashed
through the shallows and dragged it up onto the sand instead.

Sinclair stood hip-deep in the placid water, scooping handfuls into his
mouth. Parris lifted a cupped hand and sipped tentatively. Like the water
in the barrels, it tasted fresh and sweet. It occurred to him that he now
knew why: the small amount of quintessence in the water—from dead
creatures like the ironfish, or just soaked up from starlight—was magni-
fied by salt, but over time, the salt was used up. That created the water's
glow, and also its freshness. Though more likely the salt was transformed
instead of being consumed, since the water became salty again if brought
to England. Parris scooped greedy mouthfuls. The soldiers did the same.
This water might kill them if they tried to go home, but here it was the
stuff of life.

Before leaving England, the question of how to return had been the-
oretical. Now, walking on an alien land with potentially lethal water

coursing through his body, he felt it more keenly. If he didn't solve the mystery, he could never leave this place. He wondered what Joan was doing, and how she fared, and if he would ever see her again.

The thin beach sloped quickly upward. A path had been cleared through some of the brush, and they followed it up into the trees. The trunks were deeply crenellated and the greenery was neither leaves nor needles, but furry green piles of what looked like moss. The moss was hard to see clearly, because most of the trees were tremendously tall, and the dense piles cast the mostly barren forest floor into deep shadow. Where smaller plants did grow, they were moist things with radiating gills that puffed powdery spores if kicked.

Parris touched one of the trees. He stopped.

"What is it? Did you hear something?" Sinclair said.

"These are the trees."

"What?"

"Feel them. They're covered with wax. These are the trees that the beetle came from."

Sinclair scraped one with a knife, and it released a familiar aromatic smell. "Cut it down," he said. One of the soldiers ran back to the ship and returned with an ax. After several minutes of hard chopping, the tree crashed to the forest floor. Though it fell through several layers of the mossy greenery of other trees, it passed right through without disturbing them. Parris ran around to the top of the fallen tree. It was swarming with beetles.

Sinclair clapped his hands and laughed. "Look at them all."

"It's just like you said back in London," Parris said. "The box was made from the wood of this tree."

He grabbed a handful of the foliage, which was soft and spongy. The lower branches, however, were covered in stiff brown curls that crumbled in his hands, presumably dead from lack of sunlight. "Look at the branches," Parris said, noticing how the branches of dead foliage interleaved from tree to tree like a stack of half-shuffled cards. "They're competing for the sunlight. If one tree blocks the light, another tree pushes right up through it and spreads a moss pile higher up. The dense foliage completely blocks the sunlight, and the lower layer dies." He looked around the forest, tracking the passage of time as each tree grew ever higher to steal the light from its fellows. "It's a battleground."

The path followed the river, and they continued on. Parris carried the bell-box and pressed the lever occasionally as he walked. Every time he did, his own bell would ring a few moments later—an answering signal from Matthew to indicate that they were still in communication. They had agreed upon a pattern of three short rings to call for help, in case they encountered danger. They planned to work out a code to send more complex messages in the future, but for now this would do.

The sun glinted off of water in the distance. They emerged into daylight to find a large lake surrounded by forest. It fed the river to their left, coursing over scattered rocks and filling the air with the sound of rushing water and a fine mist. To their right, in a clearing by the lake, stood the settlement.

Despite the stories, Parris had envisioned a huddle of rough-hewn wooden houses. What he saw was a small but apparently prosperous settlement town, surrounded by a high wooden palisade. The houses were huge: mansions with multiple levels and stone chimneys, laid out neatly along several streets. A church stood at the center, its steeple and cross the highest point in town.

The party approached warily. No smoke rose from the chimneys, and they heard no human voices. As they entered the settlement, Parris saw that the palisade was made from the wood of the beetle trees. The walls of the houses, however, were not made of wood or stone, but of some other whitish material that seemed uneven and sparkled when the light caught it. He couldn't see through it, but the wall looked translucent, like thick glass or crystal. When he was close enough to touch, he could see the endless matrix of beveled sides, as if the wall had been built by an army of jewelers, and his growing suspicion was confirmed. The entire house was made of cut diamond.

Parris walked around it, marveling at the shifting colors as the diamond prismed the light. They explored the town like men in a trance, hypnotized by dazzling colors and scattered rays of sunlight.

They looked in each building, but found no people. Inside the church, they found the bones.

━┼┼┼━

CATHERINE was proud of Matthew. Not only had he joined her in exploring the properties of the ironfish, he'd taken a leap forward and envisioned a use for it that never would have occurred to her. Now, standing on the forecastle and ringing patterns on his bell, he looked as happy as she'd ever seen him. To her, the exciting part had been discovering the property in the first place, but he reveled in this methodical testing. She was interested to know how far away the bell-boxes could get from each other, too, but sitting around ringing a bell all day was driving her mad.

She leaned against the rail and sighed. "I wish I could have gone with them."

"On land? But there could be all kinds of dangerous things. Wild animals, quicksand, natives with poisoned spears."

"I suppose now you're going to say it's no place for a woman."

"I suppose I am." He laughed, and she smiled to see it. Somewhere on this journey, Matthew had learned to laugh at himself. "I'm just saying it's better to let the armed soldiers take the first look. We're all going to shore eventually."

"But we're missing the first discoveries. What marvels is my father seeing, right now, while we're stuck here?"

He rang the bell again. Then he said, hesitantly, "How long do you think we'll stay here, on the island?"

"We just arrived."

"I know. But what if we can't figure out how to get home without dying? We could be here for years and years. The next time a ship arrives, it could be your grandchildren who meet them at the dock."

"You have to have children first to have grandchildren."

"That's what I'm saying. There aren't many women here, if you haven't noticed. Once this colony starts up, you might find yourself with a lot of suitors."

Catherine tossed a dismissive hand. "Who would want me? My father's money is gone, so I'm poor, but I don't how to cook or clean or keep a house. Let's see, what skills have I learned recently? I can dissect animals. I can read a nautical map and tie a bosun's knot and calculate longitude. Which of those—"

He leaned forward and kissed her on the mouth. She tried to slap him, but she was off balance, and the blow barely glanced off his chin. "Missed," he said, grinning.

But she wasn't playing. This wasn't a flirtatious game, in which she pretended to be uninterested in order to lead him on. To make sure there was no mistake, she curled her fist and punched him solidly in the eye, sailor-style.

"Ouch!" He reeled back, his pride probably stinging worse than his face.

She crossed her arms over her chest and glared at him. "Why did you have to do that?"

"I thought you might like it," he said.

"It's a mortal sin."

"It is not!"

"It leads to one."

He rubbed his face. "Since when did you care so much about sin?"

"Oh, stop whining. Let me see."

She pulled his hand away and could tell from the color around his eye that blood was already pooling in the cavity. It would be black and blue for certain, probably for a few days. She wasn't really sorry. She valued his friendship, but she had enough to think about right now without trying to figure out if she loved him. Still, he did look funny. She let a smile sneak out. "You look a sight."

"It hurts."

"Craven. You'll never be a great explorer with that attitude."

"I don't *want* to be a great explorer."

She made her voice serious again. "And I don't want to marry. I don't want to plant a garden and mend clothes and feed the children while a man makes all the discoveries and gets all the glory."

She heard a splashing sound from below and looked out to see if the longboat was returning. On the deck beside them, six manticores stepped out of the air.

⊷+++⊷

THE bones were human. Most of them were scattered through the sanctuary, though they found some high in the church tower. The bones had been chewed by animals and scattered, but the fact that they were all in the church implied that the settlers had gathered there together to make their final stand. There were no weapons. There was also no clothing, not even scraps left by hungry scavengers. Had the manticores done this?

The church was made of diamond like the rest, and the long benches inside were made of gold. Almost everything in all the buildings—beds, tables, chairs—was made of some precious metal. The chimneys weren't stone after all, but blocks of silver. There was no artistry; it wasn't like visiting the rich cathedrals at Salisbury or Ely. The furniture was practical and unadorned. Parris's impression was of a group of men so saturated with riches that they didn't know what to do with them.

Even so, it was another mystery. Gold and silver and especially diamond were hard to work. You couldn't make even a simple chair out of them without a forge and a great deal of skill. Besides that, they were tremendously heavy. Parris pushed his weight against a gold bench and could barely slide it at all, never mind lift it. How had they constructed whole houses?

Beyond the church, they discovered three small pools dug into the ground and lined, one with gold, one with silver, and the third with diamond. Despite the fact that the water was still, no scum or algae grew over its surface. Dozens of eels swam sinuously through the water. At the bottom of the gold pond sat a few gold crowns stamped with the face of Henry VIII—the first gold Parris had seen that had come from England.

The others joined him at the water's edge. Sinclair picked up a fallen branch and reached in to poke at one of the eels.

"Why are they here?" Parris said. "Were they breeding them for food? There's a whole lake to fish—"

Half of Sinclair's stick was heavy and glinting. One of the soldiers reached his hand toward the water to pick up a coin. "Stop!" Parris said. He ran around the edge of the pond toward the man, but his warning came too late. The man screamed and pulled his hand out. It was frozen in place, fingers outstretched, and made of pure, shining gold.

Everyone backed away from the pond. Half of the branch Sinclair had put in the water was also gold, and he tossed it hastily away. Was it the water? Or the eels? Parris looked in the other two ponds. In one, he saw a scattering of silver coins. In the other, though he had to look carefully before he found it, a single small diamond.

The soldier moaned in panicked horror. With a great effort, he lifted the gold hand and cradled it in his other arm. Parris studied it in amazement, careful not to touch it. All the tiny features—the hair, the creases, the wrinkles around the knuckles—were gone, replaced with smooth gold like a glove. It didn't seem to be just a coating, however—the hand was heavy enough to be solid metal.

"This is worth your hand, friend," Sinclair said. "Gold of this weight would fetch ten times your wages in London."

The soldier didn't say anything, but Parris could see by his expression that he wasn't impressed.

The bell-box clutched under Parris's arm rang. He glanced at it in surprise—he had forgotten about it in the excitement of exploring the settlement. He was about to return the signal when the bell rang three times in short succession, and then did it again. It repeated the pattern over and over as they ran back through the settlement in the direction of the ship. As they reached the cover of the trees, it fell silent.

Chapter Twenty-one

THE lookouts saw nothing. One moment, the forecastle was empty but for Matthew and Catherine and a few sailors manning the ropes; the next, six red manticores appeared, still wet from swimming. They looked so much like Chichirico that Catherine couldn't have told them apart. None of them wore clothes. Matthew began sending the emergency signal through the bell-box, three quick rings.

The sailors ran, but Matthew and Catherine were trapped, since the manticores stood between them and the ladders. The manticores advanced. One of them spoke in their language, a torrent of syllables and gestures. Catherine didn't understand most of it, but she caught the word "Chichirico," and guessed what they wanted.

"He's here, on the ship," she said in their language, or tried to. She used the word for "ship" that Chichirico had taught her, but he used it for other things, too, usually human things that were distasteful. She suspected it actually meant something like "abomination."

The manticore made an incomprehensible response. Out of the corner of her eye, she saw the red beard and broad shoulders of Oswyn Tate lift slowly above the port ladder. He raised a matchlock to his shoulder.

"No!" Catherine shouted, but it was too late. He touched the match to the powder, and the gun erupted in smoke and noise. The manticores disappeared.

Tate threw the matchlock aside and scrambled the rest of the way onto the deck. He drew a knife and began slashing chaotically through the air.

"Stop," Catherine said. "You can't hurt them that way. You'll only anger them."

"I didn't miss," Tate said. "I shot one of the devils, but the bullet went right through. They're not real flesh and blood."

"They are. Please, put the knife down. They're gone."

Tate calmed down a little, but he still spun, scanning the deck. He walked over to the rail and examined a hole where the wood had splintered from his bullet. "Went right through. Didn't hurt that devil at all."

A series of splashes sounded, and they looked over the rail to see ripples spreading from several disturbed areas of water. A voice whispered in Catherine's ear, in halting English. "I go with them. I return."

She kept her face still and didn't reply.

Tate still peered over the rail, oblivious. "Good riddance," he muttered. "I hope they don't come back."

Catherine raised an eyebrow. "How can you be sure they're gone?"

+++

SINCLAIR was furious. Tate, that fool, had fired on an unarmed native who posed no clear threat. The reds might have been coming with an offer of friendship.

"You weren't here," Tate said. "They appeared out of nowhere and attacked the young lady."

"They didn't attack me," Catherine said. "They were talking to me."

Sinclair clenched his fists. He was surrounded by idiots. He couldn't leave them alone for two hours without something like this happening. Maybe the manticores would have been their enemies anyway, but they certainly would be now.

"I should throw you in the brig," he said.

"You can't do that," Tate said.

Sinclair leaned forward. "I like you," he said. "You've always been loyal. But I *can* lock you up, and I *can* have you flogged. Don't ever question my authority."

Tate looked like he might object, but he said, "Yes, my lord."

Sinclair called for the bosun and started issuing orders to unload the ship. There was no point in waiting any longer. Being surrounded by water was clearly no protection from the manticores, and they couldn't stay on the ship forever. Better to establish a strong presence as soon as possible. Any more time spent huddling on board simply delayed the inevitable. With enemies that could turn invisible and walk through walls, no place was safe.

◄+ + +►

THE soldier with the gold hand came to see Parris, complaining of pain where the flesh of his arm was fused with the gold. His wrist was red and irritated, and when he rotated it, pus seeped up from the gap. He was hot and feverish. Whatever was wrong, the quintessence water wasn't healing it, or if it was, the presence of the gold was causing it all over again.

Parris told him there was no choice but to amputate at once. With the miraculous water running through his body, the normally dangerous cut should heal in a matter of minutes. The soldier balked, despite the fact that the hand was already useless, apparently hoping a way might be discovered to transform it back. He would wait until morning, he said. In the morning, he would let Parris amputate.

By morning, he was dead.

He was the first to die that day, but not the last. Quintessence water might be able to heal common sicknesses and injuries, but the plants and animals of Horizon had more deadly weapons. While the sailors were put to work unloading the ship, the passengers started felling trees to enlarge the palisade. One man tried to pick a juicy-looking fruit he found hanging on a bush within easy reach. The fruit was covered with invisible barbed spines that lodged in his hand. They were apparently poisoned, since he fell over dead a few minutes later. Another man, a passenger with some experience hunting game, went into the forest with a matchlock against advice. He shot a boarlike creature, but by the time he approached it, it had healed from its wound and gored him with its tusks. These, too, were poisoned, and the man died shortly after dragging himself back to the settlement.

It made sense to Parris. God had provided the animals and plants of this place with miraculous water, making them harder to kill, but predators still had to eat, and prey still needed ways to defend themselves. Poison, apparently, had taken the place of brute force. It made the island seem more alien and treacherous. How many more people would die discovering which foods were deadly and which were safe?

Despite this, the new settlers threw themselves into the work with enthusiasm. After months of confinement on the *Western Star*, they reveled in the chance to stretch their legs on dry ground and build their new home. They were awed by the buildings, and everyone wanted to dip a branch into the pools and pull out gold or silver or diamonds.

The sailors, no more able to return home than anyone else, were as much a part of the settlement as the passengers. That meant over a hundred people who needed shelter. The existing town wasn't big enough. They chopped the beetlewood trees into long logs and extended the palisade into a second circle, giving the whole settlement the rough shape of a figure eight, with a short opening connecting the old town with the new. The palisade itself was a lethal-looking toothwork of sharpened stakes that any large animal would have difficulty scaling. But would it stop a manticore?

At dusk, when the sun reached its largest and brightest and the clearing blazed with heat, Sinclair called a halt to the work. He insisted that all tools be carried back to the ship. They had just gathered everything together when the manticores appeared.

No one saw them coming. One minute, the forest was silent; the next, more than a dozen manticores surrounded them. These manticores were red, like Chichirico, with the same basic size and features.

"Ignore them," Sinclair said. "Carry on with your business as if they weren't there."

Nervously, the men hoisted supplies on their shoulders and began the trek back to the ship. The manticores watched them, but made no move to engage. Parris spotted Tate, off to one side, ramming wadding into his matchlock and filling the pan with powder. He pointed him out to Sinclair.

Sinclair reached Tate just as he raised the gun to his shoulder.

"Put it down," Sinclair said. "Do not fire."

"Someone has to be ready," Tate said. "I won't fire unless they attack."

"It won't do any good. Bullets pass right through them. And if you threaten them, you may provoke them to attack. I'm ordering you to lower the gun."

Tate swore, but did as he was told.

The red manticores shadowed them back to the ship. The settlers ignored them as best they could, and all returned safely before dark.

A feast was waiting for them on board. Some sailors had found enormous tortoises walking on the beach and hauled them back to the ship. Turned upside down, the tortoises could be roasted in their shells and made fine eating. The delicious smell of smoking meat filled the ship, and the men soon forgot the silent threat of the manticores in an evening of feasting, dancing, and song.

⊷+�❦+↤

CHICHIRICO returned that night. He appeared to Catherine in her cabin aboard ship, where she was sitting up waiting for him, hoping he would come. Father was snoring in his hammock. Catherine was tired of the ship. So far, she hadn't been allowed to so much as touch her foot to the beach. Matthew had joined the men in their first day of work on land, but not her. She'd been pressed into service mending sailcloth with the other women. A necessary job, of course, if the *Western Star* were to one day return to England, but as dull as the endless open sea. She wanted to go on shore.

Chichirico seemed happy to see her, though perhaps he was just happy to be back in his own home among his own people. They spoke in a mix of English and manticore, switching back and forth in an attempt to be understood.

"Who killed the original settlers?" Catherine said. And in manticore: "*Why . . . hairless ones . . . die?*"

There followed a frustrating series of attempts by Chichirico to communicate something which Catherine couldn't understand. Finally, Chichirico lifted his central tail, the one with the needle-sharp spine at the end. "Try?" he said. He made a motion like he was drinking water. "Safe now."

Catherine understood—because she now had quintessence in her body from drinking the water, it would be safe to bond with him. But would it really? Was he just guessing? Chichirico wore a simple sling or bandolier made of twisted vines, and from this he produced the tough cylindrical stalk of some plant. He bit open the top, revealing a hollow inside filled with a metallic fluid that she recognized: mercury.

Catherine glanced at her father, still sleeping soundly. Heart pounding, she shifted in bed, presented her back to Chichirico, and waited.

⊷+❦+↤

IT was gentler this time. She slipped easily into his perspective without losing her own. The change was disorienting, but not nearly so overwhelming as it had been in England. When the ritual was done, she was fully herself, able to control her own thoughts, but with a thin strand still connecting her mind with Chichirico's.

This is how it's supposed to work, she thought, forming the words in her mind.

Yes, came the immediate reply. An idea more than a word, but her mind translated it to English. *Here, among the stars, with life in your blood, we can be kin.*

An image appeared in her mind of a crowd of manticores gathering in the woods and pressing close, touching tails. She knew without being told that this was Chichirico's experience of returning to his tribe. In the space of a moment, Chichirico summarized the story of the previous night, as clear as if it were her own memory.

His return had divided the tribe, some happy to see him, others angry. He had re-formed the bond with his memory family, but this meant strange and confusing memories—Catherine's—were now mixed with their own. A few of them resented this alien incursion into their family's memory life, some so much that they abandoned the family and began a new one.

Catherine tried to send an image back, a picture of the bones of the original settlers scattered in the diamond-walled church, as a way of asking what had happened to them. She had never seen the bones or the church, so it was driven entirely by her imagination and other people's descriptions, but Chichirico seemed to understand. He sent her back an answering image that was so strong, it swept her up inside it.

⊰+++⊱

SHE was a manticore. A red manticore, but not Chichirico. A female from his memory family. She was climbing through the forest upside down, using the hooks on her hind legs. The branches were covered with dead brown curls that smelled like honey and crunched as she moved. Catherine was struck by how different the sounds were than in an English forest. There were birdcalls, but they were unfamiliar screeches and wet gurgling noises. The rustling of animals in the treetops was muted by the dense mossy foliage, and when the wind blew, the layers of dead foliage rattled.

Catherine—or rather, the manticore whose memories she was reliving—missed Chichirico. She had been his friend and lover. She understood why he had chosen to go with the ship. The hairless ones were like weak infants in some ways, but in other ways they were strong, and more of them would come. If the hairless ones allied with them, it would make them that much stronger against their enemies.

It was an accepted practice to give over a son of one tribe to another tribe, to bond with them. The two tribes gained a new connection with each other and were more likely to keep the peace.

So far, the gray manticores had dominated trade with the hairless ones. The jewelry, ornaments, and clothing were rare and different than anything they could make, and they became symbols of rank and status among them. More importantly, though, were the metal knives and axes that could cut wood quickly and stay sharp, the traps and snare wires that could be used to catch game, and kettles to carry and boil water. The hairless ones also showed them how to brew alcohol, which had an even more dramatic effect on the manticores than it did on them. The grays guarded their nearly exclusive access jealously, and traded with other manticores deeper in the island, becoming more powerful and influential among the other tribes. They used this influence to expand their own territory and push others away from long-established hunting grounds.

After Chichirico went with them, the balance of trade had changed, and the red manticores were given preference. The grays must have decided that the best way to keep their power was to exterminate the hairless ones and take all the goods for themselves. As she crept closer to the village, she heard the sounds of their guns firing. By the time she reached the clearing, it was too late. The hairless ones had made their last stand in the church with their useless guns. As far as she could tell, not a single gray manticore had been so much as scratched. The hairless ones were all dead.

The grays raced through the village, snatching up clothes and tools and guns. They had been welcomed into the village as traders and friends, but they left it as killers.

The vision faded, and Catherine was once again in her dim cabin on the ship with Chichirico. She shuddered at the memory of the bloody corpses, still warm as the gray manticores looted their possessions.

Are the grays still strong? she asked.

In this part of the island, they are. They have had many children and taken many sons of other tribes. Many other tribes pay them tribute.

What about your tribe?

Chichirico looked proud. *My tribe does not enslave itself to others.*

What does your chief think about us being here?

He is dead.

Dead? You have no leader?

The position passes to his oldest living son.

Who is his oldest living son?

Chichirico gazed at her with somber eyes. *I am.*

Chapter Twenty-two

JOHN Marcheford mobilized a team to remove the bones from the church and scrub the pews and floors until the bloodstains were gone. They cleared some land beyond the palisade to use as a graveyard. It was impossible to separate the bones into those belonging to individuals, so they buried them all together and left a gold marker with the name of their ship and the date.

Sinclair hated funerals, but he knew he had to attend. Marcheford preached from Psalm 103: "As for man, his days are as grass: as a flower of the field, so he flourisheth. For the wind passeth over it, and it is gone; and the place thereof shall know it no more."

The words disturbed him. How was it supposed to be comforting to remind everyone that their lives were short? Sinclair could see the void again, expanding, devouring the distillery. He thought of John Gibbs's atomist theory, that the whole material world was nothing but tiny specks floating through nothingness. He hated it. It made existence seem so . . . tenuous. What if the specks just drifted away? *For the wind passeth over it, and it is gone. . . .*

One of the first expeditions he planned to make, once they were settled, was to the westernmost edge of the island. He wanted to do it, but his stomach twisted at the thought. He feared he would peer over the edge and find that the whole world was just a thin crust hanging precariously over the infinite, empty void.

When the funeral ended, Catherine and Stephen Parris waved and caught his eye. Parris suggested privacy, so they walked away from the crowd. "Catherine saw Chichirico again last night," he said.

"He was a son of the chief," Catherine said. "The chief and his older sons all died fighting the grays, and Chichirico's younger brother Tanakiki has been leading the tribe. Now that Chichirico is back, *he's* supposed to be the chief. But after all the time he's spent with humans, a lot of the reds don't even want him in the tribe, never mind as their leader. The others think his connection to us will finally give them the power to defeat the grays."

Sinclair groaned. "We haven't even moved in yet, and we're already embroiled in their politics."

"What should we do?" Parris said.

"Don't make deals with any of them. Maintain a fair trade with all, as much as we can."

"Won't that just make them all angry?"

"Maybe. But we can't please them all, either. The trick is not to make any of them angry enough to kill us."

⊰┼┼┼⊱

DIAMOND homes were far easier to make than the normal variety. Walls of packed mud, hastily erected, could be transformed into immovable, beautiful ramparts by ladling water from the ponds over them. New houses sprang up in days.

Sinclair gave Parris his pick, and he selected one of the nicest original homes near the church. At Catherine's request, Blanca continued to live with them and shared a room with Catherine. Catherine, however, barely spent two minutes inside. She flitted from place to place across the settlement, eager that no one should learn anything about the new world without her knowing it first.

When Parris began to make exploratory forays into the forest, he brought her with him. Her excitement over new discoveries was infectious. Every day they found something new. A bird that nested inside solid rock to keep its young from predators. A jet-black lizard that grew bristly hair every night to insulate its body, then shed it every afternoon before basking in the blazing evening sun. Many animals changed color or coat between morning and evening to protect against the dramatic temperature swings.

As the weeks went by, the settlement turned from a huddle of frightened passengers to a thriving town. Two- and three-story houses were everywhere, larger than most had lived in at home. Red manticores visited in small groups, but the grays never did. The reds showed the settlers which plants were good to eat and which were dangerous, in return for tools and other manufactured goods from Europe. A few people began to learn their language and engage them in trade.

Matthew Marcheford rarely left the settlement, but Parris and Catherine brought back specimens of whatever animals they could catch. It turned into a rivalry between her and Matthew to think up practical ways to use their unique qualities. Parris wasn't sure of which of them he was more proud.

They found a tiny rodent that they named a Samson mouse, because it made its den by piling up rocks three times its size. Catherine made a pair of Samson gloves with its hide and teeth that allowed men to lift objects far heavier than themselves.

Matthew, however, discovered that the fruit of the mimicry tree could be induced to grow into other kinds of trees when planted, and soon the colony had groves of priceless cinnamon, nutmeg, and sandalwood trees, as well as apples, pears, and oranges. If they ever solved the problem of getting their treasures home, Horizon would make England the richest nation on earth.

Other colonists became interested in their work and began to make discoveries of their own. Accidents were common. Parris decided to form a Quintessence Society to share discoveries and regulate experimentation. Gibbs and Kecilpenny were two of the first to join.

Sinclair didn't object to the Society, but he refused to participate, preferring to perform his experiments alone. It was typical of an alchemist, but aggravating. The way to expand understanding was with open communication, not with secrecy, and the nonparticipation of the colony's governor meant the Society could only suggest rules for safe experimentation, not regulate them.

The most wonderful of the Society's successes—discovered by Catherine this time—was a use for the sand tortoise beyond roasting it in its shell. The creature ate sand, which seemed impossible—what nourishment could it find? But two months after their first meal of tortoise, she found a corkscrew organ on the tortoise's neck that actually transformed the sand into something very much like grain on the way down its throat. The grain turned out to be nutritious for humans, too, and delicious. If the corkscrew—a bony spiral with a speck of quintessence not unlike the ironfish skull—was removed from a dead tortoise, it still worked. Soon their tables were laden with breads and cakes made entirely from sand.

"We've come full circle," Parris said at a meeting of the new Society.

"What do you mean?" Gibbs said.

They met in the church, now free of blood and bones, which doubled as a meeting place for any kind of colony business. The basic design of the architecture was simple—more like a large barn than a cathedral—but there was no denying the majesty of the high diamond walls and roof, refracting the sunlight into a thousand intersecting colored beams. Parris stood at the front, moderating conversation, while the rest sat loosely scattered in the front pews.

"We're all eating sand," he said. "Chelsey's expedition must have done the same thing. They stocked the ship for the return journey with food made from sand. Only it transformed back again on the way, including what was already in their bodies."

"Because they traveled too far from the sky," Kecilpenny said. "Aristotle said quintessence radiates from the sun and stars, and here on Horizon we're almost close enough to touch them."

"Then we're following in the footsteps of dead men," Gibbs said. "If it's the stars we need, we'll never go home."

"Yes, we will," Matthew said. "It's just another puzzle to solve."

"Not if quintessence really comes from the sun and the stars. What can we do about that?"

"We just have to learn how to take the sun and the stars with us."

There was some muttering at this, but no one could deny that Matthew and Catherine had already accomplished things that, a few months ago, no one would have thought possible.

Parris was as proud of Matthew as if he'd been his own son. In fact, judging by the time he spent with Catherine, Matthew would be his son before long. Matthew sat at his ease among his elders in the Society, answering questions with confidence, and Parris wondered how it made his real father feel.

John Marcheford didn't like the culture of the colony. He disapproved of the colonists' obsession with gold and diamonds and spices and their furor to bend the power of quintessence to their will. He held services in the church on Sundays, which were well attended, but he refused to live inside the settlement walls. Kecilpenny, who had been a vicar in England, performed the duties of Christian minister for the rest of the week. Marcheford built a rough house with his own hands several miles distant, where he lived alone and tried to evangelize the manticores and reputedly had even made some converts. He had expected Matthew to go along with him, but Matthew had refused.

This early in the day, the distant sun was still small, and the church was dim. For light, they used a jar filled with worms. They had discovered these worms living inside the beetlewood trees, gnawing tiny tunnels through the trunks. Why worms that lived inside of trees should need to give off such a blazing bright light that they needed to wrap the jar in cloth to be able to look at it at all was a mystery, but it made for a convenient source of illumination, even in the middle of the night. Kecilpenny had named them Shekinah flatworms.

"Presentations," Parris said, interrupting casual conversation. "Who's first?" He dipped his quill in an inkpot. He could have asked someone else to scribe for the meetings, of course, but he preferred to do it himself. He didn't trust anyone else to document thoroughly enough.

John Cole was the group's cartographer. He presented a map of the parts of Horizon they had so far explored, with different-colored dyes representing the beetlewood forest, the thicker jungles to the east, the foothills of the mountains to the north, and to the west, beyond the bay, a rocky incline leading up to the final, endless precipice: the Edge of the World. He urged explorers to keep better records of their travels, to add to the general understanding. There was little incentive for most of them to keep careful maps since, as long as they brought a beetle with them, they could always use its unerring sense of direction to find their way back to the beetlewood forest and home.

Tobias Huddleston, who had been a bricklayer in London, presented drawings of a predatory reptile the size of an ox that could make itself light enough to float through the air. It hunted on the western plains, using the wind to drift over the large grazing mammals that cropped the grasses there. Once in position, it plummeted, crushing its prey under its new weight. Huddleston theorized—somewhat recklessly, in Parris's opinion—that they might use some part of this reptile's body to give man the ability to fly.

Gibbs had found a toad that, unlike many Horizon animals, did not seek shelter at dusk, when the enormous sun scorched the landscape. Instead, a gland in its neck produced an oil that it spread meticulously over its whole body with its agile feet. Gibbs had extracted the oil and spread it on his own skin, reporting that it provided remarkable protection against burns and produced a cooling sensation.

Kecilpenny made a case for mapping Aristotle's four elements—Air, Water, Earth, and Fire—to the four categories of quintessence change they had so far identified. It was a traditional scholarly argument, full of symbolic reasoning and reference to ancient writings, with no experimentation or testable criteria. It was, however, decidedly Aristotelian, and raised the old argument again: Aristotle vs. atomism. Most of the Society was in Kecilpenny's camp, but a vocal minority agreed with Gibbs.

"What good is a theory that only explains half of what we see?" Kecilpenny said. "Perhaps the manticores' passing through walls can be explained with atoms, but turning invisible? Light can't be made of atoms. And what about the manticores' mind connections? Are you telling us that *thoughts* are composed of little bits of matter?"

"What if they are?" Gibbs said.

Kecilpenny rolled his eyes. "The manticores send thoughts across long distances, much farther and faster than any matter can travel."

"So can we," Gibbs said. "With the bell-boxes." They had worked out a rudimentary alphabet with patterns of rings, and though it was slow, they could now send any message at all from one box to another.

"That's not the same," Kecilpenny said.

"It's very much the same. Quintessence allows two shards of bone to be paired, regardless of how small we cut them. When the atoms in one piece are altered, the state of the atoms in the other piece changes, no matter how far apart they are. That means we can alter matter to transmit complex thought."

"In code," Kecilpenny said. "With words. It's like shouting across the room. That's not *thought*. Thought is something—"

"Different? What if it's not? What if thought is no more than the rearrangement of the atoms in your brain? Think how a manticore makes a connection with another manticore—by inserting physical material from its tail. If that material is paired with material still in its body, then what do you have? A bell-box. Possibly hundreds or thousands of bell-boxes, each as small as an atom. The arrangement of the atoms in the brain could then be transferred across those bell-boxes in a totally material way."

The church fell silent. The atomists were all nodding, but the Aristotelians were shaking their heads. Gibbs had just confirmed the main reason most of them refused to consider atomism: it was inherently atheistic. If thought was pure mechanism, that implied that the personality and the soul were mere byproducts of atoms crashing together in random ways.

If the universe was just a machine, what room did that leave for God?

"Would you deny the spiritual altogether?" Kecilpenny asked softly, voicing what many in the room were thinking.

"You don't understand," Catherine said. The silence, already uncomfortable, grew awkward. Most Society members, particularly those who came from the more exalted traditions of academia, weren't used to the idea of a woman offering her opinion in a gathering of men. Parris, however, did not correct her, and she continued. "It's not like sorting buttons in a sewing box. We don't get to argue and then decide based on who is most convincing or who shouts the loudest. Either atoms exist or they don't. The only way to find out for sure is to test it."

Parris allowed a small smile to play across his face. This experimental philosophy was new, and difficult for many traditional theorists to grasp. Learned men thought knowledge came from the books of the ancients. It didn't occur to them to test what they read. But how could the ancients have anticipated what they had never seen? Matthew and Catherine recognized this was a new world, to be studied in new ways.

"I don't understand most of what you all are saying," Huddleston said, rubbing the stubble on his face with his rough bricklayer hands. "But I understand what she said. If it's true, then it's true."

"Well spoken," a voice said. Parris looked around the room to identify the speaker, but all of the Society members were looking up at him. No, not at him—at something behind him. Parris turned around to see Christopher Sinclair. He must have entered by the doors in the back of the nave.

"Come in. Welcome," Parris said. He was surprised, but delighted. Perhaps the exalted governor was finally ready to share his discoveries and submit to the rigor of group opinion.

Sinclair walked around and sat in the pew behind Matthew and Catherine. "Carry on."

Parris waited expectantly, but no one continued the conversation. "Any new presentations?" Parris said, but again, no one volunteered. He looked at Matthew, who shook his head. Nothing new. "Governor?"

Sinclair shrugged.

"No?" He waited a moment more, but Sinclair didn't speak. "That's it, then, I suppose. Meeting over."

—+ + +—

CATHERINE watched the Society members file out, feeling irritated. She knew she should respect these older and more educated men, but sometimes their learning just seemed to keep them from accepting what they saw with their own eyes. What did it matter what Aristotle said? If he was right, then fine. But it was ridiculous to cling to what he said if it didn't match reality.

Master Sinclair leaned forward from the pew behind her and said, "I've been studying boarcats."

Catherine didn't turn around. Matthew had gone up front to talk to Father, so for the moment they were alone.

"Does the venerable Society know how boarcats mate?" Master Sinclair said.

Catherine stifled a laugh. "No," she said. "We've never seen it." A boarcat was a yellow brush pig the size of a small dog, but with claws like a tiger. She and Father had seen them frequently, but Father always insisted they keep their distance, since the claws were venomous. One thing they had discovered was that its yellow fur was due to sulfur, though what purpose that could serve they didn't know.

"I'll tell you, then. The male brings an offering to the female. It pulls the meat off a diki with its teeth and presents it to her. If she's pleased with it, she'll mate with him."

Catherine was intrigued. Dikis were fat little flightless birds with plenty of good meat. A child could catch and kill them, but they had poisonous bone ridges concealed in their feather fluff which made eating them next to impossible. "How do they avoid the spines?"

"They don't."

"But . . ."

"They slice their mouths bloody pulling off the meat. Sign their own death warrants. They drag it to the female and then die at her feet."

Catherine turned slightly so she could see his face. "I thought this was a mating behavior."

Sinclair's eyes danced with his secret. "It is. If the female is pleased with the offering, she brings him back from the dead to mate with him."

A long silence followed. Catherine watched the corners of his mouth for some sign that this was a joke.

"Back from the dead," she repeated.

Sinclair nodded once and shrugged. "You know how lethal diki poison is."

"But how . . . ?"

Sinclair shook his head. "That's all I'm willing to say."

She blew out air, annoyed. "Why tell me at all, then?"

"Because I've reproduced it. I brought a male boarcat back from the dead."

She faced forward again, but Father was still deep in conversation with Matthew. Was it possible? Father always talked about finding an answer to death, but she'd never really believed it. Though in some ways it wasn't all that different from what she'd seen the snake do on their parlor floor in London. A walking stick could hardly be said to be alive, and yet the snake's life was stored somewhere and then returned to its living body. "How did you do it?" she said.

"I'm not going to tell you. It's more complex than you even dream. But not only does it work, it's not limited." Sinclair dropped his voice dramatically. "I can bring back anything. Anyone."

Catherine's heart thudded in her chest, so hard it was difficult to speak. "You've brought back . . . ?"

"Not humans. Not yet. I don't know how much harder that will be. But it's *possible*. It will be done."

Every inch of her body tingled with the thrill of what he was saying, but she was wary. If what he was saying was true, why didn't he announce it at the meeting? "Why are you telling me?"

"Because you're the only one in this room with any sense," Sinclair said. "Your father gets it sometimes, but he's still too mired in old ways of thinking. You're too young and bright to waste your time with these amateurs."

"What do you want?"

"Your help. I want to try to bring back a human, and it's more than I can accomplish on my own. Will you help me?"

Her cheeks felt hot, and she covered them with her hands, hoping Matthew and Father didn't look her way.

"Tonight," Sinclair said. "My house."

She heard him standing up. "Wait," she said. "Is it dangerous?"

"Yes," he said. "If that stops you, you're not the girl I thought you were."

Chapter Twenty-three

CATHERINE sat in the shade of the palisade, watching Matthew use a thin saw to cut a beetlewood board precisely into one half of a dovetail joint. For a bishop's son, he'd grown remarkably good at woodworking. Since his first, poorly constructed bell-boxes, he'd watched the carpenters and asked them questions until he could copy many of their techniques.

"What was Master Sinclair saying to you?" Matthew said.

"Nothing of importance."

"Liar. I saw your face. He told you something."

"He wanted me to help him with an experiment."

"Really? Why you?"

She was annoyed. "Why not me? Just because everyone treats you like a demigod doesn't mean you're the only one who can be useful."

"I know what he's doing. He's trying to raise someone from the dead."

Catherine gaped at him. "How—"

"It's what he's been after all along, isn't it? He's not a man to waste time."

"You're just sullen because he didn't ask you."

Matthew blew the joint clear of sawdust. "Who says he didn't? You didn't say yes, did you?"

"What if I did? You're not my father."

"I know what your father would say if he knew."

"He won't know."

"Listen. Sinclair is using you. He doesn't care about you or anyone else. He flattered you and invited you secretly because he wants you to do something dangerous."

"I don't care. And don't you dare tell my father."

"He could get you killed."

"Or he could do the most amazing thing anyone's ever done! Aren't you at least a little excited? That it might be possible? He says he already brought an animal back. What if he really raises a person from the dead?"

Matthew shook his head. "It's not possible."

"Who says so?"

"My father does. I do. There's a big difference between an animal and a human being. A human being has a soul. You can't bring that back once it's gone."

"What about Lazarus? He had a soul."

"Of course. God can bring someone back, soul and all. But people can't do it."

"How do you *know*? Just because your father says it, that makes it so?"

"Don't mock my father."

"I'm not. I'm mocking you."

Matthew flushed. "You think there won't be consequences if he tries to turn back death? It's a spiritual problem, not a physical one."

"Then it shouldn't hurt to try."

Matthew fitted the wood he'd been working on into another piece, completing the third side of a box. "What if he does bring a man back, but the man has no soul? What would that be like?"

"What if he succeeds? Think, Matthew! What if, after someone died, we could *bring them back again?*" It irritated her that he kept working on his box instead of making eye contact. She looked a little closer. "What are you making, anyway?"

"A box."

"It's too big if you just want to trap a beetle."

"True."

She tried to think of what other creature would be the right size. "I give up."

"It's to trap a void."

She raised her eyebrows.

"It's about time we tried it," he said, defensive. "We can't stay ignorant forever."

"And you're lecturing me about risk?"

"We think the beetlewood might contain it. Since the creatures that pass through solids probably do so by sliding atoms around each other through the void, and since beetlewood stops them from doing it, it stands to reason—"

"Who is 'we'? You and Sinclair?"

Matthew had the grace to look abashed. "It was his idea. He suggested it to me as a line of research."

"Let me understand. Sinclair wants you to study probably the most dangerous thing we've encountered so far, something that even terrified him by my father's account. And you think he's using *me*?"

"It's not reckless. He's planning a trip to the Edge. We'll test it there, just in case, so we can hurl it over if it grows too large."

"What if you can't?"

"There's always some risk. We all risked our lives just to come here. I think we're taking responsible precautions."

"I see. It's perfectly understandable for him to consult *you*. But if it's me he includes in a project . . ." Her eyes stung, and she was embarrassed to feel them welling up with tears. "You're all the same."

"What are you talking about?"

"Nothing, Dr. Marcheford, sir. I'll just sit and learn at your feet." She brushed the tears away. "When did you get so exalted?"

"You asked me what I'm making, and I told you. I wasn't bragging about it."

She could have screamed. "I taught you how to think this way. You were only interested in quintessence in the first place because of me."

"I know it. So what?"

"So now you treat me like I'm not bright enough to understand it."

"I never said that."

"But you think it. Everybody does. They pat me on the head and expect me to embroider. You, they worship."

"That's not true."

"It is."

"You have to give them a chance to get used to you. You're different. People don't expect important thinking from . . ."

"From a woman?"

He shrugged.

"Sinclair doesn't belittle me," she said. "If the Society really values everyone's input, like they say, why does Sinclair appreciate me more than they do?"

"Don't do it, Catherine. You don't want to play with life and death."

"I don't? Why not? Because you say so?"

"What if he succeeds, as you say? Do you really want someone to have power over who stays dead and who comes back to life? The whole world would go to war for that power. Even if it *is* possible, we're better off without it."

"My brother isn't better off without it."

"Your brother is with God. He *is* better off."

Catherine felt the blood rush to her face. Matthew did it; her father did it; all the men in the Society did it. They made pronouncements. Do this. Don't do that. This is the way things are. They thought themselves so open to new ideas, but in some ways they were as blind and prejudiced as the inquisitors they'd left England to escape.

Only one person had never treated her that way, not from the first time she'd seen him showing magic tricks in an English parlor. Only they hadn't been tricks at all. They were real.

"If it's so much better to be dead," she said, "why don't you throw yourself off the Edge and be done with it?"

✛✛✛

SINCLAIR'S house was the largest in the settlement, though only he and Maasha Kaatra lived there. He referred to it as the governor's mansion, but Catherine thought that was more to remind everyone that he was governor than because he anticipated passing it down to future officeholders. It was set on a small hump of land, making it higher than all the buildings in the colony but the church.

Less than half of the mansion was devoted to living quarters; the rest was for his laboratory. All his alchemical supplies from the ship had been moved here, and he insisted that any new animal or plant discovered by anyone be brought first to him. It infuriated Father. Things sometimes disappeared into Sinclair's mansion before anyone else had been permitted to examine them.

But Catherine was going inside. She would see all the things Sinclair had been hiding and report back to the Society. Father would forgive her. Eventually.

The front door was made of thick beetlewood and fastened with an elaborate series of locks and chains. Sinclair beckoned her through, then closed it and slid home a heavy bolt.

At the sound of the bolt, a shiver of foreboding slid through her, but she shook it off. Sinclair had no reason to hurt her. This was her chance to contribute to something on her own, out of Father and Matthew's shadows. They never let her handle venomous animals or get near caustic fluids, never mind how much they did so themselves. They treated her as if she were fragile, when she'd shown time and again how strong she could be. Well, this time they could be the ones standing in the back and taking notes.

Sinclair led her through the parlor and down a hallway to a doorway in the back that led to his laboratory. Maasha Kaatra stood there, waiting for them, and followed them into the room. She heard chatterings and growls and other, less recognizable sounds before she even entered the room, but when she passed the threshold, the sounds increased tenfold. Beasts of all color and shape leaped or fluttered or shook the bars of their cages, which were lined up on tables and sitting on the floor. A tiny bird, smaller than a mouse, made an incredible screeching racket by scraping its claws on its silver beak, while a striped toad belched sooty smoke as if it had swallowed an oil lamp. Catherine gaped at them, astonished. Most of them she recognized, but she had no idea Sinclair was keeping such a bestiary. What was he doing with them all? How could he possibly study them all by himself? About once a week, she or Matthew came out with a new invention that somehow improved the lives of the settlers, and other interested dabblers had made discoveries, too. Sinclair had produced nothing. At least nothing he'd seen fit to share.

Sinclair walked straight through the room, ignoring the animals. From a shelf in a dark corner, he lifted a wooden box. On the far side of the room stood another door, this one banded with iron and a heavier lock. The iron wouldn't keep out a manticore; this door was meant to exclude other humans. He reached under his doublet and pulled a delicate and complex key from around his neck. He fitted it into the lock and rotated it three times. The door swung open.

The room was littered with experimental detritus: bones, horns, claws, feathers, beaks, skins, furs, carcasses or parts of them swimming in spirits, piles of petals and herbs, mortars and pestles, rows of jars with powders, tinctures, extracts, and solutions of all colors, the carapaces of beetles, husks left by molting firewasps, and a pyramid of tiny marmoset skulls. A jar of Shekinah flatworms illuminated a pale corpse lying on a table set against one wall. Catherine recognized John Mason, a man who had died by the river that morning when he picked up an acid salamander.

Sinclair set the wooden box on the table. From inside, he cautiously lifted two severed and dried paws with needle-sharp claws. Catherine knew those claws had enough venom to kill him before he could take his next breath. She moved a little closer, not wanting to miss anything.

Sinclair lifted a tiny blue bottle and showed it to Catherine. "You'll want this."

"What is it?"

"The tears of an animal called a seer skink. Put it a drop in each eye, like this." He mimed how to do it, and she followed his lead. She had already applied it to her second eye when the first one began to burn. Soon both eyes blazed with intense pain. She screamed and clawed at them. He had blinded her. He'd given her acid for her eyes, and like an idiot, she'd poured it in.

"Stings a bit," Sinclair said. "It'll pass."

Just that quickly, she blinked back tears, and the pain was gone. "You could have warned me," she said, and then she stopped talking and stared. The room had come alive.

Tiny networks of light crisscrossed through the air, not randomly, but connecting various items of bone and beak and skin. An iridescent bird sat perched on the table where she was certain one had not been before. As she watched, it flapped its wings, then launched itself up and out of the room through the ceiling. Bright insects buzzed to and fro. Far from being dazzled by all the light, she felt like the world had grown suddenly clear, as if the rest of her life up to this point had been viewed through a veil.

She lifted a hand and reached for a cord of light, but her hand passed through without breaking it or casting a shadow. A faint filigree of light curled intricately under Sinclair's and Maasha Kaatra's skin, illuminating them, thicker in the trunk and branching out toward their fingers and toes. She lifted an arm and saw the same effect in herself, and thought: *Blood.* Specks of quintessence were flowing in their blood, healing any injury.

"That bird," she said. "The one that flew away. It's invisible, isn't it?"

"Yes," Sinclair said. "Both invisible and insubstantial. There are some species that stay that way most of the time, perhaps even all the time. Under normal circumstances, their lives would never intersect our own."

Catherine spun, trying to take in everything. This was literally a new world, separate and yet parallel to her own.

"What do all the connections mean?"

"They mark a quintessence link. When a material is infused with quintessence, then separated into two . . . Here. Watch."

Sinclair took a tiny bone from a shelf. She didn't think it was an iron-fish bone, but she couldn't identify it. Marmoset, perhaps? He snapped the bone in half. Light flowed from the break like molten metal, and as he pulled the pieces away from each other, a new strand pulled out between them. He tossed one bone half to her, and she caught it awkwardly. The strand stretched to connect the two pieces across the room.

"Just like the bell-boxes," she said.

He nodded.

"Just like the manticore bond, too," she said. "The atoms are connected through quintessence. That's what Gibbs was saying to the Society, but most of them didn't believe it."

"People are slow to change," Sinclair said. "Only a few of us can see past the stories to the way things really are." He threw the bone aside. Unlatching a cage with two birds inside, he grasped one of them gently and drew it out. Even the bird had fine veins of glowing light moving through its body. Its head bobbed in quick jerks, but its wings were entirely enclosed in his hand. "You must see how it works," Sinclair said, "so you know how to help."

Catherine realized what he was going to do a moment before he did it. "Don't!" she said, but Sinclair closed his other hand over the bird's head and gave it a swift twist. When he removed his hand, the head hung limp, and the glowing veins were dark.

Solemnly, he laid the dead bird on the floor. "First," Sinclair said, "we need a surrogate to stand for his life."

He lifted the other bird from the cage and placed it in Catherine's hands. "What are you going to do?" she asked, but Sinclair put his finger to his lips.

He strapped the dried boarcat paws under his own hands with loops of string, the three claws of each paw attached separately to three of his fingers. Gently, as if playing a lute, Sinclair plucked at one of the strands of quintessence leading out of the living bird. The strand moved at his touch and *bent*, as if a light beam were a material thing.

"A boarcat's claw is a remarkable tool," he said. "And the boarcat female knows how to use it."

"Does she have tears like the seer skink?"

"Not that I know of. She must sense the quintessence in some other way."

Quickly, like a girl playing finger games with loops of yarn, Sinclair wrapped the strand through his fingers and stretched it toward the dead bird. He wrapped it around the bird's chest and tied it tight. Its chest began to rise and fall in time with the living bird. A second strand tied heart to heart, and light once again pulsed through glowing veins. A third tied head to head, and the bird sprang to its feet. Its head bobbed and twitched from side to side, in exact mirror imitation of the one in Catherine's hands.

"It's a puppet," Catherine said.

"True," Sinclair said. "It's animated, but not truly alive, not its own creature. The last step is to recapture its spirit."

Catherine looked up, half expecting to see a ghostly bird flying around the room. "How can you retrieve a spirit?"

"From the place spirits go when they depart. From the void."

She hadn't seen a void, but she shivered anyway. "I thought it was dangerous," she said. "Father said it almost killed you the last time."

He grinned like a cat. "Not the last time. Just the first time. I've reproduced them since then."

"But that's why you wanted Matthew to make those boxes, wasn't it?"

"Your young friend is good at making things. Such a box will be useful, but I can't wait for him."

Sinclair opened a metal tin and lifted out a quintessence pearl. Nearly all animals on Horizon had them somewhere in their bodies, so it had not been hard to replenish the supply they had collected from the ironfish. He set a dish onto a metal stand that held it at the same height as the table and poured in a few drops of vitriol. "This is the reason for the sulfur in the boarcat's fur," Sinclair said. "She runs her claws through it and collects enough to create a small void." He stood back and dropped in the pearl.

The pearl's glow vanished, as did the pearl itself, leaving a tiny black sphere in the dish. The sphere began to grow.

As it did, a faint new strand appeared, passing from the dead bird into the void, like a rope stretching out of sight down an endless well. As the void grew, the strand grew a little brighter. "This is the difficult part," Sinclair said. "This is the reason I will need your help."

Maasha Kaatra approached holding two flat planks of beetlewood. He already seemed to know what to do. When the void grew larger than his fist, he began to push it back with the beetlewood planks. It worked; apparently the void was unable to grow beyond the beetlewood. If he held the planks in one place, however, the void would bulge, becoming egg-shaped, and he would have to move them to stop its growth in that direction.

As Maasha Kaatra controlled the void's growth, Sinclair began to manipulate the strand that led into it from the dead bird. He pulled more and more of it toward him out of the void, looping it around the boarcat claws, around the bird's body, and around the strand that led to the living bird.

"Every creature has an anchor that ties its soul to its body," Sinclair said. "In death, that anchor is lost to the void. If I simply pulled the spirit back into the bird's body, it would flee back to the void as soon as I released it. That's why we need a surrogate—a living bird to give its anchor in place of the dead one's. For them both to live, the anchor must be shared between them."

Catherine felt a tug on the living bird as the strands were entangled. The strand from the void grew thin and taut, and Sinclair strained to wrap it tighter. At the other end of that strand must be the bird's lost spirit.

"Don't let it go, now," Sinclair warned.

The strand began to thrum like a lute string. Vibrations oscillated back and forth along its length, growing larger and brighter. The void seemed to open more quickly, and Maasha Kaatra was hard-pressed to keep it under control. He moved with lightning speed and grace, but every time he pushed it back in one place, the darkness leaped out in another, as if the world were a fabric tearing away from a hole. The living bird in her hand began to vibrate, too, and Catherine had to plant her feet and lean back to keep it from pulling out of her hand.

Finally, with a blinding flash, the end of the strand licked up out of the void and into the dead bird. Like a tug-of-war when one side lets go of the rope, Sinclair, the dead bird, and Catherine flew backward. The whole room, in fact, seemed to leap in a sudden tremor. Maasha Kaatra lifted his planks like two swords and clapped them together right through the center of the void. The void disappeared with a pop.

In the silence, Catherine heard a flutter. The dead bird hopped and flapped its wings. Afraid she had killed the one she held, she opened her hands, but that bird was safe as well. Before they could fly, Sinclair scooped them both up and brought them back to their cage. They fluttered and bobbed and pecked, as independently bright and alive as they had ever been.

Catherine could hardly breathe. She knew what would happen, had known the whole time, but somehow hadn't believed it. She had seen this bird limp and dead, and now it lived. Her gaze ran from the birds to the corpse of John Mason, and a chill ran down her back. Now that she really knew it could be done, it terrified her. Part of her was eager to start; the other part wanted to run home and cower in her bed.

"What do you want me to do?" she said.

"Maasha Kaatra will be the surrogate this time. I need you to control the void."

"What if I can't?"

"You saw how it was done. Just push it back wherever it grows too large."

"I don't know . . . ," she began, but the look he gave her stopped her short. She could almost hear his thoughts—that he should have known better than to ask a girl. He was the only man who trusted her to do something dangerous and hard, and here she was about to give up the chance.

"I'll do it." She snatched the planks from his outstretched hand. "You do your part. Don't worry about me."

Sinclair put a hand on Maasha Kaatra's shoulder. "Are you ready?"

His friend nodded. "Let's begin."

They began. Maasha Kaatra and Sinclair lifted John Mason's corpse and set it on the floor. Maasha Kaatra lay down next to it with his muscular arms folded across his chest in imitation. This time, Sinclair wrapped glowing strands around him instead, chest to chest, heart to heart, head to head. The corpse breathed, glowed, and finally moved, mirroring Maasha Kaatra's arms and legs like a marionette on strings.

Then it was her turn. Sinclair produced a second void, and she began to control it, awkwardly at first, then with growing confidence. It really wasn't that difficult. Another glowing strand ran from inside the void to Mason's body, and Sinclair began the process of teasing it out, wrapping more and more of its length around the corpse, and tangling it with the strand connecting the corpse to Maasha Kaatra.

Soon he was laboring with the effort, struggling to wrap each length as if hoisting a mainsail by himself with a hundred feet of rope. The void began to grow faster. It became more mutable, too, changing its shape more rapidly in response to her attempts to push it back. She tired, and the emptiness began to fill her vision. It was a hole in the world that constantly sucked more and more into itself. She felt like she was trying to patch the hole by pushing matter over it, but it kept tearing larger. It was bigger now than it had been, almost blocking her view of the rest of the room, and she began to beat at it frantically.

Maasha Kaatra had closed it completely by slapping the beetlewood planks together across the center. "I can't control it," she said. "I'm going to shut it down."

"No," Sinclair said. "I'm almost done."

The oscillating began. Vibrations thrummed back and forth from Mason into the endless depths of the void and back again. The void grew larger yet, forcing Catherine to take a step back. "I can't wait," she said, and slapped the planks together. But it was too late. She could no longer reach the center. Her slap simply pushed it back, but didn't close it.

Sinclair saw. "Run!" he said.

She stumbled backward, dropping the wood. Sinclair abandoned the boarcat paws. Maasha Kaatra clambered to his feet and stood transfixed by the glowing vibrations, not seeming to hear. "Girls?" he said. "My girls!"

Catherine tugged at his arm. "Get back!"

"They're in there," he said. "I can reach them."

"No!"

His gaze turned to her and he gripped her wrist painfully. "Murderer," he said in a terrible voice. "You killed them."

She tried to pull away, but he was too strong. "Maasha Kaatra!" she shouted. "It's me, Catherine!" The void was enveloping them. She could see nothing in its darkness. "Let me go!"

A gurgling cry came from the floor, and the corpse of John Mason struggled to rise, wrapped in glowing cords, fresh blood running from his open mouth. Catherine screamed and pulled again, this time yanking her wrist out of Maasha Kaatra's grasp. The vibrating strand connecting Mason to the void blazed like the evening sun, and then broke.

To Catherine, it felt like the floor flew into the air to strike her face. Instead of just throwing her backward, as with the bird, the whole room lurched and shook. She looked up from the floor in time to see Maasha Kaatra fall backward like a tower toppling. Where he should have struck the floor, the void was there, and he kept falling, tumbling farther and farther, like a rock into a bottomless well.

The void collapsed with a pop. Catherine lay still, afraid to move. Sinclair, too, stood rooted in place, whispering the word "no" over and over. He didn't seem to see her.

On the floor, the corpse of John Mason lay still, composed entirely of crumbling sand.

Chapter Twenty-four

THE island ended in a sheer cliff. The forest gave way to scrub and dirt, which in turn gave way to bare rock, which dropped off suddenly, straight down into blackness. The cliff continued down for miles, beyond what the eye could see, and no stone thrown over the Edge ever hit bottom, no more than did the torrents of ocean that rushed over it to the north and south.

On the side of this cliff, unseen by any human, a colony of cliff dippers flocked out of their roosts and began to hunt for food. The dippers had long necks and bills like cranes, but with a glaring difference: their beaks were on sideways, opening to the left and right instead of up and down. As they flew along the cliff face, they bent their sinuous necks and plunged one side of their beaks into the solid rock, skimming as if through water. Their prey was a fat beetle larva that curled itself inside the rock to await its metamorphosis. Each time a dipper touched one, it snapped its beak shut in lightning reflex, dragging the food out of the rock, and swallowed it whole.

Then the impossible happened. The cliff betrayed the dippers. A section of rock they had hunted for countless generations suddenly hardened, trapping several beaks inside. Feeling the sudden resistance and interpreting it as food, the dippers snapped their beaks shut, slamming their bodies into the cliff. One beak broke off, freeing its owner, but the others screeched and scrabbled and flapped their wings, unable to move. The offending section of rock rumbled and shook and then sheared away from the cliff face, slowly at first, then with gathering speed, dragging the screaming birds into the abyss. Their fellows flew after them, crying their confusion, but they couldn't keep up with the falling rock, nor reach the top again if they flew too low. They beat their wings, rising with the air currents, and returned to their nests.

⊰╼╋╾⊱

EVERYONE felt the earthquake, though no one else knew what had caused it. Catherine avoided them as she made her way back through the streets. There was no damage to any of the buildings that she could see, but then, what could damage buildings made of diamond? She reached her own home without having to talk to anyone, and was relieved to find that Matthew was not there, as he so often was these days. She didn't want to face him and his smug rightness. She was shaken and afraid. It had all gone so wrong. Her confidence that morning, that they could experiment with such deep and violent powers without risk, seemed so stupid now.

She ran to her bedchamber, grateful not to meet Father, either, who was probably out talking about the earthquake and what it meant. She was alone.

It was her fault. Controlling the void had been her job, and clearly that had failed. Sinclair had said nothing to her, just sat slumped dumbly on the floor while she slipped out. Perhaps she should have stayed and made sure he was all right, but at that moment all she could think about was escaping that terrible room.

The thought of the horrible, yawning void and Maasha Kaatra's body tumbling into its depths made her hands tremble, and she clasped them together. If he hadn't released her wrist, he might have dragged her down with him into the nothingness. She clutched her wooden bedframe, desperate to feel solid matter. Reality seemed fragile, nothing more than a colorful mural painted on a thin sheet of glass. They thought they knew so much about quintessence, but in truth they knew nothing at all. They were living in a world vastly beyond their comprehension and meddling with elemental powers more dangerous than they had ever imagined.

Voices whispered through her mind, voices she'd heard all her life, even when they hadn't been spoken aloud: *She's only a girl. What do you expect? Leave the important work to men. The thing a girl needs most is a man to take care of her.*

Catherine buried her face in her bed, overwhelmed with grief for her brother. She needed Peter now. She needed someone who would enfold her in his arms and comfort her without condemnation. Since he had left, nothing had been right. And where was he now? In the bliss and joy of heaven, not needing or thinking of her at all? Or spinning helplessly like Maasha Kaatra in an endless, tumbling void?

"Catherine?" It was Father, peering in at the door.

"Go away."

"I know what happened. At least, I know what you tried. Matthew told me."

"He's a liar, then."

"He saw you come out alone, and he was worried. He found me, and we went in and found Sinclair."

Something about the way he said it made her look up.

"No, he's alive. Furious to find us there, in fact. He wouldn't tell us any details."

So this was why he was here. Not to comfort her. To find out what she knew. It made her angry, though she had not wanted his comfort a moment earlier. "And you expect me to explain it?"

He sighed, that deep sigh he had used at home whenever he tried to talk to Mother. "When you're up to the task."

"Why wouldn't I be up to the task?" she said, louder than she'd meant to. "I'll tell you what happened. Nothing. We tried to bring a man back from the dead! " Laughter spilled out of her throat. "It didn't work. He's still dead. And not only that, Maasha Kaatra . . ." Hating herself, she burst into tears again, but when Father tried to hold her, she fought him off. "I'm fine! Leave me alone!"

"Is he dead?"

Mutely, she nodded.

"His body?"

"Gone."

Father walked away, then turned and stood hesitantly at the door. "We'll need to know more. When you're ready."

"Here." Catherine plunged her hand into the pocket of her gown and pulled out a tiny bottle of blue liquid. "This might help."

"What is it?"

She averted her gaze. "A way to see."

✦✦✦✦

THE bottle was small and only half full. Parris used a brush to transfer a blue drop onto a seashell, the smooth inner surface making an ideal viewing background. He pushed the drop around, noting its color and consistency. Matthew peered over his shoulder at it.

From a crowded shelf, Parris drew a thick book of rough paper, bound in dried skin. It was the Horizon version of the anatomical notes he had kept so scrupulously in England: an illustrated journal of the flora and fauna of the island he'd been adding to since they'd arrived. He leafed through the pages carefully, looking for a match to what he saw on the shell. It could be an alchemical mixture, of course, not even indigenous to Horizon, but somehow Parris didn't think so. Most of what they had discovered uses for had come straight from Horizon animals. Then he found it: a picture of a black lizard clinging to the side of a tree, surrounded by notes and measurements from its dissection in a small, neat hand.

"Of course," Parris said. "A seer skink. That clever fool."

"What is it?" Matthew said.

"It's a lizard with prominent blue tear glands around its eyes. Its prey is the Hades helmet fly, which can turn invisible, but the skink seems to find it by sight even so. Somehow it can see what the rest of us can't. Sinclair must have found out how."

Matthew picked up the bottle. "There's not much left."

"He must have poured it in his eyes." Parris shook his head, amazed. "Trust Sinclair to take such a risk."

"So this might allow us to see the manticores, even when they don't want to be seen," Matthew said.

"Perhaps. We don't know that it worked."

"You said Catherine seemed to think so."

"True. We should wait and see what she has to say."

"Why? Do you think it's dangerous?"

"Who knows? That's the point. How do you know you won't wake up blind tomorrow? Sinclair is reckless. He doesn't test, he doesn't communicate; he just risks everything to blaze ahead." The thought of whom Sinclair had risked this time made a hot flush of anger rise to his face. "He's a dangerous fool."

"Manticores!" The cry went out from one of the posted lookouts and was echoed through the settlement. "Manticores!"

Parris snatched the bottle and ran outside, Matthew at his heels.

The palisade was about twice the height of a man, but constructed with platforms at regular intervals to allow men to see over the side. Parris climbed one of the platforms and looked over to see a large crowd of gray manticores, as many as fifty, more than he'd ever seen in one place before. The heavy palisade gates were still wide open. The posted sentries on the wall and in the forest had given no warning. Apparently the grays had passed invisibly through the trees, only showing themselves when it was too late. They poured into the settlement, gathering in the open square, showing no sign of aggression beyond their sheer numbers.

"We'll need Catherine," Parris shouted to Matthew over the din. "Go see if she'll come." As Matthew ran to get her, Parris glared at the governor's mansion. Would Sinclair come out and deal with this problem? Or would he hide inside, alone with his failure, and leave them on their own?

Parris fingered the blue bottle in his hand. He remembered too well the scattering of bones in the church that had been all that was left of the first settlement. What exactly had happened they might never know, but if this crowd of manticores turned invisible and attacked, they wouldn't be able to stop them. Perhaps it was time for a little calculated risk, after all.

He unstoppered the bottle and, with his finger covering the opening, turned it upside down and then back again, so a small circle of blue appeared on his finger. Hesitating only briefly, he opened his right eye wide and spread the liquid inside. He blinked rapidly, allowing it to coat his eye evenly. Seconds later, it began to burn. Crying out, he staggered back and wiped futilely. It felt like his eye was being scoured away. Stupid! He didn't even know if Sinclair used it in this form; he might dilute it with water or oil. If it blinded him, it was his own fault.

The pain stopped. He looked up. Despite the bright sunlight, he could see the stars, and from them a sparkling rain falling to earth. All the physical objects around him—at least those indigenous to Horizon—became translucent, scattering multicolored light onto the ground. Each of the people around him, and each of the manticores, was the nexus of a fine web of bright strands, difficult to see even now. Lines emanated from him, as well, and as he lifted his hands and moved and turned, the threads pulled taut or loose, but never twisted or tangled. They led into the distance in every direction, away through the forest, apparently endless.

He spun, astonished, the wonder of this sight taking his attention from the danger of the situation. Sinclair had discovered this, and yet not told them? This was more than just seeing invisible creatures. It was an invisible world. He had no doubt he was seeing the connection between the quintessence of the stars and life on earth, the source of all this island's magic.

Oswyn Tate appeared at his shoulder, his matchlock rifle ready. "Are you all right, my lord?"

"Fine," Parris said. "Any sign of the governor?"

Tate pointed. Sinclair emerged from his house and walked toward the crowd of manticores. He had cleaned up and was wearing his admiral's hat. The manticores surrounded him, gesticulating.

Tate raised his gun. "You can't do much good with that," Parris reminded him.

"I just want to be ready."

"Here," Parris said, handing him the bottle of skink tears. "This is what you need to be ready."

Tate took it, suspicious. "What is it?"

"Dab a little in your eye and you'll be able to see them, even if they turn invisible."

Tate's eyebrows shot up. He opened the bottle.

"Just a drop," Parris said. "And it hurts like the devil."

Tate did, and once the pain had passed, stared around in wonder. He shook the bottle. "Do you have any more?"

"That's it. Pass it around to your men, quietly. Stretch it as far as you can. Then be ready."

"For what?"

"For whatever happens."

Three of the largest manticores wore human clothes. Parris suspected that size was a sign of hierarchy among them, and that those with higher rank were granted the honor of wearing the clothes. Such a cultural marker could conceivably indicate an admiration for humans and a desire to mimic them, but Parris thought it was actually the opposite, that the wearing of clothes was like wearing the skin of an animal one had slain, a sign of the wearer's bravery and willingness to kill a human for his treasures.

The largest of the three attempted to communicate with Sinclair, but it was not going well. Sinclair's crude sign language was baffling even to Parris, and he grew more and more frustrated as communication failed. Where was Catherine?

One of the smaller manticores jumped onto Sinclair in a quick movement. It used its hooked feet to pinion Sinclair's arms and swung itself over his head, piercing his back with one of its pincered front paws. Frustrated with the failure of language, the manticore was going to get information the way the manticore on the *Western Star* had done it: directly. Sinclair fell to his knees. The colonists watching from the platforms shouted in alarm. Tate raised his weapon.

But to Parris's astonishment, the largest manticore didn't let it continue. He struck the smaller manticore with his own hooked feet, a sharp slash that must at least have caused pain, if not serious injury. The smaller manticore squealed and fell to the ground, releasing Sinclair. It flattened itself and backed away from the larger one in what could only have been a display of obeisance.

Why? Parris knew only too well how effective that direct method of communication could be, to the point of fusing minds and memories as one. Why did the larger manticore not want the younger one to use it? Out of respect to Sinclair? Out of a desire for a willing exchange of information, not a forced one? Or perhaps something entirely different, like disgust that a ritual important to the life of their clan would be used on a human being? Perhaps the gray manticores were not as open to sharing their minds with humans as Chichirico had been.

Matthew returned with Catherine. Her face was drawn and her eyes red. She walked under the platform and into the crowd of manticores. A ripple spread through them and their ranks parted to give her room. She spoke and signed rapidly with them, with a fluency born of her bond with Chichirico.

Once again, Tate joined Parris on the platform. "We're ready," he said. "They won't take us by surprise, not this time."

"Don't do anything rash. We don't want to provoke them."

"Don't worry," Tate said. "I don't want to die. But I don't trust these creatures. If they attack, I'm not waiting for orders."

Catherine's young voice carried through the still air. "They're angry about the earthquake."

"Were their homes destroyed? Do they need our help?" Sinclair said.

Catherine made more manticore speech accompanied by sinuous movements with arms and fingers. The movements were bizarrely alien the way she made them, but Parris had no doubt they carried more meaning than the stilted signs he used when trying to speak with them.

"They say . . . I'm not sure I understand them. They say the"—she repeated an unintelligible manticore word—"is gone forever."

"Tell them we're sorry for their loss," Sinclair said.

"They say an apology is not enough. They say . . ."

"What?"

"They say we must leave the island."

Parris, watching from the platform, felt a chill go down his spine.

"Excuse me?" Sinclair laughed loudly and unconvincingly. "Is this a joke? Are they trying to start a war? No—don't ask them that. How could an earthquake be our fault?" His voice caught a bit at this last sentence, and Parris feared he knew why. Though Catherine had not yet explained the details, *something* had happened in Sinclair's house, something none of them fully understood, and the earthquake could hardly be a coincidence.

Sinclair's face twisted with scorn. "This is how these natives always are. Blaming gods or spirits or strangers whenever anything goes wrong. I've seen it before. I was at a Moluccan village when the natives—friendly up until that moment—blamed a freak storm on our presence there. They swam to the ship while we were asleep and set fire to the sails. Savages." He pointed at the manticores as he spoke, though they couldn't understand him. At least, Parris hoped they couldn't.

"They're angry," Catherine said. "Don't they have a right to be?"

Sinclair's face turned cold. "Tell them to leave our territory."

Catherine relayed the message. A moment later, the gathered colonists gasped and screamed. It took a moment for Parris to realize what had happened: the crowd of manticores had all disappeared at the same instant. With skink tears in his eyes, Parris could still see them, but no one else could.

Or almost no one. Beside him, Tate rose with his matchlock in hand. The manticores ran in every direction except the exit. They weaved through the crowd, ran through walls, leaped into homes. There was no way to know their intentions, but they certainly weren't leaving.

Tate blew calmly on the match, the slow-burning hemp rope soaked in saltpeter, to keep it burning. He dashed powder into the pan and brought the gun to his shoulder. Not that it would do any good. But surely Tate knew that, too. At the last moment, it occurred to Parris that maybe Tate knew something he didn't.

Tate aimed and pulled the mechanism that touched match to powder. The gun erupted in Parris's ear. Across the clearing, there was a flash of fur, and a manticore went down with a hole in its chest.

Parris gaped. He turned to Tate and saw his satisfied grin, and only then realized his mistake. "No!" he shouted.

"I thought that might work," Tate said. "Dip each bullet in a little beetlewood wax, and they punch right through."

Parris had underestimated him. It wasn't only the Society that could make inventions, and Tate was no fool.

At his opening volley, Tate's men began to fire from platforms around the periphery of the clearing, and gray manticores began to fall dead. The soldiers were somewhat hampered by the presence of the human colonists, but the colonists had run for the buildings in panic as soon as the manticores vanished, and clear manticore targets were plentiful.

Tate dropped to one knee and poured more powder into his matchlock with a steady hand.

"Stop this," Parris said. "Stand your men down."

Tate stuffed another metal ball and wadding into the barrel and drove it home with the ramrod. "You gave us that blue bottle just in time, my lord. Now let us do our jobs."

"So you could watch them! Not so you could kill them!"

"Better them than us."

A manticore scrambled up their platform before Parris could shout a warning. Tate swung the butt of his matchlock at it, but the wooden stock passed right through the creature's chest. He turned the weapon to fire at close range, but a prehensile tail whipped up around the barrel, pulling it down.

Parris kicked futilely at the attacker. It wrapped a different tail around his neck and threw him easily to the side, but the moment of distraction was enough: Tate raised the matchlock and the manticore's body exploded in red.

Breathing hard, Parris lay still and peered over at the clearing, now wreathed in gunpowder smoke. He was surprised to see the manticores fleeing out of the gate and escaping into the forest. The manticores had no guns, of course, but they were quick, armed with killing claws, and, to most of the colonists, invisible. They could pass in and out of buildings at will. Surely the resistance of Tate and his men hadn't been enough to defeat them.

If the manticores had chosen to, they could probably have killed them all, just with the numbers they had today. Tate thought he was defending the colony from an apparent attack, and perhaps he was. Certainly their invisible infiltration had seemed aggressive, but who knew what they would have done? Perhaps only steal more trinkets and articles of clothing. They understood so little about these creatures. Now they had fired the first shot of a war that could only end in grief.

Parris had seen through a manticore's eyes. He knew there were hundreds, if not thousands more of them living and traveling through the forests and rivers and mountain gorges of this vast island. If it came to war against that vast population, there would be no help for them. They would die.

⊷┿┿⊶

THEY closed the gates behind the manticores, but Parris couldn't help wondering how many might remain behind, invisible, to spy or kill or steal. He and the soldiers would have to search every building before their special sight wore off. And they would need more skink tears. A lot more.

The colonists cheered and shouted and clapped the soldiers on the back, as if this were a great victory instead of a disaster. Parris caught one look at the scowl on Sinclair's face and knew he wasn't the only one who saw the truth. Parris approached, Tate strutting behind him like a conquering hero with his matchlock on his shoulder.

Sinclair shook with rage. "Mr. Parris. Mr. Tate. You are under arrest for assault and murder on friends of this colony."

Parris and Tate reacted together. "What?"

"I'm not part of this," Parris said. "I told him not to shoot."

"And how did he and his men see their invisible targets?"

Parris's mouth dropped open. "I . . ."

"You are both relieved of all authority and freedom and will be kept in chains until your trial."

"I gave it to them so they could watch!" Parris said. "Not to kill!"

"Take them away," Sinclair said, but no one moved. It was Tate's soldiers who carried out Sinclair's authority in the colony, and here was Tate himself, under arrest for a crime they had all participated in. Despite his horror at being wrapped up in it, Parris had to admire the pure power of Sinclair's personality and his total expectation of obedience. For a moment he thought Tate would challenge him, would refuse to submit and command his soldiers' loyalty. Instead, Tate took the matchlock off his shoulder and handed it to his second-in-command with dignity.

Parris tried to catch Sinclair's eye. "I swear to you, I was not a part of this."

"Then you're simply a fool," Sinclair said. "Why do think I kept the discovery of the skink tears to myself? Out of greed?"

"No—"

"So I could *protect the knowledge*!" The veins on Sinclair's head throbbed and his eyes were wild. "So that fools with guns couldn't start wars that we can't win. You and your little *Society*, you sit around praising your free exchange of ideas, and what's the first thing you do when you get your hands on a secret? You give it to the very people who will do the worst possible thing with it!"

Parris felt his own anger rising. "And why were the manticores here in the first place? Because you couldn't resist playing with powers you don't understand! Instead of taking precautions, instead of writing things down and sharing them piece by piece, you rush into a dangerous experiment that kills a man. And you call Tate rash for firing his gun? You sat in that house and fired a larger weapon with less understanding of the implications. Somehow, they knew what you did. That's why they came. The problem is, *we* don't know what you did."

"Enough!"

"If you want to keep control of this colony, you'll have to include all of us. No secret experiments, no hidden knowledge. This isn't your private expedition anymore. We're all here together, and we have to know everything if we're going to survive."

Sinclair's mouth twisted in a sneer. "You're just angry that your own daughter took my side."

Parris gasped at the injustice of this. "And what if it had been Catherine who died? Would you still dare stand there and tell me you did the right thing?"

Sinclair moved closer, until Parris could see the wild anguish in his eyes—not just anger, but something approaching madness.

"It's why we came," Sinclair said, his voice shaking. "The secret of life. It's all that matters."

Parris looked around the clearing at the people watching: colonists, sailors, Tate's soldiers, members of the Society. Intelligent men, strong men in their way, but could any lead them through this storm the way Sinclair had led them across the ocean? He didn't think so. He knew he couldn't do it. If Sinclair crumbled, they had no hope.

Parris took a last step toward Sinclair, bringing them face-to-face. He placed both hands on Sinclair's shoulders and gripped them. Tate's soldiers stood transfixed; no one moved to intervene. "We need you," Parris said. "And you need us."

"We were so *close*."

"Right now we need to concentrate on staying alive. Those manticores will be back. Lead us."

Sinclair nodded. He looked at Tate, still standing by his second-in-command. "Thank you for your bravery and service to the colony," he said wearily. "Take your gun. Mobilize your men. We're going to war."

Chapter Twenty-five

As soon as the sun set, Chichirico appeared in Catherine's bedchamber. She knew what he wanted. Just like the grays, he had felt the earthquake, and somehow he knew that humans had been to blame. She didn't want to open her mind to him. She was ashamed of what she and Sinclair had attempted, and she didn't want Chichirico to know the part she had played in it. Nevertheless, she shifted in bed, presenting her back to him, and allowed him to make the connection.

She thought he would be angry, that he would show her images of manticore homes destroyed in the quake, but instead, he was elated. The damage, it seemed, had mostly been to the gray tribe's villages. He showed her a memory, though she could tell it was not his own, of a mercury spring at the Edge. The ground was shaking violently.

Cracks appeared in the earth, passing around the spring. The cracks widened, the ground tilted, and the precious mercury spring crumbled away and fell until it passed out of sight in the abyss.

The spring was in the grays' territory. To reach another one, they would have to cross red land, or else come to an agreement with another tribe. The grays were furious, but Chichirico was pleased, and even more delighted with the battle with the grays in the settlement. The manticores viewed it as a natural and expected part of their friendship that the humans should join them in fighting their enemies. Since it was Chichirico who had formed that alliance, the humans' actions had strengthened his leadership of his tribe.

Tell your father and Sinclair, Chichirico said.

She wanted to ask why he didn't tell them himself, but she knew the answer already. Of all the humans, only she had been willing to enter into a bond with a manticore. Manticores conducted diplomacy through memory bonds, not through speech. Chichirico wasn't going to trust his imperfect command of English to communicate effectively. That meant that for the time being, she was the bridge between the colony and the manticore tribe.

◄+┼+►

SINCLAIR found John Marcheford sitting cross-legged on the floor of the church's nave, surrounded by paper. The paper was rough and fibrous, apparently of his own making, and thickly inked with words and symbols. The symbols looked like stick figures with too many lines. Marcheford had fled to the settlement when his home had been attacked by manticores. These papers were all he had brought with him: the rudiments of a written manticore language into which he hoped someday to translate the Bible.

"The tail-waving component makes it a challenge," Marcheford said. "I'm using a combination of Roman characters, like in our alphabet, and ideograms, like they use in Cathay."

"In case you didn't notice, they tried to kill you," Sinclair said.

"Not all of them."

"Ah, yes. Your converts."

Marcheford had a handful of manticore converts who had warned him of the attack, allowing him to reach the settlement alive.

A jar of Shekinah flatworms stood on the floor near Marcheford's papers, though its light was dim. As flatworms crawled around the inside of their jars, they excreted a sludge that collected at the bottom. The sludge worked as the opposite of light: not just black, it actually pulled light out of its surroundings. Shadows became darker in its vicinity. Candles became dimmer. Eventually, the effect of the growing puddle of sludge would overwhelm even the flatworms' bright light, and the jars would have to be cleaned out before they could be used again.

"I was sorry to hear of Maasha Kaatra's death," Marcheford said. "It's a hard thing to lose a faithful friend."

Sinclair clenched his fists hard enough to hurt. "He was with me for eight years. He had two daughters, did you know that? His brother sold all three of them into slavery to the Portuguese. I was with a Dutch ship, but I always talked with sailors from other ships at berth, asking about strange sightings and hints of magic. When I went to visit the Portuguese vessel, most of the crew was ashore, with only two men left to man the ship. I found them in the hold, and the things they were doing to those two young girls . . . I can't describe it to you, Bishop. The men were drunk, and I overpowered them both and tied them up, meaning to leave them to the wrath of their captain.

"When I understood that Maasha Kaatra was their father, however, and that he had been made to watch from his chains, I freed him and let him have his revenge. It was too late for the girls, though. They both died. Maasha Kaatra meant to kill himself as well, but I told him about my search. I told him I meant to understand death and learn how to turn it back. I didn't lie to him. I told him it wasn't likely, even if I succeeded, that he would see his daughters again, but the idea caught in his mind. He had no home or family left, and didn't place much value on his own life. I think the only reason he didn't kill himself was the thought that he might help me reach my goal, and thus save other men's daughters from the same fate.

"I freed the rest of their slaves as well, who plundered the ship and then burned it. Maasha Kaatra followed me back, and never left my side." Sinclair rubbed at his temples. "I think that, at the end, he might actually have seen his daughters again."

"He was loyal and good. All men must die when their time comes." Marcheford said.

"No." Sinclair said. "It wasn't his time. God killed him to punish me."

"You think Maasha Kaatra's death was about you?"

"He died in my experiment, doing what I told him to."

"He died in pursuit of his own ends, making his own choices for his own reasons. The manner of his life and death was between him and God. You didn't own him. Perhaps he felt that these eight years were worth it, and perhaps not, but that is nothing to do with you. You miss his friendship, even if you can't admit it. Let yourself grieve for him."

"Listen," Sinclair said. "I tried to take something from God, and I almost succeeded. Maasha Kaatra's death, the earthquake—this is God striking back at me."

"That's not how it works." Marcheford stood up from his papers and straightened his back with a popping sound. "God isn't threatened by you. You can't fight him or steal from him."

"Let's just say I got his attention." *Life*, Sinclair didn't say. I nearly took back a *life*. The hairs on his arms prickled. This was bigger than Prometheus stealing fire. He was taking the fight to the very stronghold that gave God his sway over mankind—the fear of death and what came after.

"You think you've found something new," Marcheford said. "But nothing is new to God. He made quintessence. Nothing you can do with it surprises him."

"What if he didn't make it? What if quintessence is the raw material God used to make the world? We're doing things here God never intended. *Man* is taking command. This is far beyond the Tower of Babel, and this time we're winning."

"Yet you fear God will make you pay for your actions."

Sinclair turned away, annoyed, and struck at the air. "Listen, this isn't why I came here. You know the manticores pretty well. We need your help to figure out how to beat them."

"How to kill them, you mean."

"Only to defend ourselves. We're not going out hunting them."

"As I understand it, you fired the first shot."

"Tate did. The fool. But that's not the point. We either need to know how to fight them and win, or else we need to convince them that we're not to blame." He thought back to the confrontation in the square. "You know a lot of manticore words. Do you know what this one means?" He repeated the word Catherine had not known how to translate, the thing they said was gone forever because of the earthquake.

"It was a location," Marcheford said. "A place where they conducted the memory ceremonies that tied a young person to a particular family for the rest of his life. It stood right at the Edge, until the quake."

"What happened to it?"

"It's gone. The whole cliff face sheared off and fell."

"You saw it? You've been to the Edge?"

"Yes, I've seen it. The land just ends. A drop into pure blackness. The sun sinks into it every night until it disappears."

"So that's why they're so angry. Thanks." Sinclair headed for the door, but Marcheford called him back.

"Governor?"

"What?"

"I don't know what you plan, but I know one thing. If you set yourself against God, you'll lose."

Sinclair grinned. "That's what everyone thinks. That's why they never try."

━╋╋╋━

THEY hauled the remaining bronze cannon from the ship and strengthened one of the platforms around the palisade to hold its weight. It was positioned along the line of approach from the river, the easiest way for a human army to advance, but Parris doubted it would do much good against manticores. They could approach from any direction, invisibly. What the settlers needed most was a way to see them.

In two days, hunters collected dozens of seer skinks, which were caged in Sinclair's bestiary and milked for their tears. One of the hunters returned with a story of a large gathering of gray manticores, all of them screeching and leaping from tree to tree. Another of the hunters never returned at all.

Besides arming the palisade guards with skink tears and bell-boxes, they deployed scouts with spearhawk beaks to patrol the surrounding land as far as the bay. Spearhawks were birds with needle-thin beaks that preyed on the kind of eel they used in the colony's eel ponds. Their beaks were sensitive to the direction of nearby quintessence pearls, allowing them to sense the eels from hundreds of feet in the air, dive into the water at tremendous speed, and plunge their beaks through fast-moving creatures only a few inches wide. The beaks were drawn to the pearls like iron to a lodestone, adjusting their aim as they fell. The scouts used the beaks as a kind of divining rod to sense the presence and direction of any animals—or manticores—that got too close to the settlement.

Parris thought the settlement was secure, until the next morning, when Catherine revealed that Chichirico had paid her another night visit, apparently slipping past all the scouts and guards and into her very bedroom without notice.

"He said the grays are gathering for war. The reds are still on our side and will fight the grays alongside us. In fact, he seemed pretty happy about it. Before we fought the grays, Chichirico's brother Tanakiki was still popular, and a lot of them thought he should still be chief. Now they're all supporting Chichirico."

"What are the grays waiting for?" Parris said. "They could kill us all now. They could have done it the day Tate started shooting."

"Chichirico says they're afraid of us. We can see them and kill them, something Chelsey's settlers never figured out how to do. They don't know what we're capable of."

"Which means that when they finally do attack, it'll be with over-whelming force."

One of the smaller buildings had been converted into an experiment room for the Society, and Matthew, who barely left it, ended up living on the second floor. The first floor now doubled as a communications center. Parris found Matthew there with a group of volunteers, mostly women, sitting at tables with bell-boxes, transcribing messages as they came in from the scouts. The women were the wives of Protestant refugees, educated enough to know how to write, whom Matthew had taught the ring codes he'd developed.

"I was thinking," Matthew said. "A bell-box could be rigged to pull other things besides bells. We could set them in the woods around the palisade and trigger them from the settlement."

"What sort of things?"

Matthew shrugged. "Gunpowder charges, for instance."

"We don't have all that much gunpowder to spare."

"Other things, then. Poison darts. Or even voids."

Parris shook his head. "I don't even like you experimenting with those. We don't know how to control them."

A slow grin played across Matthew's face. "Let me show you something." He led Parris up the stairs to his living quarters. A cot pushed against one wall was the only furniture except for a table strewn with experimental paraphernalia: wooden boxes, feathers, horns, claws. Bundles of various plants hung drying from the ceiling. Sawdust carpeted the floor.

"First . . ." Matthew held up a small box. He opened it and threw in some twigs, pebbles, seedpods, and some sawdust. It was about the size of a bell-box, with a lever on the side, but it was made of beetlewood and had no bell.

"You're going to make a void in that?"

"Relax," Matthew said. "I've done it over and over."

He shut the box, turned the crank, and waited. After a few moments, they heard a sharp pop. Matthew opened it and showed Parris the inside. Empty.

"Complete destruction," Parris said, unnerved. "What's the good of it?" It disturbed him that Matthew was so interested in what was essentially a destructive force. And now he was talking about making a weapon with it. Once created, it couldn't be uncreated. It might help them defeat the manticores, but then what? Who else might get hold of it?

Matthew put down the box and picked up a larger one. "This is a double box," he said. "It has two layers of beetlewood, one box inside the other, with a gap between them." He threw some twigs into the inner box and some in the gap between it and the outer box, carefully fastened the lids, and pulled the lever. He showed Parris the result: those in the gap were gone, but those in the inner box remained untouched.

"You faced the waxy side of the beetlewood in different directions," Parris said, "so that when you create the void, it's trapped in the gap. But I still don't get the point."

"It was Catherine who first gave me the idea." Matthew said. He tried again, this time putting a piece of bread in the inner box. When he opened it, Parris expected to see the bread untouched, as the twigs had been. Instead, he saw a pile of sand.

A chill ran down his arms. "That bread was made from sand."

"Yes."

"When you activated the void, you isolated the bread from the flow of quintessence around it."

"Yes."

"Thus reverting it to its original state." Parris laughed and clapped Matthew on the shoulder. "Just like it would if we returned to England!"

"Exactly."

"If we can reproduce what it's like to go back home, then we can test possible solutions to the problem. And if the solution works in this box, we'll know it's safe to return."

"Matthew! Dr. Parris!" a woman's voice called.

They ran downstairs. One of the bell coders was excitedly waving a scrap of paper. "One of the scouts reports seeing a ship."

Parris thought he must have heard wrong. "A ship? Like on the ocean?"

"That's what he said, my lord. A ship in the bay."

A ship! A ship could mean more men and more guns. But where had it come from? How had it found the island?

They ran to tell Sinclair, and soon everyone knew. Most wanted to meet the ship at the dock, but Sinclair selected a welcoming committee: himself, Parris, Bishop Marcheford, Oswyn Tate, and three of his soldiers. When they reached the bay, they saw it at once, still tiny in the distance, but unmistakable. Parris lifted a spyglass to his eye. The ship was sleek and streamlined, majestic in full sail, shorter in the beam than the *Western Star,* and without the *Star*'s high forecastle. It was a galleon, made for war. Fluttering proudly from the mainmast was a flag, but it was not England's red cross on a field of white. It was quartered instead, with two castles and two crowned lions. Parris felt cold, despite the bright sun, and a heavy stone sank in his stomach. The ship was from Spain.

Chapter Twenty-six

THE Spanish galleon tacked gently alongside the dock, the deep bay easily accommodating her hull. It made the *Western Star* look like a child's toy. There was no point in trying to fight. About a hundred Spanish soldiers lined her decks, sharp-peaked helmets in metallic rows. There were even some warhorses tethered on the foredeck, nickering and no doubt anxious to get solid ground under their hooves again. Parris watched mutely from shore as sailors shimmied down ropes, secured them, and lowered a ramp from the main deck.

"How could they possibly have found us?" Parris said.

Sinclair was grave. "The other beetle."

"The one that escaped in my house? But it flew through the wall. No one could possibly have retrieved it."

Sinclair shrugged. "Then they couldn't possibly be here. Yet they are."

The man who descended the ramp on the back of a white stallion was not Spanish. He wore a wide-brimmed hat with a sweeping green ostrich plume, an embroidered doublet, and flaring lace cuffs.

Parris opened his mouth, but couldn't speak his cousin's name.

"Francis Vaughan," Sinclair said.

Vaughan doffed his hat and made a courtly bow from the saddle. "Sir Vaughan now," he said with an amused smile.

"The queen *knighted* you?" Parris said.

"She rewards faithful service."

"Then how do you come to travel on a Spanish vessel?"

Vaughan laughed. "Her Highness is betrothed to marry Philip of Spain. Or will already have done, by now. Spain is our ally and friend."

"Usurper, is more like," Marcheford murmured. "If she bears him a son, then England will be no more than a Spanish province."

"Mary has subjected England to a foreign power?" Sinclair said.

Spaniards disembarked and gathered around Vaughan. "Not subjected," Vaughan said. "Philip and Mary are partners, divine representatives of God to spread the glory of his Church throughout the world."

"In other words, Philip is draining the English treasury to fight his wars in France and Italy," Sinclair said.

A man pushed to the front, a giant with a head of black curls. He towered over the others and was dressed, as in England, in a simple black cassock. "Be careful of your words," the giant said. "You are subjects of the queen. To malign her royal husband is treason."

"And you are?" Sinclair said.

"Diego de Tavera, formerly of Valladolid, now sent to the island of Horizon by His Holiness the Pope. I am envoy of His Grace the King of Spain, with a special commission by Her Grace the Queen of England to redeem this colony from heresy and bring it under the proper authority of the crown."

Sinclair raised an eyebrow. "Just full of important people, aren't you?"

"Soon Their Graces will be the most powerful rulers on earth," Tavera said.

"As soon as they collect enough gold to win their wars," Sinclair said. "Which is why you're really here, isn't it? You were sent to find the gold and bring it home."

"As were you," Vaughan said. "We're here to make sure it actually happens."

Sinclair swept back an arm as if to show the way. "Welcome, then. Though at present we don't have the accommodations to put up so many fine men. Most of you will have to stay on the ship. I'm sure you understand."

"I'm afraid it's you who doesn't understand," Vaughan said. With a flourish, he produced a roll of paper, sealed with red wax and tied with ribbon. He handed it down to Sinclair, who opened it. Parris read over his shoulder. In flowing hand, the document proclaimed Francis Vaughan the new governor of the Horizon colony. "I will have your house, for a start," Vaughan said. "Then your people will provide whatever accommodations are lacking for my men."

"You should watch your hands," Sinclair said.

"What?"

"It's what happens when you pick up something you don't understand. You get burned."

"Are you threatening me?"

"Warning you."

"Enough of this," Tavera said. His deep voice resonated and made Vaughan's seem faint and shrill. "We will discuss these matters when our men are fed and housed. Sinclair, fetch a crew of men from the colony to help unload the ship."

Parris could see Sinclair was burning with fury at being ordered about, but he swallowed his pride, bowed, and left. The shore grew crowded with the ranks of Spanish soldiers. They showed some signs of malnutrition, but most looked better off than the passengers had on the *Western Star*. Parris supposed they had managed not to be swindled when taking on supplies in the Azores.

"Cousin Parris," Vaughan said. "I brought a friend with me. Someone you know well, I think." He stepped aside to reveal the small woman standing behind him. She was thinner than Parris remembered, and her clothes were ragged and stained, but she wore the same expression of cold rage he had last seen on her face.

"Joan!" Parris said. "How . . . ?"

"Tell me she's alive," Joan said.

"What are you doing here?"

"Tell me she's still alive, Stephen!"

"She's alive. She's healthy and happy and thriving. I was right to bring her; we never could have figured out how to save her at home." He didn't add that a physic with less knowledge might have tried giving her mercury as a general tonic, and thus cured her at home, by accident. "Why are you here?"

"You took my daughter away from me. I told you I wouldn't let you win."

"Then . . . it was you . . . ?"

One side of Joan's mouth turned upward in a sly, bitter smile. She reached into a bag, produced the pale box Parris had first seen in his parlor so long ago, and snapped it open. Inside was the beetle.

"How did you find it?"

"It was caught in a box of candles."

"In the storeroom! I knew it had flown in there; I assumed it flew right through to the outside." This still didn't explain everything, though. "How did you know how to use it?"

Her lips formed a thin line, and she raised her chin. "You're not the only one who can figure things out."

⊰⊹⊱

WHEN Catherine saw her mother, she burst into tears. The last time she'd spoken to her, it was in bitter argument about whether or not she would be permitted to go with her father to Horizon. She flew into her arms. Mother gripped her tightly, though, as always, her eyes were dry.

"I'm taking you home," Mother said into her hair. "A week or more to fill the ship with goods, and we can head for England."

Catherine pulled back a bit, still holding her mother, so she could see her face. She didn't want to antagonize her so quickly after their reunion, but neither did she want to give a false impression. "I don't want to go home," she said. "I belong here."

Mother's gaze flitted from building to building, their sparkling diamond walls diffracting beams of rainbow colors. Instead of awe, her face showed only a wary distrust. "Belong here? What do you mean?" she said. "This is a colony. It's a means to an end, not a place to belong."

"Look around," Catherine said. "This isn't a wooden village ready to fall down at the first big storm. This could be a city, in time. Generations living and working. And we're doing so much. We can make food from sand! All the buildings are lit from the inside at night—you should see how beautiful it is. We're finding out new things every day. All the animals here have special properties, things we can copy and learn from, and . . ." The image of Maasha Kaatra tumbling into the void played in her mind for the thousandth time. There was a dark side to these wonders. Sinclair had trusted her to do her part, and she had let him down. Now a man was dead.

Mother opened her mouth, and Catherine knew what was going to come out. *Give up this charade, Catherine. You're only a girl. Stop pretending to be a man.* But it didn't. Mother paused, checked herself, and stroked Catherine's face. "I missed you so much," she said instead.

Catherine didn't know what to say to that. She was geared up for a fight; she didn't know how to respond to a gesture of sympathy. "I missed you, too," she mumbled, even though she thought it was probably a lie. She hadn't thought very much about Mother, with all the crises onboard ship, and the excitement of arriving here and all they'd found. When she did think of her, it was with a strong sense of guilt that she buried as quickly as she could. In another sense, Mother had always been there, lurking behind her thoughts, as that voice in her head telling her she wasn't good enough, and that she was fooling herself to think so.

"The last time I saw you, you were unconscious," Mother said. "One day you were coming with me to Derbyshire; the next your father was dragging you unconscious onto a ship from which you would never return. When I found that beetle, and finally realized what it was, and that I could use it to follow you—that was the first time I let myself hope that maybe you were still alive. I thought that, if you were, you would be ready to come home by now."

"It doesn't matter. I can't go home," Catherine said. "And neither can you."

"Like Chelsey's ship, you mean? We would turn into statues?"

"Exactly."

"Your father promised me that problem would be solved."

"He's been trying."

Mother held her close. "I can wait. As long as I'm with you, I can wait." She looked suddenly grim. "Your father may find he's under a little more pressure to solve that problem now."

"You mean the Spanish?"

"Yes. Listen. Stay away from these Spanish, that Tavera especially. He's not a good man."

"But you brought him here!"

"It was the only way I could get back to you. I can't sail a ship by myself. He has a mission from the king and queen, and he'll perform that mission. Just stay out of his way. Promise me that?"

A Spanish soldier appeared behind them. "Lord Tavera commands everyone to gather in the church," he said in strongly accented English.

"So now it's 'Lord' Tavera?" Mother said.

"Everyone," the Spaniard repeated.

As the colonists crowded into the church, Blanca found Catherine and caught her arm. Her face was pale, and strands of her dark hair hung down from under her cap. Her hands trembled. "It's him," she said. "Tavera."

"Did he see you?"

She nodded. "He didn't recognize me. He looked right past me."

"We'll have to tell my father what we know about him."

"Catherine? I'm scared."

Catherine held her and stroked her hair. "I know. Me, too."

Tavera introduced himself in a deep, carrying voice. He praised Their Majesties King Philip of Spain and Queen Mary of England, and reminded them all of their due allegiance. He told them that their ship, their provisions, and their settlement were investments by the crown, and that a return on that investment was expected. He also informed them that the Protestant heresy was illegal in all English lands, and the worship of the True Faith compulsory. Almost as an afterthought, he introduced their new governor, Sir Francis Vaughan.

Throughout his speech the murmurs increased, until the church buzzed with angry noise.

"It's as I expected," Tavera said. "There's no discipline here, and no love for the Church. Only sorcery and greed. I am hereby granting, starting this day, a Term of Grace to last ten days. Any man found in possession of an English Bible after this term, or denying the flesh and blood of the Supper, or in any way rejecting the authority of the Church of Rome will come under the instruction of the inquisitors. Heresy will be rooted out."

"Amen," said Francis Vaughan.

⊰✦✦✦⊱

JOAN moved into the house with Parris and Catherine and Blanca. Parris couldn't work out how he felt about her being there. For not the first time in his life, he was dazzled by the strength of her character, the wit and nerve and fierce love that would enable her to mobilize a royal expedition to find her daughter, when she had no money or authority of her own. It was the kind of thing that had attracted him to her in the first place, so long ago. She was so strong, so certain of what she believed, so intensely loyal. He hadn't realized how much he missed her, nor how rare and beautiful a woman she was.

On the other hand, the easy atmosphere of their home, so often visited by Society members and filled with lively conversation about new discoveries, was now tense and awkward. She had, after all, brought their enemy down on them, and the fact that she'd done it out of love for Catherine only absolved so much. She was risking the destruction of all they'd worked for.

"How can you be on their side?" Parris asked.

"It's the *right* side," she said. "Mary is the rightful queen, the divinely appointed ruler of England. She's brought the old ways back."

"Has she forced the lords to give their lands back to the monks and nuns?" Parris asked.

"She can't do that; they'd all rise up against her. But she will, once she's strong enough. I believe in her, and so should you."

Parris shook his head. "This man Tavera . . ."

"He's not a kind man," Joan said. "He's more like a weapon. The queen sent him here to force allegiance."

"He's a brutal killer. And Vaughan—he seems eager for the ten days to be up so he can start torturing people."

"Recant. Give up all this foolishness and come home," Joan said.

"I can't do that."

"And if they kill you?"

"You brought them here," Parris said. "I hope your conscience can rest easy."

Did she really hate him that much? That she was willing to see him killed rather than let Catherine stay with him? He had taken Catherine away from her against her will, and he supposed she might never forgive him for that. Eventually, Catherine would have to choose for herself. In the meantime, he hoped their battle for their daughter wouldn't destroy the colony altogether.

◄+┼+►

THAT evening, several dozen gray manticores arrived at the gate and found it better guarded than they could have expected. The palisade platforms bristled with Spanish soldiers. Thinking it was better to confide in the Spanish than to be massacred by manticores, Sinclair had told them how to use skink tears and prepare their bullets with wax. He stood on a platform next to Vaughan, watching the manticores pour from the trees. Several held a tall pole upright while another clambered to the top. Gripping it with the hooks on his feet, the manticore balanced at its summit and said something to the men on the palisade platform.

"I think he's asking us to open the gate," Sinclair said. "Though we should get someone who can speak their language to know for certain."

Vaughan looked at him in disgusted astonishment. "These creatures can *speak*?"

"Not much English, but in their own language. They make sounds and sign with their tails."

"I'll teach them a language," Vaughan said. He gestured at one of the

Spanish soldiers, who raised his matchlock, aimed, and fired at the manticore on the pole. A cloud of gunpowder smoke erupted from the weapon, and the manticore fell to the ground.

The manticores turned invisible and scattered. Guns fired from several platforms, and manticores began to drop. Their invisibility didn't hide them from sight, and their ability to turn insubstantial couldn't save them from the wax-coated bullets. They were fast and agile, and several clambered up the palisade and slashed at soldiers with their deadly pincers. The Spanish were well trained and disciplined, however, and their bayonets were treated with wax as well. At the end of the short encounter, only two human soldiers were dead, but eighteen manticores lay lifeless on the grass. The rest fled into the woods, leaving their dead behind.

⊰┼┼┼⊱

PARRIS was glad not to be murdered by gray manticores, but he wasn't sure the Spanish were much of an improvement. Over the next several days, Tavera and Vaughan busied themselves asking questions from house to house concerning points of religion. They hadn't actually threatened or harmed anyone, but they were accompanied by Spanish soldiers everywhere they went. People were scared.

Parris found Vaughan at the marmoset farm, where the colonists raised marmosets for the quintessence pearls in their bones. The Spanish soldiers gaped at the tiny monkeys leaping in and out through the solid diamond walls of the enclosures, eating the moths imprisoned inside. One Spanish soldier tried to catch a marmoset and was bitten for his troubles, to the amusement of the local crowd.

Another soldier directed Parris to where Vaughan sat on a low wall, examining his ostrich-plume hat through a small pair of spectacles perched on his nose. He meticulously stroked the feather, perfecting its shape.

"You have no right to interrogate people," Parris said.

Vaughan didn't look up from the hat. "Good evening, cousin. It's a pleasure to see you again."

"Why have you been harrying the colonists?"

"I am empowered by the queen to report on how this colony has been run. Asking questions is part of that."

"So talk to Sinclair. He's the governor. He can tell you how things are being run."

A deep rumble of laughter escaped from Vaughan's throat. He raised his eyes and peered at Parris over the spectacles. "Come, now. How can I obtain an impartial evaluation if I only ask the former governor?"

Parris was taken aback by the calm confidence Vaughan displayed. He'd changed. He wore his flamboyant doublet and hose like a second skin, making his surroundings seem ridiculous instead of the other way around. Something had hardened Francis Vaughan, and Parris found himself frightened of the man.

"You make people uncomfortable," Parris said.

"It's not my job to make them comfortable. They don't tell the truth when they're comfortable."

"You take a dim view of human nature, then."

"An accurate one, I fear."

"Most people will tell you the truth, if they're not afraid to tell you something you don't want to hear."

Vaughan lifted a tiny pair of scissors from his breast pocket—mustache trimmers, by the look of them—and snipped some invisible fault from the edge of the feather. "Have you ever judged a heresy trial, Stephen? But of course you haven't. I have had that honor, and I'll tell you something Bishop Bonner told me. Everyone has something to hide. Whatever they tell you the first time, no matter how sincere they seem, they're keeping something back."

"People admit to anything faced with a hot poker. Doesn't make it true."

"Oh, you'd be surprised." Vaughan wagged his head like a tutor with a feckless student. "Rotten deeds hide a rotten core. Old men who fail to speak the prayers, young girls who look away when the host is raised—they fool the weak with their wide-eyed tears, but again and again, the truth is revealed. A Talmud under the floorboards. Books of sorcery or astrology. A Tyndale Bible in a secret drawer."

"I've heard the tales from Spain," Parris said. "Madmen and simpletons tortured for being too ignorant to avoid notice. Pregnant women burned alive along with the innocents they carry."

"Better to die an innocent and wake in the arms of God than to be reared as a heretic."

Parris threw up his arms. He knew he should walk away—this conversation was going nowhere—but Vaughan infuriated him. "By your argument, we should kill all children at birth, before they have a chance to sin."

"If they cling to the True Faith, they need fear nothing."

Parris tried to object, but Vaughan waved a hand to cut him off. "If I were you, I wouldn't worry so much about other people's sins," he said.

Parris narrowed his eyes. "What are you saying?"

"You have heard of the Term of Grace?"

"I heard."

"Don't expect special treatment for family members."

"Trust me, I don't."

"I am empowered to root out heresy. No matter where I find it."

Parris plucked the ostrich feather out of Vaughan's hand and threw it on the ground. "Don't threaten me."

The assault on his feather finally broke through Vaughan's oily calm. He jumped up from the wall and focused burning eyes on him. It occurred to Parris that a short man communicated power better by staying seated. Roused to his feet, Vaughan just looked like a pouting child. Vaughan must have realized it, too, because he smiled, sighed, and sat down again. He lifted the feather gently from the ground and set it back into his hat.

Parris wanted to punch him, but resisted. He turned to leave, but a soldier blocked his way.

"I'm not finished with you," Vaughan said. "Answer me this. The colony is rich. Why has Sinclair not yet sent a ship with gold and spices back home?"

"No treasures sent would make it home. They're only spices and gold while they remain here. Halfway back, they turn into rocks or sand or seawater."

"Surely your Society is working on that problem."

Parris raised his eyebrows. Vaughan knew about the Society already. "We don't have a solution. There may not be one."

Vaughan leaned in close and snarled. "Liar. You're all heathens who refuse to support your rightful queen."

"Trust me. Since any of us would die if we attempted to return, we are very interested in finding a solution to the problem."

"Die? Why would you die?"

Parris smiled. He could tell that Vaughan really didn't know. With special relish, he explained how most of their food was made from sand, and their water was really transformed salt water. "We bring in some meat from hunting, but we haven't grown many natural crops. All of our bodies are full of sand and salt. If any of us returns, we're dead men."

Vaughan's eyes were wide, and he looked as though he had something caught in his throat. "But . . . we've been eating the same food. You've poisoned us!"

Parris shrugged. "Welcome to Horizon."

━┽┼┾━

CATHERINE walked through the streets with Matthew, careful to stand an appropriate distance apart and remain in view of others. Accusations of sin and scandal were all too easy to earn these days, and there was a sense that Tavera and his spies were always watching.

The presence of so many Spanish had changed the settlement. The palisade wall had been extended to accommodate nearly twice as many people inside. A new Spanish quarter had sprung up in days with barracks for the men and a stable for their horses. Spanish soldiers were everywhere in the colony, buying, trading, and asking questions, but few of them spoke English very well, which made for daily misunderstandings.

The church had transformed, too, in preparation for Catholic worship. A giant crucifix was cast in gold and hung on the wall. Tavera and his priests distributed pamphlets announcing the Term of Grace and requiring English Bibles or any other items of Protestant worship to be surrendered.

Bishop Marcheford had disappeared almost as soon as the Spanish arrived. No one knew quite when or how he had left, not even Matthew, but most assumed he was back in the forest pursuing his work evangelizing the manticores. Matthew feared for his life and thought it a foolish pursuit, though Catherine could tell he was also proud of his father for defying Tavera. Stories spread through the colony and grew with the telling, of Marcheford living naked with the savages, of crowds of manticores coming to hear him speak. Most people found the idea of evangelizing them bizarre, if not sacrilegious, but Catherine had always known that the manticores were people. God had created them. Surely they needed to be reconciled to him as much as any human.

"Christ came as a human being, not a manticore," Matthew said. "How can his death atone for them?"

"Christ came as a Jew," Catherine said. "How can his death atone for Englishmen?"

Matthew didn't answer, but his face formed that look he had when he was considering a new thought: he furled his eyebrows, sucked in his lips, and looked off to one side. He got that look more and more often these days.

A year ago, he would have dismissed her argument and shown her how it was wrong without even considering it. Horizon was changing him.

They walked toward the church. Father had called an emergency meeting of the Quintessence Society to discuss the Spanish threat.

"How are your experiments with the double void box coming?" she asked.

"No revelations yet," he said. "Anything that relies on quintessence for its life or form either dies or loses its power when it's closed inside the box. It confirms our understanding that quintessence is conferred from the outside, not stored within. Even the quintessence pearls we get from the animals go dark inside the box and lose their power. That means they don't produce quintessence themselves; they funnel it from an outside source. We think it comes from the stars, but that's just what Aristotle thought. We have no data to support the theory."

"And if you could find something that kept its quintessence abilities while inside the box?"

"It depends. If it just stored quintessence for a while, and then dissipated, that wouldn't help us. Some things seem to do that, in fact. What we need is a source, something that doesn't run out, something that enables *other* things to keep their quintessence abilities in the box, even though they usually don't. If we had that, the problem would be solved. We could bring it back to England with us, and its quintessence would keep our bodies from transforming."

"If only you could put a star in your box."

He grinned. "If only."

To his credit, Matthew had never scolded her for the disastrous experiment with Master Sinclair, nor even brought the subject up at all. She was all too aware that he had been proven right, and she was grateful not to have to hear him say so. Still, she didn't want it to hang between them, a taboo subject never to be breached.

"I owe you an apology," she said.

"I was thinking I owed you one."

She stopped walking. "What?"

"You were right. If we had a chance to bring someone back from the dead, we had to try. If it were someone I loved"—he glanced at her and swallowed—"that's what I would want."

"But look what happened! Maybe we weren't meant to try." Her voice broke, and she fought to keep from crying.

"I told you your brother was better off dead. I was an ass."

He was so earnest, she laughed through her tears. "You were."

"I'm serious."

"I can tell."

"Life is precious. If there's a way for life to be restored, then it's from God. He gave it to us to find."

"We tried. We failed."

"Then we should keep trying. These men who came with your cousin: they're killers. I can see it in their faces. If we could bring people back from the dead, men like that would have no power over us."

"We can't, though. So we have to do what they say." A worry struck her. "You *are* going to Mass tomorrow, right?"

"I'm not planning on it."

"But you must!"

"Not until the ten days are up," Matthew said.

"I don't think it works like that. They'll be taking names. Anyone they notice now will be the first to go when the Term of Grace is over."

Matthew rubbed his face with his hands. "How can I go to a Papist Mass?"

"You have to. And you have to look when the host is raised, and say the prayers, and everything. You know they'll be watching."

A slow smile spread across Matthew's face. "I bet they'd be surprised if the wine really did turn into blood."

She gasped. "Matthew, don't you even think about it."

"This is our colony," he said. "Not theirs. We built it and worked for it and wrung out its secrets. We shouldn't just let them take it."

"These are serious men. Killers—you said it yourself. They'd sooner rip out your tongue than let you speak against them."

"I'm not planning on speaking against them."

"Be careful, Matthew."

"Don't worry."

When they reached the church to meet the other Society members, they found the doors locked and a sign posted: NO UNAUTHORIZED GATHERINGS, BY ORDER OF THE GOVERNOR.

"The fools," Matthew said. "Don't they know we're what keeps this colony alive?"

She smiled at his casual arrogance. "Apparently not."

"We can't just let this happen. We have to fight back."

Chapter Twenty-seven

ON Sunday, a bell tolled through the settlement, calling everyone to Mass. Soldiers went from house to house, dragging out anyone who hoped to stay inside unnoticed. Catherine meekly followed her parents, who needed no such encouragement. Father had said they should play the part, attend the service, bide their time.

As they reached the door to the church, Matthew ran up behind her, breathless, and whispered in her ear: "I found it." His hair was matted, and he had dark rings under his eyes, but he seemed bursting with energy.

"You mean—"

"Yes." He grinned. She wanted to ask more. Had he really found a way to keep quintessence alive in the double box? Did that mean it was possible to go home? How had he done it? They passed into the church, where a Spanish acolyte glared at them and held out a bowl of water. Eyeing the soldiers on either side, Catherine kept her questions to herself and followed her father's example, dipping her hand in the water and making the sign of the cross.

The church had been redecorated. The sparkling diamond roof was as beautiful as ever, but now the lectern had been moved to one side to make room for an altar draped with an elaborate cloth. The cloth was threaded with gold, and would have been impressive in other circumstances, but next to the gold and diamond surroundings it seemed drab. On the altar stood a crucifix and a single flickering candle. Tavera must have brought all these things with him from England.

Tavera himself, now draped in a blue chasuble lined with black, walked in solemn procession to the altar followed by a server, placed the chalice on it, and crossed himself. *"Introibo ad altare Dei, ad Deum qui laetificat juventutem meam."*

Without moving her head, Catherine darted glances at the other colonists. Most of them stared gravely ahead, afraid to call attention to themselves. Soldiers lined the walls, watching.

Tavera bowed low. *"Confiteor Deo omnipotenti, beatae Mariae semper Virgini, beato Michaeli Archangelo, beato Joanni Baptistae . . ."*

Catherine felt the tension growing in the mostly Protestant group as the service progressed toward the celebration of the Eucharist. Making the sign of the cross was one thing; giving reverence to bread and wine supposed to be the actual body and blood of Christ was something else. To most of the people in the room it was sacrilege, but she guessed the soldiers had been told to watch for dissenters. Vaughan stood with the soldiers, and she saw him staring at her with greed on his face. Her gaze snapped back to the front.

Father stood with a stony expression, twitching with rage. On her other side, Mother participated in the devotions with obvious pleasure. It was confusing. These men were villains, but Mother could look past their villainy and see a tradition of faith and practice that her family had followed for hundreds of years. Had the Reformers been right to dispense with the worship of the last millennium? Had God changed?

Tavera grasped the paten on which the bread sat. This would be the moment—those who were not willing to trade their convictions for their lives would look away when the host was raised. But something was wrong. Tavera was struggling to lift it. Despite his size and obvious strength, he strained as if the bread and paten were made of cast iron. He managed to lift it a small way off the altar, but it slipped from his grasp and crashed to the floor.

A few people stifled a laugh, and Tavera looked up with blazing eyes. A chill spread down Catherine's back. Tavera scanned the crowd in unmasked fury, looking for the source of the laughter. His eyes stopped when he saw Matthew.

"Seize him."

Matthew stood half to his feet as if to run. "No," he said. "I didn't . . ." Soldiers converged on him through the crowd. He turned to Catherine. "I swear, it wasn't me."

Tavera was laughing now, a low chuckle almost too deep to hear. "Bring him here."

Catherine tried to stand, not even knowing what she intended to do, but Mother held her down with a viselike strength.

A slow, amused smile spread across Tavera's face as Matthew was brought forward, and Catherine could tell he didn't really care if Matthew had done it or not. "The young Master Marcheford," he said. "I knew we'd be bringing you in sooner or later. I suppose it will be sooner."

Catherine could see the fear in Matthew's eyes. "I had nothing to do with this," he said.

"He has desecrated the host," Tavera said. "You are all witnesses." To the soldiers: "Take him away."

Matthew didn't struggle. Everyone sat stunned as the soldiers escorted him down the aisle. She believed that he hadn't done it; he'd obviously spent last night solving the problem of their return to England, not devising a way to make bread much heavier than usual, as someone had obviously done.

And what had been the point? A little joke? Make Tavera look stupid in front of everyone? Now here Matthew was, being dragged off to be killed. Tortured, if nothing else. They would want to know how to bring the treasure safely back home, and if they found out he knew, they wouldn't relent until he told them.

All too briefly, she saw his head reach the door and duck through it, and then he was gone.

⇥✛✛⇤

As soon as the Mass was over, Catherine grabbed Blanca and pulled her into the shadows between two buildings.

"What will they do to him?" she said.

Blanca looked as scared as Catherine felt. "I don't know."

"Please, tell me. What did the Inquisition in Spain do to those who resisted them?"

"There were many things." Blanca swallowed. "They were . . . creative."

"What do you remember?"

Her eyes grew distant. "They twisted ropes around people's arms and made them tighter turn by turn. They dripped water down their throats for hours, making them swallow continuously lest they drown. They imprisoned them in cages too short to let them sit up, but too full of water to let them lie down. People always talked eventually. But Matthew doesn't have anything to tell them, does he?"

"He does! He figured out how to bring quintessence back to England."

"What?"

"Just last night. He didn't even get a chance to tell me how." Catherine covered her face in her hands. "Now they'll force it out of him, and he'll try to be noble and brave, but they'll make him tell anyway."

"If they name him a heretic, they'll burn him once they wring him dry of information. The same goes for Sinclair, or your father, or anyone."

They stared into each other's eyes.

"You're going to try to rescue him, aren't you?" Blanca said.

"I have to."

Blanca nodded. "I know."

They slipped out of the shadows and rejoined Mother and Father in the crowd leaving the church. Mother gave them a sharp look, but said nothing. All four of them stopped short when Tavera, flanked by two soldiers, blocked their path.

His huge body and shaggy curls seemed to block the sun. "Lady Parris," Tavera said. "It's good to see you reunited with your husband."

Mother curtsied. "Thank you, my lord. It was a pleasure to celebrate the Mass this morning."

Tavera's eyes looked past her and settled onto Blanca. He lifted her chin and examined her face. "This is a pretty one," he said. "Who is she?"

"Our family's servant," Parris answered. "She came with us from London."

"Have we met, my dear? Where are you from?"

"From France, my lord," Blanca said, her voice shaking. "A small village near Calais."

He turned her chin to study her profile. "Truly lovely," he said. "You could almost be Spanish." There was a certain tone to his voice, and Catherine thought: *He knows.*

Blanca curtsied. "Thank you, my lord."

"A fresh young girl is a delight to the soul," Tavera said. "How would you like to work for me?"

"My lord?" Blanca flushed. Her eyes darted to Catherine for help.

"My wife and daughter have need of her," Father said. "Surely there are others."

"No, I want her." Tavera gestured to his soldiers. "Take her to my house, please."

Father stepped in front of Blanca. "You can't take her," he said. "She's not a slave. It's not right."

"Not right? Tell me, Parris, are you still mutilating corpses? Should I start inquiring around the settlement about your experiments?"

"That's nothing to do with her."

"Then perhaps I should inquire more about her instead. If, for instance, she's ever been to Castile or seen a Jewish family burned for heresy?"

Blanca stepped forward. "I'll go."

"No!" Catherine tried to hold her back.

"I have no choice," Blanca said. "You don't understand."

Tavera smiled. "Good girl," he said.

⊶✦⊷

CATHERINE knew she couldn't rescue them both on her own. She would just end up in chains herself. She needed help. Father would never let her try, and she wasn't certain whether Sinclair would turn her in or not. So she'd gone for help to the best source she had.

Chichirico shimmered into visibility beside her. They stood in the shadows, looking at the prison, which had been built only the day before in the center block of the soldier barracks. Like most Horizon buildings, it was made of diamond, and though she couldn't see inside, the walls shone with flickering torchlight from the interior. She could hear raised voices and moans. Two guards stood outside a large door. She and Chichirico were bonded, which made her a bit dizzy, now that she was up and moving around.

Go, she thought.

He disappeared again and ran toward the building. She closed her eyes, and she could see what he saw, the diamond walls getting closer, then straight through them into the room inside. Chichirico was taking a risk for her. The Spanish soldiers had massacred the gray manticores at the wall, and if the guards were using skink tears and waxed bullets, he could be killed. In his mind, she could feel that he wasn't afraid, and something more, that affection for her motivated his help.

Inside the prison, through Chichirico's eyes, she saw a single high room with evidence of ongoing construction to section it off into cells. In the center of the room, Matthew hung from his hands, which had been tied behind his back, forcing his arms up and backward in a position that seemed excruciatingly painful. His head hung forward, and he moaned softly.

Two men stood under him, one a Spanish soldier and the other a giant in a black cloak, Diego de Tavera himself. "We'll give you a few hours to think it over," Tavera said. He turned to leave, and his eyes swept past where Chichirico crouched. Catherine gasped, but Tavera didn't react. He couldn't see him.

The Society had not yet duplicated the manticores' ability to turn invisible, but Catherine had done the best she could. She'd brought some of the black sludge from a Shekinah flatworm jar and now spread it on her arms, face, and clothing. It caused a prickly sensation on her skin, and she didn't know if it would ever come off her clothes, but it made her very hard to see in the dark. The shadows around her grew deeper as the sludge drew in the light.

Catherine sneaked as close as she could along the edge of another building. She was within a few steps of the guards, but from this point she would have to cross open space. The light from inside the prison shifted, and she heard a rattle at the door. She shrank back just as it opened and Tavera and the other man came out, each holding a torch. Tavera laughed heartily, clapped the man on the back, and turned away from her. She saw her chance and slipped into the doorway behind one of the guards.

The door closed, leaving her in near-darkness. Ahead, a short corridor ended in another locked door. It was risky to shine any light, but she had to see what she was doing. She had one Shekinah flatworm with her, wrapped up in dark cloth. She pulled it out of her bag and unwound it slowly until a glow shone through the wrapping, faintly illuminating her surroundings. There was Chichirico, and Matthew, just as she had seen him.

She called Matthew's name. He groaned and turned his head, but with the darkness and the sludge on her skin, he couldn't see her.

"Who's there?"

"It's Catherine."

"No!" His eyes sprang open wide, and he shook his head frantically at her. "Get away from here. Go home!"

She followed the line of the rope that he was hanging from over to the wall, where it was tied to a hook. She untied it, intending to ease him to the ground, but he was too heavy for her, and the best she was able to do was slow his descent. He crashed down and collapsed like a doll on the floor.

Catherine rushed to him. His voice was hoarse but clear. "Please go. Don't let them catch you."

"I'm getting you out."

"And then what? Where will we go?"

"Stop arguing. Just get on your feet."

"I don't want you to . . ."

She wanted to kick him. "Get up, you idiot!"

He scrambled up and staggered, but kept his balance. She led him toward the door. She and Matthew couldn't pass through walls themselves, and there were no other exits. They would have to get by the guards again unnoticed, trusting to the sludge. She pulled a jar of it from her bag.

"Can you run?" she said.

He gritted his teeth. "If it means getting away from here, I can do it. I'm not sure for how long, though."

She took some more sludge from the jar and rubbed it on his skin. The months of shipboard travel and outdoor work had tanned him and added muscle to the once-pale and skinny body of a preacher's son.

"I'll do that," he said gruffly. He tried to continue the job himself, but winced as he moved his arms. She continued to apply it despite his protestations, and he submitted. The stuff really did work well. He didn't just look blackened; he looked like a hole in the air.

She paused at the door. Chichirico slipped through first without opening it, and she looked around through his eyes. The two guards were still there, and she knew she could never slip out without them noticing, even with the sludge. Just opening the door would get their attention immediately. Chichirico slipped back through the door to join them.

Give me the worm, he said, and a vision flashed through her mind of what he intended to do.

Thank you, she said, and gave him the wrapped flatworm. "Shield your eyes," she said to Matthew.

Throwing one shoulder against the door, she ran out between the two surprised guards. Chichirico flung off the wrapping and held the now-blazing flatworm aloft, running out to the left, shrieking. The soldiers shouted in alarm and shielded their eyes, and Catherine and Matthew ran out in the other direction. If they could reach the shadows between the buildings, they would be much harder to see. The soldiers would turn the place upside down looking for them, of course. They would have to leave the settlement and live in the forest.

She ran into the darkness, her own eyes dazzled from the worm's light, until she collided with someone. Strong arms wrapped around her and she shrieked, writhing and kicking to get free. She heard Matthew shouting nearby. A torch flared, and she saw that they were surrounded by Spanish soldiers. One soldier held Matthew with an arm around his throat. Her hair was twisted and gripped painfully. She turned with difficulty and saw the grinning face of Diego de Tavera.

"Predictable," he said. "They always are."

She could still see the dancing light of Chichirico, running away in the distance. A matchlock fired, Catherine felt a sudden blinding pain in her mind, and her connection to him was suddenly severed. The light fell to the ground and lay still.

Catherine screamed and shouted Chichirico's name. She kicked and tried to pull away, but Tavera knocked her legs out from under her, letting her fall to the ground, and kicked her in the head.

"No!" said another voice. Catherine rolled over, her head ringing, to see Father's cousin, Francis Vaughan.

"What did you say?" Tavera said.

Vaughan looked nervous. "I . . . she . . . there's no need to hurt her."

A smile spread across Tavera's face. "I'm looking forward to breaking this one," he said. "I thought perhaps the screws."

"No," Vaughan said.

"No? You think she's innocent?"

"She's just a child."

Catherine's vision swam for a moment, and she caught a glimpse through Chichirico's eyes. He had been hit in the shoulder, but he was still alive. The wound was healing quickly, and he was making his way invisibly back to the forest. She let out a breath. At least Chichirico was safe.

Tavera's smile turned menacing. "A child can belong to the devil as much as anyone. And do far more damage."

"I know it," Vaughan said. "But she's so . . ."

"Young?"

Vaughan nodded.

"Pretty?"

Vaughan nodded again, more slowly.

"You wanted her for yourself, didn't you? After this was all over, you thought . . . if she had no one else to turn to . . ."

Vaughan stared at the ground.

"I think you're right," Tavera said. "This one isn't right for the screws." He slid a pistol from under his robes and pointed it straight at Catherine's eyes. "She's too dangerous by far."

His finger pulled back against the trigger. Catherine opened her mouth to scream, but before she could, the muzzle flashed. A blinding pain slammed into her head and erased the world.

Chapter Twenty-eight

PARRIS was watching through the window when Vaughan carried Catherine's dead body to the house. His mind went blank, and for a moment he froze, unable to believe what he was seeing. It couldn't be true. It was someone else.

Vaughan dropped her on the front step, pounded on the door, and ran away like a frightened rabbit. Not that it mattered. Parris saw the bullet hole as soon as he opened the door, and his mind couldn't deny it was Catherine anymore. He shook her body, shouting at her to wake up, barely aware of what he was saying. He didn't know exactly what had happened, but the details didn't matter. Catherine had done something to anger Tavera or his men, perhaps even tried to free Matthew or Blanca, and they had killed her for it.

Joan appeared on the doorstep a moment later, her fists raining down on him. "I told you!" she shouted. "I told you this would happen if you brought her here." Her voice was sharp and cruel. "You killed her, Stephen. You killed her."

The words cut into him. It was the thing he most feared, the very thing he had come here to prevent. His son, dead. His daughter, dead. Both of them because of his own ignorant choices. But no. He hadn't brought Tavera here. It was Joan who'd done that. A great rage swelled in his chest, and he raised his hand to strike her, to drive her and her painful accusations away.

As he did so, he caught a glimpse of her eyes. They weren't pitiless and harsh like her words, but full of desperate pain. Her eyes looked so much like his own heart felt that instead of pushing her away, he wrapped his arms around her and crushed her into his chest, pinning her arms between them.

"It's not your fault," he said. "You didn't know."

She struggled and tried to keep hitting him, but he held her fast.

"You did what you had to," he said. "It was Tavera. Not you."

Slowly her struggles weakened, and she crumpled in his arms like a bird with broken wings. She was so vulnerable in that moment, nothing like the lioness that had kept him at arm's length since Peter's death. He suddenly understood that all her fierce strength was only to keep back the pain, and he saw how deeply he had failed her. Too late. He wanted to rewind the years, to see past his own sadness and recognize hers. She had been the strong one, the one who had pulled him through, and he'd wallowed in his own grief and guilt instead of paying attention to her. She'd never been able to open her shell, and he'd never been able to see past it.

"It's not your fault," he said again.

She took a deep, shaky breath and let it out. "It doesn't matter whose fault it is. The damage is done." Her voice sounded like it was coming from far away. "She's gone."

But Parris's mind was already racing ahead. His heart beat faster. "Maybe not."

⊷+⊶

PARRIS pounded relentlessly on the door of the barracks in the Spanish quarter where Sinclair was now forced to lodge. He was numb, running on a desperate need to keep moving. He pushed hope and emotion out of his mind, focusing only on what must be done. Get Sinclair. Get his equipment. One step at a time.

He thought of Catherine's body, lying ruined at his doorstep. He wondered what her last thought had been.

No. He thrust it out of his mind. He knew if he thought about her, if he admitted she was truly gone, he would go mad, just like he had with Peter. But this was why they had come to Horizon in the first place. This time, just maybe, there was something he could do about it.

Sinclair came to the door, two days' growth of beard on his face.

"They shot my daughter," Parris said.

Sinclair showed no reaction. "I'm sorry," he said. He walked back inside.

Parris followed him. "What do you mean, 'I'm sorry'? That's all you have to say?"

"It's all coming apart. All our plans, destroyed. God is winning," Sinclair said.

"God didn't kill Catherine. Tavera did. And you can bring her back again."

Sinclair's eyes were hollow. "It can't be done."

"You were close! You said you were."

"Maybe Bishop Marcheford is right. We can't win. Maybe it's better to die now than to scrabble and grasp at life and fall short."

Parris seized his shoulders, shook him, and pushed him against the wall. "This is my only child. Kill yourself if you like, but not until you bring her back."

Sinclair's eyes seemed to clear. "You're serious."

"Of course I am! Please!"

"If you haven't noticed, I'm not the governor anymore. Tavera and Vaughan have me on a leash."

"And if you sneaked out tonight?"

His eyes focused a little. "You can't go partway on this. If we try it, there's no stopping."

"I understand."

"We can't do it alone, either. We'll need your Society friends."

"I want to help, too," said a voice.

The men whirled. It was Joan, standing tall and determined, with her eyes blazing. "I'll do anything," she said. "Let me help, or I'll take a sword and start killing every Spaniard I can find until they cut me down."

"You can't help; it's too dangerous," Parris said.

She slapped him hard across the face. "It was dangerous for me to give birth to her. It was dangerous to follow her here across thousands of miles. Don't tell me I can't risk my life as well as any man."

Sinclair, now released from Parris's grip, gave her a short bow. "You are welcome to join us, madam. But there's a problem. The things we need are in my house, and I don't live there anymore."

✦✦✦

JOAN sobbed uncontrollably on the doorstep of the governor's mansion. Parris, watching from the darkness, was amazed. She could maintain an iron exterior on learning of her daughter's death, and then fake hysteria a moment later. She was a remarkable woman.

When Vaughan came to the door, she started screaming barely intelligible accusations at him. She advanced, pointing her finger like a sword. The two Spaniards standing guard advanced to hold her back, but Vaughan waved them away.

"It wasn't me," Vaughan said. "Joanie, I didn't do it. I would never . . ."

She collapsed in his arms, sobbing harder, and he led her inside, saying, "There, there, my dear." The door closed.

Parris and Sinclair waited a few moments, then made their way up to the front of the house, Parris holding a length of rope over his shoulder and several empty burlap sacks. The soldiers barred their way. "What is your business here?" said one in heavily accented English.

"The governor expects us," Parris said. "Ask him."

But Vaughan was already at the door. "Let them in."

They walked past the guards and into the house, where Parris quickly shut the door behind them. Vaughan was calm, though his face was flushed. Joan stood just behind him with a dagger to the side of his neck, where a thin trickle of blood already stained his skin. Parris had no doubt that she would kill him if she had to. Vaughan apparently agreed.

Parris bound his hands with the rope. "Bring him with us."

"We should kill him," Joan said.

"Not until we find everything. If he's moved things, we need to know where they are."

They passed first into the bestiary. Catherine had described it to him, but Parris was still amazed at the variety of animals, most of which he recognized, but some of which he didn't. A bird with a silver beak lay dead on the floor, its cage door swinging open. Sinclair glared at Vaughan.

"I couldn't stand that noise," Vaughan said.

The next cage stood empty, too. "Tried to touch my sooty toad?" Sinclair said.

"It burst into flame," Vaughan said. "Burned itself and one of my men to death."

"Oh, the toad didn't die," Sinclair said. "Perhaps you should keep your hands away from things you don't understand."

"I . . . I've kept the door closed since then," Vaughan said.

"Just as well. The animals in the next room would do more than just kill you."

They opened the next door and passed into near-darkness. Parris could hear the movements of large animals in the cages around him, but he could see nothing of them. Sinclair led the way past them into his laboratory.

Parris passed the burlap sacks around. At Sinclair's direction, they filled them with beaks, horns, and bones; jars of insects; dozens of vials of liquids and powders; and tinctures of all colors, though there was much they left behind. Sinclair lifted a wooden box down from a shelf and held it reverently.

A knock on the front door startled them. "Someone's here," Parris said.

Vaughan suddenly pulled away from Joan. "Help!" he shouted. "Thieves!"

Joan was on him in two steps. She didn't give him a second chance. She plunged the knife into his side, and he screamed and fell, his doublet immediately stained red.

"Time to go," Sinclair said. "Follow me." He hurried to a side door and flung it open.

Joan kicked Vaughan in the face. "You promised," she shouted. "You promised you'd keep her safe!"

Boots pounded through the house. "Come on," Parris said. He pulled her after Sinclair through the side door. The door they had originally come through flew open, and Parris caught a glimpse of Tavera and several Spanish soldiers before Sinclair slammed the side door and locked it behind them. In moments they were out of the house and running through the gate.

Gibbs and Kecilpenny met them in the forest with Catherine's corpse. They walked farther on, following routes they'd explored many times, heading toward a complex of caves that the Spanish would be hard-pressed to find.

Parris doubted that Vaughan was dead. In England, perhaps, that knife wound would have killed, but with quintessence water in his veins, it would already be healed.

"He promised me he would keep us safe," Joan said. "I would retrieve my daughter and bring her back with me to England, where Mary's reign would mean peace and a return to the Church. Is this what they meant by peace? Threats and murder? I'm sorry I ever helped them."

She still clutched the bloody knife in her hand. Gently, Parris pulled her fingers away from it. As she loosened her grip, she began to moan, almost inaudibly at first. She stared at Catherine's corpse, and her moan grew in volume and turned to crying—not the hysteria she had pretended at the mansion, but real, wracking, heart-wrenching sobs like Parris had never heard from her before. He tossed the knife aside and put his arms around her. She clutched at him and cried into his shoulder until his doublet was wet.

After a few moments she regained control and, after a deep, fluttering breath, said, "Let's go. We should catch up with the others."

"Are you all right?"

"Of course I'm not all right."

"I meant—"

"I know what you meant. I can walk. Let's go."

They pushed through the undergrowth. "Next time, I'm going to kill him," Joan said.

—◄+╋+►—

SINCLAIR lifted his hands with the boarcat paws and raised them over the body. They stood in the largest of the caves, and Catherine's motionless form lay stretched out on the rock floor. A jar of Shekinah flatworms made the cave as bright as day.

They began. This time it was Parris who was the surrogate. He lay down next to the body with his arms folded across his chest. Sinclair connected him to his daughter with the glowing strands, chest to chest, heart to heart, head to head. Catherine's corpse breathed and moved in tandem with Parris's chest and limbs, and the others gasped in astonishment.

Gibbs and Kecilpenny were both charged with controlling the void, and Sinclair began to wrap the glowing strand that connected Catherine's body with her spirit, coaxing it back out of the darkness, attaching it to the anchor that tied Parris's spirit to his body. The void grew faster, but Gibbs and Kecilpenny kept it under control.

"Almost there," Sinclair said.

The oscillating began. The strand vibrated back and forth between Catherine and the void.

This time, things would be different. Sinclair knew the kind of power he was dealing with now. The strand became harder and harder to pull, but instead of forcing it, he drew out just a little at a time. He couldn't pull too fast or too hard, or the void would become unmanageable again. There was no hurry.

The fact that human life was bound up in strands of quintessence, too, implied that quintessence existed all over the world, not just on Horizon. Perhaps it was too dim to notice in England, or they had just never learned how to use it. How many stories of women knowing the exact moment when their husbands or children were killed, or twins knowing what the other was thinking or experiencing from far away, were really instances of quintessential mind connection? It was a promising thought, since it implied the powers of the manticores and other Horizon animals might be learned by humans as well.

Growing in confidence, Sinclair twisted and knotted the glowing strands, just as he had seen the female boarcat do. Catherine's soul had departed her body, but the connection was still in place. Her body no longer had an anchor to hold a soul: that was lost, perhaps to the void, and he knew no way to retrieve it or make a new one. Instead, he would tie her soul through her body to her father's: two souls attached to one anchor. It wasn't a perfect solution, since it meant that when Parris died, Catherine would die with him. But first he had to make it work.

Soon the strands nearly encased her, a mummification by light. Parris gasped and reached up, and Catherine's body mimicked the action. Remembering the visions Maasha Kaatra had seen at the end, Sinclair hadn't given Parris any skink tears, but apparently it didn't matter. Parris's eyes were wide. "Mother," he said in a tone of wonder.

Joan crouched at his side, and her eyes, too, grew wide with astonishment. "It's her," she said. "She's here." Then she turned toward more empty air. "Grandmother!"

Sinclair didn't know what this was about—only Maasha Kaatra had seen spirits last time, and he hadn't survived to tell about it. He understood even less how Joan could see them, since she wasn't involved in the process at all. The two of them turned back and forth, apparently seeing presences all around them. Then they both turned toward the same place and cried, "Peter!" together in voices of longing and deep anguish. Parris struggled to his feet, dragging Catherine's body with him, tangling the strands.

"Stop!" Sinclair said. "Hold still."

The void surged, and Kecilpenny cried out. Gibbs lunged with his beetlewood plank and only just managed to contain it.

"Hold still!" Sinclair shouted.

He pulled the strands harder, stretching the weave. To his horror, the void surged toward him, as if moved by his pull.

"We're losing it!" Gibbs shouted.

Sinclair watched, frozen, as the void swelled toward him. He could see Catherine's strand stretching far, far away into its endless blackness, and then, in the distance, a bright light approaching very fast. As it grew closer, he could see something bright and living writhing inside it, like a moth in its cocoon. The bright thing shot past him on its strand and straight into Catherine's body.

A roar came from the earth below them. The whole cave shook, and then the floor lurched, knocking them all off their feet. In a gout of purple flame, the jar of Shekinah flatworms immolated. The flames became thousands of purple moths that filled the room, fluttering against each other and into the walls and shelves, dashing themselves into bits of wing and violet powder. There was an immense ringing silence. Catherine's body had been replaced with a black silhouette, a void with her shape, flecked with distant stars. Sinclair saw a flash behind his eyes and the cave disappeared around him.

When he came to himself again, the glowing strands and void had both vanished. Parris and Joan sat on the cave floor clutched in each other's arms, trembling. Gibbs and Kecilpenny were farther away, dazed, just picking themselves up off the ground.

In the middle of them all, Catherine sat up, fresh and beautiful, a beatific smile on her face. She yawned dramatically. "Father, Mother," she said in a clear voice. She beamed at them, but her smile faltered when she saw their astonished faces. "What happened?"

◆◆◆

TWO hundred cliff dippers skimmed their hunting grounds at the Edge, plunging their sideways beaks into solid rock. This time it wasn't just a section of rock that fell. All along the cliff edge where the island stopped, a deafening crack echoed. Lightning gaps streaked across hard-packed dirt, grass, forest, and scrub. Animals leaped away, most instinctively jumping toward the mainland instead of toward the void.

The crack widened. Puff lizards rose on inflated bodies and wafted across to safety. Tiny marmosets leaped from tree to tree, some missing their mark and plummeting into the gap. Samson mice screeched as their rock piles tumbled. Golden oxen bellowed as acres of ground tilted toward the Edge, knocking them off their feet.

As the surviving dippers pumped their wings to propel them higher, hundreds of miles of coastline sheared away from the mainland like a great ship sliding away from the harbor, its movement almost imperceptible at first, but gaining a horrible momentum, its mass beyond contemplation. With a roar like thunder, trees and animals spinning off its surface, the great mass of land tumbled away and dropped into the endless void.

Chapter Twenty-nine

IT felt like waking up from a long sleep. They told her she had been dead, but it was hard for Catherine to grasp. She couldn't remember anything. The last thing she recalled was being caught trying to rescue Matthew, but she had no memory between then and waking up on the cave floor.

It had all been for nothing. Matthew and Blanca were still prisoners, and she, though grateful to be alive, was no farther along than she'd been two days before. She had to find a way to rescue her friends before Tavera killed them.

Father and Mother barely let her out of their sight. They hugged her and touched her cheek and stroked her hair and told her how much they loved her so often she wanted to scream. What was there to be so happy about? The colony was in the grip of vicious men, and Matthew and Blanca . . . she didn't want to think about what might be happening to them.

It was late. Her parents insisted she lie down. They sat on either side of her, watching her, unwilling to leave. The moment she stretched out on the bed of moss and leaves, however, she realized how exhausted she was. She could barely keep her eyes open. In moments she was asleep.

⊶✦✦⊷

PARRIS sat with his hand tightly gripped in Joan's, watching Catherine sleep. He watched her chest rise and fall with life-giving breath, afraid to look away lest it stop. She was real. She was still here, tangible and alive.

Parris moistened his dry lips and swallowed. "It really was Peter," he said, not looking at Joan.

She didn't answer, but her fingers strengthened their grip.

"Not just a vision. Somehow, it was him. He saw us. He smiled." It was tangible proof. Not enough to convince anyone else, perhaps, but enough to convince him. He had seen his son. The souls of the dead really did live on. Although he knew no more about heaven than he had ever known, a great feeling of peace settled on him. His daughter was alive in front of him, and his son, though gone, still lived. Despite his weak faith, he had been given a sign, which was more than he deserved. He would trust God for the rest.

"Someday," Joan said, and Parris knew what she meant.

"Someday," he said.

Eventually, when they could barely lift their heads for exhaustion, he tenderly lifted Joan to her feet and led her to the other side of the cave to sleep.

⊰⊹⊱

SINCLAIR barely slept all night. He had triumphed. Catherine had been dead, and now she was alive. He had raised a human being to life. Every alchemist for a thousand years had searched for the philosopher's stone, but only he had really found it. He had nearly killed them all in the process, true, but it had worked. He had won. He had beaten God after all.

He gave up on sleep just before dawn and went outside, buzzing with energy and excitement. He wanted to do it again. He wanted to do it a hundred times, until it was ordinary, until no one needed to fear death again. More than that—he wanted to learn how to tie the spirit to the body so that it would never leave. After all, he didn't want to rely on others to bring him back. He never wanted to die in the first place.

A black shape moved in the darkness. Sinclair backed away and drew his knife. The soft mossy foliage on Horizon meant trees and bushes didn't rustle like they did in England. "Who's there?" he said.

"John Marcheford," came the reply. The black shape stepped out of the trees and resolved into the dark-clad figure of a man.

"Bishop," Sinclair said. "You gave me a start."

"I thought I might find you here," Marcheford said.

"Here we are. And what about you? Rumors have you doing everything from ruling the manticores to paddling back to England in a log canoe."

Marcheford frowned. "The first is closer, though I'm far from ruling them. They've come close to killing me several times. That's why I came. To warn you."

"Warn me of what?"

"The tribes are gathering. The grays haven't forgotten the reception the Spanish gave them, and after last night, it wasn't hard to convince the others."

"What do you mean, 'after last night'? What happened last night?"

Marcheford gave him a searching look. "The earthquake."

Sinclair remembered how the cave had shaken the moment Catherine's spirit reentered her body, knocking them all down. "You're telling me they felt the ground shake all the way out there?"

"It's still shaking. A wedge of cliff as big as your settlement sheared off and fell off the Edge. More has been crumbling over the side all night. Can't you hear it?"

Sinclair listened. There was a continuous rumbling sound he hadn't noticed until now, a deep vibration in the earth he could almost feel more than hear.

"The manticores are in a fury, and they're coming. Not just the few dozen grays that your soldiers defeated before. Some of these tribes have been enemies for generations, but they're on the same side now. Chichirico has tried to keep the reds out of it, but a good many of them have joined anyway."

"Good. Maybe they'll kill all the Spanish."

"They won't differentiate. They'll kill humans, whatever their nationality. I doubt they can even tell the difference."

"Why don't they kill you?"

"For the time being, I'm tolerated, but it won't last. If nothing changes over the next few days, I'll be dead along with everyone else. If they knew I was here warning you, I wouldn't last the night."

Sinclair kicked at the dirt. "Why must they blame us for an earthquake?" He was going to say more, maybe rant about savages and religions, but the look on Marcheford's face stopped him.

"What did you do?" Marcheford said. When Sinclair didn't answer, he said, "I know you caused the first quake, the one that brought them to the settlement. This one was ten times worse, and I want to know: What did you do?"

Sinclair couldn't help it; he started to laugh. "It's ironic," he said. "Just before you arrived, I was celebrating my victory over God. It seems he won't let me win so easily."

"Tell me."

"I raised Catherine Parris from the dead."

Marcheford stared for a long moment. "You . . ."

"Yes." Sinclair laughed again, a bitter chuckle. "I actually did it."

Sinclair heard a metallic noise in the forest, something completely out of place in the silent predawn. "Who else is here?" He searched Marcheford's face for signs of treachery, but Marcheford looked startled, too.

Diego de Tavera walked out of the trees, a pistol in each hand, accompanied by five soldiers, who moved to cut off any attempt at escape. Behind them came Andrew Kecilpenny.

Sinclair couldn't believe it. Kecilpenny, who the night before had worked alongside him, controlling the void. Who had slept in the cave, but must have slipped out during the night, quietly enough that no one heard him, and betrayed them all. Sinclair had trusted him. He'd shared his secrets, and for what? Now the Spanish would know everything. Sinclair would kill him. He would wring his fat neck and hang him up for the birds to eat.

Kecilpenny's face was pale and stricken. "They have my Elizabeth," he said. "I had to tell them. They—"

"Quiet." Tavera hit him with a brutal backhand, sending him to the ground with a bleeding nose. He regarded Sinclair with no emotion. "Where's the girl?"

⊰✦✦✦⊱

CATHERINE heard raised voices and ran out of the cave, followed by her parents and John Gibbs. She stopped short when she saw the soldiers.

"Ah, there she is," Tavera said. "The miracle herself." He circled, examining her. "You truly are alive. Kecilpenny told me, but I didn't believe." He brushed aside a lock of her hair and traced the skin of her forehead where she'd been shot. "No sign of any wound. Amazing."

Father knocked Tavera's hand away. "Leave her alone."

Tavera's jaw twitched. His pale, dead eyes shifted to Father. "I've been learning about your occult practices," he said. "It pays to be informed about the devil's work. Your friend Matthew has been quite instructive."

He smiled, but it didn't reach his eyes. "You'll find I know everything about you and your cabal. I've been honing my techniques for some time, but this island opens up all kinds of new possibilities. It's incredible how much pain can be inflicted on a body that heals itself immediately. There's almost no limit to it."

Catherine felt her throat constrict and fear boiled in her stomach. Matthew had been tortured, and she'd been here, sleeping peacefully through the night. "What have you done to him?" she said.

"You'll find out soon enough, my dear." Tavera turned to Mother. "I thought you were on our side."

She spat on his feet. "You killed my daughter."

Tavera laughed. "She doesn't look dead to me." He snapped his fingers and two soldiers stepped up. "Take the girl to the ship and chain her in the brig. I'll not have her rescued."

Two soldiers grabbed Catherine's arms.

"No!" Father said. "She knows nothing about it. Take me instead."

"I'll take you, too. And understand, your daughter's treatment depends on your good behavior. If you refuse to answer my questions, or escape, or even die, it will go hard on your daughter. And believe me, I can make her *very* uncomfortable."

The soldiers tied their arms behind their backs. Kecilpenny sat up, his face a mess of blood. "Tie that one, too," Tavera said.

"Please," Kecilpenny said. "I told you everything you wanted to know. You promised you would let my daughter go free."

Tavera stood over him, arms folded. "And why would I do that? You may have more yet to tell me."

Kecilpenny spread his hands plaintively. "I've told you everything."

"You think this is God's work?" Marcheford said. "Holding a little girl captive to make her father betray his friends?" Catherine looked at him in surprise. She didn't like Matthew's father very much, but he was brave, she had to admit, to speak up in this situation. Even with his arms tied behind his back, he managed to look distinguished, and his voice rang as if he were preaching a sermon to the king.

"These men are sorcerers," Tavera said. "They practice the foulest witchcraft, and everyone knows it. I've been sent here to purify the island, and I will do it."

"Elizabeth Kecilpenny is six years old," Marcheford said. "She's no sorcerer. Let her go."

Tavera actually seemed to consider it. "You've truly told me every-thing?" he asked Kecilpenny.

"I promise. Everything I know."

Casually, Tavera lifted one of his pistols and aimed it. "You know, I believe you have." He depressed the mechanism that touched match to pan, and the small gun blasted a haze of burnt smoke into the air. Kecil-penny's body jerked backward, slumped to the ground, and lay still.

"No!" Gibbs shouted. He tried to run to his friend, but the soldiers knocked him down. Catherine felt frozen with shock.

"I don't want this one popping up alive again," Tavera said. "Take his body to the bay and tie a rock to it. Make sure it doesn't come back up."

Catherine stared at Kecilpenny's ruined body and thought of Eliza-beth, only six years old, and Mary, his young wife. It was all coming apart. These men were too powerful, too cruel. She started to cry. "He did what you wanted," she said. "He helped you. You didn't have to kill him."

"He practiced the occult, like the rest of them," Tavera said, waving a hand to indicate the gathered men. A vicious smile spread across his face. "I hope they love you more than their secrets. Because if they don't, you're going in the water next."

Father gave a cry and lunged for Tavera, but the soldiers intercepted him. The last Catherine saw of him as they carried her away was the butts of their weapons driving him to the ground.

Chapter Thirty

THE dawn light flared over the treetops. Sinclair trudged through the forest, tied in a chain behind Stephen Parris, Catherine, Joan, Bishop Marcheford, and John Gibbs. At the beach the soldiers separated them, taking Parris and his family into the Spanish galleon and sending Sinclair with Marcheford and Gibbs on to the settlement. Instead of the prison in the Spanish quarter, as Sinclair expected, they brought them to the church. They chained them to the heavy altar and set soldiers outside to guard the building.

Along the way, Marcheford had passed his warning about the manticores on to Tavera, but Tavera didn't take it seriously. "We can see them, and we can shoot them," he said. "We'll send them running again, if they're foolish enough to try."

Once they were chained and left alone in the church, Sinclair asked, "How many manticores are we talking about?"

"Hundreds at least," Marcheford said. "It's hard to say."

"The fools." Sinclair yanked at his chains, but they held fast. "We're the ones most likely to find a solution, and here we are, trapped. The manticores will kill the Spanish first, and then come kill us, too." The thought made his heart hammer in his chest, and he rattled the chains in fury. "There has to be a way out. I won't die like this."

"The manticores knew," Marcheford said. "Somehow they knew what you did. They kept talking about restoring the balance of life. I thought they were just talking about getting rid of all the humans, but I think now they must have meant it literally. Somehow Catherine's resurrection is causing this quake."

Sinclair paused to listen, willing his panicked breathing to slow. He could still hear the bass rumbling deep under their feet. If pieces of the island were breaking off, did that mean the whole island was slowly sliding over the Edge? He wondered which would kill them first, the island or the manticores.

"Are you afraid?" Marcheford asked.

If anyone else had asked, Sinclair would have said no, but Marcheford knew him well enough by now. He nodded. "I'm so close. Another month of study, another week even, and every man on this island could be immortal."

"What you're trying to do, Christ has already done. It's not just a spiritual metaphor, as you called it. For those who trust in him, it's a certainty. A new and eternal life in a better world."

Sinclair was annoyed. The idea of another world on the far side of the void was attractive, but without any evidence to support it, it was nothing more than a pleasant fiction. Sinclair was not going to tell himself comfortable stories just to feel better about dying. "This world is all I have," he said.

Gibbs had buried his face in his knees since they had chained him here, but now he looked up. "What about Kecilpenny?" he said. Tears tracked through the dirt on his face. He shook his head at Marcheford. "All my life I believed in God."

"Believe in him still, as your friend did," Marcheford said.

"How can I? The universe is a machine, composed of tiny atoms with neither mind nor will. Now we find that the 'spirit' is simply part of the universe, an intelligent spark that obeys natural laws and can be manipulated by men. What's left for the divine? I've seen Sinclair perform more miracles than God."

Marcheford's voice was soft. "Don't think 'God' is just a word to explain what we don't understand. God isn't only in the miracles. He's in the movement of every atom, the fall of every leaf, the death of every creature."

Gibbs scowled. "He's responsible for Kecilpenny's death, then?"

"He controls all things. Responsibility is a different question. Diego de Tavera is the one responsible for your friend's death."

"I would kill him if I could."

Marcheford's eyes blazed briefly, as they had sometimes from his pulpit in England. "As would I."

The door opened, and Sinclair feared their conversation had been overheard. "Christopher Sinclair?" a soldier said. "Come with us."

⊷✦✦✦⊶

THE brig on the Spanish ship was larger than the one on the *Western Star*. It was deep in the hold and felt airless and dank. They locked Parris and Joan in an otherwise empty cell that stank of fish. They took Catherine away, and refused to tell them where. No one came for them, and they were given no food or water. The cell was dark, but enough sunlight seeped through the cracks that Parris could see a dim outline of Joan's face.

"You were right," she said. "I thought it was all foolishness, but you really did it. You brought her back to life."

"Sinclair did."

"I was so angry at you. I didn't care if they brought you home in chains, so long as I got my daughter back. If I had never told them about the beetle, then Tavera would never have come here, and Catherine would never . . ."

"It's all right. She's alive. It doesn't matter." He reached out a hand to her in the darkness, and Joan moved toward him, burying her face into his shoulder and wrapping her arms around his ribs. He couldn't remember the last time she'd done that.

"It's not all right," she said. "Tavera's got her now, and he'll . . . You haven't seen what they've been doing at home. Trials every day. Burnings at Smithfield, so that you can smell the smoke for miles. Men, women, children . . . and Tavera always asking questions about where you were going in your ship and what you expected to find. I thought if I told him . . ."

Parris's eyes were growing accustomed to the darkness. He could see the anguish in her face. He had never understood her. He had thought what she cared about was money and comfort, lands and rank, and marriage prospects. But here she was, risking her life with dangerous men and chasing across an ocean wilderness to get her daughter back. It was Catherine she cared about, with a ferocity he was only now coming to appreciate.

"I'm sorry," he said. "I should never have taken her away from you."

⊷✦✦✦⊶

THE soldiers brought Catherine to another cell on the ship and chained her arms to a beam on the ceiling, forcing her to hold them up over her head. It wasn't until after they left, clanging the rusty metal door behind them, that she noticed another person curled in the shadows. It was Matthew.

Matthew groaned and opened his eyes. When he saw her, he smiled. "Am I dead, too, then?"

"You're not dead, and neither am I. If I were dead, would I be chained up like this?"

"But I saw him shoot you." His smile faded, and he came fully awake. "Sinclair?"

She nodded. "He succeeded this time. He brought me back to life."

Matthew tried to get up, but his neck was chained to the floor, so he could only lift his head slightly. "Do you remember anything?"

She shook her head. "Nothing. It was like being asleep. They've tortured you, haven't they?"

A shadow of anguish flitted across his face, but he forced a weak smile. "I told them some great secrets to begin with, like the supernatural strength you can get from eating theramite weed."

Her mouth dropped open. "But it's poisonous to the touch!"

"I forgot to mention that."

"But surely they hurt you even worse?"

She saw a spark of fire in his eyes. "And what of it? You were dead. My plan was to fight them until they killed me, too. But then . . ."

"What?"

"Tavera stopped hurting me. Instead, he brought in . . . he brought . . ." Matthew's voice broke. His attempt at bravado crumpled, and tears flooded his eyes. "He brought in a colonist, a man I barely knew, and shot him. He said he'd do it again and again until I cooperated." He swallowed hard. "After that, I talked."

"Of course you did." She was amazed that Matthew had resisted them for so long. It revealed a strength beyond what she would have expected, beyond what she feared she would be able to withstand herself. "You had no choice. Those lives were more important."

"I know. It doesn't make it any easier."

"That morning at the church, before they took you . . . you said you'd found the answer that would allow us to go home."

He nodded sadly. "I told them that, too. Remember the double box I built, with the void between the layers? In the inner box, bread would revert back to sand, gold back to sticks and stones. Just like they would at home."

"But you found a way to prevent it."

"It was quite simple, actually. I put a Shekinah flatworm in with them."

She stared. "The *worm* made the difference?"

"I found it by accident," Matthew said. "I was just testing different objects to see if any had a different effect. I think we've been wrong about everything."

"What do you mean?"

"We were treating light like it was just another thing quintessence could produce. But that's not right. Light *is* quintessence in its purest form."

"Like the stars?"

"Exactly. A void is a conduit to nothing, the absence of matter or energy. A star, or a Shekinah flatworm, is a conduit to another place, to the source of life and energy."

"Then why don't we have quintessence back in England?"

"I think we do, only it's diluted somehow, or not as pure."

She shook her head. "The answer to everything. A worm."

"Now they've been gathering all the worms they can and preparing a cargo to ship back home. Once gold and diamonds start arriving back in Europe, there will be no stopping the ships. They'll come here by the dozen."

They heard pounding feet. The door crashed open, and Vaughan pushed into the room, followed by two soldiers. Each of them was holding a spearhawk beak. They spread out in the room, holding the beaks in front of them like divining rods. All three beaks pointed directly at Catherine.

"Explain yourself!" Vaughan shouted.

"About what? What's happening?" Catherine said.

"We moved some of these beaks from the settlement to the ship, to give us warning of manticore attack," Vaughan said. "Only we found that all of them were pointing *toward* the ship. As if the manticores were already inside."

"There aren't any manticores in here," Catherine said. "And those beaks point toward any concentration of quintessence, not just manticores."

"Then explain to me why they're all pointing toward you." Vaughan smiled, clearly relieved that it was only Catherine and not a manticore insurgence. "What are you hiding, cousin?"

"Nothing."

"Come, now. You and your father have discovered some device to store quintessence. You have it on your person. Give it to me."

She shook her head. "There's nothing like that."

"It will do you no good to pretend." He motioned to the Spanish soldiers. "I can have my men search you."

Catherine pulled away as far as the chains that held her arms would allow.

"Stay away from her," Matthew said.

Vaughan pointed. "Juan. Luis. Search her. Let's see what she's hiding."

Catherine shrieked and tried to pull farther away, but with her arms chained above her head, she couldn't even shield herself.

"Don't you touch her!" Matthew shouted. He yanked at his chains, but he couldn't get free.

⇥✦✦⇤

SINCLAIR had never felt such pain. While Tavera sipped a glass of wine nearby, a soldier put a white-hot knife underneath his fingernails. Sinclair was no hero. He hated the Spanish, but if it came to a choice between helping them and dying, the choice was clear. He had to live. To lose it all now, so close to realizing his life's ambition, would be pointless. If others had to die—Parris or Gibbs or Matthew Marcheford—that would be sad. But he was the only one who could continue the work. No matter what, *he* had to stay alive.

So he gave in. He told Tavera everything, from the failed attempt and Maasha Kaatra's death to his final success with Catherine. Tavera asked pointed questions, and sometimes seemed to know the answer to a question before he asked it, but Sinclair had no desire to be caught in a trap. He told the truth.

He tried to describe the quintessence strands around Catherine and what he had done with them, but Tavera wasn't content with an explanation. "Show me," he said. Flanked by soldiers, they walked through the beetlewood trees toward the ship.

"Where are the other guards?" Tavera asked a soldier on the dock.

"Down below in the brig, my lord. Investigating a possible manticore attack."

"You've seen manticores?"

"No, my lord. The spearhawk beaks were all pointing that way. More likely an animal of some kind, or a large fish under the boat, but they had to investigate."

They climbed the ladders down into the hold. Tavera burst into a cell. Sinclair, just behind him, caught a glimpse of the scene inside: Catherine Parris, chained to the ceiling by her arms, and two Spanish soldiers, grinning, their hands pulling at her clothes. She twisted away from them, and her hands *slipped* out of the chains. Clearly surprised, she nearly fell, but recovered and backed into the corner, wrapping her arms around her chest. The chains hung loose from the beam.

"What's happening here?" The sharp voice was not a shout, but it drew everyone's attention to the doorway. Vaughan jumped back, startled, and Sinclair suspected that Tavera had not authorized this interrogation. Vaughan was the governor, of course, but everyone knew Tavera held the real power.

"Leave us," Tavera said. He pointed to Matthew. "And take him out of here." Vaughan scuttled away like a cockroach in the light. The soldiers unchained Matthew and dragged him away.

"It's surprising how much sorcery you find in a place, once you start to root it out," Tavera said in his oily voice. "How did you get out of your chains?"

Catherine rubbed her wrists. "Get away from me."

Tavera advanced. "I have the only key, so I know Vaughan didn't let you out. There's dark magic going on here. How did you do it?"

"I don't know! I just pulled hard, and my hands came free."

"We'll find out, no matter how long it takes."

Catherine, visibly frustrated, started to show some fire. "I don't know! Check the chains; maybe they were rusted or something."

"You know what sorcery is, don't you?"

Catherine crossed her arms and didn't answer.

"It's power that the devil offers in exchange for doing his work. And the devil's work is to claim soul after soul and lead them away from the Church. In Spain, we would sooner burn you alive than let you tempt others to heresy."

She turned away. "That's barbaric."

"It's merciful. The fires of the stake are nothing to the fires of hell. If, for instance, we could save you, in the blush of youthful innocence, from falling prey to your father's degradations, it would be worth any torment."

"My father is a good man!"

"Oh, in Spain your father would burn in a moment. The whole colony knows him for a devil worshipper."

"He's not! He believes in finding the truth, not accepting what others tell him."

"Careful. I've seen girls younger than you go to the flames. If they're lucky, their families have enough money to buy a pouch of gunpowder to throw at their feet. Otherwise, it can take hours."

Sinclair lurked in the corner, apparently forgotten for the moment. He picked up a spearhawk beak from where it had fallen on the floor. He moved it back and forth, noticing how it always pointed at Catherine. He couldn't get it to stop pointing at her, even if he twisted it as hard as he could. Amazing. "She doesn't know anything," he said.

Tavera turned his pale blue eyes on him. "Defending a witch? That's grounds for suspicion, at the least."

Sinclair shook his head. "There's something else going on here."

"What is? You'd better explain yourself."

Thanks to the quintessence water, Sinclair's fingernails had already grown back, but that just meant they could be pulled out again. The healing was complete, but he could still remember the pain. He started to explain.

"Wait." Tavera turned to the soldiers. "Stay. Watch them closely." Then to Sinclair: "Come with me."

They left the cell and retreated to the hold, which was rotten with weathered casks and worn sailcloth. Sinclair explained to Tavera about the beak. "It's as if she has a quintessence pearl inside her."

"Like the manticores?" Tavera said.

"Like the manticores, like the eels, like just about every animal here."

"And now she emits the same energy."

"Only greater. Like an ocean full of eels." Sinclair shook his head. "I have no explanation. It's like she's tapping into the stars."

"Or like she's possessed by an angel."

Sinclair gave him a quizzical look.

"Why not?" Tavera said. "Demons are but fallen angels, and we know they can possess a man. What if she were possessed by an angel?"

"You just accused her of heresy! Threatened to burn her at the stake!"

Tavera waved his hand in a dismissive gesture. "What I want to know is, can her energy be harnessed? Could it be used for practical purposes?"

"We've no shortage of quintessence pearls," Sinclair said, and then stared at Tavera as comprehension dawned. "You want to give quintessence powers to humans." Sinclair felt dizzy with the implications. It certainly was possible that with her own source of quintessence . . .

"Think of it," Tavera said, his eyes alight. "Invisible soldiers . . . swords passing through them without harm . . . instantaneous communication through their minds. Our armies would sweep across the earth. The whole world would be brought under the Church in one glorious Christian empire."

Sinclair would have laughed, if the thought of Tavera at the head of an invincible army wasn't so disturbing. In all their experimentation, they had never been able to give a human the abilities of the manticores to turn invisible or walk through walls, nor the ability of other animals to make their bodies change texture or color or become as light as air. But what if those abilities came from having an internal quintessence pearl, connected to nerves and tissues and bone? If so, that implied that Catherine . . .

He spotted a pair of Samson-mouse gloves lying on a crate. They were common around the settlement, and now on board the Spanish ship, too, since the sailors used them to lighten the loads of anchors and sails and barrels of ale. The gloves worked that way for most things, but never for lifting humans.

"What are you doing?" Tavera said.

"Let me back inside."

Catherine stood when he entered. Without explanation, Sinclair put his gloved hands around her waist and lifted her. The gloves did their work—she weighed no more than a cask of wine. Expecting her full weight, he nearly knocked her head against the ceiling. She screamed and twisted, trying to free herself. He set her down, being more careful with her this time, and turned to face Tavera, unable to keep the astonishment from his face.

Tavera studied her. Then he reached out and pushed her, a half-hearted shove that wouldn't have knocked over a child. She flew back as if hit by a cannonball, struck the far wall, and fell to the boards.

Tavera laughed. He reached down and lifted her up again with one hand gripping her throat, a maniacal fire lighting his face. "One glorious Christian empire!"

-+++-

TWO soldiers stood guard in Catherine's cell to watch her. She tried to think, but her head hurt from the impact with the wall, and it was hard to concentrate. Her body felt all wrong. She was so light, she was afraid if she jumped, she might hit the ceiling. Master Sinclair had used a pair of Samson-mouse gloves to make her lighter. How? Had he discovered a way to transform human beings? She shuddered. For as long as they had been looking for the answer to that problem, the implications had never occurred to her. She could still feel the nauseating sensation of being lifted like an infant. When she walked, it felt as if part of her body were missing.

And what else might be possible? Could a man be made so heavy he couldn't move? Or so light he floated away into the sky? Or transmuted into some other shape or material? She thought of men with swords for arms, or with extra limbs, or mutated into horrible shapes as punishment for crimes.

Of course, not all of the applications were hideous. It would be convenient to be able to turn invisible, or to climb through walls, especially now. Catherine glanced at the wall next to her, her heart suddenly beating harder. The soldiers watched her. She leaned against the wall and pressed her fingers against it, willing them to pass through, but the wall resisted her touch.

Perhaps she had to believe she could in order to do it. But she couldn't just believe in something she knew was impossible. Could she?

It's true, she told herself. *Whatever Sinclair did to me, it made me special. I can walk through walls. I have to, if I'm going to get out of here. The manticores can do it; I can, too. The easiest thing in the world. I'll do it . . . now.*

She dashed forward and thumped stupidly against the wall. Angry, she yelled and kicked it, hurting her toe. The soldiers moved forward, alarmed.

Catherine slumped to the floor and buried her face in her hands, feeling like an idiot. Her eyes stung and her throat hardened, and though she tried to keep them back, tears streaked her face.

The door opened, and Francis Vaughan walked into the cell. "Don't cry, cousin."

She stood, hugging herself, suddenly aware of how vulnerable she was. It was the middle of the night; Tavera would be back in the settlement asleep, and the soldiers guarding her would surely obey Vaughan.

She held her head high and tried to act commanding. "I'm fine, thank you. You may leave."

Vaughan shut the door behind him. "I'm your cousin. There's no need to be afraid."

Her attempt at bravado crumbled. "Please leave me alone."

"It could have been different, Catherine. For years, I watched you grow older and more beautiful. I asked your father for your hand, you know. But he laughed in my face."

"Get away from me."

"It's always been like that, hasn't it? You and your arrogant father. He could never consider me a suitable match. No matter how high I rose, I was never good enough."

"You don't love me."

"What do you know about it? You don't know what I feel. You don't know what it's like to have no money, no opportunities. For everything you want in life to be forever out of reach."

"It has nothing to do with money or opportunities," she said.

He cocked his head at her. "You're laughing at me, too."

"No. I'm just telling you the truth."

His hand shot out like lightning and slapped her across the face. "Even now, like this, you think you're too good for me."

He blocked her way to the exit. She looked behind her, at the wall.

If she was going to pass through it, now was the time. She grew suddenly angry, at the world, at men who thought of women only as objects for their own purposes. She charged the wall, determined to get to the other side even if she had to break it down.

She went through. It was easy, like a Spanish bullfighter pulling away his red cloth as the bull charges through thin air. She fell flat on her face on the floor on the other side. And ran.

She raced down the gangplank past the guards on the dock, ignoring their surprised shouts. They both had matchlocks, but she reached the tree line before they could fire. She ran among the beetlewood trees, grateful for the soft carpeting underfoot and the lack of undergrowth.

She imagined Vaughan staring incredulously at the wall she had just run through, and a feeling of freedom and euphoria flooded her. She tried another test, willing her body to grow lighter so she could run faster, and it worked. Her feet were bare, so she tried to make the soles tougher to protect her bare skin against twigs and rocks, and succeeded once again. Easy.

Once she passed the beetlewood forest into a region with more varied foliage, she ran straight through any tree that blocked her path—a disconcerting sensation, but one that would put more distance between herself and any pursuers. After running for what seemed like an hour, but was probably much less, she stopped, breathing in gasps, a pain in her side. If only she could alter her body to make her lungs stronger and her muscles not so tired. As soon as she thought it, it happened. Her breathing became easy, and the pain disappeared.

Exhilarated, she ran on. The forest changed, becoming darker and wetter. Straight clean lines turned to sinuous curves and massive trunks with protruding buttresses. The ground became slick. Fungi pushed up through wide, decaying leaves. Soon her bare legs and feet were filthy.

She came upon what looked like the statue of a large bear: hairy, broad, and clawed, but without a bear's protruding snout. She suspected it was neither a bear nor really a statue. It was made entirely of stone, but she didn't trust it to stay that way. She gave it a wide berth and traveled on.

She didn't have a beetle. That meant that not only did she not know where she was going, she didn't know how to get back. The thick forest blocked the sun, stealing all sense of direction. She became gradually aware of presences in the trees around her. They moved quietly, invisibly, so that she didn't so much see or hear them as realize, slowly, that she was not alone.

+++

PARRIS and Joan heard shouting. Their cell door rattled. Joan's head came up, and her eyes betrayed her terror.

"Stay back," Parris said. He clambered to his feet and stood in front of the door, arms crossed. He wondered if Sinclair and Gibbs had been tortured already, and, if so, what they had revealed. They would want to know how Catherine had been resurrected. They would want that power for themselves.

The door banged open. Vaughan stood in the opening, his face working with fury, flanked by soldiers. "Where is she?"

Parris thought he meant Joan. "She can't help you," he said. "She doesn't know anything."

"Tell me."

"She's right here, but it's me you want, not Joan. Whatever you need done—"

"Don't play with me, cousin. I'll have your tongue out. Where's your *daughter*?"

"Catherine?"

"Do you have another? Move aside."

Vaughan pushed through, and Parris let him pass, confused. They searched the cell roughly, though there was almost nothing to see, and certainly nowhere to hide. Vaughan yanked Joan to her feet and moved her aside, as if Catherine might be hiding under her skirts.

Parris stepped between them. "What are you doing?"

"I told you. Looking for your daughter."

"You should know where she is. You took her. Did you lose her?"

"She walked out through the bloody wall!" Vaughan's face flushed an angry red. "You've been holding out on us, you stupid fool. Tavera knows it now. He can get secrets out of anyone." He flashed a brutal smile. "And I'm going to be right there to watch."

Chapter Thirty-one

IT was as close to drowning as Parris thought he could physically come without actually dying. Tavera's soldiers held his head in a barrel of water until his lungs burned and he thrashed in panic. He thought they would pull him out again, but they didn't. He fought against his own muscles, forbidding his throat to open, but his body screamed for air.

They had to pull him out, didn't they? He couldn't give them any answers if he was dead. He twisted his body in violent jerks, but he was bound tightly, and they held him fast. His throat muscles spasmed open, letting in a little water before he clenched them shut again. A powerful urge to cough nearly mastered him. He was choking.

They were taking too long. They weren't going to let him out. He was going to die right now, in only moments, and he wasn't ready. Instead of the peace he thought he might feel at his own death, he felt only panic. Blackness crept over his consciousness. His throat opened against his will and he felt the water rushing in. . . .

A hand slapped him across the face again and again. He was doubled over on the floor, and a soldier was striking him. He retched up water, then turned onto his hands and knees, coughing and gagging and breathing in great gasps of cool, sweet air.

"I can do that as many times as it takes," Tavera said. "I'm very good at it. I know just the right moment. My subjects rarely die, though occasionally I lose one. Would you like to try again?"

Parris shook his head, shivering and shuddering uncontrollably. "I'll help you. I'll tell you whatever you want."

"That's very good," Tavera said. "So tell me. Where is your daughter?"

"Truly, I don't know."

"That's not very helpful. Once again, please."

Parris thrashed as they grabbed hold of him again, but he couldn't pull away. He hadn't even caught his breath from the last time, and they didn't give him a chance.

⊰+┼+⊱

WHEN they finally threw him back in his cell, Joan was there to take him in her arms. When he could breathe again, he repeated to her the questions Tavera had asked about Catherine. If she truly had escaped through a solid wall, it meant her resurrection had changed her in some fundamental way that none of them had predicted. It meant she was free, though, and he prayed they would never find her.

Joan put his head in her lap and ran her fingers through his hair, crooning softly. "Do you remember when she was born?" she said.

He remembered. Joan had been in her confinement for the months preceding the birth, keeping to her bed in a darkened room to reduce any risk of harm to the child. Peter was four years old, an active boy who drove the household staff mad with his energy and propensity to run through the hallways and spill or break things. Parris had insisted on being in the room with Joan, and Peter was left in the charge of his governess.

Catherine was born, to Parris's great amazement and delight. Peter slipped his governess's care and burst into the room. He was quickly removed, but not before he had seen his sister—not crying, her eyes still shut, and slick with blood. When his governess dragged him out again, he solemnly informed her that the baby was dead. The news spread through the servants and out of the household before it could be corrected, and Parris had to present the healthy, bright-eyed child to many neighbors before they believed she was alive.

"She was beautiful," he said. He wanted to add, *And you as well,* but he didn't know what Joan would say to that. It had been a long time since he had shown much in the way of affection toward her. In fact, since Peter died, he'd been so caught up in his own tormented sense of personal failure that he'd hardly paid any attention to her at all. So he just let her hold him and marveled that it should take a threat to their lives and a voyage to the end of the world to bring them together again.

⊰+┼+⊱

THEY appeared all at once, dozens of red manticores, some in the trees above Catherine, some standing within arm's reach. Despite the fact that she had known they were there, she shrieked. She hadn't realized there were so many of them, so close.

They converged on her. She didn't struggle. What seemed like hundreds of tails lashed her arms and legs and body, then lifted her clear off her feet. They placed her in a woven sling and carried her as they swung through the trees. It was surprisingly gentle, and she felt secure, despite their speed and distance from the ground. She could distantly remember being carried this way before, as a baby perhaps, and she recognized the feeling as coming from Chichirico's memories. She made herself as light as possible. Somehow, she knew that besides those who were carrying her, there were others ranging ahead, scouting for danger.

The manticore village looked like a clutch of rolling hills. It sat in a sunny clearing. Catherine wondered if the manticores had cleared it, and how they kept the forest from encroaching. Each "building" was a dome of living wood. Hundreds of vines grew out of the ground, twisted together, flattened, and seemed to grow into each other to form an unbroken surface which sprouted tiny pale leaves. Many manticores were visible on the roofs of the buildings or in the trees.

The living buildings were large, no taller than one story, but some wide enough that she imagined a network of rooms. The manticores set her down gently and she followed them inside. There was no door or opening, but she passed through the wood just as easily as they did. Inside, it was brightly lit and cool. She looked around for the source of the light and saw a conch-shaped seashell softly glowing. She guessed there was a Shekinah flatworm inside, its light diffused by the shell into a more pleasant glow. Much better than trying to wrap it in cloth. Why hadn't the settlers thought of that?

Chichirico was waiting inside. "You're alive!" she said. "I was afraid they had killed you." She wanted to run and hug him, but his face was inscrutable. Was he angry with her?

"We must go," he said in English. The manticores set off again through the wall of the building, dragging her with them. Chichirico took the lead. They flew through the forest in another direction with Catherine towed behind them.

This trip took longer. As they traveled, the rumbling from deep underground that was constantly present grew louder. The trees began to shake visibly, not with wind, but as if the earth they were rooted in had grown unstable. Eventually they broke into a clearing, and Catherine saw that they were at the Edge, at a spot along the cliff face she'd never seen. The sun was setting, a blazing red orb so large and close it seemed that a running jump off the cliff would land her right in its fiery depths. Clouds boiled away. Sweat broke out on her face.

As she watched, a piece of the cliff face the size of a house sheared off and tumbled away out of sight. The ground between her and the cliff was traced with a web of cracks. It was just as Bishop Marcheford had said. The island was steadily sliding off the end of the world.

How long would it take before the whole island was gone? Before the human colony went over with everything else? Another chunk slipped and fell, larger than before.

The manticores set her down. They still didn't say anything, but watched as Chichirico began to dance. They pushed her forward, toward him, and she approached apprehensively. The dance was slow and deliberate, more a series of poses than movement. When it was over, he leaped onto her, flipping over to her back in one fluid motion. Instinctively, she made her body heavy so he didn't overbalance her. She knew what was coming. He plunged his tail painlessly into her back, and she gasped. The familiar connection returned, and she realized how much she had missed it.

Her surroundings became normal and comfortable. She knew the island and its creatures. She knew how to get back to the human settlement, but it was no longer so important. This was her forest. This was home.

Chichirico spoke into her mind, and she interpreted it as English words. He told her how her resurrection had put the world out of balance, and how only she could set it right.

"Is there no other way?" she said.

His silence told her there was not.

"I can't," she said. "I can't leave my family and friends to be tortured or killed. What good does it do to save the island, if I leave them to Tavera?"

"Soon it will reach our homes," Chichirico said. "It will threaten my family, my friends. We will move and rebuild, but it will not matter. The whole island will be destroyed."

"I'll do it, but you have to help me first," she said. "Help me rescue my family, and then I'll do what you want."

"We will help you. But we must act fast. Today."

"How long until the island is gone? Weeks?"

Chichirico shook his head in imitation of the human gesture. "It moves ever faster. By tomorrow night, there will be nothing left."

⊷+✛+⊶

PARRIS couldn't sleep. Joan had finally fallen into a fitful slumber, but he was afraid to close his eyes, lest he wake to find his head held underwater again. When his mind drifted, it was to panicked dreams of being unable to breathe. He knew it was psychological torture, a ploy to wear him down, but it was working anyway. He wondered if the drownings had done permanent damage to his mind.

He heard a click at the door. It eased open quietly, and the soldier who unlocked it admitted Christopher Sinclair. "Tavera thinks you're ready to talk," Sinclair said.

Parris sat up, suspicious. "What are you doing here?"

"I'm cooperating. There's no way out. If you don't talk, they'll torture you until you do, and if you convince them you don't know anything, they'll kill you."

"But I don't know anything more than I've told them!"

"I know. But I do."

Parris's head spun. "What are you talking about?"

"Did they tell you about Catherine?"

"They said she escaped by walking through a wall."

"She must have." Sinclair told him how she'd pulled her arms out of her chains, and how he'd made her lighter with the Samson-mouse gloves.

"But where is she now?"

"Someplace where they can't get her. They haven't found any trace of her, and I'll tell you, they've looked. Tavera is furious with Vaughan; he's holding him responsible. Vaughan might be the governor, but he's going to find himself on the wrong end of an interrogation before long."

"I don't understand. How did Catherine get these powers?"

Sinclair sat on the floor facing Parris. "I've been thinking about it. We all have quintessence running through our veins."

"From the water."

"Right. The manticores and all the creatures here have more than that, though. Somewhere in their bodies, they have a pearl, which can either channel the quintessence they use for their special talents, or else open a window to the void."

"But Catherine doesn't have a pearl. Does she?"

"When I pulled her soul back into her body, I wrapped a mesh of quintessence strands around her body. I think that mesh might be acting like a pearl. Even better, in fact—every time she moves any part of her body, she moves one of those strands. Once her mind started to associate her movements with the changes in the quintessential world around her, she could learn to control them. We don't consciously think of how to coordinate our legs and arms, or focus our eyes—her mind could be learning to use quintessence in the same way.

"The animals on this island all use quintessence to some degree or other to find food, escape from predators, or procreate. We thought it was something special about this island—that God created them differently. But what if they're not different? What if, over time, a partial mesh—a twist or turn around an animal's claw or horn or one its bones—formed accidentally, through chance, giving that animal some control over the type or substance of its body? That animal would be more likely to thrive, and it might teach its young how to do the same thing. Over a long period of time, all the animal species would develop such a skill, just like Catherine. Only Catherine's is wrapped around her whole body."

Parris was skeptical. He felt worn to breaking, and Sinclair's senseless talk wasn't helping. "This is pure fancy. An animal might chance to learn a behavior. It might possibly teach it to its young. But the boarcat has special claws, created for the purpose of manipulating quintessence strands. The seer skink has tears that let it see the strands. It's not just something they figured out on their own."

"Remember the beetlewood trees," Sinclair said. "Living things do what they must to survive."

"There's a limit. I can't grow two new arms to help me swim faster, no matter how badly I need them."

Sinclair waved the argument away. "The important part is that what I did to Catherine, I could do again. It wouldn't need to be a resurrection. I could wrap a mesh around a living person to give him Catherine's powers."

Parris smiled without pleasure. "Then they've been torturing the wrong man."

⊷✦⊶

AFTER Sinclair left, Parris finally slipped into a fitful slumber. When he woke, it was still dark, and Joan was awake. In fact, she was gently shaking him. Everything hurt, especially his head. When he tried to move, stars burst in his vision. Then he saw the angel.

It was a white figure, pale and shimmering in the dim light. He was hallucinating. He waved his hand at it, as if to disperse smoke.

"Father?" The voice spoke clear and sharp in the silence. Parris opened his eyes wider. It was not Joan who was shaking him awake, but the angel.

A light flared, blinding him. He cringed and covered his eyes. As he blinked away the initial glare, the light took definition as a softly glowing seashell. He studied it, bemused. What made it glow? Finally, his sluggish brain realized that someone was holding the shell. His eyes followed the slim hand up to the face.

"Catherine!"

She breathed a sigh of relief at his recognition, and then engulfed him in her warm embrace. "Oh, Father, what have they done to you?"

"Water," he said. "Food."

She helped him to his feet, and Joan was there, supporting his other side. Catherine plunged both hands into the curved wooden wall that was the outer hull of the boat. She traced a rough circle, sliding her hands through the wood like it was water, until her hands met again at the bottom. She kicked, and the circle of wood fell out, revealing the bay and the dark sky. They were right at the waterline, and a stream of water began to flood into the room through the hole.

Parris might have thought he was dreaming, but the water running over his feet was wet and cold. He scooped up handfuls and drank greedily. How had she done that? Just passing through the wood wouldn't have carved a hole. Though if Sinclair was right, quintessence was now a natural extension of her mind and body. Who knew what would be possible?

He saw one of the living boat creatures, which a Scottish sailor had named a kelpie, swimming rapidly toward them. Matthew and Sinclair were already aboard, along with a red manticore he recognized as Chichirico.

"Quietly," Catherine whispered. "Climb in."

Resting in the kelpie's concave back were loaves of sand bread, which Parris and Joan attacked greedily. Catherine lifted the circle of wood out of the water and fitted it back into the gap. She splashed handfuls of water against it and smoothed her hands over the surface, transforming the water into wood and sealing the opening. The kelpie pulled away from the galleon, silent and—so far—unseen.

Parris's mind was clearing now that his immediate hunger and thirst were satisfied. "So you can walk through walls."

"Yes," Catherine said.

"And alter your weight."

"Yes."

"What else can you do?"

She lifted her arm and concentrated. Her hand transformed to iron and then back to flesh again. She vanished and then reappeared.

"Does it . . . make you tired, or hurt, or anything?"

She shook her head. "I just think what I want to do, and it happens."

The ease of it disturbed Parris. It was a tremendous amount of power, and he found it hard to believe it could be had at no cost. "Where are we going?"

"Back to Chichirico's village. But Father . . ." Her face was strained and anxious.

"What is it? What's wrong?"

Her eyes welled with tears, and suddenly Parris saw an image, fully formed in his mind as if he had experienced it himself: the ground cracking and crumbling and falling in huge pieces off the Edge. In a moment he knew the whole of her visit to the reds, her connection to Chichirico, and what she had learned.

He clutched at his head, unused to processing such an avalanche of information in so short a time. He had been Catherine's surrogate, and they were still connected, still tied to life by the same strands of quintessence that Sinclair had wrapped around them both. It must be operating in a similar way to the manticore bond.

He tried to come to grips with this new knowledge. The island, doomed to destruction. His own responsibility in bringing it about. And worst of all, the knowledge that Catherine's new life was only a borrowed one. She still belonged to the grave, and the whole universe was bending to send her back again.

They glided farther and farther from the galleon, propelled by the kelpie's powerful tail, until they slipped around a bend and out of sight. Parris moved closer to Sinclair and whispered some of what he had learned from Catherine.

"I don't understand it," Parris said. "How could what we did be pushing the island over the Edge?"

"We played with the fundamental energies of the universe," Sinclair said. "Quintessence is the energy that gives atoms their structure and coherence, that makes them form lead or gold, solid or liquid. It's the skeleton of the world. That our interference would destabilize it seemed unlikely . . ."

"But not impossible."

"No. Consider how this island got to be here, perched at the very end of the world. What if, long ago, it broke off from a continent—Western Africa, maybe—and floated with the currents? When it reached the Edge, propelled by the water gushing over the side, it was caught by the network of quintessence strands from the sun and stars and held fast."

"Wait a minute. Caught? How would it be caught?"

"I don't know. I'm just suggesting a theory that seems to fit the facts. The animals—once simple African beasts, perhaps—changed over time to make use of the quintessence, and those which did so best survived. Until we upset the balance that kept the island in place."

"But a single human soul? That little change, and the whole island rushes over the Edge?"

Sinclair shrugged. "Who knows how significant a human soul is? We're talking about quintessence here, the essence of life. In quintessential terms, a human soul might be the heaviest thing in the universe. Usually a soul has its own anchor to balance it, but remember that hers is connected to yours. Two souls on one anchor. It must be enough to throw off the balance."

Parris shook his head, still not wanting to believe it. "The boarcats do it. They don't upset the balance of the universe. There must be another way, some step we overlooked."

"If we had time, we could research, study, try to understand more. But we don't have time."

Parris lowered his voice to an angry hiss. "You're saying she has to die again."

"There's no other way. Unless . . ."

"Unless what?"

"Unless you die first."

—+++—

THE kelpie beached itself on the sand, and they all clambered out, half a league away from the dock and out of sight of the Spanish. The moment everyone had disembarked, however, ten Spanish soldiers stepped out of the trees, matchlocks raised to their shoulders.

"Don't move!" their captain called.

"Run!" Parris shouted. Capture just meant more torture, and likely death; running was worth the risk. They scattered as the guns erupted in flame and noise, and Chichirico went down with a hole in his chest.

"No!" Catherine screamed. She stopped and knelt by his body.

Parris turned to go back for her. They had scant moments while the soldiers either reloaded or charged them, but if he didn't get her out of there soon, she would be next.

Catherine, her face contorted with rage, vanished. Parris watched in terror, unable to flee. A moment later, a soldier went down. He imagined her clubbing them with her iron fist. The soldiers had skink tears, though, didn't they? That meant they could see her. He saw a soldier with a re-loaded matchlock tracking his gun on something he couldn't see. The conversation with Sinclair still fresh in his mind, Parris let go of Joan's hand and ran toward the soldiers. *Please, God, let her be safe. If one of us has to die, let it be me instead.*

The soldiers were all looking the other direction, toward Catherine, and they didn't see him coming. Parris reached the nearest soldier and tackled him to the ground. He wrested the gun away and ran on, firing it at the next soldier, but missing. The soldiers wheeled to aim at him, but Parris ran on, shouting like a maniac and waving his hands, trying to distract them from Catherine.

Like an answer to prayer, a final shot echoed, and Parris felt fire tear through his thigh. He collapsed into the sand. Joan reached him and tried to pull him up, but he couldn't run. The soldiers surrounded them.

By the time they hauled him to his feet, the wound was already beginning to heal, but it was too late to get away. He scanned the beach for signs of the others, but saw only Chichirico's body still lying like a crumpled coat at the waterline. Catherine and the others had escaped.

Chapter Thirty-two

CHICHIRICO was dead, and it was all Catherine's fault. She knew what she had to do; she should have done it right away. It was only friendship for her that had prompted him to help rescue her family. Now that friendship had cost him his life.

Catherine led Matthew and Master Sinclair to the red manticore village, barely aware of her surroundings. She felt like a part of herself had been torn away. She'd lived life from inside Chichirico's perspective, shared his memories, dreamed his dreams. The whole journey from England, he had been there with her. Even though she hadn't known him all that long, she felt his loss keenly.

Tearfully, she told the tribe about Chichirico's death. There was no family to inform; the whole tribe was his family. The reds could spare no time for grief; they were evacuating. The island was slipping farther each hour, bringing the crumbling Edge ever closer to their home. Catherine found it hard to care. She didn't know any of these manticores. She couldn't even remember their names, except for his brother, Tanakiki, who seemed to be back in charge. She wanted Chichirico.

Enough. Too late for grief. She knew what she had to do. She slipped away from Matthew and Sinclair, hoping they would have the sense to save themselves.

⊷╼╾⊶

SINCLAIR let her go. He knew, or at least suspected, what she planned to do. The whole situation was his own fault. It was hard to admit it, but he had experimented too quickly, with things he didn't begin to understand. And yet, what should he have done? Given Catherine back to her parents with a bullet hole in her head?

"Do you know what they've done with my father?" Matthew asked. "Is he still alive?"

"Last I knew, they had him imprisoned in the church," Sinclair said. He didn't say what he had heard: that Tavera was offering him only bread and wine from the Roman Eucharist, which Marcheford—despite starving for food and drink—refused to take. The old fool. Too stubborn to save his own neck.

And now Catherine was going off to die. That wasn't stubbornness, but true self-sacrifice, the necessary giving of her life for many. It was the right thing to do. But Sinclair wasn't certain that in her place he could have made the same choice.

"Where did Catherine go?" Matthew said. "We need to leave. We should get as far east as we can."

"She might be able to stop the quake," Sinclair said.

Matthew looked surprised. He was so naive, despite his cleverness. "How can she do that?"

"Her soul doesn't have an anchor of its own; she's only able to stay alive by hanging on to her father's. As best as we can tell, that's what's causing this. Her soul is dragging us all into the void."

Realization dawned on Matthew's face.

"Wait," Sinclair said, but Matthew took off running westward, toward the Edge.

"It's too late!" Sinclair called. "You'll never catch her!"

Matthew kept running.

◄+►

TAVERA took Parris and Joan to his own house. Parris didn't understand why at first, but when Tavera began asking them questions about Catherine's quintessence powers, he understood. Tavera wanted to learn the secret of her abilities without sharing it with anyone else. Not even the other Spaniards.

Blanca was there. Parris hadn't seen her since Tavera had taken her away to work for him, and now he hardly recognized her. Her normally animated face was blank, her gaze perpetually aimed at the floor. Her bare feet were shackled, forcing her to shuffle in little steps. Her body looked unharmed, as of course it would with quintessence water in her veins, but there were rings under her eyes. She didn't look at Parris or Joan. Tavera dropped his cloak at her feet, and she picked it up without a word and carried it away.

Tavera locked Joan in one room—for safekeeping, he said—and led Parris to another. Inside, John Gibbs sat tied to a chair, looking worn and beaten and even more gaunt than usual. A ball of cloth was stuffed into his mouth as a gag.

"We'll start with a little test," Tavera said.

Blanca returned, carrying a box. She set it on a table and opened it, revealing the pair of boarcat claws Sinclair had used in the cave. She curtsied low to Tavera, backed away, and stood in the corner like a shadow.

"You will give Master Gibbs the same powers your daughter enjoys," Tavera said. "You will explain every step so that I understand it. If you try any tricks, your wife will be killed, little by little, while you watch."

Parris hesitated. If Tavera gained those powers, there would be no stopping him. And yet, how much worse could it be? He could already kill anyone in the settlement as he pleased. If he did as Tavera asked, then there might yet be a chance to defeat him. If he didn't, Tavera would kill Joan, and then he would kill someone else, until Parris did what he wanted anyway.

Slowly, Parris nodded. He could do it; the boarcat paws should be all he needed. Gibbs wasn't dead, so no void was necessary. Parris simply had to wrap Gibbs's body in a mesh made from quintessence, and everything should work as it did before, at least according to Sinclair.

Tavera, using skink tears so he could see the process, asked questions at every step, wanting explanations of the strands and what Parris was doing to them. Parris used himself as the surrogate this time, choosing strands from his own body to build a mesh around Gibbs. The process might have worked with Gibbs's own strands, but Parris didn't want to take the chance.

Without the void to deal with, the process was straightforward, and it didn't take long.

"Is it finished?" Tavera said.

"As well as I know how."

"Then we shall test your workmanship. Blanca, my sword."

Blanca retrieved a sheathed sword from its place on the wall and brought it to him. He drew it, leaving her with the sheath, and advanced on Gibbs, who paled and tried to stand. He shook his head and made muffled protests through the gag.

"No!" Parris said. "You'll kill him."

Tavera smiled. "But he can pass through walls now. Surely he can pass through a sword. Unless you were unsuccessful?"

"Catherine didn't know she could do it at first," Parris said. "She had to figure it out. It took time and practice."

"He had better learn fast. One!" Tavera raised the sword.

"Don't! At least let him try it with a wall first."

"Insufficient motivation. Two!"

"Please!"

"Three!" Tavera's sword sang through the air. Gibbs shut his eyes, but the sword passed through his body as if he were nothing but air. Tavera, thrown off balance by his own swing, fell down. He looked up at Gibbs with wonder and avarice painted clearly on his face.

Gibbs tried to run, but although his body had passed through the sword, the ropes around his arms and legs still held him fast.

"Fortunately, I planned for success," Tavera said, standing. "That rope is waxed with beetlewood oil. Quite impassable." He drew a pistol from under his cloak. "As is this bullet, I'm afraid."

He shot Gibbs in the head from close range. The body jerked and then slumped, still held up by the ropes.

Tavera's eyes were bright as he faced Parris. "Now you will give these powers to me."

⊹✦⊹

THE closer Catherine got to the Edge, the louder the rumbling sound became, and the more the ground shook under her feet. It was crumbling away more quickly now. She tried to walk out farther, but the tremors made it impossible to stay upright.

She tried not to think of what she was about to do. She wasn't sure she'd have the courage to actually throw herself off, so she just sat down where she was. It wouldn't take long. The Edge was advancing swiftly as more and more of the island fell away. A nearby tree toppled, its roots tearing loose from the ground.

Her heart thudded wildly. She didn't want to die, but she believed Chichirico, and Master Sinclair had said essentially the same thing. It was her stolen life that was causing this, and so only her death could stop it.

The truth was, as much as she wanted to live, she was already dead. She'd been shot in the head by Diego de Tavera. Her temporary return was the result of a valiant effort by Father and Sinclair to bring her back, but in the end, it hadn't worked. She only wished she could have rescued her parents and somehow said good-bye before she left. Though that might have been worse. They would have tried to stop her, and that would have made it even harder to do what she knew she had to do.

She waited, shaking as much from fear as from the earthquakes, as the rapidly eroding cliff's edge approached her position. A piece almost within reach slid away, revealing a view of the endless drop into darkness. The sound of rending rock hurt her ears. She covered her eyes.

Just as the ground underneath her began to tilt forward, a strong arm wrapped around her waist and jerked her back. She coughed in the swirling dust. Her rescuer dragged her farther until she pulled away to look at him.

It was Matthew, looking angrier than she'd ever seen him. "What do you think you're doing?"

"I have to," Catherine said, starting to cry. "I should have done it already."

Matthew took her hand and pulled her east, away from the Edge. He didn't let go until the sounds of breaking rock faded. Finally, she sat, and he sat next to her, clasping his arms around his knees.

Catherine took a ragged breath. "The island is doomed while I live. There's a . . . a kind of balance between our world and the other side. Souls aren't supposed to come back again. My soul is attached to Father's anchor, holding me here, but it's thrown everything off balance. I'm pulling the whole island over with me."

"Leave the island, then. Sail back home. Run away from it."

"And what if the problem follows me? Chichirico is dead. How many more people need to die so that I get a second life?"

Matthew grabbed her shoulders and shook her. She finally looked at him, and saw the tears running down his face. "I won't lose you," he said. "There has to be another way."

Catherine rocked back and looked at the sky. "I'm already dead, either way. If I fight it, everyone on the island will die, too. What choice do I have?"

◆+◆+◆

SINCLAIR stayed close to the faction of red manticores he thought had been loyal to Chichirico. It was hardly safe, but it grew worse when he saw one, then two, then a dozen gray manticores advancing through neighboring trees. In moments the forest was filled with them, hundreds of manticores, and not just grays, but snow-white ones, black ones with bright yellow tufts behind their ears, short and stocky manticores, and thin, spidery ones—tribes Sinclair had never seen before. It was the manticore army Marcheford had warned him about.

Many of the reds seemed to be joining it, and he realized there would be no help for the colony. They were on their own. The colonists would kill a few, to be sure, but eventually they would be overrun. Catherine might stop the island from sliding off the Edge, but it wouldn't matter to the humans if they were massacred by manticores. With a sinking spirit, Sinclair realized that if he didn't do something, he might soon be the only living human being left on the island.

He crouched in the shadow of one of the manticore homes until the army passed overhead. Fortunately, none of them stopped or even looked down, and he remained unnoticed. He had little hope that the reds would protect him if he was seen. The time for hiding was over. He ran east, back toward the settlement, following the army. He couldn't keep up with them, but that wasn't important. He only hoped he could get there before everyone was dead.

◆+◆+◆

PARRIS moved as slowly as he dared, not wanting to give quintessence powers to Tavera, but feeling like he had little choice. Everything he had hoped for this island was falling apart. Their best discoveries, in the hands of their enemies. Catherine's resurrection, failed. Even this unique and magical island itself was soon to be destroyed, unless he or Catherine died first. He hoped Sinclair and Matthew would prevent her from doing anything rash. If one of them had to die . . . An idea struck him. Perhaps neither of them had to die. Perhaps there was another way.

He steeled his face to show none of the nervousness he felt. He used his own strands to create the mesh, just as before, but this time he was careful to tangle them in Tavera's anchor. His idea would work; it had to. But the timing would be important. He would have to actually finish the mesh, which meant giving Tavera superhuman powers, at least for a moment.

Blanca wouldn't look up, though he tried to catch her eye. He didn't want to think about what horrors Tavera must have inflicted on her to bend her will so thoroughly. He concentrated on his work, guiding the strands around Tavera's torso, under his arms, around his fingers. The gestures were disturbing, almost intimate, but it was what Tavera expected, and it allowed Parris to get very close.

He tied the last knot in the weave. He was finished, but before Tavera could recognize it, he grabbed the pistol from Tavera's belt. He tried to raise it, but Tavera was faster. He caught Parris's wrist and twisted it, forcing the barrel of the gun away from his face. Parris was weak from lack of sleep and food, and Tavera was strong. The pistol began to turn, slowly but inevitably, toward Parris. His grip was slipping. As soon as the pistol's muzzle turned far enough, it would all be over. At least Catherine wouldn't have to die.

Blanca sprang into action like a statue coming to life. She snatched a length of the waxed rope from where it still lay on the floor and wrapped it around Tavera's neck. He roared and tried to jerk away, but she hung on. Her blank, subservient demeanor disappeared as she twisted with all her might. The thin rope bit into his flesh, and he choked, fighting for breath. Parris kept struggling for the gun, which kept his hands busy so he couldn't reach for the rope.

"You killed my sisters," Blanca said, her Spanish accent thick. "You killed my mother. You should be dragged into the pit of hell."

With a mighty heave, Tavera threw himself out of the chair, which toppled, dragging both Blanca and Parris down with him. The pistol clattered across the floor. Blanca shrieked and fell, the chair on top of her. Tavera rolled out of it, climbing to his feet. He kicked Parris once, twice, and then a blast of noise and powder erupted and Tavera collapsed, his face a frozen mask of shock, his chest spurting blood. Joan appeared from behind him, spattered with blood, the recovered pistol held in two hands, a triumphant look on her face.

Parris scrambled to his feet, thinking it was over, but Tavera was back on his feet, still fighting, the horrible wound healing fast. Parris grappled with him, but Tavera was pale and still losing blood. Blanca threw another loop of the waxed rope around his neck, and Joan joined her in pulling it tight.

It seemed to take an hour. Parris's face was inches from Tavera's. He could smell his sweat and see the stubble standing out on his chin. Tavera bared his teeth in a rictus of effort, his face turning blue. Finally, his muscles gave out, his face grew slack, and he slumped to the floor. Blanca and Joan kept pulling on the rope, their teeth gritted, their arms shaking, together ensuring with every ounce of their strength that Tavera was truly dead.

The skink tears allowed Parris to see the void when it appeared. It flared open briefly, and Tavera's soul, bright and writhing along a quintessence strand, was sucked into it before it snapped shut again. But Tavera's anchor didn't go with it. It was still connected to Parris. Quickly, Parris picked up the boarcat paw and used it to sever his connections to his own anchor. He cringed when he cut the last one, afraid it might kill him, but it didn't. His soul was still connected to the physical world through Tavera's anchor, which now snapped into Parris's body, while Parris's own anchor flew away, drawn by its connection to Catherine. If his understanding was correct, he and Catherine were now separated again, each with their own anchor. He was connected to Tavera's anchor, and she was connected to his.

Catherine's debt to the void had been paid, but by Tavera, not by Catherine. The balance of the universe should be restored. He only hoped it wasn't too late.

⋖+┼+⊳

THE earthquake stopped.

One moment the ground was shaking hard enough to smash rocks and uproot trees; the next, it was utterly still and solid. Matthew and Catherine stared incredulously at the suddenly stable ground. Catherine laughed and danced and hugged him, then grew somber. "But how?"

Matthew raised his hands in joyful ignorance. "Does it matter?"

"It was happening because Father and I shared the same anchor," she said. "If I didn't die, then . . ." Her heart seemed to stop in her chest, and she clutched Matthew's arm.

"Your father," he said.

"Come on!" Together, they ran back east, toward the settlement.

Chapter Thirty-three

PARRIS hugged Joan, amazed that they were all still alive. When Blanca had gone to retrieve the boarcat claws, she had unlocked the door to the room where Joan was imprisoned, allowing her to escape. If she hadn't, there was a good chance Tavera would have reached the gun first, and both Parris and Blanca would now be dead.

Parris cracked the door to Tavera's house and peered outside. There were no soldiers guarding the door, nor any people to be seen. He heard gunfire, lots of it, not far away.

"Let's go now, before the soldiers come back," Joan said.

"Wait," Parris said. "There's something we need to do first."

Joan was reluctant, but Parris convinced her. "It's the only way we can survive."

Blanca went first, standing still while Parris used the boarcat paw to weave the quintessence mesh around her body. Next came Joan, complaining that she didn't want to have unnatural powers, but submitting to it all the same. Finally, he did it to himself, a somewhat tricky operation, but one he eventually managed.

As a test, he tried to walk through a diamond wall from one room into the next, but just walked stupidly into the wall. It took him several tries, but finally he figured it out, and after that it was easy. Blanca did the same, laughing, and Joan followed, more subdued. "It isn't right," she said.

After several failed tries, they all three turned invisible—Joan and Blanca confirming it, since Parris could still see them with the skink tears—and left the house. A cloud of smoke hung over the western curve of the palisade and rapid pops of gunfire echoed through the settlement.

Here and there they saw a gray shape appear on a platform, spinning and thrashing while the soldiers and colonists alike parried with bayonets and knives. Many human shapes lay sprawled on the platform or down on the ground.

"They're fighting the manticores," Parris said. "And they're losing."

—◆+◆+◆—

SINCLAIR heard the gunfire and knew the manticores had reached the settlement. He sneaked close enough that he could see the fighting, and then returned, frustrated. He needed some way to get into the settlement, but how could he possibly do that with the gates closed and defenders shooting anything that approached? All he needed was a dead manticore and a vial of mercury. The dead manticore should be fairly easy to obtain, but the only mercury he could possibly reach was inside the palisade walls.

He heard footsteps and turned, ready to hide or flee, but it was Matthew and Catherine, both still alive. They must have run faster than he could, to catch up with him.

"Where's my father?" Catherine asked.

"I don't know any more than you do," Sinclair said. He studied her. "Do you think you could get into the settlement and back out again?"

"I don't know. Probably. Why?"

"I think I could stop this war, once and for all. All I need is a vial of mercury from the stores in my house."

She traded glances with Matthew. "How are you going to stop the war with a vial of mercury?"

"Don't worry about that."

She crossed her arms. "If I'm going to risk my life to get it, I want to know how you're going to use it."

"You remember the ironfish?"

Her eyes went up, considering, and then her mouth fell open. "You're going to cut a manticore open to find its pearl. And drop it into the mercury."

Sinclair nodded.

"You'll kill them all!"

"Isn't that the goal?"

"I mean, *all* of them. Every manticore on the island. The grays and reds both, and thousands more we've never even seen."

"Nonsense. We didn't kill every ironfish in the sea, did we? Just those in that one school that shared a quintessence bond."

"No, she's right," Matthew said. "The manticore lineage is mixed. The young are captured by other tribes and adopted as their own children."

"You're guessing," Sinclair said. "They can't *all* be linked. But it doesn't matter. *People* are dying. Not manticores. People. Whatever the manticores get, they've brought on themselves."

"There has to be another way," Catherine said.

Sinclair raised an eyebrow. "What is it?" When they didn't answer, he added, "They're overrunning the defenders right now. If we wait too long, there won't be any humans left to save."

"But it's murder."

"What the manticores are doing right now is murder. Remember the bones we found in the church? You think that once the colony is massacred, they won't come after us, too? The Spanish and English are fighting shoulder to shoulder, but they won't last long. Your parents are probably in there. Matthew's father, too. The manticores you're so concerned about are going to kill them. Are you going to stand by and let them die?"

Catherine wavered; he could see it. "Go," he said. "As quick as you can."

⧫⧫⧫⧫

CATHERINE circled the battle and climbed the palisade far from the main action. A soldier saw her, but ignored her, firing instead on a manticore in the other direction. She was inside.

She wasn't convinced by Sinclair's arguments. She knew the humans, including herself and those she loved, were likely to be killed, but that didn't make it right to murder the entire manticore race, friend and enemy alike.

She would get the mercury. She wasn't sure yet if she would give it to Sinclair, but it would give her time to think. With every soldier engaged in keeping the manticores out, Catherine entered the governor's mansion easily and found the alchemical stores. Much of them had been rummaged through, taken, or broken, but she found what she was looking for, a vial with a bead of a metallic liquid that shone dully in the light.

As she tucked it into a pouch, she noticed another vial filled with finely grained salt. The opposite of mercury, in alchemical terms. Where mercury decreased the effect of quintessence, salt increased it. An idea began to form in her mind. She filled a jar with water and poured in the whole contents of the salt vial.

⊰⊹⊹⊹⊱

As Parris ran toward the palisade, Joan and Blanca right behind him, he saw the colonists and soldiers throw down their weapons and scramble away from the wall. A wave of manticores crested the wall, overpowering those who didn't get away in time. Colonists jumped off the platforms, slamming hard into the ground, then running or limping away.

They weren't fast enough. The manticores opened the gate from the inside, and the rest of the manticore army poured into the settlement and circled in front of the fleeing men, cutting off their escape. They closed the circle, forcing the humans into the center, Parris, Joan, and Blanca among them. The manticores advanced quickly, ignoring both weapons and cries for mercy, clearly intent on killing them all.

The air was acrid with gun smoke, and the ground was soaked in blood. Parris ran at an advancing manticore and turned his skin to iron just before the manticore drove pincers into his chest. The iron skin was so heavy it nearly knocked him down, but he found he could change the material further, making it light and still just as strong. He parried several manticore blows and swung iron fists to drive them back.

Around the circle, Joan and Blanca started doing the same thing, trying to protect the humans who remained, but it wasn't enough. The manticores flowed around them, too many to count.

Parris was almost surrounded himself when Catherine came running out of the governor's mansion, something clasped in her hand. She leaped clear over the manticore mob, an impossible jump, and landed next to Parris. He parried a manticore blow aimed at her head and knocked the attacker to the ground.

"Close your eyes!" Catherine shouted. She shook a jar filled with a cloudy liquid and drank it down.

⊰⊹⊹⊹⊱

The salt was like fire, burning Catherine's throat. She reached inside herself and felt its power. She had never tried this before, but every other manifestation of quintessence had so far answered her command. If the Shekinah flatworms could do it, she should be able to as well. Catherine began to glow.

Just like the worms, she blazed out light, intuitively drawing on the salt inside her to increase it. Soon she was far brighter than any Shekinah flatworm. The manticores shied away, wrapping arms around their heads to shield their eyes. The humans, too, dropped to their knees and hid their faces against the light.

Catherine blazed still brighter. Her own eyes seemed to adjust to the light, so that the world around seemed dark in comparison. She could feel the salt burning away inside her, and concentrated all her efforts on increasing the light.

They scattered, humans and manticores alike, the manticores rushing out of the gate as quickly as they had come. Catherine made her body lighter and jumped into the air, landing on top of the palisade. The manticores, who had paused on the other side, ran into the forest.

The palisade burst into flames. It was a quintessence fire, and it burned white and bright, the flames shooting in a deadly arc all the way around the circular wall. She leaped down on the far side, as light as a leaf, and floated to the ground like a star come to earth.

She watched the manticores run until they were out of sight.

◄─╫─►

EVEN from where he waited among the beetlewood trees, Sinclair couldn't look directly at the light that burst from the top of the wall like a second sun. What could it be? Had the manticores brought some weapon?

Catherine hadn't returned. He feared she was caught or killed, and without the mercury, he could do nothing. Then the manticore army went streaking past him through the trees, paying no attention to him at all. What had happened?

He ran toward the settlement and saw the fire. It had spread from the palisade to several of the surrounding buildings, which, though made of diamond, burned brightly. Outside the gate, he found Catherine, her clothes singed and her hair flying free, crying.

"What happened?"

She shook her head. "I can't put the fire out," she said. "I don't know how."

He ran through the gate, where teams of colonists were throwing buckets of water on the fire. The roaring inferno was so bright they could barely look at it, but it seemed as if the water did nothing to douse the flames. Strangely, the fire was not hot, as though its energy were expended in light instead of heat, but when a colonist got too close, the flames shot up his leg and devoured him while he screamed, his friends helpless to save him.

Sinclair ran on. Farther in, the colonists were using shovels of earth instead of water, but he feared there would be no stopping this fire until the settlement was razed to the ground. Fortunately, all the colonists had been outside fighting the manticores, so no one was in the buildings.

But wait—what about John Marcheford? He was chained in the church, wasn't he? He wouldn't have been released just because the manticores had attacked. Sinclair ran in that direction, ignoring the fire-fighting efforts, and found the church ablaze. The flames licked high, the gold and diamond burning as readily as straw. There was no safe way to get inside. Diamond melted and ran in shining rivulets down the walls, and he suspected it was about to collapse.

Sinclair wiped his streaming eyes and cursed. Marcheford might very well still be alive. The fire wasn't hot and there was little smoke—if the flames hadn't reached him yet, there might still be time to rescue him. Though to try would be suicide. If the flames touched Sinclair at all, there would be no stopping them.

He cursed again. It was not his problem. The stubborn fool had welcomed death instead of compromising his principles. He would get what he chose. And maybe he was already dead—maybe Tavera had killed him. If he was now trapped in a burning church, it was his own fault. Besides, Marcheford wasn't afraid to die; he had said so himself.

Sinclair was. He had always been terrified of what lay beyond the veil. The black void that swallowed Maasha Kaatra was always lurking in his dreams, ready to leap at him as soon as he closed his eyes. He had sworn that that would not be his future. He would never die. He was closer now than he had ever been to realizing that goal. Why would he rush into a burning building? It was folly. Someone might choose to die for a child; that was pure mathematics. The child would have more life left to live. But Marcheford was older; what made his life any more valuable than Sinclair's? Better to stay where he was and save himself.

Don't fear the fire that can only kill the body.

Marcheford's voice leaped unwanted to his mind, and he remembered how unflinchingly Marcheford had faced the likelihood of his own death. Sinclair had always thought himself strong and men like Marcheford weak. He was forced to admit that the reverse might be true.

But no. Running into a burning building wasn't strength, was it? It was stupidity. What could be more stupid than hurrying your own death? Marcheford's strength came from his trust in God, but Sinclair didn't need God. Hadn't he brought Catherine to life again with his own cleverness and invention? He would bring life and immortality to the world; what would Marcheford bring?

He didn't want to go into that building. But neither could he walk away and leave Marcheford to die. God was forcing his hand.

He heard Marcheford's voice in his head again. *I know one thing. If you set yourself against God, you'll lose.*

"You old fool," Sinclair said. He raced into the church, not sure whether he was cursing Marcheford or himself.

The door hung loose on its hinges, and Sinclair managed to slip in without touching the flames. The smell inside was pungent, like sulfur rather than smoke. The light came from every direction now, blinding him. He was afraid of blundering into a burning brand or a portion of wall. Judging by what had happened to the man by the palisade, one touch might be all it took.

Marcheford was still chained to the altar where Sinclair had last seen him. His face was streaked with soot and sweat. He grimaced as he twisted a bloody wrist in the manacles, trying to work his way free.

Sinclair shielded his eyes and scanned the church for something he could use to break Marcheford's chains. Not very smart to come rushing in here to the rescue without bringing something—an ax, for instance—that could free him from the altar. He saw nothing. Everything in view was on fire. The altar was only spared for the moment because it was separated from the other furniture and walls. All it would take was a spark.

A spark. Iron chains would burn in this fire as readily as anything else, wouldn't they? Sinclair snatched up a wooden rod used to light candles. His mind screamed haste, but he had to be careful. He touched the end of the rod to the wall, and it caught fire instantly. The flames leaped down the rod like it was a gunpowder fuse, however, and Sinclair threw it away just before the flames touched his fingers. That wouldn't work.

How could he burn the chains without burning himself and Marcheford at the same time? A fuse—that was what he needed. Sinclair pulled the gold cloth off the altar and used his knife to cut it into four long strips. He pushed one strip through a link in the chain and worked his way toward the burning wall, tying the strips end to end. The last strip bridged the gap, connecting his makeshift fuse to the wall.

It burned quickly. Fire streaked along the strips and into the chain, almost before he could pull his hand away. Marcheford, braced against the altar, pulled hard, and the weakened chain broke where the fire touched it. He was free of the altar.

But not free of the fire. The end of the chain that hung from his arms was on fire. The flames consumed the chain, not as quickly as the cloth, but it wouldn't take them long to reach flesh. Sinclair tore off his doublet. The only chance was to smother the fire. If it didn't work, there would be no stopping it.

He wrapped his doublet around the burning chain and held it tight, holding his face as far away as possible. The flames died, and when he pulled the cloth away, the chain was clear.

"Watch out!" Marcheford said, pointing behind him.

The warning came too late. Intent on smothering the fire, Sinclair had leaned too close to the now-burning altar. White flames leaped to his legs and in moments he was alight, the fire spreading rapidly along his clothes.

"Run!" he said.

They ran for the exit. Sinclair tried to tear away his clothes, but it was too late. His flesh was on fire. The flames weren't hot and didn't even hurt, but he could feel them devouring his legs, and he understood why the colonist had screamed. In moments the flames spread up his ribs on one side.

The roof groaned and sagged. He burst out of the church into the fresh air just as it collapsed behind him. He rolled on the ground, trying to smother the flames. It didn't help. The flames covered him and ate into his flesh.

Marcheford spun, looking for some means to help him, but everything in the area was on fire. Realizing it was hopeless, Sinclair stopped rolling and looked at the sky, aware that these were his very last thoughts. Had he lived his life the way he wanted? He thought of his years of world travel, fruitlessly searching for the elixir of life. More recently, the discovery of Horizon and the long journey. He remembered the look on the boy Merton's face as he'd ordered the boy's flogging. The ultimately failed attempts to raise John Mason and Catherine Parris from the dead, the first of which had ended with Maasha Kaatra's death, and the second of which had caused many more to die. He had set out to save life, and had only destroyed it. In fact, the best thing he could remember doing in his life was what he had done just now.

Was this failure? While wandering through Asia and Africa, he'd told himself he would never stop until he found what he was looking for. And he *had* found it: quintessence, and all the great secrets of the ages with it. He'd transformed lead to gold. He'd turned death back into life. The culmination of the alchemist's art. And what good did all that do him, now that he was moments from death?

The devouring flames spread to his throat. It was more like dissolving than being burned alive. He was being distilled, like a liquid in one of his retorts, boiling away and leaving his impurities behind. The subtle spirit liberated from gross matter. Would he condense and reappear again, purer than before? Somehow he didn't think so.

Marcheford crouched near him, but Sinclair waved him away. The last thing he wanted was for the flames to spread to Marcheford. That would make it all pointless. But Marcheford didn't move. His eyes locked onto Sinclair's. "There's nothing I can do. I'm sorry."

Sinclair tried to smile, which was difficult, since the flames were now racing up one side of his face. The sky seemed to shrink and grow dark, until he imagined he could see the stars, sparkling with quintessence, an impossible distance away. Then they, too, began to fade. He could no longer see Marcheford, but he knew he was still there. "Don't be," he said, hoping he could still be heard. "It was worth it."

Chapter Thirty-four

WHEN Parris saw Catherine walking back through the gate, he ran and caught her in his arms. Joan soon joined them, the three of them embracing, each astonished that the others were still alive. After all that energy had passed out of her, he expected Catherine to be weakened, but she walked on her own strength and squeezed him tightly. He supposed the energy hadn't really come from her. Perhaps the stars would shine just a little less brightly that night.

The fire had burned intensely, but it didn't last long. Once most of the buildings in the settlement had been destroyed, it flared and died. Catherine cried as they walked through the streets between the charred and melted structures. Nearly everything was gone.

"It's not your fault," Parris said. "You saved everyone."

"I destroyed everything."

"Buildings can be rebuilt, more easily here than anywhere else in the world."

"People died because of me."

"People died because of the grays. Anyone who died by fire would have been killed anyway, and many lived who would have died if you hadn't acted. Look around you. These people are alive because of you."

The remaining colonists gradually gathered in the empty square. Of the one hundred and twenty who had come on Sinclair's ship, fewer than sixty remained. Of the ninety Spanish soldiers who had come with Tavera, fewer than forty remained. Francis Vaughan was still alive by pure chance; he had been found cowering under a table in one of the few buildings not destroyed by fire.

The Spanish ship was unharmed and already filled with treasure for the return voyage. Vaughan addressed the survivors and announced his intention to return home. He said nothing about Catherine's role in saving them from the manticores, nor did he thank the colonists for their role in the battle. The Spanish soldiers would return with him to Europe.

"Anyone who wants to get away from this nightmare may come along with me," Vaughan said. "The rest of you are on your own."

◄╌╋╌╋╌►

THE Spanish moved back to their ship, leaving the colonists to clean up the wreckage and rebuild. Only two of the colonists elected to go with them; the rest stayed. Despite the need for living quarters, their fear that the manticores would return prompted them to begin by rebuilding the palisade wall. For several nights, they all slept on the ground under the stars.

Marcheford held a service for the dead. None of the Spanish attended, but all of the English settlers did. He said a brief word about each person who had died in the battle. When he came to Sinclair, he described his life as a war against death, an unrelenting battle that he ultimately won by giving his own life to save another's. Parris didn't think Sinclair would have thought he had won the war, but Marcheford captured Sinclair's character, flaws and all, which was the best you could expect from a memorial service.

At the end, Catherine stood. "What about the manticores?" she said. "They died, too."

There were some mutterings at that, and one man said, loudly enough to be heard by all, "It was the manticores that did the killing."

"Not entirely," Catherine said. "We came here with no knowledge of their island or its magic. We disrupted their lives and destroyed what was sacred to them. We killed manticores through ignorance and fear, manticores who would be alive today if we had never come. So I say, let's mourn their dead as well."

Not everyone agreed, and a few of the colonists walked out, but Marcheford nodded gravely. He knew more manticores than anyone else in the colony, and he recited the names of those he knew to be dead, ending with Chichirico, and expressed sorrow for the many others whose names they would never know.

The memorial completed, they buried those colonists whose bodies had been found. As they lowered Sinclair into the ground, each of the colonists threw a diamond onto his body from the original barrels he had carried back from England. He had been right, Parris thought. Almost no one had believed him, but he'd brought them here anyway, and everything he had promised had turned out to be true.

⊷┼╋┾⊶

ON the fourth day, the Spanish ship was ready to sail, provisioned with Horizon water and bread made from sand, and bursting with gold, silver, spices, dozens of devices invented by the Quintessence Society, and exotic beasts of all descriptions, including a crate full of beetles.

"We could go back to England together," Catherine said. She and her mother stood on the beach, watching the Spanish ship make final preparations to sail. "It's what you came here for, to bring me back home. Now you can."

Mother shook her head. "You like it here. And you were right, you do belong. I couldn't take that away from you."

Catherine dug her bare feet into the sand, plowing little furrows with her toes. "It hasn't all gone well, though, has it? My choices have hurt people. Even gotten some of them killed. Sometimes I wonder if I should have stayed home like you wanted me to."

"You're a woman grown now. You have to live with your own choices and their consequences. That's part of life." Mother gave a sad smile. "I'm proud of you," she said.

Catherine felt her eyes grow wet and dabbed at them with her sleeve. She had never expected to hear her mother say those words. She wasn't sure she deserved them, but it helped to hear them anyway. "What about you? You hate it here, don't you?"

Mother sat down in the sand, unlaced and removed her own shoes, and tossed them to the side. "I'll just have to get used to it, I suppose."

"I would go back with you. If you asked me to, I'd go back. You could find a suitable husband for me, and I'd settle down and love him and give you grandchildren, just like I ought to."

A distant look appeared in Mother's eyes, and she didn't answer right away. Then she shook her head. "I've made that decision already," she said. "I'm not willing to leave you and your father, and this is your place. I'll learn to be content here. Besides," she said, nodding to a lanky youth silhouetted along the shore, "here you can probably find a husband for yourself."

Matthew came closer, also barefoot, letting the ripples from the bay wash over his feet. Catherine waved.

"Go ahead," Mother said. Laughing, Catherine ran off to join him.

—✦✦✦—

THEY walked along the beach away from the ship, Catherine still thinking about Mother and her decision to stay on Horizon. The approval meant a lot, but Catherine couldn't shake the feeling that when she'd trusted her own instincts, they'd led her astray. She tossed a pebble at one of the giant sand tortoises snuffling through the surf. The pebble skipped off its shell with a hollow sound and plunked into the water.

"Did I do the right thing?" she asked.

"Of course you did," Matthew said. "You were the hero of the hour. You saved everyone."

"I killed some, too. I started a fire that destroyed half of the settlement and burned alive some of the people I was trying to save."

"You didn't know that would happen."

"Exactly. Just like every other disaster we've caused by invoking powers we don't understand. We allow our greed to outreach our caution. And people die—manticores and humans both."

"You're thinking of Maasha Kaatra."

She nodded and kicked at the sand. "And don't tell me that wasn't my fault. It might have been Sinclair's idea, but I went along with all my heart."

They were quiet for a time, listening to the crunch of the sand underneath their feet and the distant calls of the men as they hoisted crates from hand to hand. In this sheltered bay, there were no waves as such, but the violence of the ocean sent water cascading down the tunnel at the mouth of the bay that translated into ripples along the shore. These slowly eroded the footprints Matthew and Catherine left behind them as they walked.

"There was no perfect solution," Matthew said finally. "You didn't create the situation. If you had done nothing, many more would have died, perhaps all of the humans, perhaps all of the manticores. A man pulled from the fire wouldn't blame you for bruising his wrist. You saved many."

Catherine sighed. "I know it." She smiled at him. "I might need to hear it again, though."

"Will you marry me?" he said.

She barked out a laugh. "What are you talking about? We don't even know if we'll survive the next week."

"Discounting that."

She laughed again, more awkwardly. This wasn't what she wanted to think about right now. A lot had changed since he'd introduced the subject the first time. She no longer thought he would discredit her views or relegate her to insignificance. And he had shown himself as courageous and principled a man in crisis as any she had known. Perhaps later, if a peace of some kind could be found with the manticores, and they could rebuild the settlement, and they could somehow weather the war among the European powers for control of this place that would be inevitable once a ship returned with treasure . . . but that might be never. Part of her was afraid to love him, knowing the dangers to come that could claim either of their lives. But refusing marriage wouldn't change that. Did she really want to delay happiness until some future moment of tranquillity that might never come?

"Yes," she said.

"Yes? That's it?"

She grinned. "Just don't try to kiss me again."

He winced and rubbed his eye. "Not a chance."

⊰┼┼┼⊱

PARRIS found Joan on the beach, watching the crew hoist the sails.

"You miss London," he said.

She nodded. "I don't like this place. There's an ocean between me and everything I understand. I have no house. I can't sleep for fear of what will happen next to threaten my life or those I love."

"Maybe we should go back."

She slipped into his arms. "You're sweet. You and Catherine both. But you know we can't do that. With an England full of men like Tavera, do you think we could live in peace and obscurity? Would they let you retire to the country? Besides"—Joan pointed farther down the beach, where Catherine and Matthew walked together, deep in conversation— "how could I take her away from him?"

More colonists gathered on the beach as the time came for the ship to leave. A stiff breeze blew down from the north, fluttering the sails. The capstan was turned, the anchors raised, and the ship drifted ponderously away from the dock. No one waved. Parris assumed his fellow colonists had all turned up for the same reason he had: to see with their own eyes that the Spanish were finally leaving for good.

"They'll come back, you know," Joan said. "Spain will send another force, with or without English help. And word will spread. The French will come to stake their claim, and the Dutch, and the Portuguese."

"If they make it back," Parris said.

Joan looked at him sharply. "What do you mean?"

Parris shrugged.

"Did you make all that up, about the flatworms?"

"No," Parris said. "That was true. The Shekinah flatworms really should prevent the problems Lord Chelsey had on his return."

"So we're giving all these miracles into the hands of our enemies."

"So it would seem."

"Then what are you talking about?"

Parris held her close. "Remember I told you what happened on our trip out here? When we opened up the ironfish and took out a quintessence pearl?"

Joan nodded. "The leviathan came."

"Would you say that those jars of flatworms on board represent a flare of quintessence greater, or less, than that of the ironfish?"

"I know little of such things, but they are certainly much brighter. I would have to say greater. Much greater."

"That's what I thought, too."

They watched the ship dwindle into the distance. Parris scuffed his shoe in the sand. "Someday we'll go back," he said.

She looked up into his face and nodded. "Someday."